An
Earth
Scorned

ISBN: 1-4392-1276-7

ISBN-13: 9781439212769

An
Earth
Scorned

Raym Richards

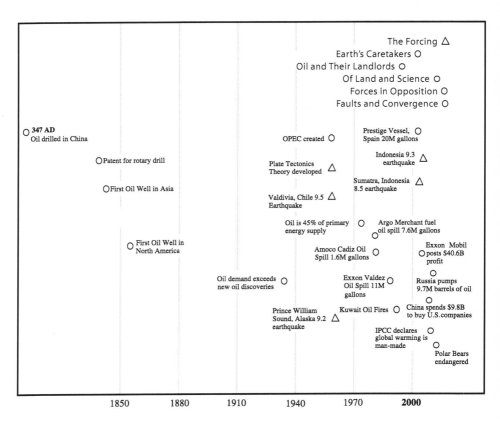

The Forcing △
Earth's Caretakers ○
Oil and Their Landlords ○
Of Land and Science ○
Forces in Opposition ○
Faults and Convergence ○

○ **347 AD**
Oil drilled in China

○ OPEC created

Prestige Vessel, ○
Spain 20M gallons

○ Patent for rotary drill

Plate Tectonics
Theory developed △

Indonesia 9.3 △
earthquake

○ First Oil Well in Asia

Sumatra, Indonesia △
8.5 earthquake

Valdivia, Chile 9.5 △
Earthquake

Oil is 45% of primary ○
energy supply

Argo Merchant fuel
oil spill 7.6M gallons
○

○ First Oil Well in
North America

Amoco Cadiz Oil ○
Spill 1.6M gallons

Exxon Mobil
○ posts $40.6B
profit

○

Oil demand exceeds ○
new oil discoveries

Exxon Valdez ○
Oil Spill 11M
gallons

Russia pumps
9.7M barrels of oil

○

Prince William
Sound, Alaska 9.2 △
earthquake

Kuwait Oil Fires ○

China spends $9.8B
to buy U.S.companies

IPCC declares ○
global warming is
man-made

○
Polar Bears
endangered

1850   1880   1910   1940   1970   **2000**

○ MAN CAUSED
△ EARTH CAUSED

Table of Contents

THE FORCING   **1**

CHRON 19H18M46.659S 360320N 1120823W   3

DAY 37. CONGRESSIONAL OVERSIGHT HEARING. WASHINGTON, D.C.   7

DAY 245. RESIDENCE OF DR. BUD WORTHINGTON. HOUSTON, TEXAS.   11

EARTH'S CARETAKERS   **23**

DAY 5110. THE CHURCH OF HOLY SAINTS. NEAR ACOMA PUEBLO, NEW MEXICO.   25

DAY 3650. RICE UNIVERSITY. HOUSTON, TEXAS.   37

DAY 3285. NEAR CANYON DE CHELLY NATIONAL MONUMENT, ARIZONA. 360453N 1090812W   53

DAY 250. OFFICE OF DR. BUD WORTHINGTON. RICE UNIVERSITY. HOUSTON, TEXAS. 57

OIL AND THEIR LANDLORDS   **75**

DAY 3650. SPECIAL CONFERENCE TO THE PRESIDENT OF THE UNITED STATES. WASHINGTON, D.C.   77

DAY 2555. CLOSED SESSION HEARING, THE CAPITAL BUILDING. WASHINGTON, D.C. 83

DAY 2190. NEADE. UNDISCLOSED LOCATION NEAR THE PENTAGON. ARLINGTON, VA. 91

DAY 730. NETL. WASHINGTON, D.C.   97

DAY 245. NEADE. UNDISCLOSED LOCATION NEAR THE PENTAGON. ARLINGTON, VA. 107

OF LAND AND SCIENCE — 133

DAY 365. GRAND CANYON NATIONAL PARK, ARIZONA. 360320N 1120823W — 135

DAY 245. AMERICAS GEOSCIENCE RESEARCH CONFERENCE. SUN VALLEY, ID. — 145

DAY 260. MIDLAND, TEXAS. — 197

DAY 183. RICE UNIVERSITY. HOUSTON, TEXAS. — 215

FORCES IN OPPOSITION — 255

DAY 152. OFFICE OF DR. BUD WORTHINGTON. RICE UNIVERSITY. HOUSTON, TEXAS. 257

DAY 122. RICE UNIVERSITY. HOUSTON, TEXAS. — 275

DAY 84. RESIDENCE OF DR. KENNETH MILLARD. RICHMOND, VIRGINIA. — 313

DAY 63. MESA VERDE NATIONAL PARK, COLORADO. 371400N 1082847W — 335

FAULTS AND CONVERGENCE — 375

DAY 56. RESIDENCE OF DR. PAUL BREWER. HOUSTON, TEXAS. — 377

DAY 49. SKY CITY CASINO. NEAR ACOMA PUEBLO. — 397

DAY 47. ENTERING LA CUIDAD SAGRADA. 360453N 1090812W — 421

DAY 46. EXITING LA CUIDAD SAGRADA. 360453N 1090812W — 453

DAY 45. WAREHOUSE DISTRICT. DENVER, COLORADO. — 467

DAY 43. ACOMA PUEBLO. 345347N 1073452W — 473

THE FORCING — 483

DAY 37. CONGRESSIONAL OVERSIGHT HEARING. WASHINGTON, D.C. — 485

CHRON 19H18M46.659S 360320N 1120823W — 487

Characters from An Earth Scorned

Earth's Caretakers

Alejandro – grandson of Amado, is the remaining family member that still believes in his grandfather.

Tom'as Juanico – 'Mr. Thomas'', Amado's boyhood friend.

Amado Vallo – an elder of the Acoma Pueblo, initiated into the Corn Clan as a medicine man. As the remaining caretaker of Earth, the sacred visions taught to him will prove Earth is ready to retaliate against the greed of mankind.

Of Land

Sarah Cannes – Ranger, working at the Grand Canyon National Park. Unwittingly, her photographic archive captured the recent changes, as the canyon prepared itself for a major forcing.

Harold Chaplin – 'Harry', ex military pilot dating Sarah with the hopes of convincing her of his commitment.

Of Science

Avey Barnes – Arthur's girlfriend is a catalyst of many things.

Dr. Paul Brewer – retired museum collections researcher, confidant of Worthington.

Jude Caine – junior student, nephew of Peter Childs, struggles to define his resolve.

Peter Childs – Geologist, proud graduate of Rice University. His work ethic complicates his dedication to friends and family.

Arthur Hyde Clarke –'Clarke', Jude's roommate. Defines himself as a black sheep resisting his family's prestige.

Dr. Ravichandran Franklin – gifted geophysicist in study of tectonics, whose cultural integrity is a formidable strength against betrayal.

Karl Johns – Geologist, and close friend of Peter. Mentored by Worthington, his deeds are greater than even he could believe.

Wren Kennedy – fellow graduate hones her skills by hacking computer systems.

Dr. Kenneth Millard – renowned geologist, founder of Geo Terra Services. Sometimes his shrewdness can be outplayed by his vanity.

Robert T Straw – 'Looks', a fellow graduate. His love for extreme sports matches his gift of foresight.

Perrie Williams – fellow graduate whose dedication to her sister remains to be tested.

Dr. Bud Worthington – Professor Emeritus, archeological theologian, Rice University. His "black books" become the diary of Earth's final ultimatum.

Oil's Landlords

Willis Colton – ex CIA, controls NEADE, a covert agency. Allowing no proxy for error, his quest for power appears reckless to many.

Doug Erls – Field man for Apache Oil. His own family heritage haunts his past and future.

Angela Gates – CIA agent, working for Colton.

Jen Rawlins – geologist, Apache Oil. Her friendships with Peter and Karl are contradictions of truth.

Jason Smith – CIA agent, working for Colton.

Things have changed,
your touch has grown strange.
I can't help myself I know that,
you have left me dyin' here.

The Doobie Brothers

Prologue

I N THE LATE eighteen century, a scale of geological measurement began to evolve, allowing mankind to chart the impressive characteristics of Earth. Embedded with principles of time measurement, the study of earth's layers emerged, giving science the ability to develop a chronology of our planet. Using time segmentations, present day geologists commonly recognize the Holocene epoch, beginning twelve thousand years ago, as the most recent event in Earth's geological history. Nothing has happened since, to induce science to recalibrate our understanding of Earth's evolution.

A Chronozone or Chron, is the smallest calibration of geological time measurement that would scientifically document Earth's next hemorrhage. Despite the constant disruption of earthquakes, volcanic eruptions, tsunamis, and the momentous destruction of the polar icecaps, no geological 'forcing' has been recorded.

A 'Forcing' is the occurrence of an unforeseen physical disturbance, triggering irreversible and permanent change. Inevitably, a forcing impacts the sustaining characteristics of the planet.

The prophecy of a forcing is known by Amado Vallo, the Earth's remaining caretaker. Encouraged by him, only a few are allowed to seek the truth, which is far beyond science to understand. Mankind and its science can only react and by recording the first Chron ever, submits to Earth's geological fate.

Without admitting its own greed, mankind will wonder if the forcing could have been prevented and naturally will look to the past – counting the number of days before the first Chron event. All other forms of time measurement become irrelevant for good reason. There's nothing else worth counting when the survival of the human race is at stake.

The Forcing

CHRON 19h18m46.659s

360320N 1120823W

"**H**ELLO! I *SAID* the bottom of the canyon has fallen out!"

Sarah Cannes could not comprehend the voice yelling at her. Dizzy from sitting up too fast, she didn't understand. Having answered her cell, a man was repeating himself to be heard above the loud interference from an airplane engine. Pulling the quilt around her to keep from shivering Sarah realized her daughter, Rylie snuck into her bed again, barely affected by the commotion. Her mom's brain was not decoding fast enough.

Rubbing her eyes and pulling hair out of her mouth, all Sarah could muster was, "Harry! Do you know it's only five-thirty?"

Determined to make one more pass at the geological anomaly below his aircraft, the pilot was trying to be patient with his girlfriend. Unwilling to risk being heard on aircraft frequency, he had no choice but to call her from his cell, "Time? Forget that! I can't describe it!" he yelled as he maneuvered to get the plane level after banking hard left. "It's gone. The river is like... gone! Get over to the public hangar. You have to see this! Your camera has to see this!"

Still processing what she was told, Sarah gained more consciousness, "Is it bad? Why haven't you called SAR?"

"Everybody is gonna' jump on this! If you get the first photos they'll be worth big money!"

"He said the river's gone. The Colorado River's gone?" she debated, running over to the desk to compose a message. And then back to the bed with more clothes, landing on it with her knees, "Rylie, wake up. Wake up!" Shaking her gently, she coaxed her daughter out of a dream.

"She was there!"

"Rylie, listen. I've got to go down to the bottom."

"Remember the concert? She told me to get on the stage...I was singing!"

"Ya, that's really cool, but listen. Alice will come get you for breakfast. Just watch TV or read until she arrives. Remember the secret knock."

The sentence was said in slow, definitive segments as Sarah pulled on jeans and covered her top half with a sweatshirt and cap. She managed to get a pony tail pulled through the back of her hat.

"I want to go! I can get dressed fast!" Rylie spurted out.

Simultaneously, her body slumped back to supine upon hearing her mother's hard rejection, "Not this time, honey. There's something going on, but it may not be safe."

"Then why are you going?"

Sarah stopped putting on her boots for a second. The answer she gave was accurate enough for a seven year-old. "People may need my help. Now stay put. Okay, sweetie?"

She sealed the last request with a kiss on the forehead and went through their front door of the small house, locking it behind her. From the porch, Sarah looked towards one of the greatest national treasures on Earth, the Grand Canyon. The light coming through the rim of thin clouds made the golden threads of her insignia shoulder patch glow like neon. Along her route she wedged a note in the front door of the El Tovar hotel baker. Alice would be up and going within the hour.

Sarah drove twenty minutes to the checkpoint, an airstrip for licensed air tours and the search and rescue teams, wondering if the few drivers she passed knew what Harry had discovered. Binoculars, GPS, digital camera, and a medical backpack were piled at her feet as she waited.

"Where the heck is he?" she whispered, trembling from the cold air while scanning the horizon. Tipping her head, she heard the down throttle of an engine as the fixed wing Cessna reached the necessary altitude above the south rim. The plane circled to land on the maintenance strip, taxied past the sole occupant on the runway, and parked. The pilot had motioned with his hand, pointing to the helipad, and immediately climbed out.

Racing fifty yards to his Bell 206 helicopter he met his passenger at the front glass.

"Get a move on!" Harry yelled, fumbling with the straps on the tail prop, talking to himself and at Sarah intermittently. She could only hear portions of it.

"I can't believe my timing. I mean, it wasn't supposed to be done until tomorrow. You won't believe it!" the pilot reminded his passenger as he stowed away her gear, rushing from one side of the helicopter to the other. "Those guys never get done with the mechanics when they say they will! Who knows why I even bothered to check this morning and test it out. This was meant for us! I'm usually asleep! Hurry up! It's changing every second!"

Both climbed aboard as he helped with restraints, activating the aircraft at the same time. He paused to yell above the turning rotors, "You're ready with your camera, right?"

She lifted it up as proof. *But what was Harry up to?*

And then she thought she figured it out, "This better not be *another* prank!"

Sarah Cannes' disbelief was about to be confronted.

Day 37.
Congressional Oversight Hearing.
Washington, D.C.

I SOLATED FROM PUBLIC scrutiny, the hearing had been an intense ninety minute barrage of questions by the Senate Energy and National Resource committee, to unlock the activities of an agency secretly rooted within the Pentagon, under layers of security clearances. The congressman hoped to convey a sense of honor. Other tactics had failed.

"Mr. Colton, I remind you that, while not under legal oath, you are bound by standard code of conduct befitting a federal employee. Notwithstanding your service to our nation's intelligence gathering efforts, you should reconsider your answer."

At stake was the covert organization's three billion dollar operating budget, cloaking the research of one-hundred and twenty-five scientists, their research and discovery protecting the viability of a single substance.

No one outside the room was aware of the additional four hundred federal agents, dispersed across the globe to infiltrate U.S. and foreign interests. Within the walls of the interrogation room, no one yet grasped the deep roots of the agency, created to defend and serve the largest monopolies in the United States, whose profits totaled trillions of dollars.

No one knew how the secret agency had begun to spin out of control, becoming septic, yet impetuous in guarding secrets and assassinations.

No one could have predicted a single substance could have conjured a labyrinth of greed that would fail to control the Earth's deadly consequence of geological forcings.

A single substance.

Oil.

The monosyllabic answers aggravated the congressional leadership, who had failed to pry loose any secrets. Apathetic to their cause, the government official testifying was the seventh individual to repeat immunity. The committee members had read the dossier of the defendant, noting the document contained nonconsecutive pages, lines of text blackened—all evidence of intentional redactions.

"Who the hell is running this operation, Mr. Colton?"

The chairman was determined to strike a nerve. So far no answer was forthcoming to allow that achievement. His colleagues had become apathetic to his repeated assaults. He answered his own question. "Well, from where I sit, it can't be you, sir. It's evident they've cut you loose. It's obvious that you're over your head."

The brisk hand from counsel, placed on Colton's right arm, didn't stop him from exploiting their frustration. They were out of their league, "The same is obvious from where I sit, Mr. Chairman."

Neither man believed the accusations.

The chairman was driven to anger and retaliated, "For the record, Mr. Colton, this committee is *very* capable. Apparently you think you're out of my reach. From where I *sit*, there has been an abuse of power including several parallel investigations regarding multiple deaths, including an agent within your own organization. If we cannot ascertain the value of your agencies' involvement in the spurious use of funds, our ruling recommendation will certainly have a negative effect on your career. I will move in favor of a judiciary hearing for the purpose of obtaining legal warrants to break the silence. Now, for the record, is it true you oversee a Pentagon funded agency referred to as NETL…"

As a kid, Willis Colton and an older brother were on display with behavior that was polished every day by one parent. His father, a WASP on the east side of Brooklyn, worked for the CIA as a reader, scanning information collected by foreign operatives. As patriarch he ran the home, allowing his wife to fit in where she was expected. The boys were given a consistent message: stand up, grow up, and take it like a man. This practicum was applied to baseball, hockey, and church.

Being coached for something greater, Willis' older brother by four years was an example of this strict methodology, until his fatal drug overdose as a young teen. It wasn't clear to young Willis what occurred or why. Just that he was alone. Surviving his teens, he faced stark realities leading him to a binary decision to become a Marine cadet. Conditioned throughout his young life to be malleable, but only for authoritative purpose, he was very capable, with a keen intellect. Everything the Marines threw at him was taken as strengthening.

Saturated in military service, the drone of self-efficacy, self-control, and self-morality were interwoven into Willis' maturation towards adulthood. Once there, he fought a human obliqueness, the result of his father's structured insistence.

If he bothered to think about it, he couldn't recall a thing about his childhood that was fun or enlightening, not even baseball. His older brother's death left the void of sibling mentoring, instantly filled by the rants and demands of his father. At times of introspection Willis searched adolescence to find a connection to his parents. Nothing. There was no personable or emotional event that he could unlock from memory. Since adulthood, he had been re-tooled to lead men towards purposes rendered honorable. Willis Colton was alone.

After a tour in Vietnam as a sharpshooter, Colton joined the Eighth Special Forces group and trained insurgents in Latin America. When the group deactivated in the seventies, Colton pursued a career with the CIA. It was a natural transition given his father's diligent career record. Willis' set of distinct characteristics—to observe, reflect, and assimilate, but remain detached at a subliminal level—was a precious asset in espionage. He was a precious asset to his employer.

Day 245.
Residence of Dr. Bud Worthington. Houston, Texas.

THE SIP OF diluted Scotch was difficult to swallow, as the evening of brooding foiled the night cap. His stomach, unsettled by macaroni and cheese, battled the alcohol. Bud had almost forgotten to take his medicine, prescribed for his bout with Crohn's disease. Holding a pill, he cared less about its risks tonight. Bloodshot from anxiety, his eyes looked through corrective lenses at the lined paper smeared with cross outs, rewording, and doodles. Plotting the uncertainty of things, the professor's doubt chased logic to the mental corners leaving the professor struggling with his motives.

As a tenured professional of nineteen years at Rice University, tortured with his expansive knowledge and disgusted with his fallibility, the list in front of him was again unresolved. Like the night before and for months in the past, the internal debate stalled progress.

"My good hell!" Bud threw the pill in his mouth, chasing it with the remaining liquid, leaving him wincing. "Tomorrow night there will be two less issues to deal with," he promised, determined to enjoy the finish of the Scotch on the back of his throat. Deferred for over six years, the list of distinctive burdens collided with their human antagonist. Tonight's version of the four objectives, always the four that evaded his control, was listed with a solution:

Paul—His health! Find "El Santo Cáliz."[1] Government is taking too long!
Seismic Volume model—desperately needs analysis! Recruit Mr. Caine.
New earthquakes—finish research! Others will overtake my lead.
Acoma Project—exploitation of the pueblo!

No amount of deliberation retired Bud's sense of obligation and only aggravated his moral compass. For years, the same item was always listed first – bring Paul evidence of the artifacts, if not the sacred stones themselves. The two men, professors of Earth science specialties, would both share in the accolades of a discovery overlooked by a truculent society of get-rich-quick treasure hunters. A discovery they nicknamed, "The Holy Grail".

Ignoring the mounting critics at the university, Paul Brewer, professor of paleontology, was resilient to their peers' judgments that Worthington had become eccentric, exceedingly unorthodox in his area of expertise. Paul, in dire shape with diabetes and a bad heart, had stuck it out because of promises both envisioned would lead to success. The final blow was when Bud was snubbed for the annual Packard Fellowship award, reserved for distinguished scientists. Besides rescuing his sagging reputation, the bounty of over a half million in cash would have easily funded the Acoma project. Bud's candidacy ended when the broad funding and prestige was handed to a chemist. The promise of notoriety from gene splitting was more palatable than finding a lost culture's artifacts.

In the aftermath of the award decision, Bud learned his strengths were perceived as overstated, and many supporters had become weary of his mutation of the fundamentals of historical earth study. The umbrage from the Packard review board stemmed from his cocksure manner and a general conclusion he lacked the cachet to be considered viable for the inner circle of professionals. They particularly didn't care for his conceited remark during the interview that "the recent shake up in physics was a sign of the times and my research would do the same for Earth science."

Shortly after the announcements, political fences were mended, and, in Worthington's case, the mending was an offer to be displaced in Guatemala.

The dean laid out the terms in his office, "This is fully funded. There's ample discovery down there. Take some time off then get back on track. Rice will support your tenure, but not your current research."

---

[1] Holy Grail.

Bud's response required a more accurate assessment from the dean, more than willing to restate his position, "Rice has no interest in this Pueblo tribe. Since fighting with Spain for centuries, very little has changed, and there's nothing new to discover. Let the anthropologists handle their eroding culture."

"I'm certain of a find that would excite the *world!*" Bud pleaded, not interested in compromise or appeasement. "We both know artifacts extend the learning of one ancestral to a future one. This one has the greatest promise to do that!"

"The rationale for inferring an actual discovery could be made is highly suspect," the dean cited. "To be honest, some refer to it as a 'magical mystery tour,' if you know what I mean."

The dialogue was a debasing of Bud's certitude. Walking him to the door, a last push was made: "Think on this one. Do the right thing."

Upon hearing about the conversation, Paul improved his own mood by mocking the board, assuming Bud's second chance shot at "El Santo Cáliz" was going to put them back on track.

"What do those Judas' know of our Holy Grail?" Paul had boasted. "We'll get it in the bag and never look back."

And what of the Acoma project? Bud queried in his mind. He feared gaining possession of the tribal relics would destroy the Acoma and their sovereign rights. The conquering Spaniards acquired Pueblo wealth by force, as did later invasions by the new Americans. Announcement of newly discovered relics would permanently disable and probably destroy the remaining fragile context of the Acoma. Bud believed scientists and news media would descend upon Sky City, the home of the Acoma Pueblo, extinguishing their humble offerings and vilify their cultural systems.

Is it anything but speculation? Bud reminded himself. All his work, an *if,* teetering for years on the basis of friendship, and a trust begun a decade ago with the remaining Acoma elder; a trust that became intertwined by ancient visions, shared by the oldest surviving council member. *Nothing is going to happen if the "sacred stones" don't really exist!*

It seemed like the friendship and trust with the elder, counterbalanced with the hope of discovery, was already strained. And nothing eroded the hope of the potential discovery greater than Worthington's premonition of anticipated failure. His own tenuous suspicions of why he *was* trusted by the elder were unfounded, yet the Pueblo artifacts were still undiscovered.

Wrestling with facts and guesses, Bud pulled out his research papers from his leather brief case and gazed at the draft written months ago, explaining the premise of his research. The elegance of the text, familiar to its author, swept away resentments:

> The effort expended to understand man and his surroundings with generations of scientific-based observations have allowed mankind to creep towards a survival-based existence on Earth. Human studies have evolved from the simplistic map brought forth by the Greek philosopher Alcmaeon, to the complexities of the human genome. In a race of time for profit, the intellectual capital of Earth science has accomplished the same quantum leaps. The first cartographer, Diego Ribero, would be impressed that man now looks from above and penetrates Earth both physically and virtually to make sense of it.
>
> Overwhelmed with the contrary goals of benefactors, Earth scientists around the world are challenged to produce intellectually-driven conclusions that also support incentive-based rationalization. To succeed, the body of empirical research is required to ignore or disregard the multitude of Earth borne anomalies that continue to arrive at our doorsteps. Studies at the headwaters of new science continue to be those in tectonics, seismology, volcanics, and their subcategories. Aptly rewarded, researchers rely on theory-driven conveniences like repetitiveness and pattern theory to enlighten the public as to the consequences that await mankind.

Bud continued reading his manuscript in silence:

> While a myriad of scientists, experts, and a host of private and public institutions invigorate the status quo, Earth continues along her way, resistant and impervious to leading research. In parallel, increasing in opposition, the protocols of human kind continue to radically affect Earth.

Once a narrow opportunity of human survival thousands of years ago, with humankind literally poised naked on Earth's exterior, an eruption of unsurpassed evolution, only a few centuries later, has simultaneously transformed the planet into a warehouse and a barge to provision consumption and waste.

More specific to the inevitable hypothesis, humankind has developed a ravenous appetite for Earth's substrate, ingesting finite surface topologies. Sustaining our existence mandates excavation in three major forms: energy, metal, and non-metallic, expanding the methodical quarry of raw material to nearly one hundred elements.

Bud looked at one of his data tables, still amazed at the rate of human consumption, indicating permanent damage to Earth's thin lithosphere:

Extraction from substrate	Tons – Billion	Time Span – Years
Coal [2]	125	25
Oil Product	39	10
Natural Gas [3]	24	10
Metal	-	-
Non-Metalic	-	-

Table note: 919,000 producing wells worldwide [4]

He thumbed forward skipping the rest of the data analysis, pausing to read one of his favorite sections:

We have embarked on a path to apply counter-intelligence to Earth studies that have identified the limitation of Earth's resources. Mandated in every industry, the objective of restating "production" and "reserve" disregards the

---

[2] Energy Information Administration, "International Energy Annual 2004", http://www.eia.doe.gov/iea/.
[3] BP, www.bp.com/home.do?categoryId=1. Use download links, by energy type
[4] Morton, G., "Oil Headlines," http://home.entouch.net/dmd/oil_headlines.htm. Also see WorldOil.com.

premise that Earth is permanently disabled or worse. In fact, the planet's resources have declined precipitously to warrant fatal reactions.

This study exhumes the beginnings of our time and seeks to validate relevant discoveries that support research perspectives related to the hypothesis of Gaia [Lovelock 1979] and strong theories such as Omega Gaia [Chardin 1959] and homeorhetic balances [Margulis 1979].
Currently as applied, Earth science enjoys the pathology to resist theories that are based on spiritual evidence. While the technology continuum strengthens that resolve, a divergence is needed to challenge the subjective conclusions of earth sciences and unconditionally reexamine the enormous physical derivatives Earth continues to place in our paths.

The words, structured as the basic tenets of his research, were reinvigorating to the author and he was recharged with determination. Renewed by morning, Bud embraced two decisions that would bring his research closer to publication and world recognition.

On schedule, arriving in his university office by six am, Bud mechanically sorted through stacks of student assignments, culling their value for his unpublished research. For years, this routine gave the professor the facts and figures needed to mount a creditable defense, expecting his theories to be challenged vigorously. Typically, he had full charge of his own office for ninety minutes until a sequence of sounds dictated Ms. Margaret Olivary's punctual arrival.

Like every other morning, he heard the outside foyer doors open, the key and lock movement of the office door, then her humming, as she printed meeting schedules, email, and watered the plants. Then she would make her first appearance in front of his desk with polite reminders to not forget important events for that day, or books he planned to take to his class sessions, and to take his medicine. Her mentoring, sometimes imposing a countdown of time remaining, brought annoyance, especially after a hard night of posturing and indecision. He mused at the amount of attention he was given for his medical condition, opposed to the babysitting his admin doled out, reminding him to consume the proper dosage and pay attention to the side effects.

"Don't be surprised if you come in here and find me comatose on the desk," he had teased once.

The professor did approve of Ms. Olivary's tea service, a ritual he thought she started to keep tabs on his workload. She routinely delivered a fresh pot early morning and mid afternoon, with his favorite cookies. The first arrival of tea initiated the morning review of the calendar, implementing changes to accommodate the variety of requests from phone calls and emails. Bud was personally loyal to the student or faculty in need, in that order. Anyone else was last in priority unless there was fundraising involved.

"Marge," he called out, "I'm ready to have a go at the schedule."

She came in moments later, setting the tea on the credenza, "Dr. Worthington, have you taken your medicine this morning?"

"As a matter of fact, with glee."

She nodded, "What changes do you need to make?"

"I'd like to have Jude Caine on my calendar. Is there a possibility of scheduling a series of meetings?"

She flipped pages of hard copy forward then back again and replied, "There are a couple slots. Morning or afternoon?"

"I'll check with him at our first meeting. Please contact him tomorrow and get it set up."

"Good. What else?"

"My dinner with Paul on Thursday night. Is it still on?"

"Yes," Margaret replied after checking.

"If he tries to cancel, make sure he doesn't."

"Okay."

"I think that's it for now," her boss signaled.

"Oh. Remember Brad Harford?" the secretary asked. "I did find the address and will be sending flowers and a personal note to his widow."

"Yes. Thank you," Bud paused. "Strange how these young scientists are unable to keep themselves healthy. He was an outstanding research climatologist, affable mind with a promising career. Very surprising to everyone, I'm sure."

"You look a bit different today. Are *you* feeling well?"

"Actually, I feel better than usual. Tired, but not exhausted."

After Margaret left, Bud went to the partially opened window to listen to the surroundings outside, full of students' voices, cars, and the spring leaves of maple trees lined along the curb, rustling in the strong breeze. Instinctively, he felt his pocket for a pack of cigarettes but ignored his craving, satisfied to watch and observe change. After minutes, he returned to his desk and wrote emails to friends that were unaware of each other's significance. Bud expected to unite them soon.

"What the hell?!" Jude Caine blurted, while grading freshman assignments.

Fulfilling duties as a research aide for Worthington, he never understood why students thought plagiarizing from the web was harder to detect. A month away from spring break was making it harder to concentrate. And, his mom called, first to check up on him, then asking about his grades. Jude thought listing them off would suffice, but that didn't stop her from prying loose more detail. Then the conversation morphed to his travel plans during the break.

"Ya, Mom. You'll get a copy of my flight confirmation. I'll send it as soon as I get back to the house."

Fending her off led to her suggesting he should just come home during the break, even though he already had a ticket. She insisted it was refundable.

"No. It's not. Yes, they said they'll pick me up. Yes. I'll call Peter and let him know he needs to call you… *if I remember.*"

He wasn't the typical ungrateful student. He respected his parents but was used to his mom trying to take control. It just wasn't his day to baby sit her, or his uncle.

"Mom. I've got to head out. Okay. Love you. Yes. I'll tell Clarke you said hi. K. Bye."

Jude thought of the fun he would have in the Guadalupe Mountains located in southern Texas. He would be joining a group of Rice University grads who had remained together. Jude had traveled with the group before, but was really siked to hook up with one of them to BASE jump. Dabbling in kites for a while, he found them difficult to transport to remote locations, and enjoyed skydiving, but that got too expensive. With his parents trying to dictate his spending habits, jumping seemed like the natural fit between the two sports. He hoped the Texas weather and wind would own up to grant them perfect conditions, even if they ended up settling for mountain biking.

"Sweet," mumbled the student, as he scrolled through the images of the trails as he checked out the "free rider" site that mapped bike rides south of Carlsbad.

Returning home that evening, Bud had a stronger will to finish his massive research project, having completed his two self-imposed tasks that day. Sitting down on a chair, worn from repetitive use, he gathered his convictions to halt the continuous churning of review. Looking at the boxes of compiled literature surrounding the dining table, and stacks of folders in front of him, he encouraged the feeling that the constant appraisal could end after ten years

"Of course I can let this go. I've got all I need!" he said out loud, convincing the sole person in the room.

He sat there, testing his decision, "I could do this until doomsday. How did I ever think I could keep a continuous pulse on the world's activities and those who research it? I've got to move on!"

He got up and nervously circled the stacks, talking through the change.

"I'm solving the other items on the list. I *can* afford to stop *this* as well, this incredibility mindless ritual. Nine iterations of research review *are* enough."

When the heat vent blew cigarette smoke and ash into the air, Bud brushed off the papers as if touching them for the last time. Some were stained with coffee, others yellowed or permanently curled. For the next hour the professor rearranged the stacks, placing his favorites into common piles. All of them chronicled analysis about the appreciable change or shift in Earth's geological affairs, describing catastrophic events of volcanoes, earthquakes, floods, and weather anomalies. Bud flipped through Jude Caines' work that he had graded and kept, always appreciative of the student's solid approach to his assignments. Familiar with Jude's academic promise, Bud hoped the student would be motivated beyond college.

Thinking of his own path, Bud wondered if their dreams were like his, holding promise then diminishing into something else. As a boy, all he ever wanted to do was lead the best archeology teams and discover unheard of treasure. With age and consequence, his choices narrowed. The necessity for a steady paycheck came by way of teaching.

"There's nothing wrong with making ends meet," his dad would demand. "Being some big shot looking for bones. It's all hit or miss. Teaching is a good career."

Young Bud gave up convincing his dad that taking risks could make a big difference in the long run. As both got older they discovered they weren't alike. Debates about priorities added to the growing friction between them. Through his college days, Bud remained restless wishing for his break, dedicated to achieving fame.

"You don't have to like what you're doing as long as it pays the bills," his dad would lecture. "I've always had a job. Stay in teaching. Everything worth finding has already been discovered."

It was meant to be empathy, when Bud received his doctorate.

"Well, the bastard's been right so far," he thought.

Early in his teaching career, Bud was the activist, using man-made travesties like the Valdez spill and the Kuwaiti oil fires, to ethically incite students' interest in Earth science, educating them about the enormity of global destruction.

After arriving at Princeton University, he taught the dominant theme of finite resources and their impact upon global economies. At the beginning of the course, Worthington liked to trigger a classroom debate by asking, "What consumption patterns will doom future generations?"

The students learned past cultures were short-circuited or self-extinct because of reliance upon limited natural resources. Filled classrooms debated whether cultures fell victim to religious beliefs such as worshiping the sun, or fell to man-made consequences such as war or dependency upon finite resources.

Intensifying the theme, the professor packaged the course as a study of ecosystems and their need for preservation. Worthington's brand of paleo-science mixed with the global specificity of indigenous cultures had no equal at the graduate level. In the late sixties, at the height of increased activism throughout campuses, Rice University approached the seasoned scholar, to supplement their new Sustainability with Earth Sciences program.

With tenure, Worthington was given carte blanche to teach and preach within the purview of the board of regents and enjoyed being among the ranks of professorial, research, and endowed faculty. His empty office, provisioned with a personal administrator on the first floor wing, was immediately filled with the multitude of books, papers, and his framed black and white poster of Einstein. Arriving after hours to personally stow away the beginnings of his speculative research, he was certain the university would accept anything he threw down.

Expanding his studies of native North American cultures, Worthington looked upon himself as an archeological theologian. As part of teaching the hierarchy of scientific discovery, he lectured on the need to understand the spiritual imprinting of past civilizations and societies, and the role artifacts played in identifying unique characteristics of the culture. Field studies encouraged students to learn identification and preservation theories. It was the blend of classroom and the focus on regional theocentric-based tribes that brought the Acoma Pueblo into his view.

Taking a deep drag and letting the smoke seep out slowly, Bud flipped through the pages, getting his attention back to the work layered on his dining table.

"Flow rate changes with lithostratigraphic implications, he read and scanned the rest of the citation. "Hmmm. From the National Energy Technology Laboratory. No doubt a federal agency. Watchdogs with teeth protecting oil and no one else!" Bud boasted to himself.

A look at his wristwatch informed him he missed his TV program, but it was early enough to relax with a spy novel. Situated in bed, he could not settle his mind, excited with the instant progress he had made just by forcing his own hand. He felt propelled from the actions he put in play earlier that morning, even though his list, his four challenges, could not be solved in days or weeks. Still, it felt like a huge leap forward and he knew there would be a deeper reliance on people—people that he would need to convince or even beg.

His eyes closed and memory brought back his first visits to the Acoma Pueblo fourteen years ago. He fondly remembered the Acoma elder who never complained about the destructive force of generations that the Pueblo encountered. The elder had endured to share his knowledge, his friends, his food, and his family. Sometimes a young grandson named Alejandro would be invited to sit with them during meals. The Native grandfather insisted the professor witness the unfettered spirit of a Pueblo child who understood the history of the Pueblo and its spiritual placement within the universe. Secretly siphoning off budget dollars every quarter, Bud had all but forgotten about the stipend he saved for the elder's grandson.

Just before falling asleep, a smile appeared on the professor's face. *The years spent with the Acoma tribe were not wasted.*

Maybe everything was falling into place because of their friendship and trust. The spoken word of the elder was the essence of that trust and friendship. Bud remembered the elder's words after they had hiked through a rainstorm in the mountain ranges of New Mexico: "I was joining

Earth in her ways. She has told us many things. We are honored to be given her wisdom."

With the last of consciousness taken by exhaustion Bud realized the luxury of time had diminished. He could no longer cordon himself off letting suspicions bind his progress. Or waste energy on the minutia of reviewing others' research. Or deeply worry about the impact on an entire culture.

It was time to bring out the truth. It was time to take a risk.

Earth's Caretakers

Day 5110.

The Church of Holy Saints. Near Acoma Pueblo, New Mexico.

THE ACOMA ELDER looked into the professor's eyes. The lower tones of the native's voice were melodic, sometimes competing with sounds of the warm wind rushing to the church windows, pressing hard against the hand-set pieces of stained glass. With creaks and small pops, the wood and plaster structure bore the brunt from the outside elements. Temperature and humidity inside the old church caused the occupants to sweat.

The cadence of speech seesawed between them and an interpreter, "Memory of her is everything. We hear and listen to the world above and below us. Others are deaf and blind to the changes of her soul."

The host shared very little knowledge during their first meeting, but this eighth meeting, with the previous visits spread across multiple years, held more promise of discovery, of a culture not widely studied or appreciated. Much of the Acoma's existence was recorded by observation from third parties. In the past, it had been difficult, even impossible to learn about the Acoma from its own population. Like other generations, the elder would never reveal his personal experience of the gallo[5] races he competed in as

---

[5] James, *ACOMA*, 70. From the Spanish decent, a footrace that transitions to horseback, of great endurance and agility with men and horse competing to catch and carry a fowl; the owner keeps it from others.

a young adult, the healing dances, or reveal his sacred animal, the dya.´t^{yu}.[6] Life and living on Earth, the storms, the toil, the learning, all remained sacred to Aacqu, and to the seventy-nine-year-old named Amado Vallo.[7]

Bud remained vigilant and treated each session as a keepsake expecting more evidence to be given for validation of a potential discovery. The professor had learned during the visits that the elder was one of the last 1,000 natives and part of the remaining population to speak the dialect called Aa´ku. A language isolate of Western Keresan, Aa´ku was spoken only by the Acoma Pueblo, one of the 300 tribes the United States government began to recognize in the mid-1900s.[8]

Today, Amado spoke Spanish, reserving his heritage language for spiritual purpose. Worthington nodded to confirm his understanding of the interpretation and responded, "I am a teacher of the earth. I want to earn the respect of the native."

The distinguished professor had learned to pause and think before responding to Amado. He shivered with anticipation. A simple statement of obligation and commitment was being translated to the only living oblate of the tribe. Bud sat motionless waiting for a response. Nothing was said. The outside noise of vehicles resonated through the gaps in the front doors.

"*¿Por qué busca Ud. la realidad de la vida?*"

The interpreter, Mr. Thomas', translated the phrase to English without much accent. As boys, with a ten year difference in age, he and Amado were part of the Corn Clan witnessing the ceremonies kept pure by ancestry. During his military service, Tom´as Juanico changed his name, from the pressure of others making fun of his culture. Many natives had done the same. A simple change deflected taunts, but deep beliefs remained impervious to mocking. When he returned to the Acoma Pueblo, he remained near Amado's side.

"Why are you searching for the truth?" Mr. Thomas' translated.

The words surprised him, but Bud remained calm. Taking a breath to slow down he spoke, "To protect and preserve ancient beliefs."

The interpreter started translating to Amado, when Bud raised his hand abruptly, interrupting the dialogue. He realized the elder would judge him from his words and they may hold false meaning.

---

[6]   White, "New Material from Acoma," 308.

[7]   Minge, *Acoma Pueblo in the Sky*, xi.

[8]   Wikipedia, "Keresan Languages," http://en.wikipedia.org/wiki/Keresan_languages.

He apologized, "I'm sorry."

"*Lo siento*," repeated Amado.

"Speak from this," Mr. Thomas' said as instructed. Quick to mentor, the elder pointed to his heart.

"I respect your love for the earth. As an individual, I must learn to protect her," Bud restated.

The elder then extended his arms and grasped the visitor's hands. The skin of the native's palms was rough; his elongated fingers encompassed much of Bud's hands and wrists.

As he felt the energy beyond the warmth of tissue, Bud was relieved and added to his commitment, "I respect your gift and must earn your trust."

Over years, the many talks between them uncovered similarities. The teachers spoke of students passing through their own forms of mentoring and bragged of greater deeds each of them coveted as adults. After meals, the men talked about their places in society, agreeing there was an erosion of respect for their accomplishments. Often nine months would go by until another visit occurred, but time and distance did not unravel their growing relationship or Worthington's pursuit of knowledge.

The few books he had purchased were repetitive in the description of Acoma history, located the farthest south of all eighteen Indian Pueblos. Less explored in text, much more was said about the Zuni, Hopi, and Navaho cultures. Bud used students and other resources to expand his understanding of the tribe and explored Acoma nuances that set it apart from all other Pueblos.

The most obvious distinction was the physical location of their entire existence, on a 357-foot mesa called "Sky City," northwest of present day Albuquerque. Bud was intrigued the Acoma tribe had survived the ebb and flow of brutality, receivership, and emancipation. Although the Spaniards arrived in the mid-1500s, the Acoma Pueblo wasn't given back self-appointed custody under the protection of the United States until 1913.[9]

Research gathered by his students showed similarities existed between all the pueblos in their ritual worship but a clear delineation remained for the Acoma. Their worship was centered on a supernatural living on earth, its strength encompassing the Sun.[10] More so, the Acoma was

---

[9]   Minge, *Acoma Pueblo in the Sky*, 83.

[10]   Mails, *The Pueblo Children*, 266.

documented to have lived prior to all other tribes, beginning in 1200 AD. Some experts believed the tribe existed before Christ.[11]

During this eighth session, the elder said he had become impressed with the steady commitment Worthington possessed. He was translated to say those who were willing to seek guidance about cultural integrity, endurance, and sanctity, had been few.

Without explaining the motive, Mr. Thomas' told Bud that for a long time, Amado had been searching for truth and honesty. To his satisfaction, the professor had earned the trust of the Acoma.

"Today was a final test of your journey. As the Acoma define it, Truth is in us." And then Mr. Thomas added, "Or it's not."

The Pueblo had already allowed a small group of students into the area for a restoration project that would reverse effects of natural erosion. Bud assumed the elder saw that annual commitment as a token of the trust he had just earned. He hoped he would be given tribal permission to explore different sites. Bud explained the essence of his research proposal and how it could benefit the Acoma. The elder seemed interested and asked the professor to stay later than planned.

Late evening, an hour of translated dialect was more evidence that the professor was being rewarded. Amado shared details of a forgotten location, telling a story passed on by his ancestors. According to Mr. Thomas', the event was unprecedented. He himself had never heard the complete legend as it was told that night. Exuberance and fatigue challenged Bud as he attempted to recount the dialogue in a small journal.

Upon returning to his group, the professor scrambled the following day trying to get organized. He quickly entrusted one of his senior students, Karl Johns, with leading the work projects, saying nothing as to where he may be going and admitting only that he was still meeting with the Pueblo members.

"There could be a breakthrough and I'm certain everyone will benefit from it!" Bud exclaimed.

That morning, Bud journeyed hours with the elder, Mr. Thomas', and Alejandro to a place the Pueblo leader had called "*la cuidad sagrada*" meaning sacred city and another time, said it was "u*na cuidad escondida dentro de otra ciudad*," a city hidden within a city.

---

[11]   Minge, *Acoma Pueblo in the Sky*, 1.

In succession, paved highway turned into improved surface, which degraded eventually into primitive forest service road. Through the foothills of canyons, scattered with pristine vegetation, the group traveled on a thin trail that followed anemic water sources, towards increasingly higher plateaus. As they hiked, Mr. Thomas' spoke slowly, giving explanations about the relationship of Ocatc, the sun, sometimes called Father and the twin boys, referred to as Twin War gods, Masewi and Oyoyewi.[12] The older Indian nodded with approval during the conversation.

"They are the spirits who tell us the meaning of what we see, hear, and feel from within," Mr. Thomas' continued to describe. "Ocatc appears with many faces. The twins were our strongest mentors in the early days."

After miles of weaving around small valleys, climbing over ridge tops, they approached an enormous box canyon partially surrounded by a fence perimeter. Rising in height over that of Sky City, smooth sandstone vaults and massive veneers dwarfed the visitors. Imagining the site in its original state, Bud perceived it as a replica of structures located in Sky City, although the ancestral engineering was advanced in design, doubling occupancy to over one hundred individual homes, complete with cisterns located outside some of the larger building structures and at multiple levels.

Ingeniously, the structure paralleled the degrees of incline of the naturally formed mesa wall that towered over the visitors. The lower rows of adobes were offset forward to create a wider base for stacking the succeeding rows above. Every two or three rows of physical construction were shifted horizontally to allow for climbing ladders or water collection. Narrow chutes to channel rain water were visible going all the way to the top. Reflecting compressed living space, Bud could envision the intended design of each two-story home.

Visually, the exteriors and interiors of the lower section of homes had been treated poorly by vandals, yet the structures stood impervious to wind, rain, and heat. The roof extensions of cedar that would span to hold yucca fiber and grasses were mostly decayed. The dome shaped hornos with mortar surfaces, were desecrated with bullet holes. Many of the door frames had been removed exposing the complex earthen layers of the vertical walls that spanned fourteen feet in width. Some ladder material lay on the ground with saw cuts.

---

[12] Mails, *The Pueblo Children*, 266.

Mr. Thomas' spoke his own mind reflecting the miserable condition of the site, "Years ago, the government told our council they would protect the area from further destruction," pointing to the steel fence that had fallen, snarled with debris. "This is what they call fixing the problem. We've asked many years. You can see their commitment was false."

The young grandson, Alejandro started to explore. He was bored after listening intently to the explanation of how the Pueblo council had, for hundreds of years, taken many issues to the governments in control. Amado rested on the edge of an empty cistern as Mr. Thomas' shared the unknown truth of the past.

"This area was to be a secondary site, one of community for *all* the Pueblos. Many Acoma and Laguna built this structure after the Spaniards arrived and left. Our ancestors had hopes of protecting themselves from further control. Our forefathers worked out agreements with other Pueblos. It would have benefited all of us."

"I read accounts of the small pox in the mid-1700s. That it was the reason for the decline in population in specific tribes," Bud reasoned.

"Yes. That's what was believed. At times, we had hundreds of workers here instead of where the government expected them to be. This was a place where we united. It was to serve the purpose of unifying the ancestors. But only because of the government, our boundaries were in dispute. Nothing but trouble for many."

"All very sad," responded Bud, feeling empathy for those past transgressions and the visual plight in front of him. All of it dampened his enthusiasm. This site was not exactly hidden, let alone revered.

Mr. Thomas' pointed to an open space that had fire pits littered with broken glass and wood cinder, saying, "In the center of the ground over there, ceremonies were performed by leaders like Amado. They taught the dances to their children, but that teaching was taken away. The last of the Pueblo was forced to the smaller Acomita settlement and their children were taken, made to attend mission and government agency schools."

"What dances were taught?"

"Healing that called on the Father, that protected the earth and our families. Dances that kept them strong here and here," Mr. Thomas' stated, pointing to his head and his heart. "The dances of the Corn Clan and maybe Initiation would have happened here. The Katcina cult bringing the spirit rainmakers would make families happy."

Suddenly, the elder's voice commanded attention. Only a few had heard the utterances he spoke in the native tongue.

"*Tsi.'mait*," he whispered, picking up pulverized dirt and letting the wind from the north blow it away. He held a flint in his hand, the leather strap attached to it, dangling from his neck.[13]

Removing it from his pouch, a Katsina prayer stick with a small feather attached at both ends was laid on the ground.[14] Amado, the medicine man, shifted his feet, transferring his weight. Another dialect was spoken that Mr. Thomas' was more familiar with.

"He is talking to the powers of the spirits. *K'obictaiya* comes from the east."[15] Then the translator lowered his voice, "He is summoning *tsa.ts*'"[16]

Alejandro was intrigued as well but ventured off again. He did not have the endurance of the adults watching Amado for more than thirty minutes. Bud did not approach Amado when he finished the impromptu ceremony, and instead walked among the lowest of the tiered stone walls. His exploration was unsurpassed if the color of the rock, sky, and living creatures could be counted as new discoveries. Dependent upon the direction of the wind, the barren site was scattered with mobile amounts of tumbleweed collected in corners of the giant adobe structures. Coated on many walls was substance that, upon closer examination, revealed it as artwork. Mr. Thomas' nodded with approval when asked if a few pictures could be taken.

Bud looked at his watch again. He was prone to forget to take the dose of his new prescription. The doctor told him the drug, Azulfidine was the best precaution on the market and a re-diagnosis would likely turn up negative for his ailment.

"What are we looking for?" Bud wondered out loud, getting back to the task of a breakthrough. "What should we be looking at for clues to discover the hidden city?"

"Only a few selected from the tribe were given the sacred truth as they became his age," Mr. Thomas' stated, pointing first to Amado, then to Alejandro. He then translated the question back to Amado.

"The beauty is in the rock," the elder was translated as saying.

---

[13] White, "New Material from Acoma," 324. Meaning Earth.

[14] Ibid., 323.

[15] Mails, *The Pueblo Children*, 267.

[16] White, "New Material from Acoma," 324.

"It would be difficult to examine this whole area," Bud exclaimed. "We would need many of my students. So that I can find my way here, possibly Alejandro can continue to guide me in your absence and I can get some manpower out here. He might enjoy it with the students."

Surprising Bud, the natives seemed apathetic to the idea and he set his idea aside, "Well, we certainly can figure out a plan for the future," Bud relented and noticed a massive thunderhead peering over the mesa's edge. "Look's like a storm is brewing. Let me take some notes, and then we should head back."

Mostly downhill on the return trip, the spiritual intricacies of the hike became more apparent to the professor as the group reached the lower summits. Before getting consumed by weather, an updraft allowed a swarm of airborne gnats to supplant themselves on the hikers. As Bud aggressively swept his face, bare arms, and clothing, neither the elder nor his life-long friend bothered to brush themselves off. While Bud had avoided the rough scrape of sage or grass along the trail, he noticed Amado extended his arms to touch, sometimes lifting his hand to breathe in the scent of the foliage. When another silent frenzy of bug hatches whirled in front of the group, the two older Indians marveled at them while looking across the landscape, speaking in low tones. Their eyes peered into the bounty of Nature, seemingly as pristine as when it created itself. As the trail led them onwards to less remote landscape, the human-dispersed trash had become more frequent, but nothing was said to diminish the natural beauty displayed around them.

Carried across from the expanding thunderhead, large drops of rain began to explode on the callused landscape. Alejandro playfully dodged the drops jutting back and forth. The wind pushed the hikers along the last segment of the hike, as the rain increased, hitting sparse ground cover. A glance back showed that sheets of water would soon coat the surface of the earth they were walking on.

Bud observed that the elder seemed oblivious to the conditions. All his senses were open to Earth's offerings. Often, the native would turn into the wind taking a deep breath and appear to hold it for seconds. He never wiped the rain off his face or the snarled strands of hair clinging to it. *It was as if he was absorbing the moisture*, Bud conjured. Instead of interrupting his host to satisfy his curiosity, the professor honored what he witnessed.

The knurled juniper sliced wind gusts into high-pitched whistle sounds signaled the guttural bellow of thunder that raced across the mesa six miles behind them.

When Bud heard portions of the elder's meditation, he caught up to Mr. Thomas', "Amado's chant. He's repeating what we heard earlier?"

"Yes. *tsa.ts*'. It is the soul of rain."

Bud stopped, letting his friends proceed down the path. He had read about the supernaturals and the unnerving faith of their native subordinates. The sky was clear when they had left mid-morning. The drops plinking on his face had been a nuance until that moment. Getting left behind, Bud imagined much of the flowing energy was largely ignored or disrespected by Earth's humankind.

When asked later about his behavior on the mountain, the elder watched for Bud's reaction to the translation given by Mr. Thomas', "I was joining the earth in her ways. She has told us many things. We are honored to be given her wisdom."

Before rushing back to Albuquerque to catch his flight, Bud mapped out new portions of his research on the hotel bed, trying to organize his thoughts. His excitement faded after a call with Paul. When drilled for details about tangible evidence, Bud had to restate the importance of the sacred city. Not entirely convinced it was a "city hidden within a city" he reconciled his chances, "With my candidacy for the Packard award, I guess it's not as strong a finding as I wished for."

As a master conservator, Paul had grown tired in the museum business appraising the leftovers from the major findings, and migrated to a university setting. He had seen many site discoveries go sour.

"It might be too early to draw conclusions about the absolute value of it. We'll give it some time to mature," Paul cautioned, but couldn't hide his own regret. "Although, it would have been nice to rub something in their faces."

The hype of locating the abandoned "sacred city" could not impede the chain of events triggered by the university. As Worthington sparred with the university president to allow him more time, his budget allocations were trimmed. There wasn't much left to salvage, considering the core of the Acoma project consisted of a field trip and a semester of free labor from students.

"I don't have any extra funds," Bud complained to Paul one evening. "And the board has clamped down on my budget. But they can't tell me how to spend my days. As long as I have students, I'll have minds to harvest."

As quick as Bud declared his defiance, he announced another surprise. "But there's another path that opened up. Did I tell you about this young Indian fellow, Dr. R. Franklin?"

"I've heard bits and pieces from others."

"He's entered the program, with a PhD in geophysics. I've heard he's an astute field man. We've got to talk to him about a potential role. I've also heard a rumor. The board has given *him* a budget."

"That's consistent with what's been shared with me," Paul confirmed.

"Apparently they see a great deal of value in him. His specialties are tectonics and seismology, specializing in reflection."[17]

"So he might have some interest once he appreciates your idea," Paul presumed.

"Yes. He's required to be here a year minimum, so there's ample time for me to lay the groundwork," Bud speculated. "My preliminary findings could get him up to speed quickly. His expertise would be put to good use integrating the data constructs I have developed."

"Does this mean you've given up on the Acoma tribe?"

"Call it postponed. There are other irons—"

Margaret knocked and stepped in the doorway, "Excuse me." She waited for acknowledgement.

"—that need attending to. Yes?" Worthington addressed her.

"You wanted me to tell you when Mr. Johns arrived."

"Yes. Thank you. Tell him a moment or so. Where were we? Yes, I think the data models are key, and I'll accept what theoretical outcomes they can offer, but they are *not* as important as what the Acoma might have for me."

"Aren't you a bit overzealous about the Pueblo?" Paul prompted his friend, as the only willing antagonist to debate the Pueblo's fallibility.

---

[17] Wikipedia, "Crustal Studies," http://en.wikipedia.org/wiki/Reflection seismology#Crustal_ studies. Reflection seismology is a branch of seismology that uses reflected seismic waves to produce images of the earth's subsurface. By noting the time it takes for a reflection to arrive at a receiver, it is possible to estimate the depth of the feature that generated the reflection. In this way, reflection seismology is similar to sonar and echolocation.

"There were no findings out there other than bullet holes and litter. Maybe the research needs to lead with science and less on Indian tales."

"I'm aware of the risk. A reasonable case for the Acoma tribe having autochthonic decedents would get attention."

"Just so you don't float yourself away on hearsay, my contacts from the museum haven't concluded in your favor. We'd never get them to settle on the Acoma being the first humans on the earth."

"With what we've shared with them, your people haven't disproved the hypothesis either," Bud weighed.

"Well, it remains open, but certainly not neutral or positive. I've got to go. You have your student waiting for you. See you at dinner tomorrow night then?"

"Of course."

Barely had Paul passed out of sight when Karl walked in and sat down in a leather chair, "How come you never invited me?"

Worthington had planned to tell his favorite student about the cancellation of programs within his teaching curriculum and termination of funding for the Acoma project, "Invited you? Where?" the professor asked.

"To meet with the holy man," was the response, presuming a partnership.

"Oh! I'm very sorry about that. It was a complicated relationship that needed to be built on the trust of two peers. We did manage to exchange a wealth of information that I've shared in part. I plan to go back soon and could use your help then, but I have to tell you—"

"I've heard the rumors. It's all over the college. No more funding."

"Unfortunately, that's accurate. We'll have to put the Acoma Pueblo in moth balls for the time being."

"After doing all that work, I'm not going to get the chance to organize the excavation of the site. If you not going back, then—"

"It's a setback Karl, but not permanent. No one has given up. Myself, nor Paul."

Karl nervously rubbed the back of his head. Even with lots of options available to him, the student was genuinely disappointed that the opportunity for the pueblo wasn't going to materialize. He had been imagining his role, bringing the crew into the area and managing their day to day existence, "With a majority of major dig sites overseas it would have been cool to make a new discovery in our own backyard. But I graduate in one semester. I've got job offers that I planned on turning down, hoping it would happen."

"Karl, I know the timing of this is disappointing. Believe me, I have the same reaction. However, we'll do our best to make a go of it. You'll be my first contact when I can get it back on track. I know you've made sacrifices throughout your tenure with me. Of course if you need my reference, I'll gladly provide it."

Worthington stood up and patted Karl's back, "Still, I have made some gains on the mathematical aspect of my research. There's another resource coming along that can help us achieve our goals. Even without the university's support, I plan to continue research on the project."

Karl looked at his favorite Einstein poster on the office wall, with its caption, "Violent opposition and mediocre minds."

Nothing was closer to the truth.

Day 3650.

Rice University. Houston, Texas.

With darker skin and curly hair, his dialect was precise, flaunting a bilingual capability. Symbolic of a young rebel but with Indian ethnicity, Dr. R. Franklin was young in age and highly educated.

The single child borne of Indian descent was expected to learn and achieve. The boy was taught the strife his parents had endured in their lifetime, themselves conditioned with higher probabilities of failure than their offspring. His birth as a U.S. citizen did not shield him from the knowledge of the pain and suffering experience by past generations. His parents did hope and pray their son's achievements would renew blessings for their spiritual kin. Instilling competitiveness through formal education, they expected their child to excel to the highest level possible.

The gifted Ravichandran Franklin eventually adapted his birthright to conform. Known as R. Franklin while in college, he immediately showed his preference to be addressed as Franklin. His father, with great anguish, acknowledged the obvious need to avoid cultural bias.

As an undergraduate, the young man was awarded an internship at MIT. His aptitude was paid in kind with the willingness of many teachers to mentor him in the field of physics. This acquired intellect was accompanied by evolutionary study in tectonics and paleotectonics. The dual majors in geophysics and seismology helped secure a teaching appointment at the graduate program at Rice University. His intellectual gifts continued to advantage his endowed purpose, to affect the spiritual bounty of the family tree. Never losing his connection to his parents, he would effortlessly relocate them provisioning for their comfort and security, ensuring they were in the center of his life.

Brushing the tip of his cigarette across an ashtray held near the office window and waiting for Margaret's punctual arrival, Bud thought again, of the first dinner meeting he had arranged with Paul and Franklin. Negatives had to be neutralized or at least addressed. Smiling, the professor was wary of Franklin, assuming the young intellectual had been warned in advance. With his amiable voice and experience in museum collections, Paul was ready to shore up any questions about Bud's reputation.

At dinner, their conversation was engaging, as it breached areas that were subtle tests of commitment, honor, and truth. Franklin was responsive when asked about his immediate plans and, with a nudge, affirmed he was promised a budget. Larger than either suspected, Bud struggled to conceal personal displeasure towards the board of regents; he thought his funds had been diverted to Franklin. He had lost enough sleep over their lack of interest in his continued explorations.

With his own influence, the topic politely shifted to Paul, talking about previous jobs and projects. He explained the methods for procuring and evaluating priceless artifacts.

"Many don't perceive the intrinsic value of the art or relic and decide to sell it to the next high bidder to take immediate profit."

"And if they were making the wrong decision, what controls do you have?" Franklin queried, as if to treat the matter like a lab experiment.

"If I knew the piece had extraordinary purchase power, a formal write-up documents my evaluation. Although I'm limited by degrees of confidentiality, my peers often ask to share their opinions. Sometimes I might attempt to influence the owner as to their potential mistake. It's a human trait that has its absolutes."

"Which is?"

"When others eventually realize what they could be giving away, all hell can break loose," Paul boasted.

The response of shared amusement was recognition that each man had dealt with the same circumstances in their careers.

Bud segued into the status of his research, feeling out any chance of advocacy, "We certainly can attest to that behavior," he admitted.

"Franklin, you may have heard I lost my bid for the Packard award a while back and it's likely going to cost me an endowment chair as well. But I'm still interested in developing the statistical modeling for that study. If I may ask, what is your opinion, assuming you've heard of it?"

Paul was shocked his colleague went to the point of conflict so quickly. Bud explained later that if there was disaffection he wanted to root it out so he could at least enjoy his meal.

"Actually, I was tipped off," Franklin admitted. "I wasn't given details. Only that you are very dedicated to seeing it through."

"Really?"

"I'd be happy to get more details from you. I'm developing models beyond others' capability to appreciate their power. It will allow for predictability with the characteristics of seismic wave technology."

"Applied modeling in the lab? For use in the field?" quizzed Bud.

"For both. You know the status quo. The standard math is in stasis. You've heard of COCORP and those findings, of course."[18]

"Of course," Bud said as he nodded.

"As you know a number of interesting threads were started there from the deep reflection experiments. Throw in Moho, the downwelling of the mantle and you have a trace of what I'm seeking in terms of scientific discovery."[19]

Franklin was prompted for more detail from Paul, just as much intrigued and willing to admit his limited knowledge of multi-dimensional seismic volume study, "As a sidebar, you can assume velocity is still the basis for all similar research. Impedance of the wave is considered a gating factor as well," explained the geophysicist, sipping wine and then deciding to share more detail. "There are possibilities for the mathematical inferences and asymmetries for a common set of data points, like the coefficients of reflection. I'm gauging other inputs, beyond what the oil industry is compelled to force on all of us. Let's stop it there other than saying it's determining the simple cause and effect, when mild forcings are presented and how rates of change are manipulated to show predictive outcomes. You can imagine the computing power I need to qualify even preliminary calculations."

---

[18]   Brown, Larry, "Unexplained Mysteries: COCORP revisited." 9, http://www.scec.org/news/01news/es_abstracts/brown.pdf.

[19]   Chapman, Jay, "California's Lost its Moho," Geotimes Web Extra, http://www.geotimes.org/septo4/ WebExtra090204.html.

"I'm sure your objective is superior to others in your field, but do you find there are competing interests trying to reach the same conclusions?" Paul asked hoping the answer would make their case. But his motive backfired.

"I suppose so. It's always a race to the finish *if* you have followers. There seems to be avenues that one can go down and unfortunately never have to worry about someone tracing their steps. But no one remains permanently disinterested in another's specific research when they learn of its funding support."

"Rightly so," responded Bud angling for a new advocate. "But funding can become a two-edge sword. I'm fortunate to still have ample backing, but I look forward to our relationship as an injection of interest, money or not."

"I'm not suggesting there would ever be budget opportunities. Our studies seem mutually exclusive," Franklin deflected. He decided to test their friends' mettle to confirm their dire situation. "But from what I was told, you lost your funding."

Bud hesitated, but his answer was defensive, "The board will come running back to us when the value is more apparent. Of course there's a line out the door of naysayers, all sheep if you ask me—"

Paul cleared his throat as a reminder of the earlier coaching he gave Bud, and his friend recanted, "—of course, I owe them their indulgence and can leave my personal opinions at home. I'd be honored to have access to your intellect. I don't need any more funding at this time."

Fresh out of subtle attempts to discover each other's motives, a final round of wine finished off the evening for the trio and after Franklin left, the other men stayed to compare notes.

"It sounded very positive to me," voiced Paul, "although I didn't intend to shed light on the dollars. I was trying to guide Dr. Franklin, showing him how the two projects have intriguing outcomes."

"Yes, I realized that. Our projects may in fact be closer in comparison, and that's something I can mentor him on. It's important to find out exactly what Franklin is willing to do for us."

"On the other hand, I suppose he could be a pigeon for the board," warned Paul.

"Yes. I have a great deal of concern about that. Keep friends close and enemies closer, right?"

Paul nodded, toasting with his empty glass, "My thinking as well."

Franklin kept his word evaluating the partnering opportunity with Worthington. After a few meetings, he outlined a commitment both men thought would serve their purposes.

As mutual trust was gained over time, the intrinsic portions of research were shared by both. Worthington revealed what the university considered to be the weakest piece of his thesis—the value of the Acoma tribe's spiritual power. Franklin talked through models he developed using the whiteboard, but the theories were beyond Worthington's interest. Interactions between them were never strained to the point of exhaustion, but many discussions caused friction, centered on the scientific method of approach and technique. And often conventional wisdom was challenged to favor youth.

Traditional baselines of scientific research hadn't changed, but the younger man was eager to preach his interpretation as if his older colleague had morphed away from required protocols. After hearing vague statements describing the value of the Acoma, Franklin coached his colleague on maintaining objectivity.

Bud hid his annoyance when Franklin offered a refresher on the common approach for objective scientific discovery, "First, I train myself to have solid comprehensive knowledge of the subject matter, which could take months or years. After I develop the theory, experiments help prove or disprove. If I get stuck—"

Worthington bristled, but Franklin ignored the attempt to interrupt, "—if I get stuck, that forces me to think differently about what I believe. In time, I change my perspective, which hopefully provides the solution."

"Yes," Bud calmly asserted, ready to challenge the accusation. "I actually went through that transformation with archeology, which *ultimately* brought me full circle back to a theoretical posture."

"*But* you have to have an experiment to test your hypothesis. You don't seem to have one. What you have are reams of geological data on one hand and the promises of spiritual discovery on the other."

"In time," Worthington insisted, realizing Franklin was motivated to debate the relevance and weaknesses of a life's work.

"If I merely collected the historical information about all the volcanic eruptions in the world, and only guessed about the levels of predictability, no one would listen," Franklin proposed. "I only get their attention when proof is offered. Hard proof from models."

"I wouldn't disagree," countered Bud. "Your dependence upon mathematics is unquestionable. I'm merely suggesting my thesis manifests beyond Eolithic discoveries. I have to think of myself as," and Worthington was pleased with his description, "a rebel of science to further the cause. Much of what I'm going to publish pushes the boundaries."

That day, their arguments became bolder, demonstrating the sheer competence of the two scientists. Worthington knew his protégée was strongly biased towards the value of simulation models and mathematical progressions. Emboldened, Franklin saw a teacher steeped in valuable field experience, but mortally wounded with credibility problems. It became a last ditch effort to save each other.

"Bud, you need a practicum or robust model to represent the primary goal of your research. Clearly you can see how your critics are attacking the conceptual framework of your study. You need to fight back in absolute terms with the mathematics and avoid the flagrant assumptions."

"I have all the data I need in my archives," Worthington countered. "With due respect to your valiant appeal, a mathematical model is secondary to my primary theory of spiritual prominence. Although there is a connection between the two, but spiritual relevance must take precedence."

Franklin shook his head, appreciating how the rigid priorities blinded the researcher, "Bud, specific to the risk of whether the Acoma can provide the needed artifacts, how can a quantitative model, with its extraordinary flexibilities, be secondary?"

"Let me test *your* bias," Bud offered, using the discovery of the first prehistoric flower, to make his point. "The first Proteaceae pushes through Earth's surface three hundred million years ago and evolves on a land mass now called South Africa. You might be aware California promotes the flower widely today. As you said earlier, the process of discovery starts with the test of materiality. Agreed?"

Franklin did, but mentally prepared himself for another adventure in futility.

"Then it is a matter of deciding *what* to discover," Worthington continued. "So, does one focus on how the plant became popular at flower shows in San Francisco?" quizzed the older colleague.

Franklin laughed out loud, "Of course not!"

"Then should the discovery be how 329 species came to survive in the regions of South Africa?"

"Possibly."

"Or, should we try to discover when the flower exactly presented in scientific terms, in mass quantities?"

"Among the choices, that last one is precisely the science that I find most plausible to expand on and I would model that."

"And for me, I find another choice most appealing—who or what *provided* the instruction for the *first* Proteaceae seed to materialize."

As Worthington paused he looked for Franklin's reaction and saw a childlike grin on his face, "I believe the root *cause* is the best choice for examination. It should be the first priority and can *only* be substantiated by the spiritual strength of the argument. There is *no* model today that will do this! Like the Proteaceae flower of today, the Pueblo elder lives by spiritual message that has been carried by the pre-generations of the Acoma Pueblo. That spiritual seed in effect predates your model."

At that point, Franklin was certain he was not going to change the views of a fellow scientist. He recognized the eloquence of the argument but remained convinced mathematical science should not be relegated to a supporting role. It seemed like a stalemate no matter how they massaged each other's opinions for mental ingestion.

Franklin remained stalwart, "Proving is seeing. You have yet to deliver tangible evidence."

"My young man, don't allow your tendencies of mathematical prowess to overrule the pure logic of simple congruence."

Franklin immediately defended his integrity, "I doubt I'm overconfident in my abilities to establish a verifiable conclusion for my research. There are *no* exclusive dependencies that I'm aware of!"

"I apologize Franklin. What I meant by that remark was there is evolving knowledge that the Pueblo relics have significant meaning. Until we have contrary knowledge, it does not diminish the perceived authenticity of the tribe's spiritualistic rituals, or their genuine protection of the Earth."

Bud patted the arm of his weary friend who had become impatient with explanations that pleased only one of them.

"We make a very lucid team. As you perfect your mathematical models, I will uncover the seed that gives them integrity. Science is not privileged to discovery in absence of spiritual knowledge."

Unknown to Worthington, the younger scientist contemplated the nature of his commitment to his colleague who was operating under the illusion his study of the Acoma would trigger a national debate. Franklin thought instead, scientific reaction would be brutal and denounce

Worthington's theories immediately. He thought even the chance of someone caring about Worthington's research was unlikely.

> Under ninety-five hundred feet of sea water, the eruption was hidden from view. It was unlike the other million submarine volcanoes around the world that produced seventy-five percent of Earth's magna. With the advent of molten rock, water pressure increased over two-hundred fifty times of standard pressure. Quick cooled into pillow lava, the massive bulk deposits added to the margin of the continent. Even though the forcing had a definitive beginning, the end was a link to other undetectable episodes.

When Bud was blindsided with the news of Franklin's departure, it was numbing. Over years, so much talent had arced with Worthington's mentorship and moved on, that he alone, shouldn't have been expecting permanence. Yet, he ignored signs, unaware of other agendas equally important to his own. Bud phoned Franklin from his office and left again to meet with him.

Feeling the sting of Franklin's announcement, Bud barely concealed emotion, but not his frustration. "I thought you were doing well here. I have to say I'm shocked. There is an enormous amount of work left to do. Where are you heading to?"

"Department of Energy. I've been given two scientists and I think an analyst or two, a budget five times the size here, and full access to terabytes of memory and storage."

Computing power. The incentive was completely foreign to Bud.

"That and it practically fell into my lap. I was contacted through the fellowship program. They said the federal government was hiring for this agency dedicating itself to Earth sciences. I sent my resume and list of projects, experience and so on..."

"You mentioned my work?"

"No. Of course not. But I did show them my seismic volume model. They were definitely interested. It took about two weeks to get to the second round of interviews."

"You seem excited with the magnitude of their IT department. Could it be summoned to complete the calculations you developed for me?"

"Perhaps. I'll have other duties obviously," Franklin thought quickly, careful to avoid a deliberate promise.

"Of course, yes I appreciate that constraint," Bud responded. "But you would potentially have the opportunity to continue our collaboration?"

"Once I get settled in, I'll see what can be done. I can't make any promises."

Bud's avuncular sense of pride did not keep his insides from knotting. He could envision a complete stop, "Completely understandable, my boy. I'm happy for your success. Your parents must be proud of you."

"Yes. Very much so."

"We must accept new prospects when they arrive and do our best," admitted Bud affirming his own mandate.

It seemed appropriate with the old memories to retreat to his office for the afternoon telling Margaret she could leave early. Sitting with a cup of tea, he battled the urge to stop. Stop the devotion. Stop the research. Stop trying to force a connection between heaven and earth. Looking around his office, volumes of his research project lay helter skelter on the office furniture,

Collecting another brief from the shelves, Bud thumbed through extracts of Franklin's calculations, and like before, he knew little about their power. Once more, inadequacy overwhelmed him. Without his research, the body of geological science had no worthy antagonist to push it beyond what the oil industry dictated. The spiritual legacy of the "El Santo Cáliz" could prove science had been manipulated by the powerful and corrupted.

"But my dedication might be my ultimate failing," Bud admitted to an empty room.

Slave to his single purpose, it was like a blindfold blocking out parallel worlds of research.

"Franklin's mathematical prowess easily eclipses the obscure link the Acoma Pueblo has to Earth's sustainability," Bud lamented. *So what has drumming up the obvious done for my ego?*

Rubbing his forehead, Bud allowed reality to take hold once more. In advance of publicizing, the authenticity of his work would be challenged, with attempts to disprove his conclusions. Then his professional and personal credentials would be assessed and background searches would amplify the negatives. Well aware, Franklin seemed on the verge of having his work in front of those same peers; Bud feared his research would never see the light of day.

His cigarette and the one before it had burned down. His research would not be showcased for months, possibly years. Delayed, because it wasn't good enough to keep the interest of a very gifted mind. Compulsively, Bud micromanaged the resource to get the best out of him. *And maybe chased him away.*

He placed Franklin's research in the same folder and returned it to hiding. Upon hearing the outside foyer doors and the lock turning, Bud realized the janitors were arriving. Brushing cigarette ashes off his sweater, Bud stood transfixed on the bold concept: proving a Pueblo tribe had been the guardian of global destiny for hundreds of years. If believed, the theory would expose risks beyond human scope. Patently familiar with Einstein's obscure path to success, he wanted his own miracle year. The deed to investigate beyond known boundaries of Earth science was agonizing. If he was to reach a realm of great objectivity, there could be no more delays.

He had to make another trip to the Acoma.

Residence of
Mr. Thomas'. Acoma Pueblo.

NEVER CERTAIN OF its power, access to the sanctity of the Pueblo enchanted Worthington. On his ninth visit, the professor was finally allowed to speak of his research, explaining the theoretical link between science and spiritual beliefs. The elder waited patiently until his friend finished.

"I understand your message," repeated Mr. Thomas'. He continued after pausing for Amado, "In our world, all relationships—wind, earth, mind, and spirit must be healthy for *us* to remain healthy. Many people are sick with the lack of these connections."

Bud thought for moments before replying, "I believe as you do. Our science is sometimes overwhelming. I am seeking to prove that the existence of spiritual beliefs strengthen the truth of science."

Worthington talked about the theory of Gaia, and the four related components to the natural elements Amado described.

On loan from Paul, Bud shared a set of books illustrating Pueblo works of art he hoped would have significance to either native, "Have you ever seen these images or in forms other than what is pictured here?" Bud quizzed.

"The truth I have may not exist anymore but is strong in my heart," was Amado's translated reply.

Worthington's passion was revived instantly, but he wanted tangible proof. When no clues were given, the men shared a traditional afternoon meal.

"I often think of our chance meeting. Me finding you and Mr. Thomas'," Bud reminisced.

He paused to give Mr. Thomas' time to finish the bite of yeasty bread, although the elder was moving his head positively while Bud talked.

"I believe now it wasn't chance or luck. Even one of my students, Karl—you remember him. He graduated but still keeps in contact and occasionally asks about Acoma."

The elder referred to his grandson by his nickname, "Soldadito. He will know him soon enough," interpreted Mr. Thomas'. [20]

Assuming a translation error, Bud was confused. The elder explained his reasoning, "What you think and to speak it out loud to the earth, gives it power."

Weeks before with prayer, the elder had a vision that the professor would arrive and would be speaking through his heart as he had done so many times. With the vision coming true, it was proper that Amado share another part of the vision with the professor and enlist his expertise.

Towards the end of the meal, Mr. Thomas' laid out an old relief map and began to translate the story of sacred stones, actual objects originally transported from the Acoma centuries ago, by a splinter group.

Mr. Thomas' explained that a smaller tribe was entrusted to journey south, back to remote areas pre-inhabited, "I'm told the government believes we came from Mesa Verde. Of course they never cared to look at our tracks. Our journeys took us back and forth in the time when many tribes were settling on the land."

Amado then revealed the relationship of the stones to his dictated belief of the sacred place hidden within the city they had explored. Bud's eyes rimmed with tears when he was given the task to retrieve the sacred artifacts. He had written off the value of the abandoned Pueblo site, unaware he had likely stood on holy ground.

"Is the spiritual future of the Acoma resting on their discovery? They are like the Holy Grail!"

Amado's translated answer surprised his guest, "El Santo Cáliz", Mr. Thomas' repeated. "The Holy Grail is like a twin. They are connected."

---

[20]   Little soldier.

The new gift of knowledge being bestowed solely to Worthington still seemed as real as anything he had been told before. He showed no hesitation to commit himself to learn more of the spiritually guided trek, regardless of the financial constraints from the university.

The moment was simultaneously celebratory and solemn for the learned professor, unable to challenge why he wasn't given this chance earlier, "Yes. I have ample resources to locate and bring these precious artifacts to you."

Anxious to share, Worthington called Paul. But for that night, Paul had been contemplating returning to New York City, tired of the pomp and circumstance of academics. The fresh details of the history, the artifacts, and the hidden city motivated Paul enough to promise he would reopen business contacts to share the pictures and notes Bud would gather.

Worthington convinced his partner there were other funding awards they could obtain, "Even though I didn't make the cut for the Packard award awards from the National Academy of Sciences or the highest honor in geology, the Penrose Medal would silence the skeptics."

Bud insisted everything was possible now. He had to move quickly to initiate a search for the sanctified stones and excavate the site Amado once called, "*la cuidad sagrada*", a "sacred city."

In his own community, the elder was passionate with the leaders who inquired about his dealings with whom they respectfully called "*profesor de la tierra*"[21] but not all of the truth could be told to everyone. Amado would be meeting with the remnants of the embattled Caciques, the centric leaders of the Pueblo. Through generations, they and their forefathers fought bravely against the federal courts to gain back twelve thousand acres that had been in dispute for over one hundred fifty years. It was a small pittance in comparison to the historical account of one million acres the Spaniards referred to as the "Acoma kingdom" in the mid-1500s.[22]

Besides accepting the degrading concept of "boundaries" multiple battles with Spain, and infractions with other Pueblos, other punishment was felt by the Acoma. Christian salvation, formal education, and cultural degradation had impacted the tribe. Cultivating the land, once a singular

---

[21]   Earth teacher.

[22]   Minge, *Acoma Pueblo in the Sky*, 138.

vocation, had become impossible for a younger Amado Vallo to survive on.

Introduced into a variety of secular school systems, he learned Spanish and was trained in other forms of labor. The practice of mixing the tribes in the schools was fortuitous for Amado when he took his bride from another pueblo. The ceremony enacted at the top of Sky City preserved the reverence of the couple to the tribe.[23]   Nothing else around their existence stood still as they carved out their lives, had a child, and tried to remain steadfast to their beliefs.

Before speaking with the small group of Acoma leaders, Amado returned to the place where Earth was silent and, like other times, prayed for healing. His mind traveled to times the earth belonged to those who understood her. The explanation that Amado was given was that Earth was wounded. Geological explanations could not begin to fathom the injury.

> Erasing centuries of careful native stewardship, the land masses shifted below the crests of exposed ridgeline. Gravity pulled hard against slopes of dirt, rock, and vegetation. The forging of smaller crevices allowed water to erode deep into the earth, leaving a natural boundary of extended fault line. The slide broke loose near the top of the hill slope, rupturing pockets of permeable soil, previously unexposed for eons. Seconds to minutes spared nothing in the path of the landslide that lay silent again, with dust moving in the direction of the wind.

Although the Acoma Pueblo had continued their silence, they remained unconditionally bound to Mother Earth, a value given by ancestors whose beliefs were absolute. In stark deference to tides of Christian bloodshed, the stories of their supernatural gods and their peaceful toil on her surface embodied the ethic that the Acoma had been the chosen ones before Jesus walked the earth. But ever since their discovery by foreigners in the sixteenth century, the sacrifices thrust upon them had been many.

They were subordinated on their own land, forced to war against other tribes who had been allies. Their labor was extracted to make others rich. The knowledge of the invaders spoiled their pure thought. The sickness

---

23   White, "New Material from Acoma," 321.

of the invaders killed them. But generations later, Amado survived their greed. There was no one like him at Akome.[24] The secret societies and ways of the medicine men had vanished, but his spiritual strength was intact, radically different than those around him.

When Amado talked privately to the tribal council they were made aware of the past and the future. In Spanish he told them the professor did not act from fear or greed like other men, "*Él trae otros con intenciones sanas. Unos pocos más vienen de su voluntad. En sus propias maneras, trabajan para la tierra.*"[25]

With all staring silently at the only man they trusted, he uttered a single word in native Aa'ku, "*Tsi.'mai*" and then confirmed in Spanish that, "much will be revealed."

Together they prayed. All were encouraged the elder's strength of vision would bring back the Acus kingdom.[26]

Even with their paths on a mutually shared course, Dr. Worthington did not anticipate it would be close to a year before he would see Amado Vallo again. The university was radically changing its policies on funding research. Even with the compelling news reviving his claims, the review board insisted the professor re-substantiate the new evidence prior to submission of his budget proposal.

One of the neutral members pulled Worthington aside, "Quite frankly, your credibility is at risk *because* of this project. We've got so many applicants that have genuine proof. So far you've brought us nothing to act on."

On the eleventh visit to the Pueblo, Bud confessed little progress had been made benefiting the Acoma, admitting he was unable to convince the university to authorize resources to investigate the recent claims of the Acoma Pueblo, "Student research validated the migration of the Acoma tribe but it did not sway the board."

Mr. Thomas' translated the elder's response, "I only have the words from my ancestors."

---

[24] James, *ACOMA*, Introduction. Meaning "people of the white rock."

[25] He brings others that are true. A few others come of their own free will. In their own ways, they work for the earth.

[26] Minge, *Acoma Pueblo in the Sky*, 2.

"The only bright spot is we were able to pinpoint the area Amado spoke about," Bud explained. "Remember the notes I took from your map?" The location is listed on the National Park registry. It took a few students a great deal of effort. The site is valid, but I learned that grave robbers had invaded the area a couple years ago. I don't know what they took, but there's still a chance of recovery."

The elder listened as Mr. Thomas' criticized the misfortune, "Like always, we've had no luck with the government. They have caused us great harm. How can you find the sacred stones if they were taken?"

"Actually, the bandits have been captured and all the stolen pieces have been released to the federal government for return to the site," Bud reported gleefully. "I've filed the necessary paperwork. We think the pieces are there, but I have no control over when I'll be given formal permission to excavate."

The irony was upon everyone's mind. The artifacts' rightful and legal owners could not secure the return of their own property without obtaining authority from the government.

Worthington returned home and sought out Paul to report that the Acoma leadership was counting on him to locate the stones. Suggesting they needed to consider what the future might hold, Bud spoke of his desire to have both of them involved in the eventual fieldwork, downplaying their poor health. Bud encouraged Paul to see the site for himself, ignoring his friend's advanced heart condition.

Paul resisted, "I'm of no help to you if I have an attack out there. What would you do?" he challenged in a raspy voice, coughing.

"Resuscitate."

"And after you failed, you'd blubber all over me because there wouldn't be any one left to interpret those stones you've bragged about."

Worthington set that scenario aside looking off in the distance, "Indeed, the stones are as the elder called them, "El Santo Cáliz."

Day 3285.

Near Canyon De Chelly National Monument, Arizona.

360453N 1090812W

OWARDS THE END of the university school year, Dr. Worthington made his twelfth trip to the Acoma Pueblo without students. Even with no progress to report and no specific contingency, Bud needed to keep the friendship intact between him and Amado. Amado had shown him the way many times and nothing had been accomplished in return.

The professor reluctantly reported the Acoma project had stopped again, "I'm still waiting for federal approval."

Ignoring the legal process would result in automatic dismissal from the university, arrest, and fines.

Seeing him doubtful and stressed, Mr. Thomas' and the elder convinced the professor to extend his stay. For him, they gathered up camping gear along with a pack mule to make a trip over to the canyons surrounding "*la cuidad sagrada,*" the city still holding its secrets.

Reaching a plateau to view the world, the pack mule was tethered and a fire started. The sky turned purple cold as Mr. Thomas' prepared a bean and corn dish while finishing another story of the Acoma, "For us the clear sky is the promise of revealing the spirit path. The Milky Way is a ladder to the heavens."

As cool air sank to the ground and flowed amongst their wrapped torsos, the small wood fire continued to burn down to embers painting the surroundings in yellow and orange hues. Completing their meal, Bud shared his failures with Amado. He explained the loss of financial and academic support. He talked of the times he resisted his father's advice to stay in teaching, "But I've taken risks. I taught rigorously, bringing new concepts and methods into the classroom. I've given to students. The university hasn't given back in kind!"

Bud's ample frustration surfaced, "It's not the outcome I expected, after years of dedicating myself to the school and students. We did good things here. The students did good things here."

Sadden, the professor's voice cracked with emotion, "I've been working the project and research on mine own for a long time and by God I'm going to find ..."

In silence, Amado slid over and put his hand on the thigh of his wounded friend and spoke without a translation, "Many have come and gone with stolen value. Many want truth for power. You are not with them."

His message snapped Worthington out of his dour mood, "You speak English?"

"Not well. Over years. Only to Tom'as when lazy. No one knows."

"But you've hidden it from others and me?"

"To take another's voice weakens the spirit of our people."

"So you understand my trouble?"

"Some. I hear your heart more."

The two men sat next to each other for many minutes as Mr. Thomas' put gear away. Except for brief seconds, a night hawk was invisible when it called to its hunting mate. Now roosting, they had seen the few red-topped Vermillion earlier in the day perching on low brush to feast on ants, beetles, and crickets. Listening to the wood sizzle and spit, there would be little or no talk now that their piece of Earth was transforming to accept nightfall. Like other campouts with the natives, their pagan focus became transfixed on the earthly gifts surrounding them, consuming her offerings, feeling the universal energies ebb and flow. Humbled, Amado remained motionless waiting on the virtual presence of the greatest of the super naturals—Ocatc.

Witnessing as much as allowed, Bud had learned to feel safe cloaked in their stillness and meditation. He knew of no modern culture that held the power to summon tranquility from raw nature, seemingly a bridge to any god.

The stars shone as the men prepared their wool beds to sleep under a canvas lean-to. Bud's last glance over to the fire ring confirmed the spiritual healer was still meditating. Later, the elder would leave as he always did, walking to a self-identified center of energy to think upon the deeds of all men. The cool air swept the natural surfaces, carrying subtle fragrance he knew from childhood. Waves of sounds multiplied then stopped, amplified then went silent. Bending to sit, the elder calmed himself, permeating the surrounding area.

No one could see the spectrum of flora and stone held in virtual position in front of his physical body. He raised a consciousness of spirit with strength and vitality through his beliefs in his gods. Leaving his mortal self for an ethereal vessel to the clouds and stars above, he walked forward into the window of space, venturing on a path known to him. His visits would invade other forms of the living.

The invigorating drops of dew on his skin brought the human flow of energy back into the body. By the time Amado returned to the cold embers, cactus wren flitted about warming up to feed. A renewal of crackling wood and smoke would greet his waking guests.

Worthington said his goodbyes the following afternoon, feeling empty with thought but full of spirit. He expressed his joy and humility, promising to return with the stones, predicting they would be found soon. When he drove out of sight the elder wiped the small tears from his eyes knowing he would not greet Dr. Bud Worthington again. More clarity of vision had been revealed to Amado, and he would start preparation for a healing ceremony asking the spirit of the twin boys for courage and virtue. Using the affirmed spiritual strength, the elder would reach into another's heart.

The professor was on a path the elder could no longer influence.

Day 250.
Office of Dr. Bud Worthington.
Rice University. Houston, Texas.

"It's only a matter of time," Bud convinced himself as he fussed over budget cut that was thrust in his face. His share of funding was still in decline each year, impacting the number of hours he was teaching.

"Marge, we have to shake up the schedule this morning," he yelled, "See if Stein wants my support at his charity event."

Expecting disappointment Margaret came into the inner office to deliver the news, "He said he has the help he needs."

"Well. I'll be keeping my appointment with Mr. Caine at ten," Bud assured as if the rejection didn't matter. "I like that young man. He certainly has some growing to do, but he's coming along, don't you think?"

"Jude is always polite. Is his friend, Arthur, coming in as well?"

"I hope not," Bud said dreadfully. "Mr. Clarke can be the biggest pain in the ass in lecture class. I can only take him once a day. My pills are much more enjoyable."

Starting to cough, he reached for his tea, "These kids nowadays are bright...and full of it at the same time," he said, knowing his comment would get response from Margaret.

"You don't really mean that, Dr. Worthington. You know these boys look up to you. Not many professors can say that. I won't turn Mr. Clarke away if he's with Jude," she threatened.

"Well, at least keep him busy in the foyer," Bud demanded. "He can lecture you instead of me this time. I find Mr. Clarke to be pretentious yet obnoxious," the professor bellowed, half-serious.

Upon Margaret's departure, Bud finished a call with Paul to lock up a time for dinner. He walked over to the open window to light up a cigarette, looking down at the sidewalks and street. With the aspect of publishing a formidable study with monumental implications, he was excited with the prospects of working with Jude Caine.

The years of accumulated books and papers in his office were invaluable research assets. With all its bookshelves, cabinets, and plaques the crowded room had become the hub for his serendipitous crusade. Downplaying the wide speculation of his retirement, he communicated to the review board, telling them of his expectations to complete the research within two semesters.

Today, is a milestone, Bud thought to himself as he approached his closed door, ready to engage Mr. Caine. *I'm going to have to confide in him, trust him. I need a fresh mind.*

"Let's get started," Bud announced as he stood at his doorway directing the student through with his hand.

"Hello, sir," Jude responded, unaware of the professor's motives. The smell of cigarette smoke interfered with his focus.

"Hello, young man," Worthington replied. "Before, I get started, do you have the full hour available?"

Geeze, Jude thought, "I just have one more class after this. Dr. Hayden's. Did, ugh, did you see something wrong with the papers I graded?"

"No, young man, I did not. As usual, they were done well," Worthington confirmed, motioning for his aide to sit.

"I've been reviewing your final. It deserves a B or slightly better. You know I don't grade on the curve. As such, it's a solid mark. I only gave two Bs and one A."

Jude immediately knew who got the highest grade – his roommate, Arthur Hyde Clarke.

"But, today, there is another item I need to discuss, and your full attention is appreciated. Promise that nothing of what I'm going to share leaves the confines of this office."

Observing Bud casually closing the office door, Jude remembered the rumors about the professor's retirement. *The professor could have quizzed other students. If he puts me on the spot I—*

"Jude, I've done a great deal of field study over my tenure as a professor of Earth sciences. And over many of those years, I've been utilizing portions of the students' research, those being relevant to my scope of interest. And, I'd add that even some of your own submissions are compiled into my effort."

"I guess that's good for me," Jude replied.

"The research I've created presents a great deal of worthiness to *our* professional interest in Earth sciences, including undisclosed discoveries yet to be funded. I'm at the conclusion of this rather critical body of evidence and, before I ask you to join me, I would like you to be aware of the...," Bud paused, thinking of a reasonable way to put it. His voice tenor changed, "...risk."

The sound of a motorbike revved past the office window, disrupting the silence.

"Oh! Join you? Risk? What kind of risk?" Jude blurted without hesitation, concentrating on the obvious. *The dirt on Worthington was true!*

He had heard the rumors from the most intriguing to the most ridiculous. Even the freshman class was up to speed on the two big ones that seemed to hold intrigue:

> The professor had a secret study that had been commissioned, but the results were so controversial, the board of regents demanded the research be destroyed fearing the oil industry donors to the university would be outraged. Worthington threatened to release the findings to the public in exchange for his professorship and tenure.

And,

> Years ago, Worthington was awarded a special project and a million dollar budget for excavating an archeological site. Instead he gambled it away playing high stakes casino poker during trips to New Mexico, using students to cover his activities. The college managed to hide the loss, and has quietly pushed Worthington into retirement.

What's he protecting all this time that's so secret?

Still pacing, Worthington's body language was mechanical, "To explain it, I suspect there could be people, people in our profession, and powerful people in oil and government that will go to capricious lengths to suppress the importance of my findings. I would insist you become fully aware of my suspicions. If you can accept the role of lead acolyte, I have items of interest that may appeal to you."

"Lead what?"

"Acolyte. A newly appointed apprentice. I hope that role doesn't alarm you."

"Uh. I guess not," the student admitted, mentally deciding what rumor was true. *Maybe there were secrets, bad blood, and revenge.* Worthington had the reputation for being a recluse, but worse, a paranoid. He went straight home, had no friends, no activities. Everyone thought he didn't trust anyone except Miss Olivary

Again, Worthington paused, still nervous about taking this step, craving a cigarette, "I've singled you out Jude, because of our continued relationship and our shared interests. I am hoping I can rely on your help to complete the final stages of calculations. We have to protect and conceal the sources from which I based the study."

Bud pulled up on his trousers and sat down opposite his guest, placing one hand on Jude's knee to insure absolute attention, "I have been recording a great deal of information into journals. Over the years, they have become volumes of cumulative knowledge. What I like to call my "black books". The description itself conveys something dark. I can assure you the contents are above board. I confess the label I gave them was because of a personal bias."

Half-listening, Jude heard words, something about "dark" and "confessing" thinking, *What if somebody asks me about this meeting!*

Leaning back, the professor continued to make his case, "The black books started out as a reference point for me in my younger years. I had hopes of publishing it as a reference manual. That goal was eventually overwhelmed with my changing career and now my black books are a work of potent material."

Worthington made his next statement with rigor, "I never took shortcuts and rigorously validated every item. Exactly what I preach to you students! But never a technologist! I didn't transfer it to a computer. I don't trust technology as much as pen and paper."

Doesn't trust technology? Jude thought. *That's paranoid!*

Worthington leaned forward again, making his point, "But you see Jude, that is the essence of the bind I unintentionally created with the research. I can ill afford to have my volumes discovered because they are the shield against those who will deny the crucial importance of the work. If the black books are discovered, their existence will promote chaos."

Worthington glanced at his watch, and got up to pour tea for himself, "Tea?"

"No, sir. Ah, how did you come to decide the books are actually so, umm, lethal? I mean you have to know this is really surprising to see, I mean I hear you, but it's hard to believe you have to hide this research."

Jude was nervous. He didn't intend to put emphasis on the words *believe* and *you*.

Sensing his creditability was being measured, Bud went over and sat at his desk, posturing authority, curt with his challenger, "Jude, you can consider this entire business authentic without the slightest hesitation. My professional ethics prevent me from imposing extemporary ideals on my students and personal ethics bar me from avarice. This whole business stems from my lifelong focus. No one seems to embrace the critical importance! The science that I'm interested in, is not in the earth itself, it's *of* the earth and what we can learn about her secrets. This aspect should be attractive to your intellect."

Taking a sip of tea, Bud continued, "You should know I have thought through many scenarios and eliminated those that could get us both in trouble. Of the ones I chose, bringing you in as a cohort, lends a great deal of comfort to me. As you may know, I don't have family anymore or many close friends."

"Are others involved besides me?"

"Jude, I have a great deal of respect for your talents and do not want to jeopardize your future. The complete answer to that will have to come later. But in two words— happily, yes."

Worthington glanced at the pendulum clock and moved his tea aside, standing up, "Our time is running out today, and *we* lose time if nothing is done past this point in our discussion. I want to show you something over here, again, as a matter of strict confidence."

Walking over to the wall of bookshelves, Bud positioned the wooden ladder. Filling all the available space, the books reached to the ceiling. Bud climbed up and selected a three-inch thick volume off the shelf. Oversized, it blended in with the other volumes to the left and right. His strength and balance was tested as he brought it down to eye level, "This is one of the black books. The other volumes are dispersed amongst the rest of my collection. I keep the entire set in the office, camouflaged within my library. As you can see, I've adapted a pseudo cover to hide the contents."

"Okay," Jude offered, trying to appreciate the significance of what he was told.

"My friend," Bud lowered his voice, "we have to review some of its secrets together, but I cannot afford to do that today. I'll instruct Ms. Olivary to set up a couple appointments, so I can transfer some key knowledge to you. I presume you are not entirely committed until we complete those tasks."

"Yes. Maybe we can get it done before spring break."

Bud climbed back on the ladder, rejecting Jude's offer for assistance, and slid the volume back in place.

"How many volumes are there?"

"Let's save that for later as well. Go ahead and let yourself out, young man and thank you for your time today."

"Yes, sir," Jude turned and left the office, not entirely surprised Olivary quizzed him.

"Did everything go okay in there? Does Dr. Worthington need a follow-up?"

"Uhh, I'm not...well it went okay. He, ah, Dr. Worthington is going to have you schedule more time."

"Okay, I'll take care of it. Mr. Clarke stopped in. He asked me to let you know he's over in the Union building."

"Great. Thanks. See you later."

Jude strolled through the door and down the steps, pulling his cell phone out. *Does she know what Worthington is up to?*

Hitting autodial, he headed east to the library, "Clarke. What's up?"

"Hi, Jude. You said you were meeting with Worthington. I hope he didn't ask you to help with the fundraiser next month."

"Nope, you lucked out; you've got it all to yourself. You know I don't have time for that kind of stuff."

"Why were you in his office?"

"Just to answer some questions on my grading. You know how strict he is."

"Of course. I never have issues with that. Well, I'll see you tonight. Remember I've got planning to do with the team."

Who's more paranoid? Jude wondered.

Sitting down in a library cube, Jude adjusted his ear buds and scrolled to an album on his MP3. Attempting to answer pretest questions from his book, Worthington's comments popped back into his head. *Whadda trip that guy is. Rumors might be true after all. But I think I know who can tell me.*

Jude kicked back for a minute to think. His uncle Peter and the group he graduated with might remember the rumors about Worthington. They would have heard or maybe even started them. *Those volumes might be interesting though but Worthington was too weird. Once the black books are discovered, their existence will promote chaos. What did he mean by that?*

Doing laundry that evening in the dorms, Jude remained plagued with the whole experience. *If it's actually new science like he claims, it might be more interesting than grading papers.* Jude started stuffing dried clothes into a gunny sack. *He's wants me involved based on what? My grades? There's a bunch of students better than me!*

The student headed back to his house, across campus, hoping Arthur was done with his planning meeting. As Jude entered, many watched as he made his way down the hallway.

"Okay, Phil, you've got the final invitations and those will be sent out tomorrow morning," instructed Arthur. "Check with Worthington's admin before you drop them into the mail. She was nice enough to volunteer to maintain the list of attendees."

"I've got that, Arthur. Thanks for putting this together, but I've got to get going."

Nodding, Arthur continued, "Okay, that's fine. Avey, you've got the agenda and a reminder to send to the presenters. It needs to be hand delivered to their offices. Is that something you can finish?"

"Yes."

"This is our final meeting before the event. Any questions?"

Two students remained after everybody else left. Jude hoped they weren't going to get caught up in needless drivel, keeping him from cable TV in the living room. Their last minute conversation tried to solve whether Dr. Triddle had time to present the updates to his white paper on "Strong Motion Instrumentation." Then, Avey, a girl who had been at the house before, said she could convince Ms. Olivary to get her boss to give up some minutes.

They need to find a life, Jude concluded as he scrounged around in the fridge. He heard Arthur shut the front door just after Avey yelled, "See ya, Jude."

Arthur began picking up folders and reassembling the paper work to avoid a rush in the morning.

"Well, did you get it done?" Jude asked acting interested.

"I think so. The event should come off without a hitch. You're not doing the fundraiser, right? Worthington didn't hand out something for you to do? I don't want to have to redo assignments and—"

"I'm free and clear of that, Clarke."

And then Jude got the urge, probably because he was tired and Arthur was vulnerable, "But I might be hanging out in Worthington's office a bit more."

"For what?"

"He was showing me a bunch of stuff he was in to."

"At least if somebody is interested," Arthur teased, "it might as well be you."

The self-promotion and countermeasures were innocent diversions of their rivalry. Practically visible to every one, their relationship was rivalry without enmity. Mutually provoking each other, challenges were a function of their core differences and similarities—some yet to be discovered or understood. So, yanking Arthur's chain was absolutely with implicit intent. And the return volley was expected.

Jude was familiar with Arthur's duty to self—to be the best, to been seen as the top of his class, to do whatever it took to be superior and have the appearance of superiority. Stemming from his propitious "bloodline" Arthur claimed to have been "mentored first and parented second" by a family who had earned power and wealth litigating in the federal legal system. The faculty was just as confused as anyone as to why Arthur would attend Rice University to major in anything but corporate law, when his family's well-publicized contributions were made to Yale and Harvard. Extricating himself from the career benefits of injected financial province, he made it clear he was the black sheep of the family, disinterested in law and wanted to be successful with his very own achievements. Control his own destiny. Make his own mark.

Despite what he once said that, "contentious debates at the table drummed the flavor out of the meal", he remained close to his family and even closer to his objective—to prove himself in a field of endeavor that wasn't handed to him or mapped out since childhood.

His goals didn't exclude the access to wealth, and although his classmates expected the worse kind of behavior from a rich know-it-all, Arthur helped blunt the perception by using a monthly stipend to defray unexpected expenses. He paid for a student's new tires that had been slashed at a frat party. He also made a substantial donation to the student's dormitory fund for athletic equipment. These simple gestures endeared him to friends that decided even if Arthur could buy his way through life he was capable of making choices that benefited others less fortunate.

The next day Worthington's schedule permitted a quick lunch so he could finish preparing for his second meeting with Jude Caine.

Over twenty minutes late, Jude arrived irritated, "I'm really sorry, Dr. Worthington. I was told to let myself in."

"No worry, Jude. I can appreciate your academic constraints."

Listening to the professor, Jude immediately noticed two of the disguised volumes lying on his desk.

"I pulled those specific volumes down as an initiation. Their relevance is more towards the future than the past."

Jude swung his book bag off his shoulder and down to the floor, shoving his ear buds into a pocket.

"Most appreciated, Jude. I wish other students felt as compelled to remove interferences."

The student nodded but was determined to take a bold move and attempt a retreat from Worthington's seemingly inchoate stacks of theories and inane perceptions, hoping his prompting would cause the professor to have second thoughts, "Dr. Worthington, I wanted to tell you before we got started. I thought this over. Your proposal. It's something that I didn't expect, ever. I don't doubt my commitment but are you sure *you* haven't made a mistake?"

"No, Jude, I'm fine to move forward with my decision."

"I don't want you to get in the middle of it and it's...," Jude struggled for words. "Well, like a false start. And then you'd want to change your mind. I'm not really *that* qualified to help you."

"Interesting! You have grasped the nature of where I was stuck for some time. I'm glad to have a suitable companion!"

Taking the student's appeal lightly, it wasn't the response Jude was looking for to get a reprieve.

Worthington picked up one of the volumes and placed it on the small conference desk between them, "Let me explain the scope of these volumes as they relate to the others."

"I guess," Jude answered, settling in his chair figuring to make another pitch against his involvement as soon as the professor finished his lecture.

"All the volumes are segmented roughly by phases. You had asked me earlier how many—there are seven to consider for our direct purposes. The phases correspond with the maturation of the research. These specific volumes document the design and explain the hypothesis. As such they contain mostly data analysis or support thereof."

Worthington opened one of the volumes. The binder contained pages of inserts stuffed with articles and printouts of other research, spreadsheets, documents, and charts. Jude quickly showed his disappointment, mentioning that it seemed like a photo album of sorts.

The collection included numerous geological oddities and anomalies of substance regarding the natural progressions of Earth and its ecosystems. Referenced with astute detail, Jude saw documentation on asexual amphibians revealing unexplainable shifts in breeding outcomes; mammal research that examined important food chain links between bears and squirrels; and predictions that man-caused extinction amounted to half of all species in one hundred years.[27]

"With the increase of permanent biodiversity change, I expanded my core interests, tracking predictions of Earth's cycles of change and the slow evolution of its physical manifestations," Worthington explained while waiting for a reaction.

"There is *logic* to this, my boy. Don't get caught up in the formality of it. Focus on the science!"

They reviewed the first volume, sometimes discussing all the detail on a single page, sometimes skipping several pages or flipping back. Worthington kept his hand inserted as a bookmark and at times used other objects. By the time he paused for questions, the book contained a drink coaster, pen knife, and various envelopes used as place holders.

"K, let me see if I get it," Jude quizzed. "You've taken the data from all of us and mapped it to your theories?"

---

[27] Farlex, "Holocene extinction event," The Free Dictionary, http://encyclopedia. thefreedictionary.com/ Holocene +extinc- tion+event.

"In part."

"So what's not finished?" Jude queried. "Is that what you need me for? Or is it the mathematics that need to be fleshed out?"

"Essentially all of it is done. Keep in mind the other volumes document different geological events from a multitude of sources. You are seeing the result of over twenty years of dedication."

"Okay. Keep going."

The first volume took almost an hour to review. The next volume was thicker, and Jude expected another deep dive. It was no longer captivating to see the energy Worthington exhibited. Some of his explanations seemed more like pleas than proof of scientific significance. The professor took forty-five minutes to explain what he said was an advanced discourse on Gaia.

"As you recall from your classes, there is this push-pull mechanism, with each of the components, atmos, bios, geos, and hydros that intertwine with our lives and the other living matter. All *that* is integrated with the bio-diversity that surrounds us. For example, the chemical structures of Earth are roughly eighty percent nitrogen, a fourth of that oxygen, and of course methane."[28]

"I only remember some of it," Jude admitted.

"Gaia is still such new science, created around the sixties and considered by many to be speculation. Some of the core theories have been manipulated a bit. I used to have quite a following for this subject at Princeton."

"Then this is what you are combining with your study, the impact on the earth and all the related effects. You have it in these volumes?"

"Basically correct. Gaia, the Acoma tribe, and the cause-effect documentation from the students. Yes."

Still, Jude thought of the massive collection of pictures and articles wouldn't meet the standards for submission to a formal body of experts. He managed to explain his perception without embarrassing the author and was surprised with the answer he was given.

"These volumes, in raw form, are really the Holy Grail regarding this subject. I doubt the combined documents exist elsewhere in the world. It would take years for someone to collect all this."

---

[28] Orrell, David, "Science of the Living Earth:Gaia Theory," 20. GaiaNet. http://www.bibliotecapleyades.net/gaia/esp_gaia06.htm.

Jude took a glance at the office clock, deciding there wasn't enough time to get into more detail, "It's one-thirty. I've got to head."

"Oh! Yes. Margaret sent you an email with the other meeting times? Are they suitable?"

"Yep."

"Okay, young man. See you next week. If you think of any questions, save them until then. That will be our last meeting, as we won't see each other until after spring break."

"You're right. See you, sir."

Upon leaving, Jude looked at his surroundings. Nearly all the books on the shelves were supported with other books. Most had sticky notes serving as bookmarks. The file cabinets, on the only wall without bookcases, had stacks of folders, large envelopes, and other extraneous sheets of paper on top. There were piles of the same mix of material on the floor.

"Is all this part of the study?"

"I know it looks like chaos, but that's mostly reference material. I didn't have room at home, although it's a bit of a risk storing it here. I can put my finger on most anything when I need it."

After completely circling the room, Jude strode past Olivary's vacant desk and hurried out of the building. He started to evaluate the whole experience realizing he couldn't bring himself to signup for the duty asked of him. The volumes they studied seemed like the jumbled mess resembling the office.

We'd get our asses kicked if we turned in that kind of work! His commitment shifted back to tentative. *If Clarke saw this stuff he'd be laughing hysterically. The rumors couldn't have predicted what I just went through!*

A week had already passed and Jude wanted his third meeting with Dr. Worthington to be the final one. Coveting his decision to back out, he toiled with another feeling, that his respect for Worthington had been compromised.

Here's this distinguished professor and he's got a scrapbook of earthquake articles and oil statistics. It's not like news in our world of geology! He's like... gone off the deep end. What a mess. In some twisted way the rumors have to be true!

Deciding the professor would have to deal with the setback, Jude wondered if his grade would be affected. *Nobody could be that fair.*

Still unable to gain courage to explain his final decision to the professor before they met, Jude headed back to Worthington's office knowing he had to come clean and hoping the professor might suddenly renege on his own.

"You're right on time, Jude," Olivary announced. "I'll let Dr. Worthington know you've arrived. Go ahead and have a seat,"

"If he's busy or something, we can pick another time," Jude offered up quickly.

"No, he's fine. He said this morning he was looking forward to seeing you."

"Great," Jude mumbled feeling his stomach muscles tighten.

"Mr. Caine. Come in, and make yourself comfortable."

The professor swept his arm in a gesture to welcome his student. Jude walked into his office, teetering on how to just come out and say it.

"Put your things down anywhere you like, young man."

Carrying one of the volumes under his arm, Worthington was more exuberant than last week and noticed Jude's lack of interest, "My boy, is there something out of sorts?"

Jude stopped rearranging his pack on the floor.

"Whatever it is, we can take a moment," Bud encouraged.

"Yes, sir, I've been thinking about what you have shared with me and all," he confessed, taking a deep breath. "I keep thinking I'm not qualified to do this, you know...taking this on in a way that's going to help you."

Bud moved closer, setting the single volume on the table next to them and motioned for Jude to sit in the leather chairs, "I see. Go on."

"Well, it sounded like you expected me to automatically accept your invitation, and I didn't want to turn you down at the beginning. It wouldn't have been fair to you."

The lack of reaction from the professor forced more explanation, "And after seeing the research, it's something I don't understand...or, I don't understand its value."

"And this perception you have is compelling enough to change your mind?"

"Yes. I guess I have. I wanted you to know this now instead of later."

Bud got up and poured himself some tea, coming back to sit in the chair ready to advise, "As a teacher and mentor for many students through my career, the one thing I've always valued in those relationships is honesty. It is a cornerstone for all of my dealings with students and this university.

As a student, you have the right and duty to exercise your judgments. Sometimes that promotes a collision between a student and a teacher, but not if we are on equal footing with the truth..."

Jude felt relief, "...and consequently, I would have no ill feelings towards you if you determined that this undertaking is not appropriate."

"I just think I would be wasting your time."

"That is a burden for me to manage, if that was the case."

Bud took a sip of tea and patted the bounded material in front of them, "I would offer in good faith, that we review a specific portion of this volume here, so you are keenly aware of the opportunity that you have professed as a challenge to your commitment. Would that be acceptable?"

"I'm okay with that," Jude replied ecstatic of his release.

"Recall the charts and tables I showed you last week – these are the results."

When he opened up the volume and turned to the leading pages, Jude noticed the binder was new, cracking as it was pressed open. He laid his hand on the fifth page to pause Worthington from advancing further.

The young student tried to grasp the meaning of the illustrated graphs, certain he had seen them before, jutting his finger towards the data table displayed on the adjoining page. Any third year student would know the formulas were common seismic-wave modes, but with an additional notation: PKI_xK_xP, "What scale is this? PK? And what is sub_x? That's not something I've seen."

"You know it as a set of standard wave lengths. But this is seismic tomography with a hybrid element. A new coefficient!"[29]

Jude flipped the page backward referring to another color-coded contour graphic, "When was this measured?"

"Re-calculated six weeks ago."

"I know these models from seismology class, but they're different! We never get to extrapolate them because they eat up computing power."

With nervous energy, Jude abruptly stood and rattled off questions. He was familiar with the equations but this version held other significance that was intended to peak his interest. "Who did these for you? The other factor in here—I've never heard of sub_x waves. Only S- and P-waves."

---

[29] Dictionary of Earth Sciences, 2nd ed., Allaby and Allaby (Oxford: Oxford University Press, 1999), 487. PKIKP waves are signals that travel from the earth surface, through the mantel to the outer core, into the inner core, and then back to the surface.

"I won't say right now, but I could share that information in the near future."

"This is amazing! I mean I didn't know you actually had live functioning models. The other day you only said the math was borrowed and we flipped through page after page of literature. This is way different!"

"Yes, it is," Worthington replied, gleaming with confidence. "With theoretical baselines and predictive emergents. There are asymmetries worth investigating *I* think. Worth spending effort on."

As Worthington leaned back taking another sip of tea, Jude started to gently turn additional pages, finding them blank.

The professor exuded confidence, "You have to admit it's a strong illustration of my work. I can appreciate if you need to take more time to conclude whether this exercise is something you can involve yourself with. For now, we've got to put these away, if you don't mind."

"Oh uh, okay."

Worthington restacked the volume, ushering Jude to his door, "It's interesting, isn't it, Jude? When you start to see the truth, it commands attention and rigor. And minutes before, there was nothing worth discovering. If you cancel our next meetings, I'll know your decision."

Submerged in new science for moments, he was suddenly getting kicked out by the old professor whose paranoia dislodged most of his peers' respect. Kicked out by a has-been who was holding the administration hostage and had gambled away hundreds of thousands of dollars.

What was the truth? Jude wondered, as he headed for his car. His mindshare was now centered on what seemed to be breakthrough science. Keys dangled in the ignition as he tried to determine his convictions. *What if Worthington is right? What if the rumors are bogus? What if I could solve the mystery?*

Putting on his seat belt, Jude drove out to the circle and took a left turn in the opposite direction of the gym. He still had control over his fate. Bolting through the library turnstiles, the energized student hurried to the second floor. Most of what he needed was in the racks or could be accessed on the web. He sat down to claim one of the computer stations, speaking softly to formulate his plan of attack, "Okay, I don't want to be here all night. If I concentrate on reflection seismology and convergent displacement then I can search key words from those and download data to figure out the sub_x variable Worthington was so proud of."

His digital search turned up three sources familiar to him from previous classes.

"Crap. I knew I shouldn't have sold those books. Hope they're here."

Taking minutes to locate them, one book's references led to other literature, taking Jude deeper into the material. A list of researchers led him to websites that had similar illustrations that Worthington put on display. None of the literature included the additional variable notation.

"Hello!" Jude huffed in frustration. "They want us to learn it, but they don't publish the model?"

Putting in his ear buds to listen to music, he slipped his student card into the reader to pay for additional connection time. Another hour passed, searching for conclusive information similar to Worthington's boast. And another hour was spent trying to calculate the sub_x component, using online tools and sample data. Jude yanked out his ear buds, shaking his head in disbelief. *Is Worthington's stuff a hoax?*

As he stood in Worthington's office three days later, Jude knew his involvement was inevitable. As far as he could go, after scanning over thirty URLs for literal interpretations, nobody had reached the level explained briefly in the volumes known as the black books. He could find no reference to the actual computation of what many routinely referred to as prognostic capability.

Ironically, this *was* the science Jude intuitively craved. He was infatuated with the idea that the hypothetical model was out there somewhere, making sense of Earth's unpredictable behavior. He had laid in bed nights before thinking about his choice. Was he in or out?

I don't want to be looking at rock piles for a living. Probably only a couple guys have actually seen the model. How did Worthington get his hands on it? And then an idea drained him. The puzzle of risk that the professor claimed was there and the reluctance to identify others involved. Speculating on the meaning of all their conversations took hold, churning in Jude's head until he fell asleep from fatigue. That morning, Arthur stared at Jude trying to guess what he was up to. Nothing was shared other than he was tired.

A smile appeared on Worthington's face. His self-indulged protégé stood there in the center of his office tired, looking forward to going back to sleep as soon as his classes were over.

"You got me, you know!" Jude admitted.

"My dear lad, you got yourself! In my favor I was merely instructive, approaching you with a good case and hoping the probability of natural curiosity would take hold. I'll presume you are...on board?"

Jude recognized it as a milestone in their relationship when Worthington used slang.

"I'm down with it," Jude confessed, expecting many would quickly assume he had been sucked into Worthington's zany world.

"I'd add that part of your role would be to bring the relevance of the discoveries to the untrained eye and mind," the professor carefully instructed. "It's not unlike us to scurry about with models and presume everybody follows along. Remember, no one immediately accepts information at face value. The debate we'll encounter is likely to be a blend of rancor and humility."

Later that evening, Worthington was at the university supper club waiting for Paul. Celebrating with Scotch and soda, the achievement he engineered needed recognition. An advocate of window dressing, Bud was just as tired as Jude, from staying up late constructing the new binder to entice his student. He gave Ms. Olivary a cash award for adjusting the illustrations to perfection. Cognizant of the achievement, the men dined and discussed next steps, well aware other peers had long since lost interest in anything associated with Dr. Bud Worthington.

In conversation, many personal recollections were repeated. Sitting in their favorite corner, looking out across a portion of the campus, their voices went high and low in tone, sometimes to a whisper. Their hands animated their claims. Finally, with enough bravado stored up, the two colleagues parted. Bud returned home going straight to bed. And, unlike other nights when he tossed and turned until his body would exhaust itself, he slept believing the energy had shifted in his favor and there would be an ignition of inspiration from Jude Caine.

Oil and Their Landlords

Day 3650.

Special Conference to the President of the United States. Washington, D.C.

NEVERMORE. BEFORE OSTENSIVE market and price strategies, the nationalist oil executives muddled together immersed in their own fiscal conundrum, with a target on their backs, put there by foreign entities.

Historical revenue projections had been twice erased by despicable acts of economic and ecological destruction. In the mid-1900s, the birth of OPEC was a Lucifer spawn in the eyes of the U.S. oil conglomerates. Many predicted the council to evolve into a potent weapon allowing the third world to accumulate permanent wealth.

The weight of an imposed Arab embargo lasted years after hemorrhaging the United States economy in 1973. The effect on global economies lasted decades. Seventeen years hence, the retreating Iraqi military force ignited the Kuwait oil fields, ranking the fire as the second largest in the world. The ensuing economic devastation caused financial havoc around the world.

Inching back to fiscal health, the U.S. economy burned through four evolutions of swapping peace for guns to involve itself in a handful of third-world wars. As the bucolic image of the Middle East was permanently erased from the minds of global citizens, Americans were no longer pampered with the luxury of infinite unencumbered access to oil.

As the global debate about the health of the Earth began to take shape, a central core of politicians remained steadfast to offer legislation to a pre-emerging U.S.-based oligopoly, whose financial stability was critically dependent upon the rule of law to remain solvent. Until then, oil had not been amongst the favored U.S. industries that benefited from a host of exemptions and subsidies provisioned by public regulatory and taxing authorities.

But as one of the first capitalistic multinational industries, oil had become a formidable conduit of disruption and degradation to the fibrosis tenets of Keynesian economics, the monetary policy of the Federal Reserve, and the foreign policy dictates of U.S. presidents. As the country limped back from world crises, there was ample reason to give the American oil conglomerates exclusive treatment. Neither the government nor big oil could tell whose prevalent nature would consume the other first. The inherent principles in democracy and capitalism had to be preserved, protected, and defended in favor of and diametrically insulated from, the U.S. oil industry.

For all time, the resonance of interference beset upon and by U.S. oil firms was not to be solved by egalitarian methods. After months of classified deliberation, a complex solution was borne without congressional involvement, but within the context of the president's powers to operate privately within the domain of the White House. The main goals were to formulate objectives with elongated impact.

When the method of favor was to be discussed point by point, serious discussion focused on giving oil what they insisted upon and not debate on choice or reason. Arriving at that point in deliberation, the pool of congressional leads was pared down to two seasoned senators, Richard Sterling and Edward Royce. During previous administrations, they adeptly put themselves on the energy committees reaching deep into pockets to satisfy special interests. Their Lone Star state constituency was pleased with the evidence of tenacity to get wins for oil rich districts. Having matured to chairpersons with hyper-influence to turn knobs on the important rulings, they now were pleased to sit across from their constituents and hand them the prize.

The sweeping reforms were generically labeled "Partnership Program Objectives" [PPO] in all government standardized documentation with the intention to avoid detection of the explicit goals below. Classified, the full text remains protected, as "top secret" under Executive Order 13292, upgraded from the Department of Energy's classification of "restricted data." Once the scope of excess was felt by government and the public, candid opinions were extracted from research notes, from analysts who researched on behalf of public awareness groups. As one senior official claimed, "This could be the worst of all bailouts, even those constructed with bipartisan greed."

Section 17.1.2.1a – "Open-ended extensions for existing and new subsidies, leased properties, and co-funded investments."

Opinion: The oil companies considered this complex set of giveaways as a right, not a privilege. The extensive list ranges from price protection at the pump to matching funds for qualified research; from streamlining lease renewals to rollbacks on domestic fees imposed by the Democrats; from removing audit and tax reporting requirements to restructuring accounting rules for restatements of reserves, within the context of "special conditions or considerations." With no sunset terms, these handouts amount to significant monetary outlays to oil, estimated to be in the billions of dollars.

Section 17.1.2.1b – "Access to foreign entities to ensure global supplies."

Opinion: It amounts to a re-enactment of manifest destiny tuned for modern times. Regardless of country or sovereign nation, its intent is to trigger a complex assessment of all global assets near and far. A debate may have centered on whether there were actual Middle East governments that were pro-U.S. and how to cultivate those sympathies to enable a technology-for-oil trade. All remaining countries, especially those who had received funds from USAID were re-evaluated strategically to resolve whether significant interests should be pursued. A de facto doctrine established the immediate reversal of decades of foreign policy mandates focused solely on countries with nuclear war proliferation capabilities. Effectively, the refocus unlocked the potential of private investment overseas with no barriers, by rich oil firms with billions to invest. See Section 1712.1b for source of investment capital.

Section 17.1.2.1c – "Price protection for existing and future reserves."

Opinion: This was the crown jewel of all other subsidies. Quotes from taped evidence were uncovered, unrestricted under the FOIA (Freedom of Information Act). An executive from the largest oil company put it succinctly:

"We get distracted because the public is capable of mass hysteria when prices spike at the pump. The American people perceive they have access to an economic system that is capable of yielding infinite amounts of oil and natural gas, with the burden of delivery resting on our shoulders. We take on the risk of investment to maintain supplies and therefore expect ample resiliency in price elasticity to provide us a moderate return. It's as simple as that."

Price protection was invoked to make the individual conglomerates *exempt* from public pressure.

Section 17.1.2.1d – "Central organizational governance to validate exploration and stability of current and future reserves."

Opinion: The passage of a plan to create a complex infrastructure is believed to house scientific research. Although it may have been enormously difficult to incubate and achieve, it's not an entirely unfamiliar challenge by virtue of another success story. We see similarities, comparing the creation and expansion of the Pentagon, whose breadth and width had most of Congress locked up for over fifty years.

Impressed with the favorable outcomes of the exacting PPO legislation, narcissist oil executives began to see their images more clearly, sensing they would have explicit authority over their destiny. They enjoyed their new power, like their foreign counterparts, telling the governments what needed to be done and not asking or begging.

The injection of funding gave credence to the furtive organization that slowly began to expand the single point of control over global independent scientific research of the earth.

Deliberate intent leveraged the idiosyncrasies of a bloated federal bureaucracy, cloaking this unique organization within an existing federal department whose public mission could blend and integrate similar purpose, same staff, and same infrastructure.

The perfect choice was to hide the new agency, National Energy Administration of the Department of Energy (NEADE), within an existing research program called Natural Gas and Oil Technology Partnership program (NGOTP) funded by the Department of Energy, Office of Fossil Energy, Office of Energy Research, the Gas Research Institute, and direct industry contributions. Under this cover, the oil executives could maintain the appearance of arms-length involvement with the U.S. Government assuming the four PPO goals designed to bulletproof the U.S. oil industry were in force. Before the oil executives were officially excused, the ranking Senator of the committee threw them another bone. NEADE and the link to its public face, NGOTP needed an executive to take the reins.

Many candidates vetted were retired military, but the oil executives liked the dossier of a particular CIA agent. The former group would have been gloating if they were privy to the agent's official record of achievement. Among other professional maturities, the sixty-two-year-old male named Willis Colton had ground experience with hard target countries in the Middle East. A summary brief classified as top secret, detailed his involvement in a successful ghost operation that vastly improved the United States chances of expanding its presence in Pakistan.

Every nominee was given a closed session. During his interview, the CIA agent was keen on the objectives of the newly minted NEADE. The big picture attitude was refreshing to the review team, hearing the dogma about America's strength and his vigorous assertions to, "…kick the right ass at the right time. China is in their industrial revolution sucking down everything in sight and has gone out purchasing our debt. To contain that threat to our security and stability, NEADE will put us back on top to control finite global assets. Ours, and soon to be ours."

Day 2555.

Closed Session Hearing, The Capital Building. Washington, D.C.

YOU GET WHAT you need *and* what you want if you are Willis Colton.

As planned, NEADE had become a generation and repository mill of Earth science projects and programs. After establishing a network of various government-based research facilities and manning them with scientists, analysts, administrators, field workers, and a host of support personnel, the oil firms were getting what was promised to them—a single point of contact to effectively regulate competition for global natural resources. But there were barriers to success, strategies that failed to deliver tactical prominence, and people that stood in the way to superior motives.

Willis Colton knew that having oil in his backyard didn't make it easier to crack open. Alaska had been slotted for its oil and natural gas reserves for thirty years with the Republicans trying to dial in the exclusive combination. The dynamics of timed oil shortages with roll backs in environmental policies, assurances from the executive branch and manipulation of public interest— all was needed to tumble into place, to unlock the national asset.

Willis Colton knew to be patient, for his job was not solely about launching a covert government agency. Having served in the CIA for eleven years primarily as a "non official cover" agent, his risk-driven assignments and experience in the Middle East were key talents applied at the forefront of fortifying United States interests in oil reserves.[30]

Willis Colton knew greed drove ambitions that had price tags, to be paid by others. On his mark, the NEADE program became a guided assault to grab turf and expand the budget. As the infrastructure in NEADE grew, so did its capacity to capture, store, and report critical scientific research findings. And control the global content of that information. No longer would the world share the success of America's premier geoscientists without the express permission of Colton's organization.

Quickly asserting his power at the beginning of his term, Colton forged a covenant with Senators Sterling and Royce. Although the PPO was in a virtual "lock-box", NEADE was subjected to fiduciary oversight. As a team, they testified many times in closed sessions with the NSA and CIA reminding them of, not fighting for, its purpose and scope. At times, the testimonial opinions of the senators were smokescreens to placate their peers with anecdotal evidence.

Colton's testimony was fact-based, laced with military acumen, and sometimes argumentative. He considered congressional advocacy a barrier to NEADE's greater value to the United States and strongly suggested there be joint oversight with the Defense Intelligence Agency. Getting traction with the Pentagon, he engineered the reclassification of security levels to restrict congressional oversight, effectively keeping the "bunch of Nancys" at arms length.

Colton's bravado rubbed off quickly on the newly assigned political aide James Hyatt, and as NEADE grew, James began to recite Colton's message to assert the program mandates as "parallel to those of NORAD." In closer circles, Colton would call it "helping the senators pull their heads out." And at other times, he recounted his own wars: "I didn't see their asses hanging out at the Ceyhan and Sangachal oil terminals, chasing down targets."

Becoming more difficult to explain the growth factors or the Department of Energy budget increases, Senators Sterling and Royce championed tactics to set funding caps just underneath audit thresholds and transfer needed

---

[30]   CIA agents with "non-official cover" receive riskier assignments, posing as professionals in other lines of work.

funding under the auspices of the Pentagon, making the money flow in without tracks.

In its infancy, NEADE, a supporter and feeder of scientific information to the mainstream, became an interdependent clearing house for the major and minor contributors of scientific, industrial, and applied research. The prime initiative was to defuse any public panic that surfaced from theoretical or unplanned sources, such as natural disasters. The presumption was *all* natural resources were at risk, assuming oil was the primary focus.

NEADE had the prepubescent power to redirect, rewrite, or eliminate scientific aberration that conflicted with its mission. Usually, global disasters contributed to the influx of significant data but also generated adverse collaboration and opinion. Eco-trophies like the heat wave in France in 2003 sparked new studies percolating the risk of global warming. Poised to do battle against highly intelligent and motivated forces, NEADE provided the opposing studies making broad accusations against the findings of many scientists who began to expose the enormous threat of greenhouse gases and critical evidence of impending global shift in weather systems.

The management and authority nucleus of NEADE remained enigmatic to outsiders. Under Colton's rigid direction, the organization continued to undergo self-imposed scrutiny from within, to shield their increasing involvement of controlling science, research projects, and grants. The overhaul was warranted on the basis of *needing* more control because Colton *wanted* more control.

NEADE's province of activities was restated as mutually exclusive, apart from its original sponsorship from the NGOTP and GRI. The latter organizations were jettisoned in favor of moving NEADE within striking distance of the only U.S. national laboratories devoted to fossil energy research, parented by the National Energy and Technology Laboratories— NETL.

At first, the Lawrence Berkley National Laboratory had been designated to guide NEADE's research progress. Hungry for complete autonomy, Colton immediately severed the foster relationship and with the backing of defense-based priorities, targeted the Brookhaven Lab whose core competency was in energy technologies, national security, and had major scientific facilities operations with links to university, industry, and government. Colton then carved out the creation of a separate lab for NEADE with the increased capabilities including forensics, dubbing it "DARON"—Defense Administration Research of NEADE.

Brookhaven Lab was considered Tier One and Two. If the lab couldn't secure the solution, the job was scheduled as an escalation at DARON as Tier Three. In-house projects security coded were Tier Four and considered as the highest priority. All Tier Four research was governed by a restricted plan of record and monitored by the executive management.

Except for quirks in the network infrastructure, DARON was completely operational after Colton overhauled the IT infrastructure. More memory and load balancing were needed to gain processing efficiency for the massive server farms that provided explicit functions such as application and web hosting, domain and proxy, and pure number crunching for a variety of scientific tools.

The entire NEADE transformation took over two years to complete and the proposed expenditures and subsequent budget overruns were never rebutted. Funding tradeoffs with other programs were required, compensatory deals were devised, and people were manipulated. Contracts were renewed for procurement of building leases, construction, lab equipment, supercomputers, client hardware, software, network infrastructure, and virtual security. Additional security consultants, technicians, forensic scientists, and training specialists were hired.

Catching his second breath, Colton and his strategy team determined the breath and depth of NEADE should be expanded on the ground, in the form of undercover agents, to provide near- and real-time surveillance. This additional manpower would feed information and data into NEADE. Once scrubbed and analyzed, a policy statement would be given to the public arm, NETL for disseminating propaganda of public or private policy to the scientific and industrial masses. The NEADE field agents would provide the closed loop communication back to NEADE ensuring effective grounding of the message. It was these accountabilities that Colton recognized as key requirements to be an *agent* for NEADE and he modeled the job positions after those of the CIA and NSA.

Upon hearing the plan, Sterling and Royce were critical of extending NEADE's role into the masses in a way that was "too provocative" and believed they had already won with big oil, saying there was no reason to go deep.

Colton was determined to take the conflict head on and appeared at a subcommittee prehearing sitting next to Sterling. After listening to banter, Colton cut to the chase.

"With all due respect, senators," Colton initiated, swallowing those words hard, "the United States has been getting bitch slapped by the terrorists because we didn't have a plan. You've all read the NSA ELINT.[31] Many global regions, including ours may go through a major face lift. Our people on the ground will keep a lid on it until we fully understand it."

While tempers simmered, the classified briefing was formally introduced to the record. It documented the probabilities of a number of risk scenarios. The overwhelming evidence from NEADE analysis was that portions of the earth were experiencing a number of unforeseen "forcings."

"The composite of these multifarious scenarios could potentially introduce an amalgamation of complex outcomes," was read from the executive brief.

According to the Tier Four lab, the early modeling illustrated potential catastrophic events on the horizon with an order of magnitude consequence. In testimony, Colton reiterated NEADE objectives were to stop the myriad of end runs by the scientific communities who needlessly broadcast scenarios of global risk, panicking global populations. He went on to speculate that the U.S. Government was at the mercy of its citizens, whose reactions to numerous geological episodes resulted in dramatic economic consequences.

With graphs and charts, analysts disclosed only Level I and II response scenarios that were historically evoked by the U.S. for geopolitical objectives:

Level I: Once rampant press coverage exploded, a federal response was expected, committing the U.S. to massive relief efforts.

Level II: Consummate legislative authority provisioned emergency funding or advance monies to support a variety of proactive or reactive measures designed, to keep our global constituency safe.

---

[31] Space Today, "ELINT," SpyTerminology Glossary. http://www.spacetoday.org/
Area71/SpyTerminologyGlossary.html. ELINT: Electronic Intelligence, a NSA acronym for information obtained for intelligence purposes.

Supporting testimony cited the global disasters of Iran, Afghanistan, Colombia, and India earthquakes in the last ten years and the Asia Pacific tsunami in January of 2004 as credible accounts of Level II outcomes, triggering a series of congressional closed door briefings. Financial archives showed there wasn't a single nation prepared to deal with the disaster in manpower, infrastructure, supplies, or cash other than the United States.

Other federal personnel provided written testimony the United States had been the leader in providing disaster recovery relief through its independent federal agency USAID, responding every year since 1961. Since 1993, the annual budget increased near three hundred percent to five hundred million dollars responding to seventy disasters last year, in fifty countries.[32]

Restated emphatically by Colton, NEADE was put in place to secure *the* finite natural resource that had been exploited, but indeed should be managed intelligently in all U.S. led responses to global disaster. As entered into the record: *NEADE's purpose is to manage all global response scenarios, especially those that are evoked due to a second and tertiary Earth initiated forcing.*

The executive summary emphasized the potential threat to the U.S. economy if the NEADE operations remained at status quo. Colton knew the U.S. Government and its prime investors would be under siege if a no-vote was approved by the committee members.

Senator Bolen was compelled to challenge the request. His state had their federal funds trimmed and the NEADE budget was the culprit, "When it all adds up Mr. Colton, this program looks more and more like another underground military operation. And may I say, at the cost of needed federal funds redirected from the states."

Colton stood up, adjusted his shirt cuffs, and moved to the aisle to leave the meeting, "You call the president and tell him that we all forgot about getting your name on your state office building and you want your money back."

"Goddamn him!" Bolen seethed to his colleague, as he slammed down his dossier.

Sitting in the chambers of a Pentagon boardroom, James Hyatt had witnessed the castigation of one of his senior mentors.

---

[32] USAID, "Annual Reports Library,"
http://www.usaid.gov/our_work/humanitarian_assistance/disaster_assistance/
publications/ annual_reports/index.html.

He instinctively stood up and apologized for Willis Colton who had just walked out with certainty, "I'll see to it sir that he understands the implications of his actions."

Hyatt was always in career survival mode recognizing any episode might force his hand as to where his sympathies lay. Until now, he was walking on both coattails. Catching up with his boss in the hallway, Hyatt approached Colton, noting that some of the committee members were coming in their direction.

Within their earshot, Hyatt haughtily advised Colton he had little chance of receiving approval, "The appropriation should have been about maintaining the basic tenets of democracy, not some off the cuff remark about the U.S. getting bitch slapped!"

Colton blankly stared at his aide for a moment, deciding if it was time to find a replacement, "You know, you're killing me, Jim. You're killing me."

Colton instinctively belittled efforts anyone put forth to preserve their namesake. He hated having to call someone "James."

"I don't have time for your prattle. I come down here and do *your* job and all you can think about is playing house with Bolen."

The aide looked sheepish as Colton moved closer, leaning over to whisper, "Like you, they're just standing up for the camera. They know there aren't enough assets left in the ground to fuck with."

Day 2190.

NEADE. Undisclosed location near the Pentagon. Arlington, VA.

WITH THE BUDGET resolution in hand, after a raucous argument in the back offices of the White House, NEADE was authorized to recruit over four hundred global agents, train them, and jettison them to the inside the oil industry, public and private agencies, and scientific societies connected to oil.

For the agents, the service was confidential with a "life commitment" to never divulge their roles. Formally they were public employees on leave to industry through the "Science Share" outreach program hosted by NETL. Covertly, they were operatives for NEADE. Colton was quick to assert he controlled every agent on the ground.

The agents were given distinctive authority to collect crucial and incriminating evidence. The information gathering was relatively complex as the agents utilized their work environment to ferret out the opposition. Laptops and handhelds were used to transmit and receive via blue tooth connectivity.

Software applications automatically encoded the data, attaining the FIPS-197 government standard for encryption. Once the uplink was established, the data packet was sent via another protocol. Through the NEADE firewall, the IP telephony gateways tested the file header then permitted the upload to store. The blade servers in NEADE decrypted the message and attachments, routing them to assigned desk specialists and analysts.

A twenty-four by seven call center and an operations bridge supported the field, managing operational anomalies and escalations. Their indoctrination was steadily reinforced as they had become a highly leveraged asset. Briefed on the severity of conditions confronting the U.S., it was not lost on them that military personnel were now on site as security. The security layers at NEADE were guarding a virtual fortress of selective data about the earth's secrets, locking them down for a very centric body of review, no longer in the purview of the congressional and public domain.

The operational core of both NEADE and NETL was comprised of scientists, who were highly motivated to solve complex problems. Those candidates met the same security standards as agents, but were most interested in the main attraction: a state of the art research lab and facilities, federal funded grants, and the opportunity to disclose research to the highest levels of government. NEADE scientists utilized the existing NETL research network at nine sites, housing fourteen major research facilities. After a complex reorganization, the projects were divided among three NEADE teams, each with a team lead—promoted from within, all managed by a program manager who was under the direction of Colton's executive team.

Most of the research teams were culturally diversified as a result of the distinct intellectual advantage multinationals had over American borne citizens. Although the research staffs were U.S. citizens, Willis Colton did not agree with the influx of international expertise representing the scientific core of a U.S. quasi-military operation. His idealistic broodings reflected a strong bias towards the ubiquitous melting pot and the increasing homogeneities of the U.S. populations. Colton believed interracial relationships and the prevailing overtures of equality resulted in diluted faith, whether representing self, God, or Country.

Many multinational scientists hired by the research arm of NEADE faced distress and childhood agonies much like Willis Colton. Their stimulus for achievement was fueled by ancestral displacements and repatriation, disparate socio-economic conditions, and the resolve to gain the freedoms that other nations lacked. A newly minted scientist had proven his mettle within three years after leaving his academic post and was promoted to lead a team of researchers. The humble parallels of youth placed Willis Colton and Dr. R. Franklin on similar paths to discover the rarest form of Earth's constant mutation.

Closed Hearing, SD 11-B, Dirksen Senate Offices. Washington, D.C.

The Rubik cube like infrastructure of NEADE was formidable, able to keep its core existence a secret. For months, other external oversight committees had been trying to make progress against different barriers. The Subcommittee on Energy, Natural Resources, and Infrastructure, under jurisdiction of the Senate Committee on Finance took the lead.

"I'm asking. Was it a fact or an assumption?" demanded the congressional chairwoman.

The consultant to the OMB paused, double-checking written notes to avoid perjuring himself, "I obtained the information from a well-known source. The go-forward plan was to consider all opportunities. At the time this was a fact-based assumption."

"At the time? *What* time?" the chairwoman drilled.

"After the creation of OPEC, during the fall of 1960."

"Let's cut to the chase, sir. Your testimony stems from this assumption, and apparently a volume of others..." the senator pressed, waving a multi-paged document. "...at *this* time, you acknowledge to this committee leadership, of a record of a vote to initiate a plan to allocate and transfer special funds to accomplish what this closed door hearing suspects to be another agency nested within a bona fide government organization and existing agency, the NGOTP, facilitated by the Petroleum Technology Transfer Council."

The respondent was snide with his remark, "You have simplified a theory of actual organics and mechanisms that honorably protect America's interests here and abroad to achieve economic stability."

The ranking member of the reviewing body covered her microphone and leaned over to her colleague, "There's no way we are going to get traction unless we can get budget records. You said the subpoenas were trumped?"

"Yes, by an NSA wrapper."

"How the hell did they get that?"

The chairwoman centered herself over the microphone and announced, "Call to order...thank you. For the record, it is in the best interest of this

OMB sponsored session to postpone further review until the appropriate documentation can be obtained to support or challenge the circumstances stated by witnesses. I hereby close this review until further notice."

With a majority of the audience vacated, Senator Sterling entered the small conference room and walked over to the consultant who was uninformed of the senator's role, putting NEADE on the map, "You may be retired by the time this starts up again, but just to be sure, have your entire archive of original files in my office before the end of the day."

The completion of the request was followed by an abrupt termination of contractors who were knowledgeable of NEADE's humble beginnings. When other snipe hunts were attempted to uncover the roots of NEADE, verbal shunts were injected into qualifying sound bites by venerable authorities:

Senator Royce: It would be utterly impossible to have a mutually exclusive agency working in the shadows, as you infer, to reconstitute the energy policy of the United States.

And,

Senator Bolen: The Petroleum Counsel is in full cooperation with the science community to further the relevance of their independent study and research. Another agency? Sounds redundant to me.

And,

James Hyatt, special aide to the office of the vice president: It would be a complete waste of taxpayer's money to siphon research away from global scientists and control the public opinion. The Department of Energy operates with the federal mandate to accelerate and redeem good science.

Some of the most hyperbolic attacks were launched by congressional leads who considered themselves "insiders", purposely holding the agency budget hostage. Simultaneously, the public watchdogs like the Cato Institute and Hudson Institute were on the scent of oil and the improprieties it conjured. It all died down after a hand-off was escalated to the vice president who, on a timed announcement, went on the record at the Institute of Petroleum Autumn Lunch where he was slated as guest speaker.

The Vice President of the United States: Years ago we did talk to the oil people. It was a fact-finding dialogue.

The planted reporter had a follow-up.

Reporter: Aren't you obligated to share your findings with those groups who hold an opposing view?

Vice President: No, we are not required to release any private conversations to impacted parties. To do so would limit our ability to test the theories and relative strengths of our economic, domestic, and foreign polices.

"One more question?" begged another.

Vice President: That is the end of it.

Sterling predicted privately in his office that either sweep week or some other notable entertainment would pop up to further obscure their organization. "Our constituents buy advertising, so the news can be margined in our favor. The bored thirty-something viewers are ready for another Hollywood breakup or a new season of reality TV."

A core of less-conservative senior leaders had joined their peers across the aisle with a different set of perceptions, regardless of the claims of the executive office. Discovering the host of interconnected oil and gas councils, agencies, and departments to be a complex arrangement of value limited to the few, these senior leaders continued to harbor questions about the authority and scope of the suspected secret agency, the manner to which funding was provisioned to it, and how its actions augmented influence by the use of those funds.

The ranking member of the minority party gave no appearance of bipartisan rhetoric: "They can't all be sitting on secrets that are beyond the ken of their peers. They can't all be the ones that know more than everybody else."

NETL. Washington, D.C.

Astep ahead, colton was finalizing another strategy to increase NEADE's invincibility. Most of the agents were fully deployed but he was ready to jump start another resource to weld personal control over scientific doctrine. Reaching deeper into the scientific community, Colton had managed to penetrate rank and file leaders and turn them. For certain duties benefiting the goals of NEADE, the researchers were allotted perks such as increased funding or access to lab resources. Dr. Kenneth Millard, a personal pick Colton planned to mentor, waited in the first floor conference room of the Long Island NETL facility.

Follow-up interviews with the affluent entrepreneur gave Kenneth time to check out Colton's "public" credentials and his relationship to NETL. The NEADE boss, insuring the ego was patently massaged, flew Millard out to meet with him and team members.

Concealing his dominating persona, Colton had been manipulative with the amount of information he provided, not sharing the extent of his domain. A neutral position made it easier to coax information from Millard, who found Willis Colton to be soft spoken, subtle, and "courageous in the sense of having strong convictions as a leader," as Kenneth explained to a personal friend.

During a previous dinner hosted by Colton, he told stories of his military career, hinting of improprieties that had global implications. With drinks,

Kenneth did not resist sharing his dealings and level of ethical prowess. As a serious art collector, Kenneth had adept negotiating skills, willing to be unscrupulous if the need presented itself. By now, Colton knew all about the man's private inventory of original paintings.

Kidding each other late one night in a bar, after rounds of drinks, Colton ribbed Kenneth about his looks. The ex-CIA agent, with his smaller stature, had close clipped graying hair and age-lined skin, and could pass for the quintessential silver-haired executive in a dark grey Jay Kos business suit. Kenneth, with naturally coiffed dark-blonde hair, dressed in the same expensive attire, was a bit taller and looked like a prominent news anchor.

"You know if you take this job, you'll start to look like shit," Colton accused.

"Willis, with due respect, you beat me to it."

That night, Kenneth mistook Colton's congeniality to be genuine.

Colton entered the first floor conference room well after Dr. Kenneth Millard's arrival. The light sconces on the conference room walls were dimly lit, their light reaching a center dome in the ceiling emitting a blue hue. The comfortable chairs of brown split hide leather, double sewn, had tooled wooden arms matching the trim on the polished mahogany conference table. In the twenty-five minutes that he sat alone, Dr. Kenneth Millard had been physically comfortable and relaxed. During the time he waited for host's arrival, he recalled his previous meetings with Willis Colton and reassessed his likelihood of being offered a position with NETL. Maybe a downside was his lifestyle as a bachelor but he was president of his own S-Chapter corporation. A potential financial windfall was worth his time to inspect and judge the obligation of employment with the government. He was self-aware that his shrewdness could be outplayed by his vanity.

"Welcome, Ken," Colton obliged, ignoring the extended hand. "Sit back down and we'll get started."

"I prefer Kenneth."

"Did you get checked in and you're squared away?"

"Yes, it's all taken care of. Thank you," Kenneth answered ruffled. "You confirmed on the phone that you're interested in my credentials."

"That's correct."

"I'd like to hear what's on the table."

Colton walked around and took a chair at the end of the conference table, far enough away to cause annoyance, "Ken, you've heard the saying, 'you shouldn't judge a book by its cover'?"

Kenneth felt his body tense, his shoulders raise, and the urge for a cigarette. From his angle, he could see Colton's concealed weapon.

"Something wrong, Ken?"

"Ah, no. Umm. Actually, you seem different. I prefer being called Kenneth."

There was no response to address his preferences.

"What are you talking about, the judging a book, etc.?" Kenneth's face winced. "I don't understand."

"Let me square it up. I haven't been completely honest with you."

Kenneth's brow dropped hesitating to interrupt, "Okay."

"And there are reasons why. But let me line out a couple items first. You are forty-two. Lived in two states. Your surviving family member lives within fifty miles, in plausible condition. You live on the fifth floor and at the same apartment address for six years. Your tastes in art and other collectables exceed your net cash flow so you're upside down bringing your net worth to under a mil. Hmmm. They *really* are just paintings on the wall unless you sell them."

Reciting, Colton's tone was flat and his pale blue eyes were menacing. Kenneth held his composure, his upper lip was moist, "You've got to be kidding me. What relevance does this have?"

"Your startup was financed but now you're solely funded by grants. Other revenue comes from consulting and speaking engagements."

Kenneth fumbled with his shirt cuffs, "Well, I've completely missed the point. I thought I was...we should probably end this."

"One year contract renewable at the end of the term. Nine hundred K per year, tax free in four payments. All travel expenses paid."

The prospect's weakness for the dollar surfaced. Resistance was low to none. "Well, that's intriguing. Discounting all your half-truths, what do I have to do? Hand over my consulting business?"

"No, Geo Terra Science keeps going. That's our gem. You keep your face in the game."

"Then what?"

"You have to lie."

The sweat on Kenneth's neck seeped into his starched collar. He used his embossed handkerchief to pat his moist skin, "These must be big lies."

"Not really. You're not the kind of person that can get away with that. I just need small lies told consistently."

"Are you some kind of government spook and now I know too much?"

"No."

Colton moved closer to Kenneth and sat on the table, "You can walk out of here. I'll go get someone else to do this. It's that easy. But seriously, where can you get that kind of return on your investment. You've got a solid reputation and a global clientele. You and I need to take that and tweak it. There's some stuff on the horizon, right down your alley. You're the expert and I need to put a face out there people trust and listen to. According to the science geeks, your name bubbled up to the top."

The speech was honed to make egos take charge over logic. And Colton never had to back pedal at this point with the others.

"So if I accept, I can't renege."

"It's complicated. A paper you'll sign tomorrow states there's a lock-out period on the restricted non-disclosure that will take effect."

"How soon do you need my decision?"

"There's a ten percent signing bonus if you ink it by tomorrow. That can clear title on some of your artwork."

Kenneth's composure plummeted, "What is it with you? Did you take my fingerprints from my wine glass? We're you in my apartment?"

"It's not that complicated. You file taxes and use credit cards, right?"

"Of course," Kenneth barked, divulging his agitation.

"Freedom of Information Act. Everything's out there. You think I wasn't going to evaluate *my* risk before I made *my* decision to offer *you* a job?"

Kenneth shook his head numbly. Colton stood and walked to the door, "I've got a hard stop. I've arranged a limo to take you to a private lunch, then back to your room. I'll pick you up at seven p.m. and we'll go celebrate."

"I need to think about this."

"Cha ching" was the last response from Colton as he left the room with certainty. His mercenary was in the bag. He wanted to coach this one. It intrigued Colton that somehow the twit managed to have contacts all over the world in the exact playground of geology that NEADE was tackling: tectonics and seismology.

Laying on the king bed after the exquisite lunch complete with a Dom Pérignon Rosé 1996, Kenneth felt apprehension and exhilaration at the same time. His heartbeat was accelerated. Lighting a cigarette, he drew a bath and broke tabs on a couple of Scotch bottles in the mini bar. In the tub he shifted his third cigarette from hand to hand, testing whether both of them were shaking. Convincing himself there was really no commitment to anything that couldn't be stopped, he concentrated on the money.

"Cash. Nobody can just hand it out like that. Colton, if that's his name, he must have major connections in NETL."

His greed drifted between calculations of how much money he would have in his checking account and what it could grow to after two or three years.

Colton's recruitment of Millard was not only special because of the instant expansion of NEADE's expertise, but to his delight, Dr. Kenneth Millard profiled with personality characteristics showing he was very malleable given the right kinds of incentives. There were always going to be contingencies that needed to be played with a respected face.

That evening during their dinner, Colton convinced Kenneth that his professional and thus social ranking would climb if he accepted the job. The goals for both men were mutually exclusive. Kenneth desired the money and status. Colton wanted NEADE's agenda promoted. Nervously, Kenneth showed up the next morning to collect a check for ninety thousand dollars.

Time in the box with Willis Colton was not as intriguing as Dr. Millard anticipated. For six consecutive weeks, finishing out the calendar year, he attended workshops providing education on the entire workings of NETL. Colton's team rode shotgun on their student, reinforcing his learning. The boss monitored his protégé remotely, checking in with him multiple times a day.

Feedback to Colton was mixed. Angela Gates, an agent reporting to Colton, was concerned that Kenneth would bolt before they turned him loose on the public tour.

"He's smart and good looking, but nervous as a cat. Always on his cell. And he's going to kill himself with those cigarettes."

"He'll settle down. He's just a public mouthpiece. There's nothing new here to confuse him."

"When are we going to start doctoring the presentations?" she tried to confirm.

"After training, when he gets a month or two behind him on the road. I don't want to give him any ammunition to shoot us with."

The next business quarter turned up some bad news for Dr. Kenneth Millard's corporation, Geo Terra Science. Kenneth was directed to reschedule all his private speaking and consulting engagements to accommodate the thirty-two NETL events. Kenneth did napkin calculations discovering a portion of his NETL funds would have to cover the shortfall in consulting fees that would have been revenue for GTS. And the calculated fee per NETL event was lower than his standard fee. Selfishly, Kenneth reviewed the possibility of scheduling some of his revenue generating events in the same cities where he was practically working for free, for the government.

According to the engagement profile, Kenneth learned all major metro areas had two day meet and greets. The dog and pony shows included segments on the NETL charter, services portfolio, and a snapshot of the Tier One research projects underway. The newly minted agent also had to attend all the major events hosted by the various societies and affiliations such as the American Geological Institute, Geological Society of America, Society for Sedimentary Geology, National Science Foundation, SAG, and major vendors of oil. Colton explained to Kenneth it was imperative that he attend and build up his network, as if representing his own firm.

"Am I representing NETL or myself?"

"Strictly NETL"

"I would normally get a fee for speaking."

"That's why I'm paying you."

Arriving back at his apartment for a few days off after training, Kenneth was exhausted. Cleaning up, he stood in front of his favorite wall art, *Moulin Rouge* by Toulouse-Lautrec. His love of modern masters was borne of his mother's efforts to provide her son a perspective of cultural eminence. It looked different to him.

"Maybe it's because I own you now" he purred, taking a sip of wine and raising his glass to the painting.

Consoling himself about the trade-offs he had accepted, his trance blocked out the ringing phone until his answering service came on.

"Where are you? I thought you'd be back by now. Please call me. You owe me a night on the town."

"I'm in no mood to do any more pleasing," Kenneth pampered to himself.

Ignoring his promise to call his fiancée Caroline when he arrived home, Kenneth poured his wine goblet full again and leaned back into his couch, finishing a cigarette. His sleep there was not disturbed until eight-thirty the next morning. The knock on his door was from the concierge service delivering the collected mail.

Kenneth brushed his hair back and speaking through the closed door directed the man to leave the box there, "Yes, it's ok. Just put it down."

Reluctantly, with no chance of a tip, the man dropped the box on the wooden entryway. The noise sounded like a gunshot, causing Kenneth to jump.

"Jesus!" he exclaimed, flashing back to a dream he had after a long day of NETL training. In his dream, Colton had come to pick him up in a limo and once inside, handed a revolver to him, "You need to use this if they don't believe you."

"I've never shot a gun."

"It doesn't matter; just point it towards them. They'll know whose boss."

Colton hit the switch to open the sunroof and started firing the gun into the dark, "It's that easy."

He thrust the gun into Kenneth's hand and ordered him to shoot. Having done so, the scientist started playing around, twirling the gun, firing it from many positions.

Thinking again how weird the dream was, Kenneth sorted through the overflowing box of mail and sighed, "I could shoot myself right now."

The freedom from oppression that week became a blur. A couple nights out with Caroline and outstanding business with his GTS associates consumed all his time. Kenneth had broached the subject of a transition with his two junior partners at the time of interviewing with NETL and some of his executive authority was shifted to them and his senior staff. Colton's job proposal was the impetus to lock in permanent changes at GTS, becoming the opportunity to sell-off a portion of his ownership, creating a partnership for two key employees.

A day before he would solo his first NETL hosted event, Kenneth felt more anxiety about the event than about the reorganization in his business. During his week off, the first two of the three conversations he had with Colton were not surprising. The first call was a basic rundown of the contacts Kenneth was directed to make at the co-hosted AGI and GSA "Earthcache" after-party. Another follow-up call in the middle of the week at ten p.m. was a basic pep talk, making sure he was familiar with the presentation content. The last call, five minutes ago was to tell Kenneth to wait at the Philadelphia airport for his mentor. Colton had decided to attend the event because "I really haven't seen you in action. I want to make sure you nail it."

"Shit." Kenneth hung up the phone, took a deep breath, and lit up a cigarette, "I don't need a fucking babysitter."

The next four months were painful, as Colton continued to redefine Dr. Kenneth Millard. Even though the student was no longer a novice, Kenneth presumed he must be the sole survivor by now if other professionals under Colton's tutelage were criticized with the same intensity. With Colton stalking every event, it hadn't gotten any easier to hit the road, do the presentations, meet and greet, and pack up for the next one.

As the front man, Kenneth was convinced his efforts were up to par. During his speaking segment on a dumbed-down version of seismic tomography explaining anisotropic inconsistencies, he fielded a number of questions, making sure to reference the services provisioned by NETL. As far as he could tell he was doing his job, but there were no accolades coming from Colton. Only constant reminders to follow-up with this or that person and to make sure the discussions integrated the most recent presentations.

Over those four months, substantial data flowing into NETL and analysis coming out of the Tier Three labs validated a series of new irregularities in earthquake prediction models. After many global sites had deployed additional monitoring stations and improved measurement sensitivity, a series of shock waves were reported that were undetectable prior to installing the updated equipment. That evidence was getting airtime and the government agency had to react quickly to soften the risks that were being touted to the public.

In parallel to that, advocates for global warming had been pipelining more facts and figures to the public. NETL was very successful with a campaign of words to discredit the scientists who were the vanguard of climate change, simply by suggesting the science was "new" and "while most scientists advocated studies to prove the impact of climate change, none of the studies were conclusive of proving temperature was the culprit."

As the planet literally churned out more forms of disaster-causing episodes, the barrage of earthly geological and ecosystem events peaked the resources at NETL and NEADE to contain, defend, and disseminate opposing material. Agents all over the country were pressed to close off the flow of information pouring through the portals of mass media. The seasoned teams knew their best defense was an offense that was pulled out and used over and over. An official "guidance" memo was circulated within NETL:

> Attack with the fear of doubt! The public is fickle when listening to the scientific debate over the effect of the changes occurring almost daily. As long as it can be proved that none of the global disruption touches them, they can be won over. Missing bees and declining frog populations don't raise fuel prices. The plight of the polar bear is unfortunate, but doesn't keep real Americans from getting an education that they deserve. Flooding and fires are cyclical but the damage is not a permanent and a windfall to our regional economies.

With opposing forces in trenches, Kenneth and his peers had to take the heat at the intellectual level of the debate. Swarming around him were councils, boards, committees, special conferences, commissions, and litigation, at all levels of governance in private and public arenas. First responders tended to be the immediate benefactors of the NETL-sponsored research. Damage control had to be applied immediately so they could quiet the downstream risk of investors, program administrators, small governments, and specific foreign interests who were safe harbors for U.S. interests. The second level was a hemorrhage of collection systems all vying for accurate assessments to filter back to their constituents. It was never simple or quick, to unplug and diffuse a statement of conclusive evidence made by an advocate with esteemed credentials, a public watchdog, or virtual material that had the half life of flotsam.

Dr. Millard and his small band of colleagues had to take the low road and smear many as conspirators. The advocates blurting news were made out to be trigger happy with their inconclusive research and accused of damaging the reputations of scientists who were loyal to NETL. It pained Dr. Millard to stand in front of those who had knowledge of his prior firm and its contributions. Many stressful phone calls started out with apologies and then Kenneth endeavored to push the conversation in the direction Colton insisted that it go.

Almost a year since leaving GTS, Kenneth was agonized, realizing things were off track between him and his employer. Fully rationalized that the money realigned his ethics, he was ready to concede that part of it could be burnout – living out of his suitcase and not at his apartment more than three consecutive days since he went full time with NETL. There wasn't much else that Kenneth was willing to take the blame for. The lies weren't working. It didn't matter how or how often he told them. His research constituents were resistant to compliance. And the public was getting smarter.

Day 245.

NEADE. Undisclosed location near the Pentagon. Arlington, VA.

ONG AFTER HIS internal promotion and now recognized as a highly-capable manager, Dr. Franklin continued to spend more time in the lab offices at night to consolidate the myriad of computations into mathematical models for validation and analysis. He was able to convince management that his seismic volume model had significant value and had revised it to significant levels. Other projects had spawned off his personal contributions, but his team remained dedicated to bringing Franklin's predictive model to fruition.

As a working manager, Franklin was personally obligated to extend the intellectual reach of his group. Like Franklin, his team members, who were "kindly" referred to as the "NEADE Indians", had modified their names as well to minimize differences between them and their American peers. Omkar Taprendra Chandrasekra whose name translated to God of heat, was born in the middle of summer. Simplified to the lowest level, he went by "TC." Navin and Vinod, both on extended work visas, erased their first namesakes of Sanjay and Mangesh, respectively. The boss decided not to complain when he was referred to as "Ravi".

Culturally driven, the scientists would never turn down an assignment even if they did not have the specific knowledge or skill set. For competitive reasons, they would merely accept working harder rather than admit they didn't know something. Franklin knew these intellectual gaps would ultimately slow their pace and he took steps to close them so his team could make the required advancements on schedule.

Throughout their project engagements, all of them acknowledged their manager's advocacy for a "system" approach to the solution, but they didn't fully understand it. Franklin, determined to reach their maximum effort, held sessions to teach them his end-to-end system.

To promote forward progress, Franklin focused them on their own model calculations relating it to a variety of other scientific disciplines. The team received many lectures on the Gaia theory. It had become surprisingly useful to comprehend cause/effect. Taking it in another direction, Franklin illustrated "snippets" from gene science, showing how the correlations of genetic markers to DNA mapping were analogous to their validation of complex seismic wave equations.

During reviews with his manager, Franklin reported progress in the lab as incremental gains, but his manager felt like it was a never ending battle to get the team moving, "Why can't your team proof these theories during standard work hours, like everyone else?"

"We're trying to John, but it's not coming to us easily."

"According to your own notes, this team you say in Britain has published their findings. We can't afford to have Euro trash coming in before us!"

"I know. The team is scrubbing it. Their research is similar, but not exactly what we're doing."

Determined, Franklin expanded his own schedule, staying later and pushing into the early mornings, mindful that eventually somebody somewhere would leapfrog his unique research. He felt the pressure Worthington must have been subjected to in the past. With frustration and exhaustion circling them, his team attempted to backtrack to maintain a level of objectivity, after logging forty-seven days straight. Given priority time on the servers for computational testing, the data utilized in the published model had not provided any advantage or breakthrough when applied to their own mathematical models.

"Did you communicate any of our preliminary findings back through NETL to validate the scientific communities' response?" Franklin quizzed his team in their work cubes.

"No, at the time there wasn't enough to go on," explained Navin. "We borrowed the data from the many articles written and started applying it but we didn't get it reclassified."

The required step to validate claims regardless of publicity hype was regarded as sacred in the scientific community. Nothing was taken at face value. And nothing was shared from NEADE that was below scientific grade. By their terms, the methodology of investigation, observance, and experimentation could not be compromised.

"You're right," Franklin admitted. "It would have been incorrect to share any preliminary result with NETL unless the specific protocol was achieved."

The decision Franklin faced in the lab that night, with classified documents spread out, his whiteboard full of hybrid calculations, sandwich papers on the floor, was to stop and restart in another place even though it felt like a time sink, a waste of precious time. They had gambled on the details of the British research model that had held promise and that strategy put them behind schedule. Staring at the whiteboard, his mind was numb, fumbling through a piece of code. Franklin wondered if they had actually missed a step. Switching to his laptop, he looked at the list of instant messenger accounts checking to see if his teammate was still online from home. It was two a.m.

Franklin: You there TC?

After five minutes,

TC: I am sir. Can I help?

Franklin: I'm going over the last run, with the quad-P curve sequences. Do you have a current version?

TC: Let me check...

After minutes more, he text back,

TC: Yes. What do you need?

Franklin: Give me the parameter list of quotients that you used for the sub_parameters of the baseline equation.

More thought and a clarification.

Franklin: Just send them to the share point.

It took minutes to send the files to their secure collaboration workspace.

Franklin tabbed over and opened the series of information. Minutes turned into to an hour. The Indian natives were very patient and respectful.

TC: Something else Ravi?

The blinking icon in his tray snapped Franklin to attention.

Franklin: Sorry. No. Thxs.

Franklin suddenly stood up and raced out of his cubicle heading for the administration station. Flipping through the slots of the magazine rack, he found the publication that had circled the floor for review. All his team's names were checked on the slip stapled to the cover. Flipping pages as he headed back to his office, he reviewed the table extract illustrations printed in the journal.

"This doesn't make sense."

Locating the contact information for the chief editor he picked up his phone and left a voicemail, "Mr. Strachen, how are you this morning. It's urgent. Could you please contact me as soon as possible?"

Franklin quickly detailed his credentials, his request, and ended with a "Thank you Sir."

In their ad hoc meeting hours later at ten a.m., his team took the news with difficulty. Five men whose average age of thirty-two, holding aggregate IQ's above 130, missed a typo. Navin, the assigned co-lead was personally embarrassed and incensed with guilt. Franklin had just explained his earlier call to the editor confirmed the mistake which would be retracted in the next volume, due out in twenty days. The chief editor was gracious for Franklin's diligence, noting most of the readership didn't have time to work through such detail.

Navin turned to his companion speaking Tamil, "Vinod. How do you say I fucked up?" meaning it to be rhetorical penitence.

Vinod repeated it in English, "You just say, I fucked up."

Giggling, he repeated it in Tamil, then he laughed loudly, "What else can I translate for you my friend!"

Emotion overtook the group, mentally and physically spent from their workload. Through the closed glass doorway, the scientists could be seen leaning over holding their stomachs, their eyes watering from laughter. The release of frustrations was a remedy for their obscure oversight. The decision was to request backup files and redo preliminary analysis with the corrected formula. When he reminded his team that another discovery was starting to take precedence, Franklin was reacting to the urgency.

"Our colleagues up stairs are working to prove the characteristics of the "enhanced" magna."

"Sounds like old science to me," Vinod said.

"Not so," their manager corrected. "It's believed to have unknown properties, but more importantly our work is primary support to identify the location of this substance. Let's focus our time to prove or disprove the speculative notations in the journal first."

The time in the lab was not all in favor of NEADE. Another benefactor awaited Franklin's final calculations. He had many reasons to explain his change of heart and decided to make a pact with an old friend.

Franklin became so obsessed with his own achievements, he ignored rumors. When he was working for NETL, he believed his efforts would expand the boundaries of understanding Earth's untold warnings. To the contrary, he heard "agents" were gathering information to control public opinion. He heard the grumblings of old and new colleagues that personally experienced the pressure to rewrite their findings. After being promoted to NEADE, Franklin refocused, but rumors persisted. They all pointed to control and power. Over months, Franklin was certain his research would be altered for other purposes. Still, he needed the infrastructure of NEADE to complete his work, but there were very few that could be entrusted. Maybe one man deserved the chance to announce the truth to the world instead of a man's government hiding it.

The extra nights in the lab, the four hundred extremely grueling hours of study and reflection actually expanded Franklin's intellectual growth and understanding of the dynamics of his model. Yet to be validated, he was unaware of any similar or parallel efforts in the world that significantly replicated his theory. Privately, he had diagramed the solution many times on the white board, erasing them to force objectivity. Reciting the theoretical implications clarified his vision but he had many assumptions and doubts about the model's value to mathematically predict the earth's physical forcings:

The new PK sub-coefficient sustains accurate measures. But it only suggests where the velocity is occurring in the earth. Strength may be a function of velocity but I can't measure it, so I can only predict that a constant force occurs. But I know nothing about the magnitude of its force. The earth is revealing herself! But how?

Reaching this extreme level of cognitive discovery, the lead scientist found eating and sleeping difficult. Franklin's outward exuberance at having a clearer shot at success was more a demonstration of relief for two separate reasons: the promise of understanding Earth's inevitable forcings, and the assurance to his patron of his competence and shared vision. Like Worthington, he had become a rebel of science to further the cause.

Midland, Texas.

HERE WAS NOTHING better, after wading in the oil-soaked grit, than to drink a few cold ones at Double Saddles. Like every blue collar generation before them, the oil rig crews filled the bar, coming in off shift or on payday. With minimum air flow, the wooden frame one-story housed the bar, kitchen, a couple rooms for group parties, and a corridor to the bathrooms. The odors of dripped, spilled, and splashed Shiner Bock and Lone Star permeated the wood surfaces. Running on quarters, the workers liked the three cramped pool tables and the music coming from the Rock-Ola Centura jukebox, loaded with forty-fives. A third of the sixties- and seventies-era tunes never rotated into play unless wrong buttons were hit or drunks wanted to piss somebody off. The rest of the vinyl was country white noise that broke up the chatter and the yelling about who slung more pipe, hit more fluid, was more pussy whipped, or who was "gonna get theer fuckin' ass kicked." There was always wild speculation on whether the stone squirrels got it right or wrong with their seismic studies. And once in a while the head toolpusher told a real good story.[33]

Of the hundreds of rotary rig sites owned by Apache, Doug Erls was lead foreman over a fraction of them. Like all other crews, his men worked in shifts to build and drill. In constant motion they found oil, piped the

---

[33] Skinner, Les, "Oilfield Jargon," World Oil, (September 2005). http://findarticles. com/p/articles/mi_m3159/is_9_226/ai_n15649426. Stone squirrels are the geologists that are assigned to the oil rig. A toolpusher is the man assigned to supply all the materials on the rig.

flow, and kept it coming by replacing valves, gaskets, chain, or rebuilding entire pieces of equipment. It took a lot of man-hours to manage the profit margin of their stakeholders.

Doug, considered a "big sprocket" by his men, was being edged out by new technology and science. Most of the manual grime and grit learning in the field gave way to computers, sophisticated tools, and software systems.

The old timers, like Doug's grandfather, made their reputations with muscle and a good eye for the landscape. Crews used to make guesses from experience, shifting the bore direction when they examined and smelled the mud. Each year a major advancement in technology made the foreman's job easier, saved money, and made more money for the oil corporations.

Aware the supply of oil was finite, oil companies kept thousands of production wells active, pulling fluid from the deep strata of rock below. In the past, the science of drilling was an exercise in gravity. Just plop down equipment and start boring. There wasn't a reason to be concerned with the exact location, size, or relative direction of the well hole. Wandering off course didn't present a problem. Throw something, it would stick.

Overwhelmed by an apparent decrease in abundant supply in the seventies, big oil struggled against subterranean geographical barriers. Soon, a host of technological advancements were enabled by science and engineers who were controlled by oil conglomerates. Precision plotting with GPS could calculate diameter and hole symmetry. Multipurpose drill bits were manufactured with advanced cutting, steering, reaming, and cleaning to gain efficiencies in time over cost. For hole opening, alignment, and challenging wellbore geologies, the drill bits gave companies cost per foot savings. Based on the assay reports of core samples, custom machined titanium bits could be calibrated with multicast layers of metal and diamonds of significant thickness to coincide with the hardness of the earth's sediments. The drill bit was engineered to penetrate the most durable material. After the surge of science and engineering prowess, if oil was present somewhere below the surface of the earth, there was very little that could stop it from being taken.

Measuring or predicting success of a well was taken from calloused hands and put into databases that could be mined for information to recalculate profit. The oil well was no longer limited to producing mud and sludge, as the eyes and ears on the ground were trained to capture sensitive data. For the new explorers, their mark in the ground would be deadly accurate and the wealth of discoveries could be obscured from public view.

But, no matter how much automation could be forced and integrated into the science of drilling a hole into the earth, a human being was still needed to get the right amount of equipment in the field and deploy those assets to make the money. A worker was needed to feed drill pipe and change bits. Another worker was needed to monitor the gauges to discreetly control the process of drilling. Brain and muscle were needed to manage the activities of the crew and to make economic decisions about the day's work.

The land-anchored oil rig was a mass of steel and labor requiring significant coordination by those educated and uneducated resources. The motorhand owned the viability of all the rig motors at the site. The drillers, derrickhands, and the toolpushers repeated operational choreography that brought the well in. Even the unskilled roustabouts with menial tasks of scrapping paint and digging trenches, were essential to the rig crew. Everybody in the field was a stakeholder, with retirement benefits on the line. Every worker was aligned to the financial plan that required every hour to be spent in a productive way, with no waste. No equipment would break down, causing delays. Nobody would get injured. Day after day, year after year, decade after decade, wells had been planned, sited, tested, and moved into production to reap financial rewards.

All of Doug Erl's accomplishments were the same as the last, as he guided his men from one site to the next, plodding the course planned by his mentors. He had repeated the same steps until they seemed like the overplayed vinyl records at Saddles. All the words to the same song on the same record played in the precise order, selecting all the records every day, with precision. He had seen it all come and go in the field. Bosses who were hot heads and others, shit for brains; crewmen who were religious nuts or dopers; advances in the technology of drilling mechanics and tooling; the pain-in-the-ass safety devices and programs; and the endless environmental pressure from the greenies, injecting their goddamn ethics into every aspect of their work. Until the oil ran out, the life cycle of a rig crew was infinite. Start it up, finish it out, shut it down, clean it up, and move on. To Doug, field life was one big continuous play with no unplanned variation left without an explanation.

But still on the maps and financial statements at Apache, a single site kept haunting his sleep. Recorded in the Railroad Commission 8A, and reported on the Department of Energy's EIA-23 form, the oil rig was formally listed as "Shafter Lake." There were crew celebrations at Saddles when the minor field was formally classified on the books. The men nicknamed it "Kilgore" after the namesake, the world record holder producing over two million barrels of crude on a single acre.[34]

The only milestone worth joking about was when Shafter Lake broke the record number of consecutive safety days. The talk in Double Saddles the night of the accident was not about production hype, but about production loss. The site failed to produce a single barrel of oil. No one involved could or was allowed to put their finger on the root cause. Apache management said to do so would waste time and money.

In the project log, the preliminary analysis declared the site a qualified as a "deeper pool test."[35] Jen Rawlins, one of the trusted field geologists for Apache, analyzed and evaluated the oil reserve potential with numerous extension tests and dutifully signed off. Following policy, her well studies were prepared in advance assessing the volume of liquid and gas to set the geological boundaries of the reserve. Like clockwork four months later, Doug Erls would be on the site ready to proceed, after hours of planning meetings with divisional management.

His favorite planning phase was partnering with Jen, to have her underscore the potential risks of the drilling site. They had quickly gained mutual respect for each others' skills—his years of field experience and her education and determination. With her graphs and specimen reports, Doug integrated her field notes that looked above and below the ground and combined her current analysis with historical drilling data from the Nash book.[36] He was confident of her skills knowing she always collaborated with the site preparation production coordinators.

---

[34] http://www.lone-star.net/mall/txtrails/kilgore.htm.

[35] 4. Petroleum Technology Transfer Council, "Drilling Well Classification System," Tech Transfer Tech, 2nd Qtr 2003, Vol. 9, no 1 (2003), http://www.pttc.org/newsletter/newsletter_past/1qtr2003/v9n1p4.htm#2. Drilling well classification by Lahee established in 1944.

[36] Petroleum Strategies, Inc., "The Nash Books," http://www.petroleumstrategies.com/nash.html. The Nash Books are a recognized source providing concise, accurate daily lease and well production information for each operator in every railroad commission district throughout Texas, reporting on the following elements: field,

When Jen came aboard four years earlier, the betting in the locker room was against her. Too many school brats had already passed through, cutting their teeth on crews like Doug's and then waltzed into management with someone else's ideas. The grim rumor was females whored their way up the greasy ladder.

Her long hours at the pretest sites didn't convince everyone that she was different. Anybody had to do that just to keep up. It was her ability to share what she learned, coming back to the field men to validate what she found or to test a hunch. Doug liked her because she shunned the big players, never running to corporate management when there was a problem. She stayed close to the action in the field and respected the men who did the dirty work. The good ole boys learned there was little variance in what Jen's work predicted and what actually came up from the ground. By the time she approved a site, a map of the hidden underground had already been projected on board room screens. But Shafter Lake, nicknamed "Kilgore" seemed to be everybody's undoing.

Kilgore Drill Site, Texas.

In the remote area of Gaines County, the ancient land of the Permian Basin, every aspect of Kilgore had been green lighted. Conditioned, the drilling teams' focus was all about earning money. An aerial view across Gaines County exposed a union between farm and oil well, each site redundant from the other 253 structures. Like fresh stitching, the right angles off county roadways led to single or multiple wells of circular fields, irrigated by giant pivots covering six million acres. Farm land nodded to new production of oil and gas with wells averaging from two to sixteen thousand feet deep. Forever changing the earth, it was a permanent swap—deep penetration instead of surface plowing. Slash piles of chain sawed branches, shrub, and mangled grass once covering the well plot, would never grow back.

As the risk of investment soared, Apache's motivation was to move quickly through classifications, from test mode to a wildcat, indicating a significant flow of oil. Further in-ground assessment could trigger an MIR classification, meaning crews would be going into twenty-four hour shifts, "moving in rig."[37] It was damn hard work, but it meant steady paychecks

---

formation, wells flowing, gravity of crude, last six months production, and depth of discovery well.

[37] DOB Magazine, "Nickles Energy Toolkit: Well Data Legend." http://www. dobmagazine. nickles.com/common/well_legend.asp.

and job security. The end goal was to hit the pay and classify it as an oil well or an O&G, adding natural gas to the discovery.[38] If real fortunate, the crews would be blessed with a new pool wildcat.[39] That meant bragging rights at Saddles for finding another untapped resource.

Like surgeons, field site preparation required pieces and parts, large and small, to be laid out ahead of the main event. From the labor intensive process of ground prep and cutting in the cellar, to rigging the power, and mechanical systems, the crews delivered to precise time tables.

In early stages, Kilgore was laid out like an operating room, as seen by Doug standing on top of a plateau, giving a panoramic view of the dust fatigued site. From where he stood, the air was clean, unencumbered by diesel exhaust. His perspective, the plotted area showed the organizational benefits of planning. Job satisfaction was more appealing from where he stood, giving him the sense of power and control— and being in control. But Doug was always nagged by paranoia. He never had *absolute* control. Gazing blankly across the jig-sawed farm land intermixed with nodding donkeys, he let his upbringing creep back in.[40]

He had stood on other earthen rises with his dad and grandfather, unwittingly receiving mentorship and the bloodline of the oil business. At the time, it was considered play, watching the working men who had duties to earn their living. Progressively receiving more exposure to the general purpose of being a field man, Doug was sculpted into an expert. There was a code of sinewy ignorance, the brawn over the brain that had kept his grandfather and father in the fields long after wear and tear broke them down. The son, following with initiative and encouragement from elders, climbed out of the skin defining the head knockers – the men who drove other men.

One final gaze from the ridge brought on a chill to Doug's neck and spine. Ignoring the source, he flexed his upper torso to shake it off, letting his shoulders settle back into the armpits of his jacket. Control and predictability was still the order of the day, especially given the status of the Kilgore, in startup mode with something to prove. He had spied a dust track, kicked up by trucks that were hours overdue. It was time to head back to

---

[38]   Ibid.

[39]   Ibid.

[40]   Slang for the pump jacks used to pull oil from a producing well.

personally direct the unloading of titanium and diamond drill bits that were about to arrive.

As Doug sipped his beer, his deep focus slowly made it back to real time, sitting alone in Saddles.

"Hey, suga, watcha dreaming about?" the bar maid asked as she wiped off half the table, popping her gum. "You haven't moved from your seat since your boys left. That was ten minutes ago."

"Just thinking, I guess."

"I hardly notice your limp anymore, Dougie."

"Thanks. Wish I could say the same. I gotta head home."

"Take care."

Sinking back in time on the drive home, Doug remembered the fall out from corporate and wondered if Jen was made the scapegoat for the failure of Shafter Lake, their own Kilgore. Announcing she was quitting, she moved up, taking a head geologist job at a drill bit manufacturer, whose lab and consulting services provided technologies that helped their clients save and make money. He always thought Jen could land on her feet no matter what was thrown at her.

Driving on to his property, Doug thought of the other test wells that came up dry around Kilgore, with another three in a row before the new guy was fired for incompetence. And the ten or so the company wrote off, located on the expansion property north of Shafter Lake.

"The shit we get ourselves into for the sake of a buck," Doug said quietly as he headed to the back porch door. He glanced back as if the city followed him home. He wanted to move farther out north from Midland. Traffic and housing had crept up around their property lines since they had built the home and improved the acreage. Unlike his employers, there wasn't any time or energy set aside to prospect another area.

"Honey, I'm in the living room," he heard Kate call as he pushed through the screen door and into the kitchen.

"I put your dinner in the fridge. Want me to microwave it?" Kate cooed as she came to greet her mate of twenty-five years. "Any news on the company barbeque? Are they going to move the date again?"

"Nope, everyone is thinking they're going to cut back though. You know they always claim there's going to be a slump. The boys said we'll just have one here instead," Doug fabricated to get a reaction.

"Oh they did, huh?" Kate responded, mocking a challenge. "We'll have to see about that."

After his meal, they spent the rest of the evening on the porch swing.

"When is Connor coming home tomorrow? He's got to rake out the horse stalls."

"I'll make sure he gets them done. You know he'll be up in that tree fort half the night with Timmy. They've become best friends this year in school."

"He's growing up fast, Kate," And then Doug spoke out loud, sharing a thought his father and grandfather would never have had. "I'm not sure I want him following my footsteps."

She wasn't too surprised hearing this. She knew when he came in the door, his typical nature was off. She spoke, taking her husband's hand in hers and started to massage it, "Been thinking about your job and all the other stuff again?"

"It has changed so much faster than I thought it would," he confessed. "I remember my dad's frustration, and I guess it's my turn. I think I'm keeping pace with it, but then I realize I'm really slowing down."

Taking a long pause, listening to the cricket's unabated song, he sorted out his feelings. "It's not the actual work or the people. It's the job itself. Sometimes I wonder if we can keep taking oil, and the next minute I know it's the only thing I have to make ends meet. I'd hate to have Connor depend on it like our generations, then have it disappear. I'd like to see him on a different path so he won't have to go through the churn."

"Doug, you know after so many years of doing the same thing, it's tougher to see value in it. It's been a good provider to us and I'm glad we have the life we do. We've done a good job putting money in the bank so Connor can go to a good school. Look at what Jen did with her career! So there are other options out there."

Doug was quick with a caution, "Remember, those folks depend on the oil business. It's just like the car industry, with all the mom and pop shops feeding off it. One bullet to the lead cow and the whole herd loses its way."

He blew air out slowly from his full cheeks, subtly weighing consequence. The tangibles didn't matter. Power was always full throttle in the oil industry and like the substance from the ground, it was altered and honed for gain.

"Funny you bring up Jen though," he said. "I was just thinking of her earlier today. I should give her a call and checkup on her. I haven't heard from her in a while."

Doug placed his arm around his wife wondering, "Ya think by now she would of whipped somebody inta shape for marryin'."

"Partner, there's no man on Earth worth marryin' unless we get to break 'em in," Kate chimed. "Like Daddy always said, that's just good horse sense."

The half moon shined back at them as they laughed, peering out over the dimly lit fields that continued to the horizon. The natural effect of the night and their mood lasted until yawns forced them to bed.

Kilgore Drill Site, Texas.

Doug and his crew settled in for dinner and within them, their energy was as peaked as the oil trapped below the surface of the earth. After mess hall, Doug held a meeting before the lead men turned in for the night.

"If that don't be all," said Charlie, with about the worst Texas drawl anybody could conjure up. His lower lip was stuffed with RedMan, a mixture of chew tobacco and molasses syrup.

"They done changed the mainince schedule on the rig operashin a geein," followed up by a healthy spit on the ground. "How are we gonna fit in the extra lockout on the big drill modar?"

He spit again, "Shieeet, that'al take another six man-herrs."

"No news there, bud!" winked Randy. "You'll just hafta do more ass kickin' than normal."

Out in the field for three weeks before rotation, the small group of ten foremen fed on laughter and a couple back slaps, promoting their good spirits.

"And you'll be punishing your men if you go over schedule," mocked Chet, the chief foreman.

He was referring to the absolute need to avoid working during daylight. Even though it was early in the summer, the heat gain rose off the ground and hit the men about chest high. With heavy gear on, they were prone to fatigue. The best scenario was to work most of the hardware into early morning hours, break for the day, and then finish after dusk.

"Ya but you all know I've got the toughest assignment, getting us on track and staying there," Chet reminded them.

"Uh huh, that's why they call ya a computor geek," Charlie teased.

"No, he's a computer god!" Randy corrected.

Maintaining tradition to stay with the same employer for a lifetime career, most of the rednecks had put in over twenty years of hard labor. For them, Texas was big enough to settle in and stay put, with a keen interest for bass or Gulf fishing. With a little push from his boss, Chet learned the formal process of collecting field data, collaborating with what the men called "the cell", a temporary location for the computer and software operations, usually manned by a savvy technical analyst. Chet got along with all sorts of folks so he was a natural pick to take on the extra accountability.

"You guys will have more time on your hands on the count of you won't be making it to church," Doug added, his accent washed out compared to Charlie. Again, the group responded with a mixture of laughter, silencing themselves to finish up.

"Alright then," continued their boss. "We've got a couple items to square up, and then we can punch off the clock. The good news is management has put an incentive in front of us—to meet or beat our schedules and they'll kick in some bucks for a party and some bonuses." Amid the whoops, Doug continued, "But everything is by the book, no shortcuts."

Sweating and frustrated, Doug sat on the edge of his bed waking up a second time since he kissed his wife goodnight. Whenever he dreamed of the Kilgore operation it seemed like moments ago, not months.

"How long before this nightmare goes away?" he pleaded to no one, urging himself to go back to sleep. Kilgore was waiting.

As Kate collected laundry from Connor's room, last night's conversation with her husband lagged in her mind.

"Why are his pockets always full of trash," she complained when she saw pebbles, metal pieces from a bike chain, and an old lure fall onto the carpet.

Kate knew Doug wouldn't get around to calling Jen. Not because he didn't want to talk to her. He would really enjoy hearing from her again, but he wouldn't do anything about it. She knew Doug had his head set on the job and once he dumped mental stuff out of his pockets, he moved on. Kate decided to take control.

Jen would be a bit of fresh air for him, she considered while shoving in a load of wash. Setting her mind, she got the address book out. *Let's see, she should be back from lunch now,* noting the time.

Dialing, her assertiveness was rewarded with Jen answering the call in person, "Hi, this is Jen, can I help you?"

"You sure can, honey," Kate replied glad not to be leaving a message. "This is Kate Erls, are you free to talk?"

"Are you kidding?" Jen answered, her voice reaching the same spirit of elation. She hadn't heard from Kate or her family for over a year. "Of course I've got some time to talk with you, girl! How have you been?"

"All fine, Jen. Doug and Connor are both growing. Doug out and the little man up."

Both laughing, Jen felt endeared to Kate because of her female persona. She enjoyed being mentored by Kate and willing to take advice if it was given. On her part, Kate made the same space for Jen as she would have her own daughter. The spirited girl reminded Kate of herself. Younger, not in need of scolding, but shaping. Needing love, not lectures. Needing respect, not rituals. The phone dialogue covered a collage of topics, all mutually shared to permit each other an update into their lives.

"Honey, I've got a huge favor to ask you," Kate inserted as they both paused.

"Anything!" Jen immediately insisted. "You know that! What?"

"I was talking to Doug the other night. You know how he feels about you, and that hasn't changed."

"You know I miss that guy," Jen acknowledged. "He must have time on his hands, worried about my life." She laughed.

"Well, actually I think he's kinda in a rut with work and all. I was calling to ask you if you could see your way to call him and just chat—now mind you *this* call is on the hush!" Kate insisted.

"Is it serious, I mean is he at risk losing his job or something?"

"No, no, honey. He's sorting through some of history, like what the company stands for and probably looks at his left leg and wonders what he could have done different," Kate surmised. "You know how he lets that stuff gnaw away at him. If his men ever knew the size of his heart, they'd probably try to get a skirt on him."

Jen caught her breath after laughing, "Of course, I'd be happy to call Doug! But let me look at my calendar for a second," she offered then confirmed her thought. "You know I might be able to squeeze a couple free days on the end of a trip next month. I could change a flight time and head your way."

"That would be really fine, Jen! More than I dared ask for. You know if it works out, we'll have to let a couple of the boys in on it. They would be so upset if you sneaked in here without so much as a howdy neighbor."

"That works for me. They owe me anyway!" Jen kidded.

"Tell you what, dear, I'll call you in a couple days or so and make sure you're coming. We won't let Doug in on this for the time being," she reiterated.

"You can call my admin and she'll have my itinerary."

"Honey, this worked out just great for us then. But, I've got to let you go. A boy needs his mom," Kate explained, hearing her son coming in the house.

"Okay, this was so good of you to think of me. I can't wait to see all you guys!"

"Okay, honey, take care. Bye bye."

When Kate's family finished up dinner the next evening, Doug was mindful of his spouse's contributions that day.

"Ok, mister," Doug directed to his son, "you and I have the dish detail."

And expecting Connor to complain, "Don't say a word or I'll add another chore. Your mother cooked us a great meal and we owe her back, right?"

"Daaad, why do I? I still have homework!"

Looking at Kate, he hoped he had a line in the sand, "He didn't get it done?"

"No, Mrs. Apple assigned him some extra math. You go ahead and get going on it," she redirected and stood up to clear the table. "Your dad and I will get this, but you owe me big time!"

"Thanks, Mom!" He ran off only thinking he got the better chore.

"You're spoiling that boy, Kate."

"This is what they call reverse psychology. Now he's doing extra homework and he's happy not to be doing dishes. I get to be with my man, no interruptions," Kate said coyly.

"Looks like a win-win," Doug quickly agreed. "I don't get many of those these days," he winked, bringing over the rest of the dishes to the sink.

This used to be a special time for them before Connor was born. Standing together, washing up supper dishes, looking out the window, talking about their day. It used to spark a romp upstairs every now and again, no longer a commodity with another person around. Taking a deep breath and exhaling Doug started to ponder his work day.

"Are ya going to doze off there before you scrub that last pan?" Kate ribbed.

"Heh, no. I'll finish it. You're lucky the young professor is still awake. I'd show you a thing or two about dozing."

And with that he put his soaking hand on her backside and squeezed. Kate responded by turning her body into his and put her arms around his shoulders, "Doesn't mean we can't get warmed up."

Her warm brown eyes looked at her man squarely and she kissed him passionately. They embraced for a moment and then both patted each other. With the kitchen work done and considering it was the right moment, Kate announced the plans she made with Jen.

"Are you kidding?"

At first, Kate couldn't tell if Doug was surprised or stressed, "I haven't seen or heard from her. Hard to believe! How'd you get a hold of her? How long is she staying?"

"Well, it turned out she can do a stay over from a business trip. We talked on the phone and figured it out."

Doug started to show as much excitement as he did for his favorite football team, "I guess it is...ya, I guess it *is* great! It will be good to see her and get caught up."

Then he started debating the idea, knowing there was some fixing around the property.

"I know you think you have to go out and make everything new. She's coming next month, staying over a long weekend. You've got more than enough time to put polish on the fence," Kate chided.

Doug put his arm around Kate and gave her a hug sideways, "You're a little sneak, but I won't hold it against ya."

NETL. Washington, D.C.

LEANING BACK IN a leather chair, Kenneth Millard's fingers twitched as he dragged on the remains of a cigarette, peering up at the blue hue on the ceiling. Colton would be coming through the door, who knows when. Hard as it seemed, his boss had become even more impersonal towards him. The one unearned payment on his contract did not improve his motivation to work for NETL.

The handle on the door moved and Colton was quickly inside the meeting room. Walking over, he slapped Kenneth on the back, "How are ya, hump!"

Let the acrimony begin, Kenneth thought, pulling out another cigarette.

"How's that girlfriend of yours doing? I hear she hits the road with you on occasion. That must be sweet."

"I didn't think that would be a problem."

"You're right. No worries. Tell me, are you going to stick this out? We've got to start turning the screws and you need to be out there doing it."

Kenneth did not look into Colton's face sitting directly across from him, "I don't know. I was thinking..."

"Let me tell you my thoughts," interrupted Colton. "Right now, I've sunk over six hundred K into an investment. It was risky but I figured with some personal effort it would ramp. And actually it did...for about two fucking seconds, then I see this drop off."

"That's not my—"

"Hold on. Let me continue. For a while you were the perfect student. Then I get reports that you're hanging in the bars with your woman. That's cool. We need a skirt closer sometimes. Then I hear she's working the crowd and my student is over at the bar getting hammered. Not Good."

Kenneth relit his cigarette, "I had a splitting headache. I told her to go back to the room. I lost track."

"I can tell you we didn't get our message out that night and maybe there was a replay at a couple other events before that. Then it gets back to me, you did the dog and pony in San Francisco, and afterwards you're back pedaling with a couple key guys, making excuses for NETL."

"Your people sent the slides late and I did them cold turkey. The numbers didn't make sense and I was cornered on it, so I fudged on a couple facts. That's what it's getting down to right? Facts? It's all bullshit! You've been hiding shit all along. There's too *much* lie to cover up!"

Approaching Millard, Colton squared up his body, "You're killing me. I warned you when you started we needed a liar. You bought into it and said you could do it. That bonus check cleared pretty fast."

"I was doing it at first. I guess I'm not good at it like you."

"That's about to change. You still owe me the rest of your contract. We're going back to class and get this lined out again. It's about the clock now and I don't have a backup."

"I read the contract before I signed it. I can sit in jail."

"Let's not be so quick to lower ourselves. You steady yourself up. We'll rework the plans, you deliver, and you're free."

Colton put his hand employee's shoulder, "If you're sitting in jail who'll watch over your artwork? I'll see you tomorrow bright and early. Enjoy the ceiling."

On Colton's exit, Kenneth kicked a chair into the wall, "Goddamnhim!"

Taking a raspy breath, Kenneth coughed, holding his chest. The sound echoed in the small hotel bathroom. Staring into the mirror that night, he was trying to build up his resolve. In less than four months he would be free of Colton. He couldn't worry about Colton's outrageous demands. He had to focus on what he was good at, get back to the basics and focus on tactics.

"I look like shit."

He knew his vanity could sometimes outpace his shrewdness.

After his meeting with his protégé, Colton had a planned briefing with his people, "Angela, I need you to trace Millard. I don't want him doing something stupid."

Colton also tapped a business analyst he had wrapped around his finger, "You get the assignment to bring Ken up to speed on the global situation."

"You want to let him in on NEADE?"

"I kind of enjoyed pushing him, but now he's just a paper cut to deal with. No. Just to NETL's boundary and tell him it's coming from their lab. He hasn't seen all of it. But I need to throw him a bone. Pump up his ego with some horse shit, but don't expose NEADE by name."

Kicking everyone out of his office, Colton made some calls and reassigned the more prominent field agents to take over Millard's share of the event calendar. He then laid out another roadmap that put Millard in with the best and the brightest. He shut his office doors to finish briefing Senator Sterling, and silence objections.

"We need him, but this will be his last chance to get his peers on a leash. In the name of science, sooner or later, the early warning systems in the middle of the freakin' ocean are going to start going off," Colton warned. "When they do, we've got to be able to contain the flood of bullshit."

Later that week, Colton went to see Millard after the promised briefing on the latest research from NETL. Kenneth was suspicious of the obvious steps taken to boost his interest. He observed security checkpoints and guards monitoring rooms. He had been given access to briefing books with confidential wrappers.

"I hope you have been duly impressed with our situation."

Kenneth's formality with his boss was thin to none, "You could have told me up front instead of hiding it."

"I suppose so, but you could have done your fucking job, so I guess we're at the same intersection. See Ken, what you don't get is we're tired of getting led around by our balls every time the earth hiccups or a wave wipes out beachfront. We don't have unlimited reserves any more to throw a thousand different ways. And everybody wants to know ahead time. That's all I've heard. If they had an extra five minutes their grandmother could have been saved. The answer is if NETL had been fully deployed we wouldn't have been bled dry by the Asian tsunami. We can't allow it any more! NETL is an attempt to funnel all the theory and facts into one pool, with a centralized database to sort out fact from fiction, determine the risk, and protect the right things."

"Right things...who decides that?"

"Us."

"Why? What's going to happen?"

"I can tell you we've been working on the *when* for a couple years. That's why we needed you and some others, to keep the scientific masses from peeking in the window, while final progress was made on the time scales."

"I know your data. You're pushing fiction and keeping the rest a secret?"

"The *what* is still a mystery, that is what and where. The NEA...NETL teams and other labs are focused on it," Colton explained. "One team on the what and the remaining group on the when."

He used harsh words to describe the little progress the program managers had accomplished with their sixteen hour rotations. Interrupted by a knock on door, Colton left abruptly after reading a message.

With him gone, Millard stared at the blue hues of the ceiling and began to see a way to flip the odds in his favor, making an outside call, "Yes, I said dial into the GTS conference line as soon as I hang up. Don't ask questions! Just do it."

Kenneth left the meeting room, hailing a taxi as soon as he got down the exterior steps. Relaxing with a smoke, he reconnected at a nearby pay phone, "It's me. Are Dave and Bryan there in the conference room?"

Waiting for the audio, he took a deep drag on his cigarette then exhaled, "Hey, guys, sorry for the emergency meeting. I need your help on some things."

Kenneth walked through a short list of documents he needed express mailed to him, "I realize this will take some personal time and I'd appreciate your candor if there's no mention of this."

"We've been getting some calls, saying your government data is biased. Our own data even contradicts what you've been preaching at your events. I don't want to say I told you—"

"Yes, you and Bryan...were right. I had no idea they were going to massage the facts."

"Why don't you quit. We could use you back here."

"I'm planning to. I've got to wrap up a couple more trips and then we can figure out a plan. Anyway, I've got a plane to catch. Remember, keep this quiet for now."

The following months were measures of relief for the agency chief and the scientist, who felt he was on a longer leash. Colton's temper and impatience minimized further personal contact with his protégé. Neither could stand to deal with the other directly. While Colton discarded his original expectations, Kenneth set new goals to finish his contract obligations, presuming his plan for redemption was going to succeed.

Of
Land and Science

Day 365.

Grand Canyon National Park, Arizona.

360320N 1120823W

S ARAH CANNES WAS up in front of the crowd every morning by ten thirty and made the same salutatory announcement during the height of the season: "Welcome to the Grand Canyon, folks!"

Her short drive from Hermit Circle, to standing room only on the South Rim, was the formal start of her public duties. Waiting for stragglers, she checked out her gear and answered the same questions before her speech: Her length of employment? Would they need water? Has the canyon changed since she started working here? How many in the group today? Was it okay to wear sandals? Are there mosquitoes? Are there snakes? Did she know the temperature? Was she married? Did she know the length of the hike? How deep is the Grand Canyon? And did she have extra water, sunscreen, Chap Stick, Band-Aids, shoe laces? And once, did she have an extra pair of socks?

To fend off more interruptions and the second surge of inquiries, the ranger launched into her fifteen minute monolog:

"I'm Sarah and I will be your federal guide today for a three-mile loop. Let me start by explaining a short history of the park. I'll take questions at its conclusion," she said, smiling.

There were always tourists waving hands, intending to prove they were smarter than the rest. The ranger continued to ignore them, by repeating her mandate. "I'll take all your questions in a few minutes. Thank you."

She projected her voice, "Hopi guides led the first Europeans to the canyon near the mid-1500s, followed by an expedition by Major John Wesley Powell in 1869, under the direction of the Smithsonian Institution. Many legislative bills failed to protect the Grand Canyon as a national park, from the late 1800s until 1919, when my boss, the United States Park Service, began its administration of these lands in August of that year."

Sarah paused to let more people join the group and then continued, "The rock you are standing on and that which encompasses the entire park is actually referred to by geologists as the North American Plate, one of seven very, *very* large plates that have shifted over centuries. The Grand Canyon is thought to be the combined result of continental drift, erosion, and volcanism. The micro layers of the plate consist of limestone, sandstone, and shale."

Hands were back up but Sarah did not break stride in her delivery, expecting to start the hike promptly on schedule. "If you want to do a deep dive into the geology of the park I recommend visiting the bookstores. Let me wrap up by reciting some raw numbers."

Sarah rattled off her memory of information about the length, width, and elevation of the park; length, width, and depth of the Colorado River; species of plant and animal found in the park; and the Native archeology, and finished with citing the classification of geological structures throughout the park.

Always on time, UAL flight 718 was above the crowd in their atmospheric groove at twenty-one thousand feet. The ranger paused, permitting attention to wander upwards. With no clouds, the extraordinary bright white fuselage glowed against the carbon blue atmosphere. Tracing the canyon, the pilots had the opposite perspective looking down at the glaring ribbon of clear water that flowed away from Glen Canyon dam, muddied when it joined downstream tributaries.

The fourth year park ranger finished her speech, "Like the Forest Service mission of caring for the land and serving people, our mission, as set forth by law, is to protect and provide access to our nation's natural and cultural heritage, and honor our responsibilities to Indian Tribes and our commitments to island communities. The Department of the Interior is proud to be the administrator of this one of a kind park. It ranks sixth in the top one hundred wonders of the world. It's so impressive the State of Arizona has its namesake as a nickname. Let's work together to preserve it!" [41]

The guided tour was going to be one of those with blessings attached to it. Rylie would be participating with Mom on the short hike, one of the two times a week she was allowed to join. Sometimes she was introduced as her daughter or tourists made the connection on their own, noticing the similar French rows in her brunette hair. The Rim loop was a favorite of Rylie's because she could see "the whole darn thing," a full visual inspection of the Grand Canyon from top to bottom, looking across to the north side ten miles away.

The little girl hoped to see the tiny orange dots, rafts in the Colorado, thousands of feet below. Eventually, the activities of tourists taking pictures, discussing geological detail with the ranger, or taking in the sights would signal an end to Rylie's adventure.

"Folks, wrap up your photos. We need to group up and make our way back. Please stay within the designated…"

This summer, Rylie had a man in her life. Someone she had begun to like. She sat still on a bench listening intently, waiting for Harry's plane to pass by.

He had taught her his itinerary: two flights in the morning, one of them for the sunrise, a couple afternoon flights, and then sometimes as a backup shuttle, a trip to the bottom for injured hikers. Upon hearing the faint buzz eclipsing conversations, the girl imagined herself flying in the seat next to Harry. Her vision became more real, when she spotted a plane floating midway through the giant slice in the earth. Breaking the spell, a small gopher scurried across her path and hid in blooms of wild daisies. After tracing the animal's path, Rylie followed the group back to the top, anticipating making cookies with Alice, staying with her into the evening. Sarah was hosting an adult's only party for Harry and for her own part, seemed to be hurrying the crowd to stay on schedule.

That night, the birthday celebration went longer than expected, for a man of thirty-eight who had an ample supply of free drinks and low tolerance to alcohol. The full glasses on the table had courtesy sips extracted from each. Everyone began picking up their belongings, leaving

---

[41] http://www.doi.gov/secretary/mission.html.

Sarah and her steady some time alone. Returning from goodbyes in the parking lot, Harry wasn't walking straight.

"I ordered you some coffee. Drink this down, will ya? We need to go."

It was one o'clock in the morning and Sarah wanted her house chores done early that day so she and Rylie wouldn't get stuck inside all weekend.

"Do you want to drive up to Page with us in the afternoon for a movie?"

Harry laid his head on the bar. "If the spinning stops, sure."

"Are you going to barf?"

"If the spinning stops, sure."

Sarah tried to move him off the seat.

"No, no. Let me just sit here for a second. Tell me again how Mother Nature kicks ass, to take my mind off my dizziness."

Sarah started laughing, "Man, you are wasted! You never remember anything I say. I should take a picture to freeze the moment."

"I'm just tired."

"That's what a man says who's not in touch with the feeling of being hammered."

Harry raised his head and took a swig of coffee, "What was it you said? That Mother Nature has balls?"

"Keep it down!" Sarah whispered, slapping him on the shoulder. "You're taking it out of context. If you remember I was feeling a no pain when I said it. I was referring to disasters, like you at the moment."

"And yet, you try everyday to put lipstick on one of her biggest screw-ups."

Sarah wrote on her application for National Park Ranger that she would not consider any other location even if she had to be put on a waiting list. After splitting from her husband of three years for his extra-marital affair, a term-based appointment in Arizona ensured she and Rylie would never see her ex again. Motivated to leave town, she worked in the stock room of the local paper mill earning enough to keep up with groceries and daycare. She had funds from the sale of the boat and cabin to pay for the remainder of her two year tuition at SUNY-ESF.[42] Upon finishing the forestry degree at the top of her class, she was able to leave Wanakena, NY for good.

---

[42] The College of Environment Science and Forestry at the State University of New York.

"Harry, we have to scoot. I've got to get home. You're going to Scott's right?"

When she started work at the park, the staff and crews went out of their way to make her feel welcomed.   Her boss, a handsome woman of sixty-three warned her politely of the risks of getting involved romantically with the staff, "What happens at the Grand not only stays at the Grand, but it keeps showing up for work every day. You best keep your legs together."

Her first six months of employment at Grand Canyon Village started in late fall when Sarah became one of ten permanent federal employees and a resident of a town of fourteen hundred. Sarah's concerns about Rylie's education were easily diffused after meeting the principal of the Grand Canyon Unified School District. She was instantly intrigued when she heard him say he believed they were providing world class instruction.

The glare of the car headlights lit the fences and sagebrush along the road towards a friend's house.

"Harry, you should really think about getting your emergency medical certification. You could go on rotation with the SAR team in the off season. I'm almost certified. It would be a kick if you made the crew."

"I'm really thinking I'd fail the test right now."

"You know what I'm saying. You keep telling me your business sucks."

"No. I keep telling you the *public* sucks."

A trained air force pilot with a military tour in Kuwait, Harry Chaplin was injured in combat leaving him with two fractured discs. Languishing on his commission for a year, he jumped at the chance to buy out his buddy's flight business after helping out one season.

Sarah pulled up in front of the home Harry stayed at when it was too late to fly back, "Are you going to join us tomorrow?"

"It depends on whether I get a call. Stop by anyway."

"This long distance thing is a bit weird, you know," she commented. "Me on this side of the rim. You on the other. Me stuck here. You flying back and forth."

"Jacobs Lake *is* the true gateway to the natural beauty of the Grand Canyon. You folks on this side are in it for money," Harry countered, starting to sober up.

"You can't live in the back of your hangar for the rest of your life. Count it up. Fifteen more years and we'll have to build a handicap ramp for you."

"I was counting on *you* taking care of me."

Harry leaned over and, instead of kissing Sarah, laid his head on her shoulder. She put her arm around him placing her palm on his forehead, "Let's see how you do." And then she lifted her arm and shoulder causing him to slide off. "Hit the road, Jack. We'll pick you up at three. No grease under the fingernails."

Sarah watched her boyfriend weave across the section of pavement. Air flight was the single enabler that allowed their relationship to continue. His home on the north side was a metal warehouse with a certified runway. He had designed the building with a studio and a hangar to store his two aircraft, toys compared to his military expertise with the Kiowa Warrior he piloted as a military captain.

She leaned on the steering wheel thinking whether their relationship could go anywhere. She was the one braking hard most the time. They met each other at the local dance. Harry was there as MC, fundraising for library books. Leading a chain of would-be dancers to the beat of the conga, he seemed like a natural with kids. Excited, Rylie ran right over and joined the group as it snaked through the gymnasium. That time, Sarah was cordial but fended off Harry as she had done with other single men since her divorce.

It wasn't until New Years Eve, that family memories gained an edge on her celibacy. In her past was an ex whose interest in the web-based dating services led to faking business trips to bed women in neighboring communities. Sarah didn't leave any opportunity to forgive and forget. The day she found the images on the PC, she called her mom and cried.

All of it closed and boxed away, Sarah was resistant and resilient towards anyone trying to find a way to her heart. The man she just dropped off had a fighting chance. He had made genuine attempts to break through her barriers. He once arranged rocks on the service road spelling "Kiss Me." The ugly bridesmaid Halloween costume with a "hire me" sign was amusing. And she thought it was sweet the time he flew above her house, towing an "I'm Yours" sign complete with a red heart, explaining later it was something he found in his storage shed.

The ranger unlocked her door quietly and walked over to jiggle the babysitter awake, "Oh. Hi, dear. Did you have fun?" Alice whispered while getting her knitting together.

"Yes. We did. I was glad I could go."

"Did Harry blow out his candles?"

"Yep. He said thank you. Everybody liked what you did with the swirls, making them look like clouds below the toy helicopter. Thank you for staying with Rylie."

"It was no trouble, dear. She's my favorite, you know."

"Mine too! Can I walk you over?"

"No. I'll be fine," Alice put on her coat and scarf. "Don't forget to get me those spices."

"I won't," Sarah promised as she hugged her elderly friend of seventy-two.

"Okay, dear. Night."

After making sure Alice was on her way, she thought how lucky it was to have restarted her life at the park. Asleep in less than fifteen minutes, she conjured dreams in color.

Taking tourists down to the bottom of the Grand Canyon on bobsleds, she yelled out instructions for the novices as the more daring shot by her, "Don't miss any of the turns," she warned, looking down at the group snaking through the rock pillars. "Mother Nature keeps changing them."

Then hooting, she went airborne with another chain of bobsleds behind her, yelling, "If we make it to the bottom, there's birthday cake!"

She could recall nothing else, waking with a headache at four. Her eyes opened again when she heard the singing from her daughter's video.

"Ohmigosh! It's ten?"

Moving slow at first, Sarah tried to get back on schedule. Finishing all the chores, they rushed to get over to Harry's just after three. Rylie ran up and knocked but received no answer.

Her feet didn't move until her mom coaxed her, "That's okay, honey. We'll still have fun."

"I guess," her daughter said, unconvinced.

Driving off, Sarah reached over and rubbed the back of a disappointed girl. She still wasn't smiling after a happy meal and entering the theater to see one of her favorite movies. With popcorn, they walked down the aisle and veered off to the side to claim a row of empty seats.

"Do ya think the seats are better over there?"

Rylie looked over and jumped into the aisle making her way to get a hug, "Harry! I knocked and you weren't home!"

"Nope. I had to fly out to Fredonia to pick up a patient. This is *my* favorite movie so I couldn't miss it."

"Cool! Mine, too!"

Sarah squeezed by Harry, kissing him, "You were in big trouble mister. You left early from Scott's?"

"Kinda. I was a little foggy."

The talk around the staff was that Harry and Sarah would get married eventually, *if* Harry didn't lose interest. Alice felt the same way about the couple, chipping in as a surrogate grandmother whenever she was needed.

She never missed a chance to mentor Sarah and did so again when her spices were dropped off, "He's kind to Rylie. She needs a father to help her along."

"I know single parenting isn't the best way to go at it. I'm just not there yet," Sarah replied protecting her feelings.

"Harry needs it too you know, the caring. His heart's in the right place."

She took Alice's hand, "I've got to get going. You're coming over for dinner right?"

The mother and daughter had Alice over at least once a week.

"Yes. I'll be there. My turn to bring the main course."

"What's that I smell?"

"It's corn chowder. Even with the colder weather ending, it'll be tasty. Harry's invited?"

"Of course."

"Good, it's his favorite. I'll bring the recipe with me."

The odds started against Sarah that evening. Although Alice could be just about anybody's grandmother, her conversational pitter-patter put the other adults on the spot. She was bold asking what the couples plans would be for the upcoming summer, how much Rylie trusted Harry—when the little girl was out of earshot watching videos—, and how thoughtful Harry was with the help he gave to them. Fooling around to make a point, Harry rubbed his fingernails on his shirt, and then blew on them. Another time out of Alice's view, he wagged his head side to side, pursing his lips.

In the kitchen, Sarah slapped his butt, "Brown-noser," she whispered.

Expecting Alice to begin heaping praise on her and her photography, Sarah guided the conversation away from her talents. But when Alice glanced away, Harry mocked the sudden shift of attention with a frown.

Rylie figured out Harry was just causing trouble and tattled to Alice, leaving him to her scolding, "I don't think her pictures are something to laugh at, my dear. They're very good."

Sarah rubbed it in, "Ya, that's just how mean he is sometimes."

Unable to defend himself, Sarah had Alice's ear, "He does that a lot."

"That's not good, Harry. You should respect her beautiful work."

"I do, Alice. She's a bit selfish about protecting her interests. I say she should sell them and make it big somewhere. What do you think?"

Alice had no allegiance, "Harry's got a great idea there Sarah. Someone would snap them up if you let people see your talent."

Shifting the conversation again Sarah cut off the next compliment, "Anyway, did anyone realize how fast the canyon is changing this year? My pictures from over a year ago showed spectacular dihedrals. My retakes of the ledges are completely different. Mother Nature is constantly changing its beauty but I think the erosion is accelerating."

Harry maintained his interest between bites of dessert, giving his view, "From what I've seen, the aerial photos taken by the geological service back that up. Major landmarks aren't there any more, with new spirals and levies appearing all the time."

"Alice, you've been here for over twenty years, right?" Sarah asked.

She nodded.

"Have you noticed big changes?"

"It's like me, getting older with more wrinkles."

They laughed while Rylie shared her perspective, "If it keeps getting bigger at the top, we'll have to move."

"It's probably getting wider, but not necessarily as fast as the river is grooving it deeper every day," Sarah advised. "The Corp of Engineers keeps tabs on it."

"They do but not as often since their budgets have been cut," Harry added.

"Anyone want tea or coffee?" The hostess interrupted, so she could jockey Rylie into her room for bedtime.

Upon her return, Sarah was still thinking about the enormous configuration of the canyon, "I sometimes wonder about the force it took to create the canyon. How would it have been to have seen that?"

"Gee, I was going to talk about the trash," Harry joked.

That earned him another slap.

"I'm serious!" Sarah responded. "It would have been awesome!"

"I'm glad we get to have it in our backyard, but if Mother Nature is planning on changing it, I hope I'm not around!" Alice boasted noting her age.

Sarah choked on her mouthful of tea when Harry responded saying, "Yeah, but we might still be here. Who's going to stop the bitch when Mother Nature says, Do over!"

"Harry," Alice scolded politely. "The things you come up with!"

Day 245.

Americas Geoscience Research Conference. Sun Valley, ID.

ATTENDING THE TENTH annual Americas Geoscience Research conference, Peter Childs finished downloading email in his room, looking for a client acceptance of his recent bid.

The symposium had four days of forums, classes, and vendor presentations. At least a third of the topics was related to or specifically addressed the science, research, and field implications of climate change. Presenters were sponsored by universities, private think tanks, and public institutions. The predictable appearances were the USGS—the gatekeepers for oil, Energy Information Administration, and a host of the industry leaders including the largest petroleum company in Europe. The vendor hall was full of equipment ranging from wide format plotters for producing color mapping schemes to imagery collection from satellites and specialized boring tools from drill manufacturers.

Peter doubted if the rich ski bums that packed these rooms in the last season of the year were any more boisterous than the crowd of professional scientists, researchers, and specialists. With over fifty geological sciences represented, Peter knew many of them by name or at least the company they represented. Standing at the doorway, he peered into the crowd looking for Jen Rawlins, a childhood friend that he still hoped to see once or twice a year.

"Excuse me."

Peter felt a slight pat on his shoulder, "It is you! I wasn't sure. All these people!" the engineer said waving his arm.

"Hi, Glen. I figured I would run into you at the World Sat booth. I was going to ask you about your experience with their software."

"Still trying to make up the investment," the consultant admitted. "Maybe we'll get it paid off if we score more work from Halliburton."

Peter expected the conversation to end but Glen continued, "I heard you got the Hughes job. They must like you."

"Yes. That's actually why I decided to make the trip. I wanted to hook up with Dave Howell and Bryan Carey at GTS and get some subcontracting lined out."

Glen saw a member of his party wave him over, "I'll let 'em know if I bump into them. Good luck with it. Let me know if I can get on board."

"Sure. See you in conference."

Through the week Peter attended sessions that discussed Earth's evolutionary progress. He expected Jen was signed up for some of the same, but learned she left the conference early the day before. Disappointed, he concentrated on the seminar information and eventually carved out time with Bryan and Dave, both confirming the interest to take on the assignments but couldn't commit immediately due to a recent reorganization at their firm.

Dave mentioned one of the remaining founders had taken a sabbatical, "and surprisingly it ended up permanent! Confidentially, we sort of lost touch with Kenneth. He's presenting here, but we don't support his conclusions. You might hear differently, but GTS is officially under new leadership. We'll be glad to take on the project though. Did you know we bid and got awarded the summary phase?"

"No," Peter answered, concealing his surprise.

Too late to take back his offer, he had just inadvertently handed them another chunk of the same contract. There was tons of business being snapped up by the conglomerates who subcontracted it out to smaller firms, who then sought the same expertise to deliver a solution.

He came seriously close to going into partnership with his best friends, Looks and Karl, both with similar college majors. Peter thought back on it as a near miss. The idea was cooked up after the three of them shared a college semester project in their junior year. They completed the class objective, classifying and mapping global disasters, creating a data array with the hope of proving statistical significance. As students, they labored to research and populate a Mercator projection world map with colored pins tracking floods, forest fires, then earthquakes and hurricanes. Far past the beer-fueled effort to get a passing grade, the mapping activity continued as a hobby, until college graduation. Karl still had it mounted on his wall at home, recently adding orange and purple pins for volcanoes and tsunamis. It was a focal point for his guests. If he could get the observer in front of his PC, the replicated virtual model was even better.

The concept of planning a business together fizzled as Peter learned more about the inner workings of his close friends, as "risk takers and slackers", he remembered thinking. Looks was a sports extremist, risking his life to get a rush. Karl was an idealist fortunate enough to be connected with old money. He was also a conspiracy nut always conjuring with theory or scenarios beyond what was common knowledge.

Towards the completion of their senior year, when they confronted Peter, he gave Looks and Karl an earful, "Hey, I'm sorry, but it's nothing against you guys. I just don't want my livelihood resting on a partner who jumps out of airplanes or somebody whose survival planning for the next something-gate."

Peter evolved to be the most prolific of his college buddies. His close friends of over ten years knew of his passion and drive, or overdrive. Landing jobs and gaining experience, each had matured in ways that placed them on different paths. Looks had started in Metallurgical Engineering, a damn wizard with mathematical modeling, but pulled out the program and dove into climatology. He said monkeys could do the math with software so he wanted to move into something he could get predictive with. The notation was not lost on any one who knew him. His final career landed on climate effects on land masses using his background in morphogenetic zones.

Karl graduated with a geology engineer degree like Peter, but studied paleoseismology. Late in his career he began favoring ancient aspects of major disturbances, mostly related to climate. Peter avoided the obscure specialties wanting to churn out knowledge for profit.

Karl pounced on him once for taking the middle road to make a living, "And you've got no problem with ethics if it comes down to preservation or ecology?"

"I'm still a greenie at heart, but there's no way I'd turn down work from anyone that wants to give me a paycheck. A box of conspiracy would have to drop out of the sky," and he paused to add effect. "Like that's going to happen."

Sitting through sessions in the vendor hall to evaluate technology improvements in hardware and software applications, Peter was curious about the reorganization at GTS but decided to participate in a roundtable discussing best practices for consultants. If he had attended Millard's lecture he would have noticed the video portion of presentation was a combination of sound bites, with animation schemes. A fourth of the crowd cleared out before an explanation of the services and support by NETL. The technical discussion of, "Recent Developments in Predictability" lasted a long thirty minutes, causing the rest of the attendees to leave by the time Q&A started. The glossy brochure near the exit was generally ignored.

Afterwards, Dr. Millard and his fiancé tried to enjoy themselves that evening at an upscale bistro, but the evening's romance was ruined by a redundant problem.

Caroline was perturbed at Kenneth for not sticking up for himself, "Tell him to get out of your way. They're your clientele, not his," she proposed.

Her male partner took a big sip of wine and corrected her, "By all intents and purposes, that's not entirely accurate."

"But you said these were people you would be doing business with!"

"That would be after I retire from this," Kenneth reminded her.

"I don't understand then."

"I can't go into the detail now Caroline! One more session tomorrow and we can get dinner in our rooms and relax," he insisted.

"You promised we would go out. Remember? The Mint Club in Ketchum?"

It held the possibility of glimpsing Hollywood's best. She rubbed up against Kenneth's body, her cleavage showing beyond the faint outline of her bra through a silk blouse. Deciding the seduction wasn't worth it, he made up an excuse to work from his room.

The next day, Caroline pressed her fiancé for a commitment and watched his eyes wander, "Yes, yes. We'll talk about it. I must get going. I promise we'll go."

He leaned in, to kiss her and was allowed to place his lips on her turned cheek. Her exuberance was replaced by contention, left to smolder.

"I'll be in the bar, if you get there," she fumed, walking away.

Shedding Caroline, Kenneth remained in the back corridors, concentrating on his adversary. Every day he had received complaints from his boss about his presentation skills and that he hadn't spent enough time with their benefactors. He was told he "absolutely had to make himself available for ad hoc discussions," with the directive that his "girlfriend" was not to continue to swarm around him or the guests. Kenneth thought about the earlier debate he had with Colton.

"Ken, you make her disappear or I will."

The scientist reminded Colton he didn't like to be called "Ken" and justified her role, "I think she's helping in a way that makes me more approachable."

"You're not going to cheapen this. This isn't some roadhouse beer bust, Ken. As much as you'd like our investors to have their dicks in their hands, I'd rather give them cash and have their research."

Colton glanced at his watch as he paused to answer his cell, "You have one more session, right? Keep the crowd engaged this time."

His temper simmering, Kenneth knew it was his cue to leave. *Asshole*, he thought as he recalled the ridicule.

With his session about to start, Dr. Millard moved inside the convention room noticing many were attendees from earlier presentations. Suspending his annoyance with the strip and pin spots above and the piped-in soundtrack, Dr. Kenneth Millard showed no apprehension taking the podium. The next two hours went splendidly as the scientist-consultant presented an interactive demonstration illustrating NETL field analysis. He used to complain to his team about the specious nature of empirical evidence he lectured about, but tonight he worked the crowd hoping for a return on investment for *himself*.

When the group Q&A extended the session over the time limit, Kenneth anticipated the questions brilliantly, titillating a few of the observers whom he believed would engage him after the presentation. Wrapping up the session, Dr. Millard paused to look across the audience, felt his breast pocket for his business cards, and moved off the stage to mingle. After shuffling on to his third group, he looked for Colton. Taking a breath to calm himself, he approached another clique of scientists eager to understand the implications of NETL's bold statement that, "the earth was in fact in a stasis period, predicted to last over five hundred years."

Dr. Millard was asked to reiterate the summation he gave earlier, "Withstanding the studies of climatic forcings, the current influx of increases in tectonic plate motion is predictably that of an anomaly."

The attendee, introducing himself as a career scientist, questioned the affirmation, "We have precedence that indicates the group of recent tectonic energy is foreshadowing a major forcing. Why or how do you explain away all the research indicating potential thrusts across the major geographical boundaries?"

Seasoned with over forty presentations Kenneth had the immediate answer, albeit it was rote from practice. In fact, Colton made him memorize a scripted response, developed to manage those scientists who disagreed with the research presented. Colton and his team strived to control the dialogue, rebuffing challenges from researchers who objected vigorously. Countering with incentives, their motive was to gain access to others' data research that would be invaluable to refine their propaganda.

Colton dictated the discourse, cadence, and body language Kenneth was to use. The practice sessions in front of Colton's people were humbling and mostly humiliating, bringing back memories of childhood barriers Kenneth encountered as a momma's boy. After his mother stopped indulging his fretting, he had matured, no longer needing medication.

Now in front of his distinguished guests, Kenneth shifted his weight forward to the balls of his feet. He raised his hands slowly and placed his extended finger tips gently to the edge of his chin as if he were praying.

Tilting his head slightly, his eyes stared right at the scientist and then downward as if casting doubt, "There must be something wrong with our models, according to your claims."

Pausing again to purposely blunt the subsequent response, Kenneth would continue, "It would be exemplary if I could get access to your data. The comparisons might reveal why we have significant deltas between the two data profiles."

Human nature took over. If there was objection to the proposal, Kenneth would contradict the challenger, citing the quality of the professional staff at NETL and lay claim that the research was touted as the watermark for worldwide scientific consumption.

Tonight the imposing scientist took the path of least resistance avoiding confrontation and remained neutral, weighing the offer of collaboration, "I suppose we could share our findings. I'm not sure our budget has any room for serious analysis."

Preconditioned, Kenneth initiated the negotiation phase, stepping through it quickly so he could attend to as many groups as possible. The offer of his card ended the dialogue, "At your convenience, call my admin and we'll figure out our share of the expense and get it on the calendar."

Although his handshake was the termination of the script, for some time the gesture had become disingenuous. He felt his own shallowness but getting to this point in the drama was compelling. The façade was continually unbearable at first, but Kenneth believed he deserved the payoff. Before he could even attend the conventions as a NETL employee, before he could participate in the presentations, before he could host the sessions in front of his colleagues, he had to transform himself to meet Colton's standards. He deserved the payoff.

Avoiding a likely round of brunt critique from his boss, Kenneth finished his discussion with the small cadre of geologists, sifted through a few large groups and then ambled towards the door. Arriving at the bar with eyes darting, expecting to apologize, he had missed Caroline by forty minutes. She decided at the top of the hour, one hundred twenty minutes before midnight, to accept a ride to her desired destination. He stayed put accepting a trickle of drink offers until the hotel bar closed.

The next morning, the conference meetings neared completion with individual breakouts. Peter wandered around hoping for a chance to talk to Dr. Millard. Unable to find the NETL scientist, he returned to his room to finish remaining business and pack for three days of early season mountain biking.

While online, Peter noticed his email to Jen had gone unanswered, "She must be on the road."

After sending a text message, he stretched out on the half patio overlooking the barren mountain draws scraped into ski runs, his mind winding down, letting thoughts bounce into each other. Thinking back on his college days something crept back into memory – that Karl had not been too far off his idealist predictions.

When their group was hanging out perfecting how they would rule the world after college, Karl predicted the mode of discovery and enlightenment was going to change for the worst and claimed there was already a sellout in Earth sciences. At the time, Peter suspected his friend had been encouraged by Professor Worthington's theories of ecosystem collapse and cultural degradation. Like Worthington, he debated his claim.

The lean years with the Carter administration and then a surge of unfettered prosperity with the Republicans, provided fresh conspiracy material for Karl to hype. But in those days, it was heresy to claim that the shared intellect of Earth sciences was for the sole benefit of the oil giants. Since many college programs were wholly dependent upon their financial support, Karl appeared as if he was biting the hand feeding the students and faculty.

With his focus returning, Peter sorted through the pile of handouts he had collected. The packet from Kenneth Millard's presentation was a stunning example of Karl's predictions. It included a DVD, a glossy binder with full-color ads, trinkets with logos, and coupons for drinks and guest services at the hotel.

"It's all bling," Peter complained to an empty room. He checked his email with the free high-speed connection. *What the hell. Let's see if there's any real science here. Fifteen minutes.*

The DVD he viewed, was produced with actors and a host of other gimmicks to reinforce the message NETL was promoting. In the reference section, URLs and a list of publications could be obtained from the web.

"What have they done with the data then?" Peter questioned as he went online and ran his browser. When the homepage of Millard's employer reported an error, another search of the brochure turned up a direct link to the funded research.

Peter could see its content was in opposition with other research advancements that he was familiar with, "Maybe this is an old version. Time to hit the trail."

He ejected the media out of the laptop and tossed it into his brief, distracted with the promise of great scenery. With no reply from Jen, Peter sent an email before signing off:

> *WWY? This conference was really marketing fluff. Everyone is bought and sold for! According to some of the old timers, funding for the little guy is drying up. I may be retiring earlier than I thought.*
>
> *Peter.*

Almost last in line, Peter sat waiting to shuffle in the queue, his thighs sore and forearms scuffed from biking. Standing under the frame of the plane door, the steward was already quietly instructing passengers. Most of the first class was seated, and the line was backed up with economy buyers struggling to get their luggage stowed near their seats.

"If passengers will be seated immediately and place their seatbelts around them, we can depart from the gate," inter-commed the stewardess who had already given one courteous reminder that the plane wasn't going to move until all passengers were belted in.

As the bottleneck ahead of him dissipated, Peter reached his first class seat, lucky to have scored an upgrade. He noticed the Ivy League class ring worn by his seatmate and the huge gadget watch half-covered with the monogrammed white shirt cuff. The man's closely cropped hair of speckled black with gray was trimmed nicely, showing taunt facial skin with squint lines on the upper cheek bones.

Peter sat down and adjusted the seat buckle, passive about striking up a conversation but decided to be polite, "Hi, I'm Peter Childs."

Annoyed, the seat companion looked up from his reading and said nothing.

Staring without blinking, the man maintained his silence. His rude posturing ticked Peter off so he insisted on starting a conversation, "I just finished a conference in Sun Valley. I'm looking forward to a short break."

Without the slightest indication of paying attention, the passenger responded, his interest peaked, "What conference?"

Peter gave the passenger a synopsis of the event and was surprised with the reaction.

"Did you attend Dr. Millard's presentation on the science of phase velocity?" interrogated the stranger.

"Your name was?"

"Mr. Jones."

"I remember his presentation was sponsored by a federal organization. I missed it. To be honest, it looked a little thin on facts."

Jones's eyes narrowed and his brow shifted forward, "I heard the methodology for the study was authenticated with the aid of NETL. If there is an insinuation of low confidence on your part it is apparent your colleagues don't share your perception."

"Generally, I take conferences with a grain of salt," Peter replied, deflecting the tone of arrogance. "It might be speculation on my part, but there seems to be competing motives behind Dr. Millard's work."

The plane crept to a stop waiting for further instructions.

"You sound like you're a supporter of Millard's research. What's your line of work?" Peter inquired.

The engines had revved for takeoff.

As he began to repeat his question, he was bluntly interrupted, "It's a hobby of mine," Jones replied. "I'm aware of Dr. Millard's previous affiliation. I wanted to meet him personally."

With that, the gentleman made an obvious gesture to end the conversation, signaling the attendant to ask for a pillow.

"Well, good to make your acquaintance," ended Peter. *Not.*

"Attendants, please prepare for takeoff," updated the pilot over the inter-comm.

Peter pulled out a paperback thinking, *who does this for a hobby?*

The hour and a half flight was ending as the attendant began announcing gate information. In minutes, the wheels touched and the plane's initial bump on the earth ended the flight. When the bell tone sounded, Peter stood to open the overhead door. He noticed a jacket neatly folded.

"Is this yours? I can get it," he asked politely

"Please, don't bother."

Anticipating a positive reaction, he had begun to lift it. The passenger ticket sleeve in the vest pocket slipped out, but he pushed it back in.

"Okay, sure. Sorry."

As the backlog of passengers deplaned, Peter noticed the man he conversed with, was already on his cell phone, "Hello, Dr. Millard."

Willis Colton's tone was menacing and he was unwilling to wait for a response, "Do you know a Peter Childs?"

"Yes, I believe so."

"Does Mr. Childs represent anyone?" Colton demanded.

"I suppose he could be a free-agent consultant—why?" asked Kenneth.

Impatient and wanting an accurate assessment from his charge, Colton persisted. "Does he have a following? Does the industry respect him?"

"Uh, I suppose—"

"No! We don't suppose anything in our business Ken. Is Peter a respected colleague or is he a flake?"

Enraged, Kenneth recited what little he knew of Peter's broad and specific experience.

"He wasn't very impressed with your work," Colton sneered. "One more time. It is *your* responsibility to get people like him aligned with the research protocols and the science of NETL."

Colton lowered his voice maintaining his strict tone, "Is that clearly understood Ken?"

"Yes," Kenneth replied, clenching his free hand.

"Ken. This is getting redundant for me. If you have difficulty performing these tasks I'll take you up on the offer to terminate your contract early, with consequences I'll insure are painful."

Colton ended the call.

"What a fucking jerk! It's Ken-neth!"

At home for less than forty-eight hours, he slammed the phone down on the India settee. Already barraged by Colton, he had already received emails from him.

His fear surfaced again, "What have I gotten myself into!"

And wondered why it had gone so badly for him, "I'm not a fucking God. I can't force people to believe all this shit!"

He had made some progress with his plan to utilize his own data to expose NETL and Colton. His old partners followed through with the package, but that favor wouldn't be repeated. Hoping he hadn't started the effort too late, he had begun to rely on other sources for information. Adeptly he had contacted other agents, feigning lost luggage or that he was hampered by slow upload connections. His requests for copies of their presentations gave him additional information he wasn't supposed to have.

He forced other exchanges by acting as if he was under Colton's orders. He asked for researcher's names claiming, "It drives me nuts but you know how he is. He says if I can't pull my head out of my ass, the actual researcher will have to bail me out."

They were helpful to give him names which led to deeper contacts with NETL. To expose Colton, he had to have an army behind him.

Kenneth nervously lit a cigarette and inhaled hard. He had been seduced by the payoff, by his addiction to money. *Something's got to break in my favor!*

He jammed his cigarette into the ash tray and lit another one, "Colton will keep kicking my ass until he's eliminated!" he murmured as he threw himself into a chair.

He would have garnered the NETL clients on his own, but Colton had taken those prospects away. Their interests were already bought and sold.

"Shit on him!" Kenneth yelled. Perspiring, his anxiety was ripe as he shut his eyes and silently vented. *I don't need some fucking idiot telling me what to do. It could have been my research. They're the ones who wanted to control the public. The P- and S-waves are so extreme in the wrong direction. No one is going to believe them. I've got to find someone who's willing to help me expose this.*[43],[44]

The last gate check-in and flight landed Peter Childs in El Paso. He was looking forward to getting together with his old college group.

Coming off the jetway, he auto dialed Karl Johns, "Hey where are you?"

"I'm double parked over by rental down at the end."

"Ok. See you in about fifteen minutes."

Spring break was supposed to be the magnet pulling the group back together. This outing had confirmed Karl, Looks, Perrie, and Jude.

"Hey, dude!" Peter shook hands through the open window and threw his gear into the rear seat.

"I saw your email? You say Perrie Williams is coming? I thought she was stuck on the island of Hawaii."

"She switched programs. Something about her professor knocking some sense into her."

"That gig was pretty sweet though. What a place to be a slave to your work."

"No doubt."

Karl cruised out of the airport byway and headed for Route 62.

"You in shape to do some mountain bike riding?"

---

[43] Dictionary of Earth Sciences, 2nd ed., Allaby and Allaby (Oxford: Oxford University Press, 1999), 533. Referred to as secondary, shear or transverse waves these are elastic in nature where particles oscillate. S-waves cannot travel through a fluid, potentially indicating a shear zone, an area of intense rock deformation.

[44] Ibid., 441. Referred to as compressional wave; it is the wave most studied in reflection and refraction seismology. P-waves are the fastest of the seismic waves.

"Just knocked off a few rides in the White Clouds. The weather was awesome but sections are still in snow pack. There's a bunch of free riders setting up a park. It's coming along. What have you been doing?" Peter asked.

"You might know these guys from Project Nature Connect?" [45]

Peter nodded.

"I know it's not solid as something you would venture into," Karl confessed. "But their hearts are in the right place. They have accredited courses on nature-based organic psychology and connecting behavioral transformations."

"Sounds interesting," Peter feigned.

"While I'm on the subject of coursework, would you like to head into Mesa Verde and do a little remapping of an Acoma Pueblo site, in a couple months?"

"I dunno."

When Karl explained the project, Peter became reluctant, "It's not a project if it's a *favor* for Worthington."

"Don't get your undies all wrinkled. He's had this permit for years. He just wants to have the area checked out. It might end up all bogus. You know he trusts us."

"No. He trusts you! Remember? We didn't get along."

"It's because you think he's the antichrist. The guy is a visionary."

"No. He's a junk scientist. And I'll add freakin' paranoid. Don't tell me you've forgotten all the rumors?"

"Did you have nasty mouth cereal this morning?"

A number of traffic lights heading east jammed their afternoon commute heading out of El Paso.

"You can't down the man because he looks at things a bit different than others."

"Understatement," Peter yelled above the road noise from the traffic.

"Regardless, he still needs a good set of eyes at the site. And you've got the software I need to log the locations. I've got an old friend up there as well. We haven't done a goodwill project together since college. Whadda say?"

Peter looked out the window for a moment. He was thinking back on their trip to Michoacan State in Mexico to teach English to fifteen year-olds.

---

[45] Project Nature Connect "Institute of Global Education," http://www.ecopsych.com/.

"Promise me you won't carry it to extremes," Peter half-kidded. "Nobody should be forced to look at you naked, standing in the middle of the stream washing your clothes."

"I'd forgotten that one. No problemo."

Guadalupe National Park, Texas.

KARL LOOKED AT the five small tents and complained, "The group is getting smaller every year. Spring break isn't what it used to be," he lamented.

"Why?" Jude said coming out of his tent into the cold air, clad in a t-shirt and running shorts. Glad to see an additional tent since he went to bed, he stared into the flat light that stretched across the east horizon. The fog line on the upper ridges emulated liquid held by surface tension, unable to burst towards the valley. The rising temperatures would soon suffocate the moisture. Camping sites made of compacted substrate were carved out amongst few Texas madrones, alligator junipers, and cactus.

"The whole group rarely shows up anymore. I guess it's harder to convince them to come out for a common cause," Karl clarified.

"When's the last time everyone made it?" Jude asked.

"Oh, about three years ago. We went over to Lake Powell on the Utah side and did the houseboat gig. Everyone had a blast. We rented a ski boat and some jet skis."

"That's a sure sign…water was the attraction," Jude guessed.

"Could be. Wren and Jen both had conflicts with work this time. But that's the point. Creating some space between it and here," Karl hoped.

A Rufous-crowned sparrow was paired with another in the junipers warning its mate of danger. Letting go from the force of the breeze, the rain drops fell from the branch tips, silently blending into the grass and gravel. Mule deer foraged within yards of the human community, keeping distance from the larger parking lot that housed the daily stream of RVs.

Karl picked up four empty jugs and split the five water bladders with Jude, "Let's get these filled. We'll be heading out soon if the group gets moving."

By the time they filled and carried the load back, the rest of the group was up and about. Waiting for the water to boil, Peter prepped the oatmeal with fresh fruit. Looks didn't get in until everyone had gone to bed and was stretching out while talking to Perrie.

She yawned, "I didn't hear you at all. I just crashed after reading. But I heard the rain pattering early. It was mesmerizing."

"No kidding. I zonked too. I'm sure the jetlag will catch up to me today," Looks admitted, yawning as well.

"You were where?" she asked.

"In Paris working on a fraction of the Kyoto ratification."

"Awesome!" Perrie hooted showing admiration. "Are you going to get some recognition from it?"

"It's a firm that signed up for the accountability to the treaty. It's more of a dot-the i-cross-the-t exercise. So...no," Looks confessed.

"Knowing you, you got some skiing in," she presumed.

Jude had been listening while installing the bladders into the packs, "No kidding! That sounds like a sweet gig!"

"Actually no, again. My friend that I stayed with was hoping we would have time, but his company flipped some timelines around so we ended up working our day off. The snow was pretty wet."

"Who's the client?"

"The prime is the Pew Center. They're driving the business end of the climate warming stick. I tied in with a couple U.S. firms with connections in France."

Perrie scrunched up her face and said, "Why would they hire you? You're still doing land mass something aren't you?"

"Ya. Close. Land mass configuration topology. The morphology stuff, inclusive of all the 3-D. This firm is ready to submit a couple white papers. They are looking to improve the formal explanation of problematic impacts to world climate changes. Besides the obvious ones, land mass changes are a hot button. You never really know what's changing beneath us, then all of a sudden, boop! A volcano shows up or a sink hole appears."

Jude was intrigued as well, "I can't wait to finish school. You've got it nice, working for yourself."

"It didn't start on autopilot. There were some lean months. You've got to have something to sell," Looks explained.

"Don't let Karl hear that," Perrie joked.

"Breakfast is served," announced Peter.

Everybody sat down at the picnic table to dole out their own portions and finished breakfast quickly. From its perch, a juniper titmouse floated to the ground to search for tidbits.

"Let's get these dishes washed up, packed up, and head out," Karl demanded, anxious to start the hike.

All the unnecessary gear was stowed in the remaining vehicles and two other cars rolled out of the camp area headed to the Permian Reef trail head. By email everyone had agreed to a firm agenda. The strenuous nine-mile loop was the first activity to consume a day with a night over on top. Everyone in the two vehicles had either made the trek before or had studied it. The second endeavor was a full day of mountain biking with a three thousand foot gain on the La Cueva twenty-five mile single track near Carlsbad. On the third or fourth day depending upon the weather, Looks and Jude were going parasailing or BASE jumping. The rest of the group decided to lie around and catch up with each other. The final day would be a mass departure with the group splintering off to go back to their jobs.

From the moving vehicle the hikers could see hillsides and steeper inclines dotted with agrito, desert buckhorn, and juniper. Deep within McKittrick Canyon below the Permian Reef, was a flourishing spring with trout and a variety of oak flora unique to the high desert plains of Texas.

Winding up a steeper incline, a flat parking spot with a forest service sign-up station became visible. Everyone loaded up their gear while viewing the acres of erect eight-foot-high stalks of lechuguilla, speckled across the landscape of cactus and brush. Their flora remained withered until a future storm.

"It smells wonderful! Temple would go nuts," Perrie exclaimed. "My work doesn't have these benefits. I always smell fish!" she said laughing.

Unfamiliar with Perrie's background, Jude was going to ask about Temple, but the others took over the conversation.

"You were into analyzing the database of the Loihi eruption, right?" Looks asked.

"The funds are dying up," she replied. "Loihi is not going to reach the surface anytime soon. Do you remember Charlie? He called me the other day. Wants me to help him do big wave research."

"Capps?" Peter confirmed. "Isn't he a bit of a crackpot?"

Jude immediately thought Peter disliked almost anyone who wasn't in his line of work.

"Well, he's out on the fringe," Perrie answered. "But he considers it a privilege. He said I could study volcanic slag anytime. Just put it on Tivo he said."

"He sounds pretty cool to me," Jude wagered.

"He said big wave theory is turning out to be a predictive tool of sorts," Perrie added.

"Will you have to move from Hawaii?" Karl wondered.

"You gotta go where the work is. But it will be closer to my family. Temple would be excited. I haven't said anything to her."

"How is she these days?" Looks asked.

"She's doing great for her age. She's forty-three now. My folks have some weekly help with her but the routine is still demanding."

Karl came over to help Perrie adjust her pack, "I thought they were looking for a halfway house to give her some experience."

"It ended up that they missed that window. Years of my parents being the primary caregivers made her too vulnerable to change and with autism the current thinking now is to get a good teacher when they're young."

Jude was intrigued with Perrie's comments, "Don't mean to pry, but what did you mean she would go nuts up here?"

"Depending upon severity, most autistics get all their primary sensory inputs from sources other than sight, so like their sense of touch and smell can be extremely sensitized. If Temple were standing here she would be whirling around literally trying to consume all the smell of the trees and rock."

The group started up the narrow trail constructed with erosion bars that temporarily trapped rain water to hydrate small rodents and birds. Their hiking boots scattered the piles of crushed leaves that littered the leeward side of each switchback.

"Really!" a couple of the men exclaimed.

"She would be ecstatic, but she'd disregard all aspects of safety."

"You mean like getting lost?" Jude pried.

"No. More like spinning off the edge of this trail. She's impulsive sometimes. When we try to control her she becomes defiant."

"Whoa. I guess that would be tough to deal with all the time."

"There is one place she likes very much...the ocean," Perrie said proudly.

Jude became captivated with the subject, having little exposure on how people deal with handicaps. As a caregiver, Perrie seemed calm with the whole thing.

"I'll bet she enjoys the sea life. Has she seen the reefs?" the young student questioned.

"That's her favorite part. To float on top, looking upward just above the water level, then down below at the coral. The change in the line of sight is puzzling to her."

In a straight queue, their boot treads ground the fine gravel and rock, erasing the faint tracks of deer. Daily storms cleared all the minor imprints restoring the trail to pristine conditions. Karl often paused to collect the shiny candy bar wrappers and cigarette butts.

"I'm never surprised at the trash along the trail. Like they think it will disintegrate," Karl complained and added, "We'll punch out another quarter mile or so and find some shade. I think there's a good vantage point up ahead to see the top of Wilderness Ridge."

The trail had changed in composition again with loose gravel replacing soil. Portions of the path spanned across a series of branching fault lines, a million years old. Karl picked up the pace to reach a suitable rest area with an outlook to the basin floor east and north.

"What's our gain?" Karl asked, directing his question to Looks.

Jude had been watching his altimeter on the way, "1730."

Peter stepped over to see the instrument, "When did you get that?"

"A couple weeks ago."

Perrie placed her hand on Looks shoulder, "Somebody is rubbing off on somebody?"

"He needed one for parasailing," was Looks quick explanation.

"Count me out!" she resisted. "I'm firmly in opposition and enjoy working on the negative side of sea level."

"At least we have our bases covered, huh?" Karl joked. "Can you dig this view?"

He pointed towards the rocky ledge with the series of switchbacks below them, "The valley floor, called the Permian Basin was created two hundred fifty million years ago, discovered by a scientist named G.G. Shumard." [46]

---

[46] Guadalupe Mountains National Park, "Roadside Geology Guide."

Perrie was the odd "man" out on geological jeopardy so she taunted them. "Now don't all answer at once, but how old is the rock we're on. How did it form?"

Peter posed the challenge to his nephew. "Let's see if Jude knows."

"Hey, I'm on spring break."

"No excuse," prompted Looks with his big smile, "Take a swing. If you get it wrong, we'll just toss you off the edge to appease the gods."

Jude rubbed the back of his neck, "Let see. The basin was originally the Delaware Sea and takes that name. And I think it was connected by a channel."

The youngest male looked at the sky trying to gather facts, "I can't recall the name, but I do remember the Capitan Reef, which is the exposed part of the mountains. The reef is limestone and the result of faulting twenty million years ago, which gives us the highest peak in the state, and the namesake of the park at something like eighty-seven hundred feet."

Jude looked at their expressions for feedback and remembered something else, "And just for Perrie, the basin had diverse marine biology. I'll blame Professor Weld and Worthington if my answer is not in the ballpark."

"Not bad for a novice," Karl soothed. "Whadda think, guys? Pass or fail."

Peter voted fail, indicating the explanation of the basin was flawed.

"Studies indicate three arms of the basin existed, Delaware, Marfa, and Midland, connected by a channel leading to the Permian Sea. And it's not limestone, but fine-grained fossiliferous. And when did it fault?"

"Like I said, about twenty million," Jude repeated.

Even in the simplest of matters Peter's rigidness was evident. Looks took it down a notch, "He's barely over the wire but with a solid answer on the overall picture."

"Ditto," Karl agreed, "It's impossible to cover all the nuances."

"More like twenty-six," Peter stated.

Looks started laughing and responded to Perrie, "We can only guess at the timing of when the mountain range was created, but for these materials to evolve, melt, cool, possibly under adiabatic conditions, it could add another couple million years or so. Then we could also throw in an isothermal as well."

"Okay, we'll postpone the sacrifice. He likes to jump off things anyway. We'd just be playing into his hands," Karl announced. "Let's head up the rest of the way."

Another long segment of hiking put them on the back side of the Permian-aged Capitan Reef. Sweating, Jude sat down taking a hit of water. Perrie did the same.

"At least the view is spectacular," she said feigning disappointment. She knew from her own studies that the reef contained a multitude of fossilized sea creatures. "Fossilized osracods, bryozoans, and sponges went extinct at the end of the Permian period during the Paleozoic era. Bor-ing!" she teased, elongating the last word.[47]

"I'm offended," Karl mocked. "I would consider this on par with your ocean bottom phenomenon of vents."

"You mean a hydro-thermo vent field? Really!" she asked holding up her hands to symbolize weighing the choices, "Extinct trilobites versus crystallized chimneys called black smokes that are one hundred eighty foot tall, produced by seven hundred fifty degree magma coming in contact with saltwater? You have my apology!"

"Trilobites are extremely rare. And this park has lent their name to the Geological Time Scale. The only one in the United States," Karl recited. "I got that factoid from Worthington, over a decade ago."[48]

"Here's an unbelievable phenomenon. Worthington getting up here," Jude quipped. "I think he's a pack-a-day smoker."

Amongst the group, Karl had the most direct involvement with Worthington, "He made it up here a couple times that I know of. But you're right, he'd be toast now."

Perrie took off all her gear, stood, and stretched, "So before we start setting up camp, explain all this."

They all walked over to the exposed ledges and inspected sections of the reef, pointing to specific features, lecturing on other aspects, like fault zone and bank-ramp complexities.

"I feel like a tourist," she admitted, "but smarter. Feel free to ask me anything about mid-ocean ridge, abyssal plain or big wave research."

Jude marveled at the aggregate knowledge possessed by his uncle, Looks, and Karl. Between them they spanned earth geophysics, structural geology, global tectonics, tectonophysics, and biogeochemistry. As consultants they held over thirty man-years of applied field knowledge. That and their egos explained their debate of when the reef and its vertical position had actually occurred. Peter explained "recent" in geological

[47] Guadalupe Mountains National Park, "Geologic Time & Rock Formations."
[48] Guadalupe Mountains National Park, "Roadside Geology Guide."

terms could be a couple million years relative to the age of the planet, "which is estimated at just less than five billion years old." [49]

Perrie encouraged their lack of unity for fun, "That's not much of an estimate. If you can't come closer, I'd say you're saying the same thing."

That set off another round of arguments. The contention shifted to the capability of science to further refine existing epochs.

Karl decided to summarize, "Nobody knows exactly. It's not down to an egg timer. We're all just observers at this point in time. Maybe Jude's children's children will get a crack at it."

Intimidation swept over Jude, feeling like his college studies had only scratched the surface so far.

This has all been discovered and debated before by someone else. And they just spent an hour fussing with numbers no one would bet their life on.

He was in search of something new. *Worthington's black books are so freakin' weird*, he thought, *there's no way I'm bringing it up.* He shook it off and looked up at the carbon blue sky and the seven thousand foot peak ahead of them.

After an early rise, the camping party traced the trail back down to the parking lot, switching clothes for biking gear and vacated the park to their next destination. The following evening, the group had finished their mountain biking and their conversation was laced with physical fatigue, talking of work and how their lives had evolved in ways unpredictable. Deciding they better get their tents pitched before there was no energy left, they traveled to Brantley Lake. Their headlight beams reached beyond the multicolored fabrics of dome tents already inhabited, illuminating a small fraction of the three-thousand-acre park hosting two hundred archeological sites.

Tired but excited for the coming day, Jude stripped off his clothes and lay on top of his bag. His ideas and thoughts drifted in and out. Wanting to go to sleep, he clasped his hands together and said prayers. A routine since childhood—it didn't count if his fingers weren't laced together. Often he fell asleep thinking about forgiveness, truth, and his mastery of life or lack of. He thought about Perrie's situation, the magnitude of her contribution towards her sister. The honor of having someone need you. Something

---

[49] Wikipedia, "Earth," http://en.wikipedia.org/wiki/Earth.

beyond acknowledgement of the need. *Was it privilege? Dinner was good. Karl was sure on one!*

There was plenty of entertainment between the oddity of the Pringles can gadget and background history on Worthington's devotion to the Pueblos. Karl promised to send a web link that explained how a Pringles chip tube could pick up frequencies.[50]

Worthington's devotion to the Pueblos was fascinating the way Karl explained to the group, "When you study the pottery and the buildings, your vision expands to the way they thought about life and how they perceive the earth."

Karl told of the ambitious Eastern pilgrims who ventured to a five-thousand-year-old city to embrace Krishna and a female consort, Radha the Gopi. Peter's eyes rolled as Karl recalled Bud lecturing on the importance of finding those who are teachers of the spirit soul.

"That's because he doesn't trust anyone else at Rice!" Peter half-joked. "He was so paranoid back when we were there!"

"Give him a break," Karl advised. "I really think Worthington believed spirit teachers are the only ones left capable of explaining their ancient beliefs."

Jude wondered what started the conflict between Worthington and Peter.

Karl is so into Worthington and Peter so against him. It's obvious who I can trust, the college student decided, thinking about the black books.

After removing the rain fly from his tent, Karl laid flat looking at the stars and listening to the crickets. And to the coyotes howling in the distance. He thought of how the group had hung together since college. *Everything is order with randomness and chaos at the same time.*

Karl met Peter in a study group. Looks was on a mountain bike ride with a mutual group of friends and they ended up enrolled in the same program at Rice. Becoming friends with Wren Kennedy was a pure accident. A laptop was begging for repair. Jen and Perrie became friends during labs and study hall.

Karl realized the coyotes sounded as if they moved closer. His thoughts returned to his friends. It seemed the group made it through college unscathed coming out the other side with jobs.

---

[50] Flickenger, Rod, "Antenna on the Cheap (er, Chip)," O'Reillynet.com, (2001), http:// www.oreillynet.com/cs/user/view/wlg/448.

When his thoughts went deeper, he wondered if it was the seesaw between individual identities and friendships that eased the conflicts, strengthened commitments, and supported hard choices. Even dating Jen was risky, learning of Peter's childhood bond to her. Too much energy would have been wasted. *But how cool that we all survived, got our degrees and split up, but we're still together at least once a year.*

A need persisted, Karl confessed to himself. *I need to see Dr. Bud Worthington with all his pomp and circumstance. That office and his chairs. It would be so...*suddenly Karl sat up.

The coyotes had shifted to the north side of the tent and since their last howl it had been quiet. He heard light thumping on the ground. With his night vision light, he grabbed his sandals and silently vacated his tent in the direction of the last sound. With the back drop glow from the few tents that were lit, he ventured slowly increasing his distance to one hundred meters, then cupped his hand around the flashlight, letting the emerald beam seep out in front of him.

The light embraced the landscape, exposing nothing that moved. Then Karl saw something invade his circle of illumination. Twenty feet away. *How could it be?*

He blinked to clear his eyes thinking the fuzziness of green light distorted the animal shape and pattern of its fur. A coyote would have been thinner and taller. Then the animal suddenly barked at him. Karl wasn't sure what he heard.

"K'aika! Samuti."

The bike ride took its toll on Peter's lower half and while stretching, his thoughts were centered on Jude's safety. And concern about his sister's reaction if Jude was injured, even slightly. Convincing her on the phone was impossible. Peter naturally mentored and protected Jude, but he and his sister differed on the depth and width of accountability she expected of him. He stood his ground interrupting his sibling's pleads.

"No" to talking him out of it, Peter demanded. "Jude is legally an adult."

"Yes" to Jude gets my help when he needs it. He insisted, "I'm not babysitting him though."

Then Peter made the obvious suggestion and wished he had not, "If Jude and you differ on extreme sports that's a conversation you should have with him."

"Peter, I'm asking for your help," she insisted. "He won't listen to us."

Continuing to stretch, Peter was convinced his sister left him no place to land. Pleasing Mom would piss off Jude and vice-versa. It was impossible to deflect all of his sister's concern or mitigate all the risk Jude would encounter throughout his life.

I've got to take a leak, Peter realized. The air cooled off his skin as he walked away from the illuminated tents. Finding a suitable location he released, peering straight into the darkness. Abruptly reacting to a scuff sound, he jumped backward peering at the dark silhouette. In a matter of seconds it transformed into Karl.

"You scared the shit out of me!"

"Not intentionally, believe me. I was out trying to spot the coyotes, but I swear to god there was a bobcat out there and he barked at me!" Karl exclaimed breathing quickly. "Then it just walked away."

"Ah...that's quite a ...a bobcat? No way!" Peter replied in disbelief. "Remind me not to let you drive at night without glasses."

"Didn't you hear them earlier? They circled the campground," Karl described. "There are prints over by the truck. That one was real quizzical!"

"Nothing that I heard. I was stretching in the tent and I guess lost in thought."

The two stood still listening briefly as Karl shone his light around the area where they were standing and found another set of marks, "See! He came right through here within a couple yards of you."

"Geeze! What is it with you and animals? Remember when those peacocks chased you?

Karl returned to his tent thinking about the weird sound the animal made. *Maybe it was choking on a bone or yawning. Seemed like it talked.*

So many memories came to mind of her sister growing up. Perrie set her book down leaving her flashlight on. She barely heard voices. This trip would have been thrilling for Temple, but a lot of work managing her.

She yawned feeling relaxed but invigorated. Recovery time tomorrow would be spent taking a short hike, reading, or writing in her journal. Her thoughts turned back to her sister's caregivers. Her eyes watered remembering her parents were on duty even now. Taking a chill, a good sigh came out of her knowing Temple would be hers to manage soon. Switching off her light and closing her eyes, Perrie wondered if Temple ever thought of her, her image or her touch, the tone of her voice, the resonance of *her* energy.

Laying on his back meditating after stretching, Looks let his mind settle. He had laid out the topology maps and reviewed the plan for tomorrow. Like tides, air current ebbed and flowed specific times of the day dependent upon the sea level barometric pressure. Temperature influenced the strength of the flow. Looks savored the role of bringing Jude along in the sport of BASE jumping and wanted his student to be as capable as he was, tracing the same transition from parasailing.[51]   For both sports, much of the study and preparation of the science, safety, and equipment blurred together. Although Jude had carte blanche with the group since he was eighteen, most of his time was spent doing activities with Looks. Tomorrow was a set of milestones. *A pass/fail test of knowledge and maybe a jump from another key object.*

Failing on a variety of crucial checks and inspections could turn the event into a day hike. Setting his alarm, Looks got comfortable and dozed off.

After his watch chime woke him, Jude laid still in his bag thinking about his weird dreams. Everything of color in the tent was dulled from dim light on the horizon. A light gray shadow grew on the tent wall.

"You awake?"

Jude lowered his tone as well to answer, "Out in a minute."

He quickly got his shorts and t-shirt on. Grabbing his day pack and water supply, Jude came out in mime fashion partially unzipping the portal, his torso passing through one section at a time.

Looks whispered, "We'll snack on the way."

As they drove north, stars were still visible in the lower western horizon. Heading south back into Texas towards Fort Davis, every bit of the time was used to quiz Jude on a myriad of topics. When Jude's answer was weak Looks walked him through a decision process reinforcing his learning. The student was flustered with himself for not recalling the detail, much of it required for safety.

"You'll force it into memory Jude. It takes experience and ad hoc scenarios to get it jammed in there," Looks explained. "The key is to have a level of self-reliance that is sustainable when you get into trouble."

---

[51]   The acronym for jumping off fixed objects, building, antenna, span (bridge, dome, arch), and earth (natural formation).

Jude took the statement as advice and then as prophetic in nature, "I hope you're not predicting anything."

Being around Looks on and off for over eight years, it was a question worth asking. Jude had heard all the stories that got Robert T. Straw his nickname. He wasn't some freak of nature talking to ghosts. He saw the big picture or facets of events others didn't and was always in the right place at the right time, knowing what evidence to collect or what to pay attention to. Sometimes it flashed as a reaction to certain people. Sometimes it was about timing or events occurring in natural order.

Looks shook his head. "Only that you better learn it."

Hours of hiking to the side ridges of Mount Locke, they stood catching their breath.

Looks revealed why they drove to the Davis Mountains, even though they had perfect drops in the Guadalupe range a few days ago, "Too many eyeballs on the ridges," he cautioned. "We could get hauled in by the rangers. These gorges offer perfect lift from the upstaging currents and you get a nice pillow effect. Doesn't hurt that road spurs are everywhere so we don't get stuck bushwhacking our way back to the car."

They repacked after laying all their gear out inspecting every knot, clip, and strand. The climbers braced themselves into the wind standing on the granite ledge that had over three hundred feet of shear drop, with a sparse landscape of low brush. They already discussed the landing areas and contingencies for injuries.

"It's perfect," Looks validated. "Keep checking your readout. It's plus or minus like we talked about on the way here. It's always a go-no-go. So it's worth taking the time to see how sustainable the conditions are. I leap first so you can see there's a float out there you can trust. I'll try and punch it back up and maybe stay aloft. That's when you want to go out, then maybe we can glide down together if the wind holds up."

Jude took a long deep breath and let it out slow to calm himself, "I can do it."

"Remember, don't overcorrect," Looks instructed. "It's all subtle movement. Keep your back to the wall and steer away. Good Luck."

Later that evening, Karl built a campfire and they circled the chairs around the pit to get toasty warm before turning in. The outstanding digital pictures everyone studied were of Jude floating near the edge of outcropping, showing his chute fully expanded against the landscape, and a landing. The shots were a surprise to Jude when he had reached the valley floor the first time.

Looks ran over and hugged him, pulling out his camera for another shot, "It's like Christmas. If you knew it ahead of time, the gift is spoiled. You nailed the E! Sweet!"

The first jump was surreal to Jude and he was jacked to try it again. Reconciling, they repacked and circled back to the original spur and hiked to the take-off for a final plunge.

"Are you going to do a show and tell for your mom?" Peter asked half-kidding.

"I think I will," Jude immediately answered, but still not sure.

Looks was admiring of Jude's accomplishment, "He did great today. I'm counting on many more if everything continues to go in his favor."

Everyone assumed it meant the parents would start to loosen up on their son's choice of hobbies.

Jude changed the subject so no one would begin to speculate, "Karl, tell me about the Pringles can again?"

"I'll send you the diagram. Wren demonstrated it to me."

"Well that figures," Perrie declared. "That girl's got everything else wired, why not junk food containers!"

Karl spoke above the laughter, "It's basically simple. The cylinder is foil-lined making it a decent collector of sound waves. With a couple alligator clips and a pair of ear buds from your music source, you've got home surveillance in a can."

The fire popped from the drams of sap squeezing out of the burning logs. Perrie cautioned Jude, "You're already doing sick things with Looks. But don't start hanging around Karl and Wren. That would be sick and wrong."

"Hey now. It's all good," Karl defended. "Nothing wrong with some extra tools in the bag."

"That's an understatement!" Peter added. "Is there anything you haven't sampled on your way through life?"

Karl faked indignation, "I've had certain freedoms that have allowed me to pursue knowledge."

Looks added, "Translation—Trust fund babies can afford interesting choices."

"I'm glad you're on our side though," Peter responded. "I'd hate to have you on some executive board wheeling and dealing against the environment."

"I'll take that as a compliment," Karl assured everyone.

"Ditto," Looks concurred.

Peter stood up and moved like the monster stutter-stepping in front of the fire, his shadow bouncing off the tents. "Mix in a number of hobbies," he teased, "Along with massive amounts of college credits and you've got Franken Karl!"

Looks piled on, "That explains why you and Worthington hit it off. You're his monster to do his evil bidding."

"Here's a toast to whatever the glue is that holds us and the earth together," Perrie announced, getting Karl of the hook. "I'm gonna miss it for a whole 'nother year," she lamented, tilting her head back and staring into the stars. "We need to make sure Wren and Jen get signed up next year."

"Can't let them stray too far from our pack," Looks offered.

"No doubt," agreed Karl.

The next morning they patrolled the camp to pick up old litter. The cars were packed with drivers having a full day's travel ahead of them before reaching their destinations. Looks was stopping at his parents home in Salt Lake City, then to Boulder to check on his house before heading back to Europe for a couple weeks. Perrie decided to take a couple more days off and surprise her sister. Peter was back on the road consulting for Hughes. Jude had school resuming, which prompted condolences from everyone. Karl was the odd man out with no immediate engagements.

The campground remained vacant after their departure to El Paso. Near midnight the waxing crescent of lunar light spread on the ground with no hindrance from tents or other man-made objects. Coyotes migrated through camp again leaving prints where man had laid the night before. No human saw or heard them.

DARON Lab. Arlington, VA.

"THAT'S GOT TO be included in the status meeting today," Franklin insisted, sitting with his teammates debating how much information they should give to management.

"Like I said," Vinod repeated. "If we show them the preliminary calculations they will expect an improvement the next reporting cycle. I can't guarantee that until I refresh the database. You know it takes time."

"I understand," Franklin replied with empathy. "There is risk, but if we don't show progress, our workload will be reassigned. If we lose this Tier Four project, we won't get another one."

All of them became defensive, complaining in Kannada and Tamil dialect. Their team had far exceeded the performance goals compared to the other research groups.

"We have worthless plaques to prove it," TC grimaced.

"Let's agree we must maintain our resolve as one," the boss assured. "Let me take responsibility to communicate our findings and I will avoid promising further advances."

Reluctantly, everyone nodded. Franklin knew he would have a stiff battle to win in the briefing room.

When Franklin returned to his desk there was an email asking him to attend an emergency meeting with his manager. The message emphasized *immediately*. His first thought was concern he would be late for the status meeting. Calling his manager, he was told that meeting was cancelled and he should come right away.

Thank God I didn't upload to the main server, he scrutinized, expecting his voice to crack when he said, "Yes, sir. Be right there."

Hands shaking he hung up the phone. His pulse quickened as he unlocked a filing cabinet to retrieve prepared Fed Ex packages – one containing an expansion brief and the other, a single envelope. *What could they have found?*

His eyes darting, Franklin quickly located TC and Navin in the break area. His face was drawn, pale, and wet, "The meeting is cancelled so you need to get working on the next steps."

He actually felt relieved for his men having another twelve hour cycle to make some additional gains. Franklin had debated his next move months earlier. To him it was an act of civil treason.

"Ravi, you look horrible!" exclaimed Navin.

"Take these and walk out the door and deposit them in the FedEx curbside depot over on Mission. You know where that is, right?" Franklin demanded.

"Yes. But how will I get through security?"

"Allow them to inspect it. I put the material on non-letter head and stamped it 'NETL Approval.' They will let you through."

He looked at his coworker and hugged him, "Don't fail me, Omkar."

"What's the matter? You are ill?"

"I've got to report to Shepard's office. Don't worry. Everything will be fine. Pray for me my brothers."

This was an intrinsic signal to them that he had severely compromised his personal values. The two men were shaken after Franklin left them.

"Do you know where the FedEx mailbox is?"

"No."

Quietly returning to their cubes, one retrieved the location from the carrier's homepage and whispered in Kannada, "I will go. You set up a meeting tonight in case to figure things out that will be needed."

"Yes."

Franklin stared at the elevator without pushing any buttons. *If I run they will catch me. I can't involve my team. I have rights. This is America. I get one call. I'll be fine.*

He got on the elevator, went down to the first floor and walked slowly to Shepard's office and through the door, "Hi, John. What do you need?" Franklin asked, concentrating to keep his voice steady.

"Here, Franklin, sit down. How's your team doing?"

The employee took the single chair facing away from the door, "Fine, sir. They are fine. A bit tired though."

"I can imagine," Shepard replied with eyes glancing upward. Franklin saw his entire frame stiffen as his boss pushed back from the desk to get immediate distance. Within his periphery, the scientist knew persons had approached on both sides. He was careful not to flinch. In his memory were stories of military brutality given to undeserving human beings triggered by the slightest transgression. Franklin swallowed. Shepard stood up and moved off to the side.

"Franklin, I'm sorry. I was told to bring you down here."

"Dr. Franklin, please stand up slowly and place your hands on top of your head."

The scientist followed the order and was seated with wrists cuffed. He had so many thoughts. Most of them fearing for those he had helped or became friends with, and concerned all would be confronted and detained. He pushed out all mental invasions concerning his parents. Shepard was told to leave and it was another twenty minutes before Colton arrived quietly appearing before the detainee.

"Dr. Franklin, I have your file here and some other facts. Do you want to go first?"

Franklin thought deliberately and firmly responded, "No, sir. I don't know why I'm here and being treated like this."

"You have been breaking the law, Dr. Franklin. Based on security reports, you've have been sharing highly restricted government information with civilians."

Franklin did not answer. Colton set the folder on the desk, "You could be put in prison with punishment set to the fullest extent. According to our logs, with what you shared, that could add up. You could explain your illegal activity and lessen the impact of a criminal investigation."

"I do not know what you are referring to."

"You are denying sending and receiving classified information to a Dr. Bud Worthington and another resource totaling over fifteen incidents?"

Franklin remained silent. His composure was reinforced with an adolescent recollection of his grandfather telling of his hardships with racism. Remembering his grandfather's voice made Franklin stiffen his resolve and disallow his fear and shame to take over. He knew before this was over he would be discredited, his intellect no longer symbolic of his family's strength and honor.

Colton made a call on his cell, "Did you find anything?"

Getting his answer Colton leaned over within three inches and stared into his captive's eyes.

"You fucked with the wrong tribe, Mr. Franklin, or should I say Ravichandran."

An implied betrayal of his American birthright, Franklin unexpectedly felt impassioned against the harshness and cruelty his ancestors must have endured.

"You and your kind will never have true allegiance. Put him on the plane."

Shepard was instructed to meet with Franklin's team as the captive was being led down a stairwell into a maintenance hallway. With three military police, he exited through emergency egress and was helped into a government van.

"Franklin is finishing his meeting with the administrators and is being assigned to a special project."

"He came up to us," Navin started to say. Underneath the table, he felt his teammate's foot press on top of his, "and said he had a meeting with you," quickly completed TC.

Navin feigned a cough and took a drink of water.

"He didn't say anything else to you or ask you to do anything or make calls for him?"

They all knew Franklin was in trouble. Before their manager had reached them, TC and Navin had rounded up their colleagues bringing them up to speed on what they had witnessed. Their solidarity was instantaneous. All of them shook their heads indicating no help was given.

"When is Franklin returning to us, sir?"

"I'm not sure, but I'll update you as soon as I know. In the meantime, you'll continue working on the project assignments you have and report directly to me."

All the scientists nodded in support.

"Oh! One more thing, do not disturb any of Franklin's cubicle contents. We'll be packing his personal effects and distributing applicable material to other teams. Okay. Meeting over. Thank you gentlemen."

On another secured floor, Colton wasn't convinced of the security chief's finding so Martin Wolmit was getting grilled in front of the director's agents, "There's no evidence the other members of Dr. Franklin's team were directly involved. We did a thorough scrub and they did not have the same security bit on their systems, thus Franklin never shared the files with them," Wolmit assured the group."

"What else?"

Colton's team was listening intently. They would have to expose Franklin's activities.

"We are working on his client system and office servers to extract target data that apparently was methodically removed, probably with a software tool."

"And?"

"We're also comparing time stamps and content on the emails with other simultaneous traffic going in and out, to rule out other players."

"No subtractions without my approval," Colton stated. "Angela, you ride shotgun on these guys. Smith, you work with Shepard and go through Franklin's cubicle."

Wolmit got the hand wave telling him his part was done. The executive waited for the technical resource to leave.

"Does their shit really work or am I getting it in the ass?"

Angela Gates responded first, "I checked out the operating procedures and went over the encryption methodology with some consultants. It's robust and it *did* give us this lead. The logs indicated Franklin had sent files that had the embedded security parity bit. With our level of security on the headers, the bit matched perfectly."

"Why didn't Franklin get tapped on his first pass? Why cycle fifteen times before a system alert?"

"I was told the parameter wasn't loaded into the FFS table integrity check and checksum header. Like it was ringing but no one was home."

"Shit, what do we pay these people for? They're killing me," Colton complained looking at Angela for a confirmation that he wasn't dealing with flakes. "Is the security team up to par or did we get low bidder?"

She shared the same apprehension and qualified the weakness. "They were going through their six month end-to-end standard operating procedures and equipment lists, knocking on virtual doors. That's essentially what got them in the ball game. They definitely need some tightening up."

Colton rubbed his eyes, "You know Franklin moved up through the ranks?"

"Yes, we both read his file. Jason thinks he was paid off."

Colton was surprised with the inference, "Smith?"

"That's what I think could have been an obvious motivation but I have no proof."

"Let's turn it up and get a look at the bank statements. Ken would be impressed with our capability to stretch the FOIA. You guys have it. I've got a plane to catch. Call me."

Jason was indignant after Colton left, "Thanks a lot for hanging me out there!"

"Hey, we can't afford to leave anything out. You know he'd be coming back to that sooner or later."

It was more than twelve hours since Franklin was shuttled from NEADE headquarters to the Air Force C-17 with coordinates of 19°54'0" N 75°9'0" W. Strip searched and all his valuables removed, he wore an orange jumpsuit with a code stamped on the sleeve and letters on the back. Other than an awareness of boarding a military plane he could not discern his whereabouts. Handcuffed to a tie-ring, he was fitted with a parachute and harnessed to his seat. There were other soldiers aboard besides the third set of MPs that now accompanied him. The sour smell of human sweat did not overpower the payload of diesel fuel and toxic solvent.

The constant resonance from the engines relaxed his mind after the hurt and emotion filled him. Anything he could say to his parents would not alleviate the shame that would be engulfing them. He hoped TC and Navin were able to smuggle the packages out of the office. He was glad for his slip up, that there hadn't been time to update the main files. Sensitive to the amplified risk, Franklin never approached his men and told them of his dereliction. Over months he agonized how he would ultimately keep the answer from the NEADE. He knew the contents of one of the packages wouldn't be squandered. For his team's sake, the prisoner wished they would *fail* without him.

Looking at her cell phone lying on the desk she saw Colton's number on her display. At one-thirty a.m., Angela wasn't asleep and neither was Wolmit.

"Why fifteen, why not one hundred?" Colton demanded.

She knew not to interrupt her boss.

"It's obvious he was going strong with no roadblocks. Why did he stop?"

"Hold on."

Within twenty seconds, Angela was responding to her boss, "Marty says the security breach broadcast the infraction as soon as they uploaded the fix. The gap in time between that and last transmission was less than two months. I'm thinking he either completed his work and or changed methods to cover tracks."

"Someone needs to be thinking about his voice communications and figure out the jump Franklin made and why."

"Yes, sir," she answered and glanced at the security chief. "Marty says he'll take it."

"You tell him he'll be sitting next to the Indian if I don't get some solid answers."

The call ended before Angela started communicating Colton's last order.

Work was the farthest event from TC's mind as he walked back into NEADE eighteen hours after he pushed the packages through the door panel of the FedEx drop box. With implicit mistrust of everyone at NEADE, the leading research team had become paranoid, knowing even their own areas had been searched. Shifting exclusively to their native dialect, the four employees completed a scheduled rotation in the lab, submissively communicating in low tones. No one believed Franklin would be coming back.

Expecting their movements were being observed at work they avoided grouping together. They bypassed computers and phones at home, and instead contacted Franklin's parents by passing notes through friends. The shared hope was to discover Franklin's location.

Angela scrubbed her face and put on some light cover to mask dark lines under her eyes. Freshening up in the bathroom did not help much. Her sleep had been scarce over the last four days. Even when she had sack time many of Wolmit's staff called her to provide status updates or ask for clarification on a next step attempting to avoid harsh fallout.

Before returning to the conference room for another checkpoint Angela looked at her image in the full length mirror. She knew the breach of security had strong implications for her boss. His energy and power was seductive to her but there were signs of incompetence. Millard, "the golden boy" as Jason put it, had consumed Colton's time and concentration. The file security fiasco could have been avoided if her boss had been more attentive to NEADE operational transition plans. She would have to fix the problems he created.

Angela entered the conference room to get updates before the call. "What have you got me? Colton's going to dial in about thirty minutes."

"We snagged something and it'll be worth his time."

Wolmit had four of his staff in the meeting to drill down to details. As explained to Angela, scrubbing the email account for additional clues they validated a majority of the file headers contained the parameter indicating a file insert or attachment was present.

"There were five file inserts to fifteen emails," Wolmit reported, letting one of his staff members take over.

"Knowing the owner attempted to permanently remove the email file with its document insert, we checked the temporary file locations, those that the OS encrypts but doesn't clean up. They contained a version of the insert, one that is cached in virtual memory for efficiency. We had to take..."

"Okay, what's the answer?" Angela requested looking at her watch. "Were you able to retrieve anything?

"Yes. Out of the five file inserts we retrieved three."

"What are they?"

"We don't know. I mean the data doesn't make any sense to us. You'll probably need someone from the lab to decipher them."

Angela nodded in agreement, "What else?"

"There's another software switch in the email," Wolmit replied. "That data bit initiates functionality in real time to manage adjacent text. The data bit is specifically..."

"You mean there's a list of the previous emails below the response?"

"Exactly. Once the bit is tripped, the application keeps track of the archive of related emails. We leveraged that construct to prove Worthington must have been replying to Franklin's email," Wolmit said excitedly. "We used it as a..."

"To find other email?"

"Yes! You're catching on fast!" From the email headers we retrieved those erased files as well."

"How many?"

"Four more."

"Doesn't sound like you got them all considering fifteen were sent."

"The odds of a one-to-one are unlikely. Figure on the industry average of one multiple response for every third email that doesn't get answered unless..."

"We've got five minutes. Anything else?" Angela prompted.

"Worthington was sharing some .gif files. You know, images."

"Jesus! You should have led with this!"

"Well. It was our last finding. We were able to restore those images. Data cleansing operations don't do a good job with images. They're scattered on the drive and get missed simply because there..."

The conference phone hummed indicating a caller.

"I get it. That's good. Don't take Colton down that rat hole."

Angela conferenced her boss, "Morning, Colton."

"Who's in the room?"

After names were given out, Colton kicked everyone out except his own lead and Wolmit, "Let's go. What have you got?"

The rendition was shorter than the dry run. The call ended with Angela assuming she was in good form.

"Nice work, Marty. Tell your guys thanks."

After Wolmit left the room, Colton surprised Angela with the order to take the rest of the week off.

"You nailed this. It's time to get some slack back in your schedule. On your return I want to run something by you. Ship those files before you leave. I sent you an email with the address."

"Okay, Colton. See you in a few days I guess."

A day later, Smith shared his findings on Franklin's financial status. Nothing excessive showed up.

"We sure don't pay these guys much considering what they're working on," Smith explained to Colton on the phone.

"Okay, so figure out another angle. Gates is out for a couple days. I need you to stay on top of Wolmit. I've got some time in the box with Millard. I'll see you two on Monday."

The weekend was nonstop for Franklin's team, fully engaged with critical mass outside of work. Their boss had been gone for thirty-six hours. Notes had been received and they had met in singular fashion with their colleague's mother and father in the mall. Tears streamed down their faces as they learned what might have happened to their only son. Their instincts meshed with the instructions requesting that they do nothing and allow the scientists to work silently and gain as much knowledge as possible before going public.

Colton and his team met again with Wolmit early Monday. The discussion had its moments. The ebb and flow of technical information conflicted with Colton's temperament.

"What's the point?" Colton interrupted getting perturbed.

"That Dr. Franklin stopped sending email."

"Not news."

"Exactly. But that didn't preclude other activity."

Colton glanced at Angela his eyes threatening. The look was "get this guy under control or I'm going to put a bullet in his head."

Angela took over, "Marty, we know that. The point."

"We literally received another email from another source yesterday! It appeared to be a reply based on an attachment. Here's a hard copy."

Pleased with his finding, Marty passed around the paper.

"Okay. Who was it?"

"Can't say for sure. It appears the sender was trying to avoid detection.

"We'll dig into this. What's the status on the picture inserts?" his host asked.

"Well, like I was saying last week, inserts were in the emails received from Worthington."

"Yes, we all remember," Angela prompted.

"Basically, there are versions of the file, like shadow images that are left to handshake with the original version. This insures the encrypted version still has integrity by matching checksum and other variances…"

"To the point, Marty?" Angela reinforced.

"We just kept testing the shadows with reverse encryption until we got one."

Everyone stared at the image Wolmit projected to the large screen.

"It's a blurred picture of four pieces of stone or rocks with hieroglyphics."

"Are you sure it's from Worthington and not some other random garbage?" Colton quizzed.

"Positive. And it's not digital, so we're guessing a scanned image or a picture taken with analog."

After Wolmit left the room, Colton's staff brainstormed and Angela summed up the consensus, "We know Franklin shared some portion of his project with Worthington and then there's this other source thanking him in the recent reply with Franklin's work attached. It's likely he needed Franklin to do calculations he shared and they're using them for something. The artifacts from Worthington might be related to the calculations."

Jason played devil's advocate, "Maybe they're not related, exactly. Franklin is not taking money so this is part of their discourse. The background check I ran showed these guys were real cozy in school. So maybe they were just catching up?"

Colton became disgruntled, "We're just finding out about this tea party now?"

"Franklin came from NETL so he passed the security checks when he got promoted," Smith explained.

"So he waltzes in to NEADE and starts sending love notes to his professor. We don't have a clue until our security gets a wake up call. Unbelievable!"

Colton paused. Another set of orders were forthcoming, "Worthington's on the verge of something and needs calculations to finish it. He's tight with the community from what I hear. Okay, Angela, you stay."

Angela shot a glimpse to Jason as he was packing up his laptop wondering what was going on. Waiting for the door to shut, Colton rubbed his face looking tired but and addressed Angela.

"I know you think Ken Millard is a flake, but I have to go to him with this one."

Angela interlaced her index and middle fingers, "Worthington and Millard are like this?"

"Not yet, but they will be. Worthington is still sending to Franklin so he's not spooked. Millard is the only professional that can get his nose in the door. He needs to pull his fucking head out of his ass. I can entice him to do this."

"Send one of the other capable scientists."

"We can't trust just anyone. I'll control Millard. You and Jason did your share of solid work."

It was a blunt signal to let go. Angela was frustrated handing this off.

"Has Millard done anything right? Look at what his own people say about him!"

"I only need him to open the door. He knows nothing of the backdrop. We'll reel it in."

Colton wasn't honest with the timing of the re-assignments. During Angela's absence, Millard and Colton met right after it was discovered Worthington was involved. It was critical enough to force Colton to travel to Millard's city meeting him in a hotel suite.

Colton was more forceful with Kenneth, pitching the new role to snag the university professor, "You've got nothing new here to worry about. He's a potential client that does a bunch of fundraisers and never leaves town, so he's any easy mark. You represent NETL. You make an appointment and fill him in on our services. My sources say he might be interested in using our lab."

"I'm going to offer him time in the lab?"

"Yes. And access to our scientists. But he has to jump through a few hoops to get there."

"Like what?"

"Same drill as the road-shows. He's got to have some research that we're interested in. You need to find out what that is."

"Find out? He's not going to just hand it to me!" Kenneth presumed.

"It doesn't matter. I need it now. *You* have to find it. Who knows there might be some reward there Ken."

Kenneth hoped Colton saw the usual contempt of his expression. By the time the meeting ended he invented a reason for declining to dine with his boss. The Lexipro medication was making him drowsy, but he was ecstatic as he got in his car to return home.

I can't fucking believe it.

Kenneth managed a smile on his face while lighting up a cigarette. *I needed a break and Colton hands me one!*

It was late evening and Kenneth was still thinking about the connection he needed to make with Worthington, "Finally! Someone out of Colton's reach. He must really have something of value. We can strike a deal once I tell Worthington who and what Colton really is."

His wine glass empty, Kenneth uncorked another bottle to continue his celebratory mood. With a buzz and numbness he thought of a strategy to approach Worthington. It had to be on an absolute professional level but he needed to transition it carefully. *When Worthington agrees to partner, that will give Colton his little tidbit! Then I can convince him I need help to expose NETL.*

Another long sip lent conviction to his plans to expose Colton. *I need this. I am almost home free.*

Kenneth was feeling at the top of his game. *Who's going to look like shit now?*

Falling back on the couch, Kenneth's dizziness progressed into a deep sleep with the quixotic mixture of drugs and alcohol.

The meeting suited Colton's purpose as he sat and drank at the bar, glad Millard wasn't there. He didn't regret giving a final assignment to his agent, having enough justification for recalibrating Millard's value to NEADE. The lengthy trace on his protégé turned up salient clues proving his fragmented loyalty. A share of his payments was spent to prop up his ailing business and promote his business partners. Millard was taking prescription medicines for anxiety and pain relief. He was increasingly sloppy at the remaining calendared events. Colton had quit attending. The latest find bugged Colton the most. *What did he learn from contacting the NEADE researchers?*

Colton always knew he couldn't absolutely trust Millard. It became a matter of how much was left to manipulate.

Kenneth wanted to be at the top of his game the next day, but it was physically impossible. With dry heaves, dehydration was worse because water wouldn't stay down. Cold compresses to the forehead didn't help the dizziness and his hands were still trembling. If sleep could bring him back to normal that's what he would do and postpone the arrangement of a first meeting with Worthington. The celebration may have been premature, but he could do this. Millard put an ice pack on his forehead.

How do I convince him that my...the world is falling apart?

It took three days for Dr. Kenneth Millard to get himself moving forward. Other personal business had been delayed. His answering machine was full. And his plan spawned from the bottle didn't seem as lucid.

The first pass at Worthington's admin failed to get a meeting scheduled. Even a phone conversation was denied. Kenneth suspected a possible check on his credentials worked against him. Pacing his floor, Kenneth reworked his approach in a manic state. The ashtray was almost full. His open prescription bottles were on the counter. He was sweating.

Unwilling to fly to Houston without an appointment, Kenneth hastily contacted GTS and asked to speak to Dave or Bryan. In a conference call he pleaded with them to contact Worthington on his behalf. The shock of them balking at the request built quickly to a stronger form of defiance. It escalated when Kenneth made executive demands, and then learned his own team didn't want him back at GTS given his failing creditability. Their ultimatum was they would leave the firm forming their own start-up, leveraging from the firm's assets, including its eroding client base. Kenneth would be left with huge financial exposure.

After a series of agonizing callbacks, a negotiated compromise guaranteed Kenneth's permanent departure from GTS. They would have a contract drawn up and mailed.

As Dave put it, "a good intersection for all of us."

Late in the evening the phone rang. Kenneth's eyes welled up, his emotions raw. Shaking, he answered. "We got you an appointment for next Thursday at two p.m. You should be getting the papers tomorrow by UPS."

"Uh. Yes. Well, Thank, uh…"

The call ended abruptly.

Distraught, Kenneth walked to his bedroom and lay on his bed needing recovery time.

DARON Lab.

NEADE was getting pressured from all sides. After the security breach by the NEADE scientist, routine entry and exit became more rigid. Employees felt the increased oppression and adjusted to yet another wave of reactive control. Franklin's men became more committed to their purpose and the boundary of their personal space narrowed. Navin stopped saying "good morning" to everyone on his floor. He and his "brothers" stopped making direct eye contact with anyone, reserving it for their own group.

Nobody on the team was motivated to extend themselves, to think out of the box, or apply ingenuity. They didn't feel empowered to achieve. Even though their workload was more crucial to NEADE, they treated it as trivial.

Shepard was unprepared to take over a team that was unconditionally loyal to a high achiever. Signaling that they could be reassigned to the NETL lab, the manager failed to motivate them with a disincentive.

The threat lost intensity when the manager ended the meeting trying to reconcile, "Okay, you know and I know no one else can do this. We're counting on you to finish. It's your duty to do so."

Their grass root efforts outside of NEADE was consuming their real passion, even though success was nothing measurable. The idea of going to the police kept surfacing but they agreed there were too many unknown risks. The group maintained an open prayer to their God of energy, Shati and God of power, Ganesha, he who removes obstacles. Franklin had not been seen or heard from for thirty-seven days.

U.S. Naval Station, Guantanamo Bay.

Mirroring his brothers, the scientist prisoner restricted his actions in kind, lowering his head when spoken to, avoided direct eye contact, and shortened his answers to "yes" or "no." Franklin instinctively repelled the dialogue with an individual who suddenly became his cellmate. Like a fictitious movie character, the young migrant had a sad tale, was too friendly, and wanted to share information. All too obvious for Franklin. Once the young fellow was removed, Franklin was relocated to an isolation cell with a steel door vented at the bottom. The form of incarceration was copied for all the foreign militants. Built on forty-five square miles, the facility was hosted by eighty-five hundred active duty personnel whom continued to enjoy their work, school their children, visit their credit union, and play golf, having mandated deference to the activities within the prison.

Franklin was confined to his cell except for meals. A light over his bed automatically dimmed at his guess of around midnight. To his surprise, paper and pencil were provided and but taken away by evening. This insignificant offering became his tools to sharpen his intellect.

His daily writings were an exercise in accuracy as the prisoner continued to drill on equations over and over, the same ones taught to his men. Habitually, Franklin sketched the boundaries of the mid-ocean reefs, speculating where physical impacts would take place. The formulas were a matrix of predictive attributes related to computations of seismic force. With a hybrid binomial distribution with associated probabilities to negate random factors, the scientist improved his theory. With study and practice he equated the strength of each attribute with wave velocity and impedance computations. Exercising the matrix every day, over and over, a domino cause-effect series of unforeseen events was no longer obscure. After his self proclaimed study time, when paper and pencils were collected, no one interrogated him about the scribbles that blackened out numbers and symbols.

At lunch one day, Colton appeared unannounced and sat down across from his prisoner. The image of Colton leaning into him, disparaging his U.S. citizenship hadn't faded.

Franklin ignored Colton the entire time, except at the moment he was told Worthington was going to be approached, "Forty-two days, seven hours ago, I accused you of sending classified information to the public, namely Dr. Bud Worthington. That accusation stands. Now that you've had some time to yourself, why don't tell me what you and Worthington are up to?"

Franklin took a bite of his sandwich, his eyes never looking up from his plate, "We're going to pull Worthington in and interrogate him. It won't look good for his career, although you could influence that either way."

Franklin raised his head and stared through Colton, "He is a distinguished professor at Rice University serving as the adjunct professor at the Weiss School of Natural Sciences. He has mentored more than seven thousand students in his career, receiving the highest of accolades from his peers. You may be able to discredit my professional career, but never his."

Another ten minutes of threats from Colton did not pry another response from Franklin. Led back to his cell, he hoped Colton was infuriated, going home empty handed. He thought of the consequences of his silence, if torture was a conceivable path to break his resistance. After the lock bolt triggered behind him, Franklin took his pencil and knelt, pinning himself under the stainless steel sink. The manufacture label was now a coded calendar. The prisoner prided himself that he was only three days off in his calculation compared to the number of days Colton had provided.

Office of Dr. Bud Worthington.

Worthington was weary of Dr. Kenneth Millard. The sudden interest and the method by which the meeting was scheduled had prompted a defensive strategy. Worthington instructed Margaret to turn down the first attempt from Millard, learning he was from a government agency, and then realized it was the same employer as Franklin. The second attempt to schedule a meeting came from strangers highly qualified in the profession of geology. Worthington rationalized he should confront Millard and gauge the potential risks on his own. He was relieved Jude was off campus.

"I'd rather have the enemy in front where I can see them," Worthington mused as he got his late afternoon cup of tea, biding time. He looked up at his bookshelves when informed his guest had arrived.

After a polite handshake, Kenneth sat down as Worthington returned to his position behind his desk, "What brings you to my office, Dr. Millard?"

"Dr. Worthington, you and your research were represented on a number of documents from our office and out of respect for your position in the academic community I wanted to meet you in person."

Kenneth persevered to explain his rationale for contacting a few of the venerable contributors to the study of plate motion, observing that Dr. Worthington had been identified as such. He made a tenuous connection to the value of his host's research.

After they moved to the smaller table, Kenneth launched a presentation from his laptop, carefully watching Worthington's response when the falsified data was discussed, "I know some of these figures seem abnormal. I can assure you NETL is working day and night to correct these data anomalies."

Finishing a review of NETL's service portfolio Kenneth placed a marketing brochure in Worthington's hands, "Can I answer any questions or concerns? Did anything appeal to you?"

"Not specifically. Although I'm always interested in why the government is taking a particular stance in science, especially in the topics you presented. I'm not versed in the services that you claim to be of utmost importance to me. Possibly there are other candidates that better suit your needs."

"Well, sir, the U.S. Government has vested interests in matters that have potential impact upon the public. We want to ensure our funding and other resources are applied to the right matters at the right time. You are no doubt aware of the current studies concerning tectonics and some of the advance categorization taking place to formulate government policy. Surely that addresses some of your areas of competence."

"Yes, I suppose so. I'm keenly aware of these activities but question the intentions."

"I share those same concerns."

Kenneth sensed he could guide the conversation towards his own motives, "We're almost out of time. I'd like to ask you to share dinner with me. Possibly we can explore the opportunity for additional funding for you and the university. There are other details that should hold your interest as well."

"I'm terribly sorry, but I have other plans. Feel free to leave that information or mail it to me and I'll make time to review it."

"Our or rather my offer is complex in some ways and it's something I generally review in person, not practical for a mailer," Kenneth replied with small laughter. "Just the same, I'll be in town for another couple days. Can I schedule another short session with you and talk again?"

Worthington balked as a ruse to force an impasse, "I'll check my schedule and have Margaret call you this evening. That's the best I can do."

"Okay, thank you very much for your time."

Millard left his card and Worthington graciously nodded, guiding him to the outer office. Closing the door he browsed the glossy brochures, "Data anomalies indeed! The man is hiding something else besides his own inventions. We'll have to see what is being offered up tomorrow."

He glanced up at his bookshelves feeling the meeting was a harbinger, making his research even more prodigious.

Worthington opened the door again, "Cancel my nine tomorrow morning and put Dr. Kenneth Millard there for thirty minutes. Don't book an adjacent meeting. I'll need a break afterwards."

"Okay, Dr. Worthington. I'll call and let him know."

"Delay the call until you leave this evening."

Kenneth left campus with some apprehension, but as he sat down for dinner, a recollection of their discussion raised his self-assurance. *Dr. Worthington seemed amenable underneath his obvious defense,* Kenneth thought. *I can explain how I started with NETL, and tell him how my doubts grew.*

Kenneth cautioned himself as he took another large sip of wine. *It's okay to celebrate, a little.*

The gesture of lifting his glass as a salute to his partial victory was a thin veneer as his cell chimed in his vest pocket. Taking it out, he blindly answered presuming Worthington was calling. It was Willis Colton's number that appeared on the display. The failed routine to let the call roll to voice mail proved costly. *Shit! But I've got nothing to hide.*

"Yes," Kenneth answered, trying to sound positive.

"Did you meet with Worthington?"

"It went well. I'll see him tomorrow."

"We're you able to get him set up in the lab so we can exchange information?"

"Eh, no firm commitment yet. That's what I'll work on tomorrow."

"You need to bring me something tangible out of the meeting."

Kenneth's mood sunk, "What?"

"I want research from Worthington in my hands. We talked about this before."

"Actually, you said you wanted to know if it existed, not have it in hand."

"Same thing," Colton stated, impervious to Kenneth's fussiness. "Ken, I can come down there and run the meeting if you can't do it."

Kenneth threw his head back, "Why do I need to actually take something from him? He may not trust me. In fact, I know he doesn't trust me or the government. He said so."

"That's why I hired you. Nail this Ken and you're home free. We can't keep hanging our dicks out."

Kenneth cupped his hand over the cell, noticing people responding to his raised voice and mannerisms, "You know what? You have no fucking clue! I'll do what I can."

He snapped down the lid to his cell, feeling the acid in his stomach. Another emotional episode was building. Opening the vial from his vest pocket, Kenneth picked through his pills. His doctor told him to medicate ahead of mood spikes. The waiter returned with water, noticing his guest was upset.

"That won't do. Bring me another glass of wine."

That evening, Kenneth's greatest fear was Colton's threat of showing up. Inebriated, he got back to his hotel and fumbled with voicemail, noticing his phone lamp was lit. He had turned off his cell when he hung up on Colton.

"Shit, its Mr. Pesky calling back to put me in jail," he chuckled as he fell back, the bed catching his full weight. He managed to retrieve the voicemail learning Worthington had booked him for nine a.m.

"Damn it!" The scientist pulled out his prescriptions counting on them to get him through the next eleven hours.

"Can I get you some tea, Dr. Millard? Did you not sleep well?"

"Ah, no thank you, um, sir," Kenneth replied, clearing his raspy voice. "I had a difficult night, you know traveling and...," clearing his throat again, "...sounds."

In comparison to the first meeting, Kenneth looked haggard with dark circles under his bloodshot eyes. His hair wasn't completely combed and his clothes were the same ones he wore the day before.

"Basically, Dr. Worthington, I need your help."

"Sir?"

"I mean to say that, as an employee of NETL, I found out they are reporting information that's not entirely true. My real motive for contacting you was to ask for your assistance."

"In what way?'

"Well, in two ways really. First, I'm at risk explaining this and as I said...," Kenneth tried to gather his thoughts and fumbled. "I need any information you have, that or I mean related to what I presented. I could. No. I mean I would represent your work at NETL to set the public record straight.

"And the other?"

"The other is...," Kenneth took a breath, but started coughing. "...the other is I need *you* to expose them."

"You'll understand if I'm confused."

"Certainly! You have a right to be confused," Kenneth responded with empathy. "I'm confused myself. I don't sleep...sleep well because of it."

"You have to agree that your proposal, in light of your circumstances is suspect."

"It is? I mean it shouldn't be seen that way. My own objective was to come to you knowing you may be able to help."

"Is there someone that you can say sponsors your effort here?"

"There's really no one. But I'm under extreme pressure to provide you services from our lab!"

"Why?"

"So you can be influenced to start sharing information."

"What information?"

"I don't know. They think you have something."

The visitor's body language became rigid and he began to perspire. Worthington believed his intuition was solid after all. He was glad for his efforts to counsel Jude months ago about suspicious attention of others.

"Who are you referring to?" asked the professor.

"I've got a boss that expects me to deliver something tangible to him."

"If you are not able to secure it, are you in danger?"

"Uh, I'm not sure. But that's not the point. If *we* work together, this whole organization can be exposed," Kenneth pleaded, clearing his voice.

"Dr. Millard, on the basis of the information you've supplied me, I could not professionally commit any attention to this matter under these circumstances. I'm not even positive about *your* credentials."

"Look at me!" Kenneth demanded, holding out his trembling hands. "I'm laying it out for you. I know I sound desperate. I...I actually am. I had a consulting business called Geo Terra Sciences. You may have heard of it. It's a viable geosciences consulting firm. It's the only thing I have left, that is, left of my profession."

"It's fair to say your contemporaries don't speak highly of you."

Kenneth felt cornered and took a deep breath, "Yes, I know they called. I asked them to. They have their reasons, but we did part ways."

Worthington leaned back in his chair. At arms' length this scenario was exactly the one he always believed would occur. It was like looking into the future and getting a solid glimpse of fate should he mistake a foe for a friend.

"You admit you are currently employed by NETL."

"Yes, sir."

"Do you know of a Dr. Franklin?"

Kenneth thought for a moment, "Who is he? What's his connection?"

"He works at the lab at NETL."

"I know a lot of folks there and have worked directly with the lab. I...I've toured the lab and met the scientists. I can't recall the name. Does that matter?"

"Unfortunately, to some degree it does."

"Wh...Why?"

"It's germane to how we proceed. But we're out of time today. I think the best path—"

"Wait...! Can you give me something that would suffice to say you're interested in the lab? I need something today."

"As I was saying, I think the best path is for us to go back to our constituents. I'll contact some independent sources and proceed from there."

"Dr. Worthington, I don't have that kind of time to...ah...to waste. With all due respect, I *need* you to help expose these people. We don't really have much time. They're changing the truth! You must know it could become a matter of survival."

Kenneth sunk down in his chair. Worthington knew all too well what Millard was indicating. But this was not a man he could trust.

"I'm really sorry for your plight, young man. I will do some thinking on this. I know you are in a precarious position, but I will have to delay. I'm really sorry. You are troubled and agitated. Some rest should—"

"I can't fucking sleep! Don't you get it?" Kenneth stood up aggravated, raising his voice. "Look at me. They've done this to me. I...I can't lie anymore. I've lost everything!"

Worthington backed away as Margaret opened the door, "Is everything okay, Dr. Worthington?"

"Yes, I hope so. Dr. Millard was just leaving."

Everything was out in the open. Worthington became conscious of a broader horizon that exposed an actual threat to his research. He thought carefully about how to spread out his risk. Millard failed, leaving himself vulnerable. With consequences, his departure was watched and a call was made.

"Where is that pathetic son of a bitch now?"

The answer given wasn't complicated.

"No, don't bother picking him up. He's off our books."

Colton made another call to Angela. There was no humility expressed, just more marching orders.

"I'll tap into it and get status. Then what?"

"Close him down."

She was more than happy to pull the pin.

Day 260.
Midland, Texas.

BEFORE THEIR GUEST'S arrival, the Erls prepared the spare bedroom and fixed the eyesores that Doug "needed to get done anyway." Their chores behind them, the family stood in the lobby of Midland International waiting for Jen Rawlins to show up.

"Hey, there she is!" Doug broadcasted, getting his family's attention.

Kate set down her paperback as Connor ran over from the pinball machines. Jen spotted them and quickened her step to greet them with hugs.

The group piled in the car and had small chat all the way back to the house.

"Ya, she's doing okay," Jen confirmed. "My mom is doing fine. She even helped out with the local campaign this year. Her neighbor's son was running for councilman. That's helped her stay busy and be in the thick of things."

While Connor played Nintendo, the parents managed to pry into Jen's love life. She had broken off her last relationship and it was way behind her.

"Men can be such babies," she protested, quick to exclude present company. "I've got so much I want to do and sometimes I'm like all bound up with these relationships. I'm not ready to settle."

"What about Peter? Is he still on your list of potential bachelors?" Doug tested.

He had met him and the group when they came to visit Jen at Apache, "Your college friends seemed pretty bright and outgoing."

"Funny you should ask. I was considering going on spring break with them. We used that as a time to all get back together," she explained. "I got an email that they were headed to Guadalupe National Park. It was tempting, but I had project deadlines."

As passengers stared out at the passing landscape, moments passed without conversation.

"Anyway, Peter and I stay in touch. A month ago, he was at the same convention I was. We didn't get a chance to connect. He's always traveling. I'm always traveling. Eventually one of us calls to check up on the other."

Doug turned on the two lane road off the state highway, bringing them close to home, "I just remember some of that group. Was it Karl?" Doug asked. "He was an interesting guy."

"Karl is that and a bit more. He kind of goes off the deep end. We used to kid him all the time."

As they settled in that evening, Kate decided to make some tea sending Jen and Doug out on the porch.

"I miss these evenings out here," Jen said dreamily. "I sit on my balcony just staring out at the stars."

"Say, when are we going to see some of the boys?" Kate asked, returning with beverages. "What did you figure out with those old coots, Doug?"

"We're going to meet some of them down at Saddles. It gets us outta the house one night. They were sure shocked to hear Miss Rawlins was back in town."

"That's alright by me," Jen agreed. "It will be nice to see Chet, Randy, and Charlie again. Is Tracy still around?"

"Naw. Feels like they let him go ages back. He couldn't man a paper bag and a fly swatter at the same time."

Doug grabbed her knee, showing his brand of affection for her, "We sure realized that's when we missed you. It's sure changed since you left. Paperwork was all messed up for a while."

"You two stay put. I'm going to go tuck in our little guy," Kate interrupted.

Doug looked up in the sky for a bit and took a breath, "All sorts of problems cropped up over time. We've got some agency crawling all over us for data on a number of drill outs. I've had to hire a feller to dig back a year or so to get more info for them."

"Who's that? Is it mandatory for everybody?"

"Not sure. The teams have been shifted around a bit, but I think every crew has the same requirements. It started right after they fired Tracy. There was a rumor going around that he had uncovered something and you were being contacted. I never paid any attention to it...just bullshit when you get down to it."

"Nobody ever called me. I thought we did pretty good out there trying to keep things by the book."

"I'll tell you, Jen, the bosses never see the detail we have to wade through."

"Well, I realized that when I was going back to them with results and they started to question the accuracy. That's what got me nervous in the first place. I decided to start looking for another job."

"You and me both," Doug agreed. "I can't tell you how many times I've been ready to take retirement, knowing I can't afford to."

"I'll end up sticking it out with Apache. It's a paycheck at the end of the day. I can't kick that it's been a decent career."

"Were you trying to cut loose from them? I took you for a company man. I mean you always talked about your dad and grandfather."

"It's still part of me...DNA. Isn't that what they call it? But, on the whole, it's going downhill pretty fast since last year with all the drilling failures."

"If I'd known, I would have been trying to get you on with me. They've got good benefits and everything. There's some room there for..."

Doug sensed welfare, "I'm not looking for a handout. I can't compete with the younger crowd, and I don't want to move the family."

"No, that wouldn't happen. I'm talking about consulting! You could do it from your home and still be out in the field. *Really*, let's explore this. It might work out!"

He knew from Jen's enthusiasm that if she got hold of something it would be tough to stop her, "Hmmm. Let me sleep on it. I'll keep an open mind," he promised. "How about we turn in?"

"You go ahead. I want to enjoy the stars a little more. Thanks for letting me stay with you and Kate. It's great to see ya."

"Same here, kiddo. Night."

"It's good to have her company, isn't it?" Kate said sleepily as Doug slipped in beside her.

"Yep. I'll pat you on the back tomorrow."

With her arm on his waist, their orchestrated movements culminated with Kate snuggling her mate from the back. He fell asleep wondering how much of Kilgore would be flooding back.

Kilgore Drill Site, Texas.

It was a patient readied for surgery. Substantial bracing was embedded into the earth, securing the foundation of the drilling rig to the ground. Ignoring the variety of birds sailing in and over the site during the late afternoon, overflow ballasts were locked in place and inflated to specific pressures. Receiving hoses and other pressure tubing was laid and cabled into parallel bundles. Noise was coming from the engines, air guns, and commanding voices directing the unloading of site supplies.

By nightfall, Kilgore had electricity flowing supplied by trailer generators. The derrick was airborne and final connections secured to masting cables that streamed from the corners to support the erected metal structure rising above the landscape. The decking was anchored and the rest of the drill rotating equipment was dropped into place. Like a circus moved to town, it was ready to receive customers. Apache had bet big on Shafter Lake, deciding to bring in permanent infrastructure.

Groaning, Doug shifted in his bed. His dream vision blurred what he saw—somebody approaching. Conjured by his snoring, the generator noise temporarily halted when Kate nudged him gently.

The next morning, Doug and Jen were up early getting the horses prepped to take them out. While Doug instructed her, they still talked about work on and off when the mood hit them.

"That's what it seems like sometimes...a circus," Doug's voice drifted off.

He came back around the horse and cinched up the billet strap. Chimney moved her rear feet, backing Jen against the frame of the stall.

"Whoa, girl," Doug said in a low voice to the horse and motioned to his guest, "Come on over here and take the halter."

She slowly walked around and put her hand inside the halter strap and stroked Chimney's nose, cooing her, "That's it, girl, that's it."

"Blow in her nose a little to give her your scent and then you can bring her out gently to the fence and tie her off."

Doug watched as Jen performed the instructions then he followed along side with his horse, "She'll settle when she figures out Smoky is going. If the execs paid as much attention as this horse has, we'd be in a different spot right now."

"Doug, it was already coming down wrong before I left," Jen revealed.

The two rode down the lane and across the highway. There was a three mile right-of-way towards the electrical towers. Within constant view were the man-made boundaries of fence, road, pipe, and suspended cable. Nothing surrounding the two riders was unclaimed or untouched.

Jen waited until Doug had caught up after shutting a cattle gate, "Remember when I told you I went to Steve Donald to close out some of the legal issues on Kilgore and I said it might shut the project down?"

"I do," Doug said flatly.

"Well, it wasn't that at all. I lied. I had been propositioned a couple times to modify the EIA-23. It would have required other supporting documentation to be changed."

"What idiot proposed that idea?"

"It started with somebody in Finance. And they said someone in the reserves business unit asked them. It turned out to be Tracy."

"Tracy? He wouldn't have the authority! Where did he come from anyway?" Doug asked

"I don't know, but there was constant pressure to fix the records so I decided to start looking for other work."

"Legal wasn't called in were they?"

"No. Legal was like confused! After I refused to do it, I wasn't going to wait around."

"I figured you had your reasons. You know you could have counted on me."

The horses half-trotted up the road for about a mile. The gusty wind coming out of the west made Jen's cheeks pink from the wind chill. Coming to another gate, Doug positioned his horse to flip the plate on the walk-thru gate and kicked it open with his foot.

"Here, take this. It's pretty chilly on the eyeballs."

Doug held out a neatly folded bandana for Jen. As she wiped her eyes, Doug realized they were wet from tears, "Hey, it's okay. I understand. You were in a tight spot and everything. You couldn't take a chance."

"No...it's not that I couldn't take a chance. I didn't allow myself to take the chance and let anybody in. You probably would have been able to settle me down and figure it out."

Jen teared up again, "Look at me. Some blubbering baby. I needed to let you know. You were really great, Doug, and I felt like I could pay you back when you hinted you were ready for a change."

"I know opportunities don't show up every day. But it's a bit of a chore figuring out the choices. I'm just about there with these guys though."

Taking a big breath, Jen gained her composure. The horses meandered up the wider part of the road that had been cut into a hill, giving the riders a wider perspective of the watershed. Major drainage points with shallow inclines came together, and beyond the airborne haze, laid the man-made boundaries where protected land mass met leased property. Evidence of native flowers and the brilliance of crimson sage stopped, and cultivated soil, over-grazing, and permanence of man's existence started.

"Really, Doug, I think there's something there for you. Maybe even for a couple of the guys, but it's going to have a short window on it."

"These days I'm beginning to believe everything does."

After they ran the horses a bit more, the two riders turned around as the sun moved behind the cirrus clouds. In flight, small flocks of Chestnut-collared Longspur surrounded them, following the fly hatch. Their warbles were faint and close at the same time. From a distance, horses and riders could see the glimmer of the Erls stable light that attracted June bugs and millers. As the hoofs clapped down the lane, crickets chirped.

Dismounting, Doug quickly released the front and rear saddle rigging, and then had Jen repeat the process. After he stored the tack, each horse was walked to their stable and the feed bags were filled and hung.

"I need to do this more often. It's surprising how you lock up after sitting tight in one position," Jen exclaimed. "Do you think we can go out again? But I'd hate to put Connor out."

"We can make time. He may think he wants to go but he'll have other things going on."

"He sure has grown up. It's pretty amazing to have kids isn't it?"

Placing his arm around Jen, Doug led her out towards the house, "It sure is. Wouldn't miss it for the world. Now *he* may not think it's so great when I tell him he has to brush out these fellers."

Both laughing they came through the porch door. Kate had already heated up chili. And to their surprise, Randy was sitting at the table.

"Well I'll be," Jen shouted.

Randy stood stepping around the chair grabbing Jen, "¿Señorita, cómo has estado? Nos preguntábamos si volverías por lo menos a ver el destino en que nos dejaste." [52]

In a sultry voice, Jen cooed back. "I've been fine. Sí señor, he vuelto a salvarlos, o si nada más, a restaurarles el orgullo." [53]

"I called Randy to say the party was on at Saddles and he just showed up!" Kate declared laughing.

Jen took Randy's straw cowboy hat lying on the table and put it on her head plopping herself down in a chair.

Filling the rest of the evening, Jen brought everyone up to speed on her latest field assignments and the little she could share about the upcoming technology in bits and drilling fluid. The men tried to pry anything loose that would give them an edge.

Going to bed that night Kate shared her impressions about Jen, "That girl sure is smart as a whip. She'd be quite a catch for some young man."

Putting down his hunting magazine, Doug stretched out on the bed, "But he better be her equal. It wouldn't be a big leap for her to make someone look stupid."

Jen's sleep was full, but she woke early out of habit. She quietly dressed and visited the barn to check on the animals, finding Connor working, dressed in pajamas with his boots on.

"Hey. What are you doing up so early?"

With a pair of sleepy eyes, his face was a mixture of shock and embarrassment, "I always get up early to feed the horses and stuff. You surprised me!"

Jen sensed that she was in his territory, "I was going to give your horse some company. I couldn't sleep any longer. Can I help you get them fed?"

"Uh, sure if you want."

"Tell me where you want me and what I should do."

As they made their way through the process of filling the feed bags, Connor became more comfortable with his temporary helper.

"It's weird. I don't usually see anybody out here when I'm doing this."

"Even when the weather gets bad or in the winter?"

---

[52] "Miss, how have you been? We've all wondered if you were ever coming back at least to see what fate you left us in."

[53] "Yes kind sir, I have come back to save you, or at the very least restore your pride."

"Nope. Dad used to check on me, but I guess he thinks I've learned it. Kinda like school."

"What do you mean?"

"Seems like I get a lot of help when I can't figure out math. Then after I do everybody quits bugging me."

"You know, Connor, that happens to me...and your dad. Matter of fact, that's how people are. Everyone lends a hand to help you out and sometimes it seems like a hassle. But then after you figure out how to do it they move on to the next person. You know the great thing is, eventually you'll be helping other people out."

Connor cocked his head, "I don't think I'm there yet."

"Hey, actually you are...you're teaching me!"

He got a grin on his face.

"Chimney's lucky to have you. And I'm lucky to have you, your mom, and dad as friends. Maybe we'll get a chance to team up again."

"I guess so."

Finishing the barn chores the two walked back to the house having figured out both knew chess, and decided on a match after breakfast. Connor was thinking that his Saturday was turning out better than expected.

Doug's dreams of Kilgore kept repeating, covering a lot of ground in a short time and were vivid in detail. He had dreamt the abstract parts again. The drilling activities had become a hodgepodge of random images on a backdrop of mountains and blue sky. Witnessing the ecology being destroyed, with a sense of doom for his involvement, his arms became heavy, useless when he reached out. The drill shaft was modulating into the earth, plunging viciously out of control with the cables snapping and whipping the ground. Dust was choking his men. The hum of the motors increased and subsided. It all broke down, but on higher ground there were men laughing playing pool. Jen suddenly appeared near the drill. She was running with Chimney and Smoky. She tied the horses to a fence and disappeared into Saddles. His leg throbbed and he jerked forward. Suddenly awake, he could hear the hairdryer in his bathroom. Kate had already showered.

"Morning you two," Jen yelled standing at the base of the stairway. "We've got breakfast goin' down here. Ya better hurry up before Connor and I eat it all."

Eventually everyone piled into the kitchen and had what Connor called, mountain man burritos—a concoction of eggs, hash browns, chunks of bacon and pork sausage wrapped in a warm tortilla.

"Jen and I are going to town for groceries and other girl errands," Kate announced. "While we're gone you men get your chores done. We don't want to be late this evening to supper over at Saddles."

"Hey, do I get to go?" Connor begged to be part of the crowd.

"Sorry bud. Your mom and I are going with Jen. You're staying over at Tim's house."

"Aw, geez, Dad, why can't I go. Jen said—"

Kate interrupted, "Not this time. We don't want you hanging out in a bar all night. You would be bored right off the bat."

"No I wouldn't. I'd be doing stuff with Jen."

Doug was surprised hearing that from Connor, "She'll be here a couple more days. Let's get out to the barn and get the hay stacked near the stalls."

Knowing Connor couldn't push anymore, Jen winked at him and before she left, they set their plans for the next day.

As Jen and Kate traveled down the highway, the conversation wandered settling on the males in their lives.

"I was surprised Connor finally warmed up to me."

"He's at that awkward age now. Not sure about girls, but still wants to like his mom."

"I envy that. I always wonder how different my life would be if my dad were living right now."

"That had to be the hardest thing for a young girl," Kate empathized. "You and your mother had to be closer than ever to get through it."

"We were. It seemed like she got stricter. I guess there was more to worry about for one parent."

"I'll bet that's so. In a sense she probably felt if one little thing slipped it would be impossible to fix. Your mom's got to be proud of you."

"She is. I think she's waiting for me to move forward and have a family. It's not there for me. At least not that I can see."

"You never know dear. It sneaks up on you. I felt like that at your age. Then Doug showed up."

She pulled the car into the strip mall parking lot.

"It goes so fast you don't bother to remember all the time without them."

Kate paused a moment looking at Jen, "Whoever it is he'll come through soon enough. Let's go get *our* things done before the groceries."

That evening, Jen stood in the doorway of Double Saddle with the Erls, pausing to remember. She could see a couple of her old work mates in the dim hazy light. The thick vitality of the place hadn't changed at all with all the odors and sounds. The jukebox was blinking and the hanging lamps over the pool tables were swinging, hit by cue sticks. The waitresses moved around the maze of old tables and booths with folks leaning on chairs or against the walls.

"Hey, Jen!" Mindy yelled coming towards her. "Well, my gosh, girl, look at you! How have you been?"

Mindy handed Doug her loaded tray and put her arms around Jen, "The boys said you were in town. They didn't say nothin' else! It's great to see you!"

"You too! You're still going to beauty school?"

The waitress ignored Doug hinting to take the tray and hugged Kate, "Yep I am. Going to get outta this hell hole in another five months."

"That's super!"

"Okay, mister. Hand that back to me before they put you to work. Get over there and see the boys. Clare's gonna take care of the bunch. See ya here and there."

The arrivals sifted through the patrons to reach old friends.

How could I ever forget this place, Jen thought to herself. *Just like normal.*

The whole group made a showing. The crew leaders and their wives, Randy, Chet, Charlie, Charlie's boy Chuck, and some of the other guys that worked the oil. When everybody got situated, the menu of beer and food merged with men conversation of oil, water, or equipment. The women shared the changes in their families, election year politics, and recipes.

Saddles started to clear out a little past nine with younger folks leaving for other hangouts and older folks getting back to their families. Kate decided to leave, telling Jen. "I'm going to take off. The boys can give you and Doug a ride home. There's not too many evenings I can lie in a tub and enjoy a book."

"Sure. We won't be too much later. Thanks for the day!"

Kate leaned over Doug from behind giving him a kiss and whispered in his ear. He smiled as she gave her goodnights to the group.

When the waitress left with another drink order Charlie got around to saying what was on his mind, "We kinda all thought Apache had given ya the boot an' all. Ya know, makin' it tough to get back on your feet."

Jen decided to let them in on why she left so suddenly, "I never really told anybody, but I didn't get fired. I bailed because of a legal issue. I felt bad leaving you guys but I couldn't take the chance."

"If that don't beat all! Those dumbass suits don't know how to protect their good folks when it comes down to it," accused Chet.

"No kidding," Randy agreed as he leaned back on his chair. "We figured it was about your field work, seeing that they were pulling records for a number of the well sites you surveyed."

"Doug said something like that."

"About a week after you left, a couple guys showed up and started going through our stuff and you know, asking who done this or that."

Doug was reticent up until that point seeing the wheels turning in Jen's head, "I didn't mention that to you earlier, Jen, you know when we were out riding. All the crews started to get pummeled with review work. It wasn't just your work, but Ed's and Roy's."

"What were they looking for?"

"Well, maybe it had something to do with your leaving?" Chet pried.

Jen paused, wondering about time and place, but went with her instincts and lowered her voice, "Guys, you know this stays here in the group, right?"

Her eyes darted to see their reactions, "Tracy was trying to get me to falsify some reports."

Randy shifted his weight quickly slamming his chair forward leaning his chest on the table, "But you never did, right?"

"No."

"So what were they looking for since it wasn't anything Jen did?" Randy asked.

All the men slid their chairs closer to keep the conversation private.

"If that don't beat all! You fellers need ta know something," Chet declared, but he looked right at Doug with a real serious look and shook his head like he'd messed up.

Randy couldn't help but put a dig on Chet, "What'd they do? Offer you a limo to drive up to the site?"

"Hell, they'd let him chew in there too!" Charlie mocked.

Jen laughed, wanting to hear what Chet had to say, "You guys haven't changed. Still can't hardly stay focused. What happened?"

"A while after they were pullin' records some other office guys came around asking for the drill heads from all the wells."

Startling Randy, Doug shot forward in his chair, "Are you shittin' me? You never said anything!" he accused barely managing a whisper.

Chet knew his boss would be upset if his authority was trampled on.

"Well, the way it went down was they came around and I don't know to how many of us," Chet slowly confessed, "they flashed their company badges and said everything was confidential...no, restricted."

Doug pulled his chair tighter to the table. "How many heads did you turn over?"

"Six in all. I inspected them before I boxed 'em up, took copies of the shipping orders, and sent them off."

Doug rubbed his chin trying to discover the motive, "What's goin' on? Jen, they never tapped you for more information?"

"Not one call."

"Did they take the bits after they came back from the lab? I'd expect them to wait until the lab finished calibration checks to tie them back to the field data," Doug clarified.

"That's what was so cotton pickin' stupid of me," Chet admitted. "I should of stalled and said they had already been sent. Instead I told them we had to ship them off to the lab. They said they needed them now and that they would take care of it.

"I've heard a couple rumors floating around that are probably close to the truth after hearin' this bullshit," added Randy.

Chet took a big swig on his beer and saw their server making her way back to the tables. His hand motioned to stop all conversation.

"You boys alright back here?"

Doug spoke for the group, "You bet, Clare. We'll go for another round."

"K, hon. Be right back."

"Anyhow I heard a couple months ago that a team went out and stuck pipe smack dab into the middle of some of our sites. I figured it was a stupid rumor but what if they've been backtracking since they pulled records and all."

"That could be the injection program identifying sites to pump in waste gas," Doug presumed.

Chet ignored the suggestion, "Hell, when they made off with the heads I was tellin' them the Kilgore units were useless. Never got a spec of oil on those bits that failed."

Randy turned sarcastic, "Did you tell 'em no oil, but it had Doug's blood on it? What a bunch of dill rods."

Jen and Doug's eyes met. She thought she knew what he was thinking, but he was having a flashback to when the drill collar broke free and thrust into the left side of his body hurling him backwards. The men said he anchored his left leg to stay upright but the collar seemed to explode backward when the shaft shot upwards, its energy transferring to the support columns.

The whole east side of the rig pulled up, shearing the plate support bolts. The platform was immediately compromised and twisted as the one inch steel cabling slacked on the opposite side. The tie downs, with reverse tension, bore the extreme weight of the shifting derrick, skewing the angle of the gigantic mast. Once the pipe shaft went airborne it took less than a minute for the entire rig to collapse.

Luckily, Doug's body had been thrown back over twenty yards. The cable stretched, coming down in a loop slapping the ground, snagging the kelly apparatus. The whipsaw effect of the cable catapulted pipe, hose, and a section of the turntable into the air landing fifty yards opposite the side of the rigging. Like a giant garrote, it would have cut Doug in half. Chet and some of the crew ran back to get Doug after the structure fell.

Everyone at the table noticed Doug had checked out for a second or two.

"Whoa, I sure didn't mean to bring it all...," Randy apologized and patted his back. "Sorry, boss."

"No, that's okay." A sweat bead traced Doug's sideburn. "I was just thinking."

Group fatigue mixed with beer had settled in.

"How about we call it a night?" Jen offered.

"I'll second that," Doug replied quickly. "Jen and I need a ride home. There's a number of things we need to get aligned on back at work. I want to know who's getting what shoved down their throats. Okay?"

It was meant for everybody, but Doug could tell Chet was going to take it personal.

"Chet, let's you and I tie out one on one."

"Okay, boss."

Clare returned with their last order, "Hey, where y'all goin'?"

A chorus of "sorry" with Doug's instruction to put the bill on his tab, got them out the door and into their trucks.

When they were dropped off, Doug stopped Jen before she opened the porch door, "I need to sleep on this, but let's talk in the morning. Do me a favor. Don't mention anything to Kate for the time being."

Doug assumed he wouldn't be sleeping any better than previous nights. His mind was filled with a myriad of complications, deliberations, and minutia. Deprived by the new turmoil, Jen couldn't sleep believing her future would be altered and intertwined with the friends she had left behind.

The next day after packing a lunch, Doug, Jen, Connor, and Timmy took off for Gilmore's Pond to pole fish for crappy and bluegill. While the boys circled the four acre earthen bank, the grown-ups set up chairs and a camp stove and started to untangle their own biases.

"So why is this bugging us?" Doug asked.

"It just seems weird! That's all. The problem didn't go away, did it?" Jen asked rhetorically. "I quit and somebody still wants the information doctored. And then your guys say the Kilgore drill heads are taken. Come on!"

Doug stood up to see the boys across the pond, "There's a whole piece to this that's been eating at me. After I got out of the hospital I tried to participate in the accident review. I figured there'd be a couple departments involved."

"I expected to be contacted too, to explain the misfire. Think about it! Not one drop of oil from Kilgore!"

"Exactly. But there were only a couple meetings and that was it. Tom, you remember him, he ran with it and then the whole issue disappeared."

Jen nodded.

"He pulled me in with some third-party guys," Doug recalled. "When I asked him about any follow-up he basically said it was 'a closed matter'. That's why I was shocked when Chet said he handed over physical evidence.

I'll bet there's no way to trace where the hardware went. We'll probably never see those heads again."

"Who were the guys in the meeting?"

"I can't remember. I'll have to look at my notes. Feds I think. They kept asking me how I was doing. Was there anything I could remember that I hadn't mentioned? I figured they were saving their butts."

"When I got asked to fix the records and didn't," Jen remembered, "I got reassigned to another project."

Nervous, Jen got up and shoved hands in her pockets, "Let's walk around the pond and see how the boys are doing. I can't sit still."

Doug continued to piece events together, "Up to the point of the accident everything was by the book. All the checkpoints passed. The only thing was we were rolling a new version of measurement software."

"That wouldn't be a deal breaker," Jen commented.

Then Doug froze and then quickly turned, facing Jen. A virtual segment of time and motion had just bubbled to the surface, "The tent, the cell! I just remembered! It was gone! Probably because I almost got my head taken off!"

He became energized with his memory, "I was watching from the tent, with the analyst. It was Steve. He had just taken a pulse on the drill head and graphed it. The system showed we were ready to pull out and slap on another bit,"

Doug recited becoming animated, "But you know Chet. He comes racing over like he can smell the stuff and says we needed more down shaft. The graph! We looked at it…and Chet's looking at us wondering why we don't agree with him. It all happened in seconds."

"Was it a software bug?"

"Chet, he was convinced it was. Steve started running diagnostics while we were in the ground. The numbers were coming on the screen. I can see them now as plain as day!"

The foreman's speech turned rapid, "The system showed we were in pay sand. The recalculation showed about the same but it's like we were in dead space or something. I walked over there. I guess to prove it to myself, and about one minute later, I'm up to my ass in alligators."

As Jen was rapt with her friend's revelation, he felt relieved with the resurgence of suppressed memory, "Maybe that's what's been rolling around in my head. You can't believe the dreams I've had!"

"It must have been. Waiting to burst out!" Jen guessed as they were just coming up on the boys.

"Hey, guys, have ya caught enough to feed us dinner," the dad joked.

"No way! They're too puny!"

"Well, make your way back to the truck. It's about high noon. We'll start cooking some grub. Jen and I are going to keep going around."

"K, Dad. Timmy, grab your pole. We'll go the opposite way back."

"Let's keep testing this," Jen insisted. "You're standing there seeing the bore shaft going down."

"That's an understatement! I've been seeing it for eight months in my sleep!"

"If there wasn't oil," and Jen paused to collect her thoughts. "Chet said last night there wasn't any on the head. Then is it possible the whole down rig jammed without hitting anything?"

"If oil was heading towards the surface we would have seen the alarms going off in the software," he clarified.

"A software glitch then?"

"I don't think so. Our above ground equipment is failsafe for lockout inspection so there would have been the audible alarms."

"You're right," she said, trying another angle. "Okay then. So what about the drill hitting rock it wasn't engineered to drill through? It would have basically...bounced off?"

"My hell if that's what happened that would explain a lot," Doug replied. "The end of the pipe was sheared on one corner and cracked in half. Chet and Randy said they saw those shafts when the area was cleaned up. The inspectors were probably told to hide that scrap as well."

"Assuming the physical evidence is gone along with the drill heads, who's doing this?"

"The Department of Energy," Doug answered flatly. "They control everything. Who else would it be?"

"Let's assume they took the physical evidence," Jen instructed. "All we have is the fact there was no oil in the area that I mapped almost a year earlier. Randy said they were making sure of that, by punching in a bunch of outpost holes."

"Then somebody might care enough to examine the evidence they took."

"To make sure," she speculated, "that it wasn't some kind of anomaly."

"If it's happening more than once, there's a negative impact on the books," Doug reasoned. "And somebody would be explaining to the stakeholders why the leased land isn't producing."

"Yes! That might be it! Like everyone else, Apache has leased vast amounts of land for exploration over term and had projections on the balance sheet. Now if it's worthless, they would be required to adjust the liquidity and downgrade the asset. The feds would eventually see all the do-overs."

"But why take the back road to hide it?" he quizzed. "It's not uncommon to have the variance? Hell, all the companies revise their reserves thirty or forty years back to cover the asses."

"Maybe it's more than just a variance. And they don't want the investors to get wind of it."

Back at the truck, Doug started heating up the fixings for lunch while they kept testing scenarios.

"Legally, Apache would be walking a thin line if they hid anything like this. They wouldn't be stupid enough to fall into the ruts left by Enron."

"You'd think so," Jen agreed but then her eyes drifted upwards looking at the horizon.

"Doug!" she grabbed his arm. "Turn it around!"

"What?"

"Turn—it—around," Jen repeated slowly. "What if Apache and other companies aren't doing this? What if the feds are behind this? What if they're driving it?!"

"And? It's not like that's never happened," Doug chided.

"Yes, but what if the feds are coming in here and to our competitors? And maybe we're, I mean your company, is a new entry. Maybe Kilgore is statistically important. They don't care about your accident. Your accident is the only reason *we're* paying attention. Your accident exposed the dry run. That's why Apache just walked away. They were told to!"

"There were three more failures in section 8-A. But the dork they let go could have caused those. You were gone by then and we basically had shit for brains working for us."

"But Ed and Roy didn't go brain dead. Their estimates stood up to mine!"

"You're saying you guys went out to these properties, tested the strata, and everything came back and said green light," Doug tested.

Jen tried to link the order of events, "Then you go out, set up you rig and bingo, no oil."

"If I were the feds, I'd be saying you don't know what the hell you're doing. Go back to school."

"But that's just it," Jen replied. "It has gotten more sophisticated with integrated technology end to end. There's no such thing as a pure wildcat!"

"Careful now," Doug cautioned light heartedly. "You're stepping on my heritage."

She ignored his rhetoric, "But you see what I mean? Why are we making more mistakes now? Up to a point in time, we were batting above five hundred. Let's see. Kilgore was way out on the perimeter years ago, pulled up and mapped sixteen months prior to that. And the other ones were probably mapped slightly ahead of it and mothballed, or pending review. Poof! All of a sudden no oil! The probabilities are upside down. We keep pulling oil out of the ground. Maybe the jar's not *half* empty. Maybe it's empty!"

"I've heard all the peak oil hype from the greenies and the oil firms, one saying there's not enough oil to go around and the other saying there is if they get to tap all these places. They keep telling each other they're full of shit."

Doug finished his beer and crushed the can to relieve tension, "And who's going to tell the feds that they're full of it?" he claimed. "Funny. I was talking to Kate the other night saying we needed to get Connor on to some other path. Maybe we're done here in the region. Hell, maybe in the states. I'm too old to go up north to the national refuges."

The oil man caught himself, "Ya know. That's something my grandpa and my dad would have done. Picked up and moved to the pay sand. I'm not like them."

Doug remembered them coming home, their faces covered in sweat and muck. The smell of their clothes. The permanent stains on their hands with fingernails full of grit. Their stories. Years and years of human toil. They were not men of power. But decades ago, their creed and men like them conveyed a guttural stoicism, protecting them from greed. These weren't the people Doug was dealing with now.

"We have to be careful," Doug cautioned with worry.

"You know my old group might be interested in this. I can guarantee at least one of them will get excited."

"Who? Peter?"

"No. Karl. He's out there mixing with people who know better."

Day 183.

Rice University. Houston, Texas.

L EFT OVER FROM spring break, Jude's two gear bags laid on the other side of the bedroom. Since classes had resumed, putting the gear away was not a priority. As usual he had assignments to concentrate on, but every night, an extra chore consumed his free time.

On his flight home from Texas, Jude decided to gamble. All his thoughts were about Dr. Worthington, the controversy surrounding him and the lack of answers. *If the professor had stolen from Rice, he would have been fired. If he had a scheme, the whole thing would have been shutdown when Peter and Karl went to school. And if not, how could he hold the university hostage this long? Were they just waiting, hoping his old age would deal him out?* Jude wondered as he stared out the plane window. *And for what? If the black books held any secrets, there had to be more!*

"So far, the details Worthington shared were worthless," Jude spoke softly as he walked through the parking lot to his car. "Except for the volume describing the new coefficient sub_x. And that's way out of his league!"

He's not stupid though Jude thought, driving home. *How could these rumors still be out there?"*

The student decided he could dig deeper. He could befriend Worthington to learn the truth. He could put the facts together and maybe even prove the professor wasn't a flake. Jude decided to gamble.

Expecting to learn more about the man, Jude monitored the professor's location and activities. He filled the often empty role as in-class teacher's aide. Usually skipping half or more of the faculty-hosted workshops, the student showed up at the ones hosted by Worthington. He added fundraisers to his agenda, those that Worthington planned to attend. For good measure, multiple calls to Ms. Olivary served as a double-check on Worthington's schedule.

The admin was slightly aroused with Jude's frequency of appearances, "I'd say you're trying to outdo yourself or your roommate."

After thrusting himself into Worthington's business, Jude wasn't sure what he was learning other than the professor was going through the motions. He was close to admitting to himself that his gamble had no payoff. Returning to the house, he found a package on the kitchen table addressed to him. Compliments of Karl, a note described the contents:

> *Jude—Here's the contraption I told you about. I decided to build it just to prove to myself that it actually works. I threw in the cheap radio as well. Amazing that the can picks up as much as it does. Surprise your friends with your geeky ingenuity! Enclosed are the parts list and the URL, in case you break it. Karl.*
> *P.S. I ate the chips.*

Learning that it was capable of collecting radio waves and conversations within a half mile, and after testing the Pringles can antenna out on some of Arthur's phone calls, Jude immediately saw the contraption for what it was—another way to snag information from Worthington. Satisfied its disguise would shield him from detection, he sat outside Worthington's office near dusk and heard bits and pieces of cell phone conversations from the building's occupants. The device even picked up the dialogue between Olivary and her boss before she transferred calls. When the office windows were lit, its occupant shadow could be seen moving about. On schedule, the light was turned off.

Yep, Jude confirmed looking at his watch, *six-thirty...the dude has some serious habits.*

Passing through the same foyer doors on the east side of the building, Worthington would walk past the Weiss College Master house, drive out of the parking lot on to Main, and left on McGregor. As long as he got out of the office and on his way home, that was considered a hall pass and Jude ended the surveillance. Considering he was getting sucked into the professor's paranoia, he remembered the professor's warning: "I suspect there could be people, people in our profession, and powerful people in oil and government that will go to capricious lengths to suppress the importance of my findings."

Ironic, Jude thought, completing his fourteenth evening in his car. *I'm practically one of them.*

As a virtual stalker, the student was starting to change his feelings about the professor, about the rumors, and about the old man's total immersion into his research. Jude felt he didn't prove anything but he *felt* different about the man who begged him for help.

I have to stop this. It's not getting me anywhere, Jude thought wearily as he pulled up in front of the house.

Arthur Hyde Clarke realized there was something different about Jude too. Something was wrong. His roommate was gone all the time. Jude's friends were calling *him* to find out where he was. He showed up home looking exhausted and nervous. Expired milk and eggs sat in the fridge. A case of ramen noodles was gone.

Coming in late again, Jude suddenly started talking about his future and how he didn't want to waste time on worthless stuff, "I know what I don't want to be doing for the rest of my life."

"What?"

"Get in a rut. You know. Start working and figure out that you hate it."

That night Jude couldn't help himself, following the professor to his house and watching him through a window. There had to be more to Worthington's fear. There had to be a reason he was paranoid.

The resident switched on lights, then brought an unfinished sandwich to the table. That was dinner. He sat in a chair flipping stacks of paper and folders. The smoke from a lit cigarette floated to the ceiling gathering above him, in a cloud. Nothing spectacular. Nothing dangerous. The student-turned-stalker walked back to his car believing the professor had nothing. Nothing to bargain with. Nothing to keep the university at bay. There were no powerful people interested in what Worthington was doing. Jude knew he was the *only* one. Watching. Watching someone who was very alone.

And then the confession came without encouragement, "Clarke, it's scary to think of what Worthington has accomplished and to see from the outside that his days are being wasted. And then it gets to a point where the trap door could open up any minute. I can see why Peter hates him. From the outside it looks like he's taking up space."

"What? I mean, uh, sure?"

"I don't know if it's more from me feeling sorry for him. I'd hate it if I had to do the same thing over and over, right down to cleaning the same dinner plate. "

And more explanation followed. It was like a boil bursting. He needed to release. Arthur wanted to get to bed but was shocked at what he was hearing. A cathartic release of contradiction and validation. Jude told him about the office meetings and the black books and how worthless they seemed at first, and then how they snared his attention. Then how he wavered again, hoping to figure out the truth. Then about the package from Karl and how he was using it to spy on the professor.

"I can't imagine myself having to balance everything I learned, on one hope. Bud is really getting creepier. Like he's even more paranoid. He's fretting about a guy he's never heard of. Who in their right mind would get freaked out about that? Instead he is worried about *why* the guy is contacting him? Maybe Peter is right. The university has carried Worthington. He's no longer valuable to anyone."

"So what are you going to do now?"

"The good news is I'm stopping everything. I'll just have to wait it out with Worthington. The bad news is I think you should see how this Pringle can device works. It's really cool."

"Hmmm, maybe the upside is you can put that on your resume."

The next morning, Jude tested Arthur to make sure he was cool with everything, "You know I appreciate you listening and everything. I'm not going off the deep end or anything like that. It's not like I need a stalking order against me," Jude said, laughing.

"I didn't call the cops if that's what you mean."

"Well, I still have to meet with Worthington. Although I dissed him a bunch last night, he might lose it if I don't show. He's convinced his research is going to save the world."

"Is it? You didn't sound convinced last night."

"One minute, I'm not. The next, I am. I forgot to tell you about the seismic tomography model that's bugging me. I couldn't find enough detail to trust it."

"Anyway you still owe *me* for listening on my calls. I want to see it work."

"No kidding?" Jude ensured.

"My parents wouldn't be thrilled, so count me in."

His meeting with Worthington didn't provide the chance to explore the sub_x coefficient model. But Jude launched into his concerns, insisting on covering more details. The professor was feeling charitable and gave in by answering only two of the questions Jude felt emboldened to ask.

Worthington claimed the model was incomplete, "because it was on loan from another source, I've already given you that knowledge. But I promise to share the author in due time. I am protecting the source based on a prior agreement."

Then he answered the second question, with surprising honesty, "And the gentleman who you say makes me paranoid? In fact, I would agree with your assessment. It is a source of concern because of a transaction I agreed to a year ago. I made a commitment to a prominent journal that I would publish a portion of my research. They are aware of the premise of the research. I was hoping the visitor was connected with the journal in some way, but he isn't."

The professor gazed over to the bookshelves, "As to the agreement with the publisher, I did delay my submission because of timing and resource issues, hence my invitation to you. I'd like to share more but some of these items are simply out of bounds until they are relevant. I do appreciate your vigorous nature, but you'll have to respect my personal privacy. Let's get back to our chores."

The River Walk. San Antonio, Texas.

ETER WAS WILLING to make a concession with his flight itinerary, especially for her. At her request he was going to see Jen Rawlins in San Antonio. In person. This time, no cells. No emails. Peter hadn't sat down and talked with Jen for over two years. Like the near miss at Sun Valley, their friendship was hemmed in by text messages and voice mail. Peter wondered why this time. *Why now? Why did she say she needed my help?*

She had never asked Peter for help before. Not when she was twelve and accidentally stuck her tongue to the frosty pole of a ski-lift chair. Not when she was fifteen and blistered the entire roof of her mouth with melted cheese. Not when she was seventeen and during high school lunch, someone hit her hand just as she put a forkful of cake in her mouth. Every time Peter was right next to or near her.

He told her not to, but she ripped her tongue off the pole and it bled. He told her to drink cold water, but instead she grabbed the cheese and peeled it off the roof of her mouth and with it, came a layer of skin. When the fork actually stuck in her palate, she pulled the fork out and swallowed the cake because she didn't want to gross people out. After a tetanus shot, she insisted on going to sports practice. Peter told her it would be better to go home and rest.

She didn't need help with her homework. She didn't need help defending the two-on-one break that kept her high school basketball team's opponents from winning in overtime. She didn't need help finding her first professional job out of college. She didn't need help in the field, working in the foulest of conditions with the foulest of men.

But this time, intuition led Jen to ask for help. She delayed calling Peter when she got back home from the Erls homestead. The more she played it in her head, the more it sounded like a bunch of rednecks bent out of shape. She followed up and figured the answers would slough off the hype created by Doug and his crew. But that didn't happen. The answers got stranger. What she learned scared her. She couldn't shake the feeling that they had stumbled on a secret. *What if the government was involved, hiding change? Hiding an inevitable change?*

She reached deep at self-preservation. Everything of value slipped out of the way for a moment. Years of emotional integrity was overwhelmed by paralyzing fear. A candle-lit tub and wine induced a remedial retrace of a childhood without a father. Sometimes she spoke out loud and laughed at a memory.

As a teenager, she had to make tough after losing her father to testicular cancer. Her mom survived day to day as a widow. Struggling, they reached their maturities in spite of the fracture left in the family.

Studying a photograph he had in his wallet, Peter marveled how a woman's intellect and physical features seem to intertwine, blending to become matured and perfected. At adulthood, Jen was physically strong, balanced with seductive warmth, sometimes the envy of her gender. Peter felt muscle tighten in his throat. Memories of them together had been tucked away.

"Drop me on the next corner." *What could she possibly want or need?*

The driver pulled up to the curb on top of a sewer grate and its stench immediately sifted into Peter's face as he opened the door.

"Thirdeen-fiffdee," said the cabbie, whose smile gave away missing teeth.

Walking west, the sun was segmented through the picket line of skyscrapers. Passing the street vendors, Peter headed down a stone braced staircase. Rounding the lower tier of moss covered pavers he spotted her sitting in front of a bistro. Jen stood up and with one step met Peter, firmly placing her arms around his shoulders and kissing him on the cheek. The sensation of the embrace lasted longer than the physical act. As they separated to sit down, the emotional soothing was apparent for one of them.

"Have you ordered any food?"

"No. We can stay here or walk down the River Walk and pick up something," Jen replied.

Surrounded by restaurants, the water canals were jammed with large taxi boats. The noise from tourists competed with the water lapping the sides of the canal abutments.

Peter raised his voice to be heard, "How's your mom?"

"She's good. Moving out of the house. She couldn't use all the space and most of her friends were leaving the neighborhood," Jen reported. "Oh! Remember the park? They ripped out the old steel playground equipment and put in all plastic stuff."

"So the neighborhood is changing, huh? Same with my folks. They seem to be handling it. How's Michael?"

"We're not seeing each other anymore. He couldn't take what he considered long *delays* in our relationship."

Jen emphasized "delays" as a way to show indifference to it, "He couldn't free himself to spend time with me in the field much like I didn't care to sit at home waiting for him to get off work. Men are such babies when they're out of their element."

"I know what you mean," quipped Peter with a smirk coming across his face. "Men really don't want to chase women around oil rigs and outhouses before they bed them."

"Apparently not."

Jen looked at the sky through the tree branches. The clouds had gathered into a dark bundle and the cooling wind had shifted. Peter noticed her bangs were slightly airborne showing the small brown freckle on her tanned forehead.

"I tried to find you in Sun Valley," Peter admitted.

The first drop of rain hit the ceramic top making a plink sound, just as Jen felt another tiny drop on the corner of her mouth.

"I was there but couldn't stay long because I had a connecting flight to my corporate office. I was glad to leave. There was a big league jerk at the bar."

Peter expected the verbal blast that followed.

"This guy hit on me in the bar the first night. You could tell he had a girlfriend but she was busy with some of his other buddies. As I pointed that out, he tried to cuddle up to me with that hurt-save-me look. Can't imagine why his girlfriend wasn't paying attention to him."

"Social behavior *is* one of our downsides," Peter joked.

"I don't have respect for anybody that needs to keep their egos at full tilt. If men are idiots then he was their king!"

"Geeze, he must have really pissed you off!"

"I just hate slimy stuff," Jen stated moving off the subject. "Are you ready to order?"

The evening storm progressed, forcing the strolling crowd to migrate into shops and restaurants.

"Were you shocked that I asked you to come to the Alamo?"

"I was. Are you shocked I'm here?"

"No, I'm not," Jen said smiling.

The waiter came over and urged them to move inside.

Jen continued her story after they were seated, "When I called you, I was convinced that we had a big problem on our hands. I was out visiting Doug. You know, the Erls in Midland?"

"How are they doing?"

"Fine. Everything was fine until we all sat down in the bar and started to reexamine a year and half worth of activities. It looks like there's stuff going on that defies logical explanation."

"So."

"That's how I approached it when I got back. It just seemed too big to be real. Then like I promised Doug, I made some calls, did some extra research, and it got me spooked again. That's when I called you."

Over dinner, Jen rattled off the conversation at Saddles and the following day at the pond with the boys.

"It's a lot to take in but that's the gist of it. Whadda think...so far?"

"And you were sober when you called me?"

Retaliating, Jen hit Peter's arm, "I did some checking with our two labs to see if they had become an unofficial depot for the government. They said no. One lab is development and test for R&D. The other lab is warranty break/fix."

"If this thing was none of your business, maybe they couldn't say."

"Well, I know these guys pretty good and there's some trust there. But without me asking, they volunteered more information. Analysts, in two different conversations, in the two labs said they have been getting spent drill heads back from the field, from customers. The equipment was sent back under the premise it failed in the field. With normal procedures the labs collaborated because of the multitude of tests that were mandated."

"And?"

"They found residue on the heads that doesn't add up."

Peter sensed Jen was building up to something, "The residue is peridotite, but not consistent with upper mantle material." [54]

She paused for effect knowing Peter would leap to the same conclusion she did, "And so they hit a mineral lattice that showed some compression. Mostly olivine right?"

"Same thing I thought. The residue was a cubic mineral."

And she let Peter go down the same path she did, "Then they found other enriched rock, like lamproites. That's textbook, drilling into a developed intrusion pocket, probably centuries old. No big whoop." [55]

"But this is the catch. They did find something else. Magna, barely chilled."

"It's got to be a misread. There's no fresh magna in the areas that oil companies drills into," Peter disputed.

"They sent the samples, heads and all back to the feds. They swear it's conclusive!"

"Magna composition, and fresh? Without a volcano? How come we're not reading this in the papers?"

"Hey, I mapped an area like that. According to them, there wasn't any sign of intrusion. These labs are in the process of retracing their steps and planning on sending people out to the sites where these drill heads were used. They're not going to take any chances."

Peter was still calm, surprising Jen, "What's got you so hot and bothered then?" he asked.

Jen set her fork down, pushed back slightly from the table, and pulled her hands downward across her face, showing exasperation, "I know. I know. But I felt it for a moment. The start of a whole shift in our knowledge about the earth. Like a global paradigm shift on the physical level. What if the

---

54   Rader, "Earth Structure," Geography4kids, http://www.geography4kids.com/files/ earth_composition.html. A dark-colored, coarse-grained igneous rock that is made up mainly of olivine and pyroxene, with very little quartz or feldspar: http://geology. com/dictionary/glossary-p.shtml. The upper mantle has Olivine (a very special rock), compounds with silicon dioxide, and a substance called Peridotite.

55   Delta Mining and Exploration Corporation, "Diamond Exploration," http://www. deltamine.com/diamond_properties_exploration.htm. © 2003 - 2007 Delta Mining and Exploration, Corp. Primary (as opposed to secondary or alluvial) diamond deposits are mined from either kimberlite or lamproite rock-types which originate deep beneath the earth's crust. Diamonds exist at more than one hundred kilometers depth within the earth's mantle and are transported to the earth's surface by extremely rapid volcanic eruptions ("diatremes"), which form these rare kimberlite and lamproite pipes.

mantle properties are changing? What if the chemical composites are now reactive at levels we drill in to? And is the earth changing on a different scale, maybe accelerating its pace? It's only four thousand miles to the center.[56] When you think about it that's not a lot of girth, considering total mass. I thought what we've done to her? What if the truth is changing? Everything we take for granted, our studies, our knowledge, and the future."

Peter felt her intensity, "Now I can see why you called."

"Well, not so you could calm me down if that's what you're thinking. I need you to take this information back to the group and figure out if it's a false alarm."

"You know that's not what I meant. I'll talk with Karl and the gang."

Jen got restless from the distractions in the restaurant and thought Peter considered this whole thing a waste of his time, "Look, when are you flying out? We can go to the company apartment tonight and finish up there…it's a studio."

"Finish?"

"I want to show you a couple URL sites."

Her greenish-brown eyes were always sensual. The synergy of her collective features was mastered by her but lavished on only a few.

"Yeah, that sounds great," replied Peter a monotone.

They headed for the parking lot and continued sharing some of their recent activities.

"You know you missed an awesome spring break in the park," he claimed.

"I appreciate the pictures. It looked like everyone had fun and stuff."

"They all asked about you. We didn't know you were too busy saving the world," Peter joked and as soon as it left his mouth, he knew there was going to be retaliation.

Jen threw a hard punch into his shoulder, "You'll see who's going to save what. You're definitely on the couch, mister."

"Hey, that's a surprise. I didn't know there was an offer!"

Jen blushed wondering how that slipped out of her mouth, "That's what you get for thinking."

---

[56] National Aeronautics and Space Administration, "Earth Fact Sheet," http://nssdc.gsfc.nasa.gov/planetary/factsheet/earthfact.html. The Equatorial radius (km) is 6378.1. The Polar radius (km) is 6356.8.

When they reached the small duplex, she gave a quick tour and they both ended up in the kitchen.

"We sure had a fun time in the park," Peter repeated.

"I heard ya the first time. You really missed me did you?"

"I was counting on you."

"Oh, really. In what way?" Jen said moving closer to guest.

"I don't know in what way, just that I expected you to hook up with us."

"Grab those big glasses for some wine and let's get online."

Showing Peter the URLs, Jen clicked on bookmarks of studies on Earth's core and lower mantle, "Don't you guys pay attention to any of this stuff? How could this not be on someone's radar?"

"Because maybe no one has all the pieces. It is entirely possible that there are people on the globe trying to figure it out," Peter said sarcastically.

"Ya think?" Jen fired back, "But look at it. We might be moving too slow. You can't sit here and not wonder."

"Like I said I'm willing to walk it around. It's possible there's something on the radar. But you know Karl's going to jump all over this."

"I wish he wasn't getting it secondhand."

"You don't trust me?"

"Yes, but you better not leave out the important parts. When are you going to talk to him?"

"Actually pretty soon. He talked me into going on a field trip to map out Pueblo artifacts."

"What for?"

"You remember Dr. Worthington."

"I remember your opinion of him."

"He called Karl. Apparently they've been in touch."

"Sounds like a boys' night out."

"We're headed towards the high desert in Colorado. Karl knows this caretaker up there and we're going to use some ATVs..."

"Like I said, sounds like a boy...."

"You're welcome to come along to keep us straight."

"Thanks, but I'll be busy earning a paycheck."

"Lucky me! I turned down a project to do him a favor."

After finishing their research, the conversation circled back around to Sun Valley.

"I got your text message. What did you mean everybody was bought and paid for?"

Peter gave no answer to explain why the Millard research appeared to be taking scientific proof in the wrong direction and avoided adding fuel to Jen's fire, "Oh, nothing. I can't remember what I was thinking about. Just trying to get out of there."

After the late news broadcast finished, a hug signaled the end of the evening. Peter ignored the awkward kiss almost on his mouth, wondering if the hide-a-bed could deliver needed rest.

Before dawn, a dream prompted him to consciousness. He felt confined and confused for seconds before getting his bearings. When his hand brushed across her stomach, he realized Jen was sleeping next to him. Peter took a deep breath, having no good choice but to reposition. Calming his urges, he lay awake listening to her. All the memories came flooding back. He could see her face change as she matured. What did she really want from him?

Remembering what she said about the truth changing, he fell back asleep uncertain whether he could accept any truth. He had lost her once and didn't want to go down that path again.

Mesa Verde National Park, Colorado.

371400N 1082847W

KARL AND PETER welcomed the landing, anxious to exit the plane and get to the car rental. They sat across from each other, but their seatmates were troublesome. The overachiever sitting next to Karl pulled out a laptop but fidgeted the whole trip. In narrow seats, Peter was compromised sitting next to an obese teenager.

"Nice. You've got a hybrid SUV," as they read the display board of member assignments.

"I had some extra points and since we're on dirt, I wanted to test the suspension," Karl replied.

"You've got a map right?"

"Ya. But I got GPS too. I'm riding shotgun though.

"I thought you'd be driving?" Peter resisted.

"I want to check out the ride as a passenger."

"I didn't see that one coming!"

Starting at Albuquerque, heading north near the Sante Fe National Forest, their journey crossed the southwestern corner of the Jicarilla Apache Reservation. Taking them over two hundred miles along the San Juan River, they ventured into the Navaho Indian Reservation and then back north into Colorado and the reservation boundary of the Ute tribe.

Stopping in Cortez for gas and groceries, the route into Mesa Verde National Park was the last leg. Spanning fifty-two thousand acres, eight thousand of them designated wilderness, the park domain held thousands of protected archeological sites, hundreds of Indian dwellings, and millions of associated artifacts.

"You know I was telling you Worthington left me another call just before spring break to make sure I was still on board."

Peter nodded glancing at the documents in Karl's lap, "Did he send you any of that?"

"No, I put it together. He's had this place on his list for over ten years waiting for his excavation permit to be approved by the secretary of state. The start-stop times are six months to three years so he didn't want to go too early and fail on the reporting requirements.

"National Park Service has shrunk over the years. They'd probably never find out," Peter hinted of a way to circumvent the rules.

"If you get on their radar there's a twenty-thousand dollar fine."

"So we go in there, do a little validation, and you're going to file the paperwork?"

"Bud has admin help for that. I want to give him the confidence he needs to get the excavation kicked off. He'll eventually have a federal field officer assigned to this. They require a sketch or a mapping of the area, so he'll be that much farther ahead after we do this."

"You were always on his hook," Peter accused.

"It needs to be checked out because robberies, so he called me."

"His slave."

"Hey, dude, the man's gotten pretty old," Karl defended. "He can't do it anymore. He's probably on some major meds by now."

"I guess so. We went on how many trips with him?"

"About five or six. You maybe two. They were a blast! Do you remember Mike falling through the tile roof and he freaks out when he lands in all the burlap, like he's got skeletons on him. What a wuss!"

"He wasn't bothered that night after tequila shots," Peter remembered.

"Man's best friend!"

Karl motioned for Peter to take the left turn going to Wetherill Ranger Station, the namesake of the mesa. They had already checked in at the main gate, to get their vehicle permit and lock combinations. The Wetherill road was still closed for the season.

"It's better to slip in here without a lot of tourists coming and going. It's nasty already without someone swerving into you."

Enjoying the shear drop-offs, they were on steep and demanding pavement paralleling Long Canyon. Dull green against the thriving rabbit brush, the interspersed Pinyon pines and Utah juniper were at uniform height as the vehicle surfaced at the top of a ridge. Sprayed across the ground in patches, larkspur and Indian paintbrush exploded with velvet buds.

"So I was saying, Worthington's trying to get the rest of his research done and he needs these relics. But I can tell he's holding his cards close."

"That guy's been working on it for years. I think we probably helped him some along the way. I can't believe the university hasn't forced him into retirement! He's not kept up or published anything even before we were there!" Peter sounded off.

"Maybe. But the dude's righteous though…I mean think about it. He's had all of us at some point bringing information to him. He's a walking encyclo-dictionary in the field. He probably got a couple students working on it full time."

"We're supposed to map the pieces and his students to get the glory? How about getting my name in the paper," Peter mocked.

"Mapping is all we can do legally. We don't have the final permits in hand."

Peter nodded, "Only kidding. You said you know the caretaker?"

"Man. It was pure synchronicity. Lloyd's been hopping all over for the Forest Service and gets assigned here a few years ago and then Worthington dials me up to the same spot. You'll like him. He's a character!"

Reaching the second gate, Karl opened the combination lock and swung the heavy iron barrier to the side. Its absence would allow the public to flood into areas of archeology digs. The road, worse as they left pavement for good, had deep powdered dirt accumulated in the ruts on the curves. It covered the windshield as the tires hit it.

"So much for the intermittent wipers…these are never set to the right speed," Peter complained, coughing just before another wave of dirt powder hit the driver side window.

"Crap, we're going to be suffocating in here!" Karl yelled as he clicked the fan speed dial back and forth, as if to magically produce more output beyond its limit. "The GPS says take the turn."

As their car approached the top of a plateau, a welcomed head wind jettisoned the dust behind them. Thick groves of heavily seeded juniper produced a sour pine smell. Only one bank of cumulous thunderheads lay to the southeast, covering the top of the La Plata range seventy-five miles away.

"Lloyd's hangout is up ahead somewhere. According to the waypoints, we've arrived."

Peter stopped the car in what appeared to be a pull around spot. A road in another direction had a swing gate with a welded padlock box. Barbed wire fencing extended out to both sides to block intruders. An old forest service plank, spiked to a large juniper, warned, "Road Closed". When the doors were opened, a barking dog suddenly appeared on the passenger side.

"Good dog. Come-on. Good dog. Get down now," Karl repeated, coaxing the happy dog.

His bark was patently intermittent as a reminder intruders were still around. Peter followed Karl on a path worn into the duff, weaving through the grove until the path became wider affording a view of living quarters.

The trailer was situated in partial shade with open ground to the side and behind it. The classic Airstream Tradewind, dulled and rust-spotted, was a summer home for one resident. A breeze had already evaporated the moisture off the foot-high grasses, still too green to produce any seed. Chirps and clicks from bird and squirrel were audible between the barking. By this time, the dog had run to the back of the trailer after scratching at the front door.

"Maybe he's not here. Or he's gone off somewhere," Peter tested.

And then there was a clank sound.

"He's here," Karl said, pointing to the back.

When Peter's gaze showed confusion, Karl filled in the blank, "He's throwing shoes."

Both visitors walked around the trailer finding Lloyd Barber stooped over with a rod in his hand, picking up a horseshoe. A bona fide pit with backstops and a worn path between two end points proved where Lloyd spent hours after he tended the high fenced garden. Covered in ten mil plastic, seedlings of radishes, beets, and small rhubarb struggled in the arid soil. A couple scrawny apple trees showed early effort displaying tiny leaf buds.

As he turned, the caretaker's aging was visible with his permanent grin line surrounding weathered cheek bones. The brim of his ball cap was tilted to one side.

"Hey, fellers!" he greeted in a western accent showing his smile.

Lloyd switched the rod and shoes to free his shaking hand. The gesture satisfied the dog, getting in the middle of the three men, "What can I do for you? Are you looking for the trailhead?"

Karl's hope of Lloyd recognizing him by sight was only that, "Hi, Lloyd, I'm Karl Johns, Gene's boy! Do you remember me?" he asked, raising his voice after seeing the hearing aid in Lloyd's left ear.

"You're who?"

"Gene's boy. Gene Johns!"

Still, Lloyd was not showing any recollection.

Something to jump start his memory, Karl thought. "Remember, you lived in Salt Lake City and you and my dad were neighbors?"

"Of course I remember," he responded, looking beyond the two visitors expecting more people to appear. "I lived in Salt Lake City. You're Gene's boy. Mike."

"No," Karl said, speaking louder and simultaneously thinking, *yelling doesn't fix memory loss*. "That's my brother. I'm Karl. Remember you used to throw horseshoes in the park and I would help you pick up on your turns?"

Lloyd's eyes settled slightly and his smile got bigger showing a metal filling in the tip of his front tooth. Yellowish tints on his teeth were further milestones to his age.

He held up the sawed off golf club shaft, "You see what I replaced you with?"

"We're up here to see you, Lloyd. This is Peter Childs. He and I went to school together."

"Where's your dad?" Lloyd asked, expecting a grand face-to-face. Karl didn't know whether it was the right time to say his dad had died of cancer. "He's not with us...uh, we brought some groceries and things. Can we get those in your fridge?"

"Do you boys need supper?"

"We do."

"Duke, git down," Lloyd ordered.

With a fluorescent tennis ball in his mouth the dog pawed Peter's thigh. Prying it loose, Lloyd underhanded it to Peter, "Throw it over towards the shed. He'll get busy on it."

Lobbing the ball hard, it hit the galvanized metal roof and bounced off with dull resonance plunging into the junipers. Duke bolted towards the throw, barking happily. He was playing the game that had been on permanent hold.

After the groceries and cooler were brought in, Lloyd and Karl toured the length of the trailer catching up on shared memories. The resident had no idea why he was seeing visitors today other than to revive stories of throwing shoes and winning trophies that littered the place. Opened mail lay scattered among the small stacks of paperbacks that decorated the floor. Lloyd had always enjoyed those stories, now puzzle pieces of his past, growing up on a farm.

After burying his wife, Lloyd started enjoying the job of caretaking, allowing him to silence most of the past. He always loved his dogs as they were a good trade off for losing lots of friends to disease and old age. He didn't mind being stationed in wide open country, with simple trail duty and gate tendering. He had a radio band for weather and a satellite phone for emergencies.

His boss, Mary Sullivan, visited twice a month bringing mail, filling the standard grocery list, and to make physical inspections of the protected sites.

"I tell you, Lloyd, I was always wondering how you managed to throw those doubles in the tourneys. You never freaked out under pressure like some of your buddies," Karl praised as they came back to the table. "Let's get some stuff cooking. You still eat earlier, right Lloyd?"

"Yup, bothers my stomach if I don't."

Duke was let back in and headed for the couch. He was not going to give up his habits and ignored Lloyd's prodding to get on his dog bed. Jockeying around the cramped kitchen Karl pulled a meal together.

"There's good odds I won't kill us, Lloyd," chided Karl, starting to dish out portions.

"Don't bother me none," Lloyd uttered never lifting his eyes from the electronic blackjack game he was playing.

During dinner Lloyd continued to talk about Karl's dad, now with the knowledge that he had passed away, "It's a damn shame. He would have liked it up here."

"How long have you been doing this, Lloyd?" Peter asked with the intention of lightening the mood.

"About eleven years. Four years in this spot."

"So I was telling you, Lloyd," Karl transitioning to their purpose, "Peter and I wanted you to take us up the road to the dig site. Do people try to walk to it from the main road?"

"Maybe. But that's why there's a lot of strong gates," the old man replied.

"Probably because of the robberies?" Karl asked.

"Well, the gate out there went up before I got the job and I don't unlock it unless there's good reason. Mary goes up there to make sure no one stole the ground," exaggerating to make a point. "Her boss says she has to inspect it, so she does. Especially after those fellers were convicted for taking some pots and stone utensils. I'm sure she already knows about you two being here."

Peter and Karl were familiar with the siphoning of native Indian artifacts from practically all the reservations.

"Literally nothing's sacred. There's no stopping it," Peter said. "The greed is too great when there's a one of a kind collectible. The feds can't put the manpower together to sting the diggers, middlemen, and collectors. As soon as it's advertised, the piece disappears."

Karl agreed but was worried, "It's a real crap storm out there. Lloyd, are there any pieces left or did the entire site get wiped out?"

"Mary doesn't think so. She would fill me in from time to time on her visits up here. She says there's inventory records from early on that explained what's there. I've never seen them."

Karl told what he had, "Actually I've got those and a newer copy, but I'm also checking to see if the original records were converted to the CSI database. I'm waiting for an answer from the DBA at the University of Colorado."

Karl saw Lloyd's startled expression as he asked, "You can get that information? What's a CBA?"

"No. DBA. A database administrator. There were a couple tries at mapping all the digs in this park, as recent as '71. Most parks relied on the Midwest Archaeological Center, but Wetherill was mapped by park personnel."

"So you know your way around these fellers to get the records?"

"I know my shit" Karl laughed as he said it.

Lloyd slapped his knee and smiled, "Well it's starting to stink in here. It must be you."

Peter choked on his drink and Karl laughed harder. It was good energy with Lloyd and Karl thinking they were at the top of their game.

The early evening sun painted mosaic patterns through the blinds, onto the back wall of the trailer. With the lowering temperature, birds were on wing to take the last insect hatch.

"Do you want to stretch your legs, Lloyd? Peter and I were thinking about a short hike from the trailhead."

"That'd be fine. I'm good for about a mile or so and Duke hasn't had nothin' interesting to do for awhile. Leave the dishes and we'll come back and have some ice cream with the goodies. I don't miss that too often," Lloyd offered, smiling again.

Out the trailer, Duke barged in front of the men racing across the yard and turned back to wait.

"Come on, Duke," Lloyd raised his voice, "This way."

The group walked to the trail split and started single file. Activating his GPS, Peter took a reading so he could reconcile the waypoint with his mash up. It was a new application that allowed the user to subscribe to land surface maps and combine content from multiple sources. The dimensional map illustration included topology and grid coordinates.

The men and dog paced themselves up and over a small knoll as the wide trail narrowed, grooved in from the sides. The small weeds and grass showed Mother Nature's persistence to reclaim her territory in areas where foot traffic had diminished over the years. As they reached the second outcropping of rocks, the trail width tapered again and in sections was invisible. The smooth reddish brown Cliff House sandstone laid in massive sections on the ground separated thousands of years ago from the parent fault fifty yards away. Cool to the touch, the exposed rock above ground was eroded smooth on the edges and weathered with a light sheen of moss and lichen. Their footprints could have been tracing those of the two cowboys that first discovered the area in the late 1800s.

Nose down, Duke was ahead of his companions inspecting gopher holes but nothing flushed. For more than a half of a mile everyone listened to their own hearts beating at the eight-thousand-foot altitude. Even as his body tried to accommodate the demands of the short hike, the caretaker didn't complain.

"Lloyd, did you say there was sort of a look out up here?" Karl spoke quickly on his exhale.

"Yep, up here," Lloyd struggled to answer short of breath. "The trail goes out under the snag you see ahead and then climbs, ending at the top."

Although the thermal currents had shifted to flow uphill instead of down, they weren't persistent enough to cool off the men. Most animals in the food chain would be moving to the ridges to pick up predator scent.

"I remember coming up here and saw a bunch of deer right over there. They were still in velvet, in no hurry until they smelled me. I haven't hunted since my boys went to high school."

"How old are your kids now?" Peter asked.

"My kids? Well, I have a couple boys, both in their fifties, and two daughters mixed in. I haven't seen them in a couple years. They don't travel out of their way much to come see me..."

As Peter was nodding, Karl moved up the trail to get a glimpse across the deep draw, remembering the map topology. He thought the access road to the Navaho dig site might be visible, so he continued to walk up the trail out of view from Lloyd and Peter. Most everything around them was transitioning to survive the night as the mountain shadows began to touch the valley of the Ute Indian reservation.

"They have their own lives though and nothing's going to change that. I get letters and pictures. I hope to see them this fall," Lloyd lamented. He looked ready to start walking again.

"Do you still want to make it to the lookout?" Peter checked.

"We can still do it, but we'll have to hurry going back. It gets dark quick up here."

They reached the snag and started up the last section of steep embankment. With some aid Lloyd shuffled up the incline. In minutes, they stood on top of the rock, surrounded by mineral, plant, and animal.

"It's sure beautiful up here," Karl remarked

"Absolutely," added Peter.

They could hear small birds reclaiming the pines, upsetting a Pinyon Jay whose high pitch 'caaa' echoed in short bursts.

"Hey, I can see the trail up to the dig site," Karl noticed. "I'm guessing it's about four to six hundred yards. Is that it, Lloyd?

Visible with the remaining light, the trail was on graded terrain facing them. Against the backdrop of the lower brush, the path was glowing in subdued yellow-orange hues.

"I think so. There's nothing else in there. I remember those dirty pot-lickers. They tried to get to the dig site from over here, disguised as backpackers. That might've worked, but I'm sure they found out there's snakes in those lower draws. The risk of getting bit on the ass was reason enough to take the road."

"You weren't here when they were caught were you?" Peter questioned, confused from Lloyd's earlier explanation of what Mary told him.

"Sounds like they got smart but it didn't help them much in the end, huh, Lloyd?" Karl clarified.

Peter figured Lloyd's hearing aid was at fault and dropped the subject.

"Let's head back," the host prompted. "Do you fellas like fudge on your ice cream?"

At daylight, Karl looked crumpled on the couch. Uncovered, naked enough to show the tat on his butt check, he exposed a circle with a blue curvy segment and a matching green one. As he snuck by him quietly to get to the kitchen, Peter was amused at the variation compared to his own mark.

Suddenly walking through the front door and letting it slam shut, Lloyd made a loud announcement, "Still kind of chilly out there. Damn four-wheeler is cold-blooded. I should have started it yesterday afternoon."

The odor of mixed oil and gas was spreading. Lloyd's damp hands were soaking of it.

"What's that smell?!" Karl yelped coming out of sleep.

Standing nude he moved his hand in front of his genitals and tried to avoid looking like a prude. Lloyd averted his eyes out of respect and headed to the sink to wash off.

"Way to go, dude," Peter deadpanned. "You promised I wouldn't see you naked on this trip."

Breakfast and packing a lunch were chores in the way of getting out the door. Anticipation was barely resilient to the delay of getting the large four-wheeler running. Lloyd had to be convinced to wash his hands again. It was another miracle that he finally remembered where the gate keys were located. With some back and forth turning, the bolt popped. Eagerly, the young men swung both sides open and Lloyd drove the four-wheeler through. The men reversed their action and secured the lock.

Talking over the engine noise, Peter felt compelled to check, "You got the key, Lloyd?"

He patted his pocket confirming its location.

Karl stepped towards the front, touching the handlebars, "Do you mind if I drive? With the weight and both racks loaded, it'll be hard to maneuver. You can sit behind me, and Peter can sit on the back rack."

Relieved that he could just navigate, the camp host immediately shoved himself back. Karl and Peter climbed aboard coaxing Duke up.

The first three miles of terrain were easy on the passengers as Karl clutched and shifted. Peter twisted his hips cradling the dog firmly as they started to gain altitude. At first, the road followed the geographical boundaries of the mountain, and then it became a series of switchbacks to avoid an inactive creek bed. Gambel oak invaded the path, causing the riders to get the brunt of the whiplash as the four-wheeler pushed through.

Peter's remarks about how difficult the trail must have been for ancestral groups impassioned Karl to remind them how foot travel would have taken a full day for the tribal hunters and gatherers as they collected food and water. Between himself and Peter, they talked about the tribe's need for critical knowledge to be passed through the tribe every day so they could survive.

"The tribes would need to be hypersensitive to sustain their physical, mental, and spiritual health," Karl emphasized.

A thousand years later, a triad of men accelerated the vehicle through the expanse of wilderness, to reach a destination by that same civilization. Covered by the shade of the highest section of the Wetherill Mesa, the sun had not peaked over the forge of a smooth rock wall that rose from ancient ocean and shoreline deposits of sand and mud. Anchored into the earth, the one-hundred-million-year-old massive structures were eroded from water, penetrating the softer shale. The twelve miles of sandstone foundation, surrounded by cactus and colorful globe mallow, could not be replicated by man and his knowledge.

A small metal post marked the boundary of the site. The architecture of the tribal structure was like a fortress for protection against peers and a greater enemy—Mother Nature. Over three acres of rock was hand carved from the base wall, extending upwards over hundreds of feet. Many of the front edges of the outer support walls were crumbling. Still void of sunlight for another hour, the air was heavy with moisture. Voice tones carried with a echo, disturbing a rock squirrel who scurried off chattering news of the invasion.

"It smells like there're bats around," Peter reported as he carried two packs over the first set of walls, with Duke on his heels. "Lloyd, I'm going to set up some markers. You can help me if you want."

"Sure."

Peter unwrapped the pin flags and fighting with the plastic shipping band, pulled his knife out to cut it. The blade slipped and nicked the flesh of his index finger, "Damn it!"

The bleeding became more of a nuisance as Peter smeared blood on whatever he touched. Eventually all the flags were anchored in the ground according to the proprietary coordinates downloaded for the site.

"Next step," he signaled to Karl.

Karl talked out loud assuming Lloyd would be interested in their process, "We have to triangulate to make sure we haven't drifted off the scale. We're using a diffuse sensor because the light beam will scatter. We measure to the coordinate map and the markers will be adjusted until we pinpoint the objects below the surface."

"What pieces are you going to take back?" Lloyd asked as he took a swig of water.

"None. We're just evaluating to make sure the pieces are still in the ground."

"Well, you know a lot of this ground was disturbed. I'll bet you come up empty," Lloyd wagered.

"That's what we'll try to prove, but only virtually. By the time were done, we'll know what is earth substrate and what isn't."

Collaborating to recheck the coordinates, Peter recorded the data while Karl moved the PSD detector to another spot. Summarily, the coordinates showed the location of the relics according to the updated inventory sheet. Working nonstop, the three men finally took a lunch break. Duke remained busy with gopher, squirrel, and lizard scent, coming back to see if everyone was still present. The sunlight filtered through the needles of sparse spruce, raising the ambient temperature in the lighted areas. Making them barely visible for the survey, the shadowed areas camouflaged some of the flags.

"Did you get a bandage for that cut?" Lloyd asked.

"I did. It's fine. Not enough blood to bring out the dead," Peter joked.

Karl studied his documentation, speaking aloud, "Worthington's targets are six, seventeen, twenty-eight, and fifty-six. We just have to finish locating those off the major points and we should be done."

Smaller markers had been set out representing the proposed locations of the artifacts. It took time to triangulate the exact location of the four pieces. While Peter recorded the additional waypoints into his laptop, Lloyd retrieved the pin flags. Karl finished taking digital pictures of the area.

"Did we get everything?"

"Yep," responded Lloyd. "You boys sure have learned a thing or two since. I hope everything pans out."

Loading back up, they made their way back down the trail towards the closest man-made habitat.

The next morning, dim light entered the trailer waking Peter up early. Losing the coin toss he had to fight Duke for the couch the previous night. Wrapped in a blanket with his laptop, he reviewed the field coordinates collected the day before, making sure there were no keying errors. Although his attention wandered about what Jen was doing, his inspection didn't find any errors.

The visitors finished breakfast and packed the car for the return trip. After ending small talk, Lloyd hinted if they didn't mind, he would need a place to visit sometime before winter. Karl felt obligated to give him his business card penning in his cell number.

"You really gave him your cell?" Peter checked when they drove off.

"He's family."

Home of Doug Erls. Midland, Texas.

AFTER A MAJORITY of passengers deplaned to make other connections, Jen called Doug from her plane seat.

She had minutes before new passengers would board, "You okay to talk?"

"Yep, I got your message yesterday and moved some meetings."

"Great. I was hoping this would work out. I'm stuck in my seat in Denver waiting to fly out. How are Kate and Connor?"

"They're great. Actually, I think Connor misses you."

"Heh. He's a pretty cool kid."

"We think so."

She jumped to the reason for the call, "Were you able to dig a little deeper at Apache? Anything from checking your notes?"

"I looked at them. I did meet with those guys but nothing was written down."

"No business cards?"

"Turns out I don't have one. Jen, these were pretty bare bones meetings. Had I known then—"

"Don't worry about it. Just trying to snag more evidence. I got caught off guard too."

"It's not a total loss. Chet and Randy checked with other teams without tipping them off. They're being audited too. The rumor mill thinks its layoffs."

"Do you believe that?"

"No, it's just a smokescreen. Something Apache is probably fanning instead of putting out."

She wondered if they arrived at a dead end, "I suppose they can cover their tracks if they've got everyone looking somewhere else."

"I'm going to talk to a couple managers and see if there's documentation I can get my hands on," Doug pledged. "The interns or admins might know something."

Background noise of passengers made it difficult to hear and Jen switched the cell to her left. "Good idea."

"Speaking about interns," Doug laughed, "Has Karl gotten back to you?"

"There might be a delay," she admitted and heard Doug sigh. She tried to be more positive. "I've told them everything. But they just had some consulting work to finish. I'm sure they're working on it."

"I guess he was surprised to hear what we found out?"

"Karl wasn't really available so I got Peter to take the lead."

"Do you think they get the gist of what we uncovered?"

"Ya, they do. Surprised wasn't the word I would use, but they'll get back to me."

"I'll be honest. This stuff is starting to spook me. Us having to sneak around. It gets down to whether we trust our employers and our government."

"It's weird, I know, but we're doing the right thing," Jen replied.

"We might end up on the short end."

"I feel ya. Peter and Karl will do the right thing. Who knows? Maybe it will be a dry hole."

"Remember you told me you and Peter hardly crossed paths?"

"What? Oh. Uh huh," Jen uttered.

"That's not causing you any grief is it?" he wondered.

"Not at all. I think everything is okay."

"Just making sure. I'd hate to cause problems where there shouldn't be any," Doug assured.

"I'll get it done. It's just going to take some time."

No one talked for a second or two. By now Jen had a seat partner.

"I've got to go, but my offer is still good you know."

"I'm better off sticking around here while I can still get my foot in some doors."

"Let me know when it's the right time."

After ending the call, Jen was uneasy. If Peter didn't take her seriously Karl had too. *He would come through, dragging. But why would he have to? They all got along. Nothing could shake their friendship.* She remembered believing her and Peter used to be like soul mates, growing up together. Having the same interests made them that way. They did things for each other. Respected each other. Loved one another. Why weren't they in love?

Our souls need more time, I guess.

Jen put her bag underneath her seat. She leaned back peering out towards the runway watching luggage go in different directions, wondering if Peter ever took a moment to really *think* about them. As the plane taxied, tears pushed to the edge of her eyes. Blinking, her cheek became moist. *Does time ever run out for souls that have endured?*

Jen didn't know if her love for Peter was lingering from adolescence, a gesture of familiarity, or real love not explored. The thick pain, freezing the sinewy tissue of her neck and shoulder muscles, felt like guilt bubbling to the surface. She held back the surge. *Not here!* Another tissue wet by lips carefully removed smudged eyeliner. The air vent cooled her face.

Landing, Jen pushed "1" auto-dialing her mom. The conversation delayed her drive home. She sat in her car at the airport deciding not to be in a hurry. Her heart was at an intersection she didn't understand. The tone of Jen's voice signaled her mom the call was more than touching base. Something was on her daughter's mind. When Rose kept the focus on her daughter, Jen shared nothing about her recent involvement with Doug, but her emotions changed when she started talking about her past relationships and she eventually circled back to Peter.

"I always thought you and Peter would remain friends," answered Rose to whether Jen had side-stepped the relationship. "But I never expected he would be the *only* one for you. That would be something for you to know."

"I guess I'm not sure either but he's popped in my head recently."

She shared a portion of her recent encounter with Peter in San Antonio.

"I'm listening to you, Jen. You're at point in your life where you feel some choices have to be made. Maybe they do. You're a wonderful person. People see that."

Jen's voice cracked when she said, "I just feel like I've missed something."

Rose could imagine the face of her offspring and she saw her again as a young girl completely bewildered at the time of puberty, "You probably don't remember, but you and I talked about this in seventh grade and again in your sophomore year in high school. The words are different, but I hear the same thing."

Jen tried to recall it, "Was it about Peter?"

"It was and wasn't. Just concerns about this boy or that one."

"It seems I'm stuck in the same place."

"Honey, it's not who you love, or when you fall in love. It's *that you love*. Someone will trigger that sensation, greater than it's been before and it'll work out."

The stress Jen boarded the plane with was less dense and easing since talking with her mom. The matter of turmoil dissipated when she showered. As she read before bed, the whole matter of energy and love was supplanted to the back of her mind. Her mom had second thoughts though, wondering if she should have shared other information. It *would* have made matters worse for her daughter.

U.S. Naval Station, Guantanamo Bay.

Underneath his clean linens, the exteriors of arms, legs, and backside of Dr. Franklin were abused. His beard was uneven and spotted with gray hairs. His dark wavy hair, normally combed back and away from his face, hung into his eyes. A few strands appeared braided only because of constant twirling. Showers and soap were available every other day, but his skin was chapped and his sandaled feet were cracking around the end of toes and heels. With white specs underneath, signals of the improper diet, the nails on his feet and hands were uneven and chipped and the surrounding skin dotted with welts and bites by insects airborne or crawling.

Void of any predator, the infestation of the walled cells was inevitable. At night, the small lit corridors attracted small insignificant life. The winged tataguas and sometimes swarms of the smaller cocuyo entered through worn mesh. Completing the food chain, hormigas, or ants, would appear until more spray was laid down in the corridors. Franklin learned that killing them was a waste of energy and the accumulating residue was sticky. For limited comfort, his blanket was the only shield. Comparing himself to others during forays, Franklin discovered he was one of the few prisoners at the bottom of the pecking order. Assuming a caste system delivered prescribed amounts of pain and abuse, he was certain Colton had ordered the stoic existence to force a purge of his knowledge.

Underneath garments, his was a body void of fatty tissue. Partitioning his day into four segments while accommodating meals and bed check, there were exercises to warm the muscle, an array of math and physics calculations, doodles and drawings for creativity, and meditation to allow him a release of guilt and pain. Toning his body and soul, he craved the routines of pushups, crunches, and a variety of yoga positions. He felt better physically, regardless of topical ailments that masked his mental resolve.

Usually sleep was filled with dreams of the parents, coworkers, and friends. He missed them dearly and hoped for a reciprocal act of longing. Franklin had sought out pity but now preferred his kin would pray for his strength and survival. A weak spot grew in his soul for his mother and father. Had he impugned everything they sacrificed for him? Had a lifetime of encouragement been exploited by him? *If I could only explain my discovery to them! Would it be enough to offset my disgrace?*

Possibly. But only if Colton and NEADE was denied. He had to endure the suffering for all of them. He expected his peers would know to protect his parents even though he worried for their safety. His fellow scientists would be answering his parent's questions and attempting to resolve their fears, but it could only be a temporary measure. He had to survive.

Logic reminded him that if he were ever set free it would be from two likely events. The true purpose of NEADE would be discovered and reckoned, or his model-based predictions would come to term. Truth. The young doctor was counting the days.

He and Worthington had to be the ones to deliver the truth.

DARON Lab.

The team of scientists that Franklin once commanded had mixed success. They continued to steward their immediate and extended families. Receiving day to day attention if wanted, Franklin's parents were consoled. Remaining resistant to collaborate at work, the NEADE Indians were challenged to provide the solution to a model they didn't understand. Shepard was grabbing at straws trying to get them to make progress on their Tier Four commitment. With Franklin's call records, he reinitiated contact with the chief editor. Upon learning of their failing, the remainder of the lab team was made to prove how they corrected the anomaly.

Advised by Colton, Shepard threatened the team with the loss of visas for some of their relatives. TC became vocal and in a closed room, countered the threat by insisting he and his team would walk out.

Navin calmed him down after Shepard left fuming, but he got an adrenaline surge from standing up to the man who had something to do with Franklin's disappearance, "That arrogant son of the bitch. That'll teach him to bring a knife to a gun fight."

The others were not familiar with that boast and having to explain it diluted the victory, "Who taught you that phrase?"

"Ravi."

A round of hand slapping ensued. They sat in the conference room shaking off the attempt to bully them.

"I'd say we are close to breaking it open," TC boasted. "I'm sure Ravi was able to do this. He called me the night before he was caught you know."

"TC! You did not mention this? The night before the error was found in the formula?"

"He did. He spent a considerable amount of time in the lab every night after we all went home. Sometimes I would come in the morning and back up the system manually. Ravi was not good about keeping updates on his server. I started making copies of files to help him. So I have versions of some of his work."

His peers were impressed with the opportunity as TC continued, "I was not willing to share any information that would put anyone else at risk. Now I can see that we can work on this in order to make some gain *against* NEADE. We really can't afford to lose our jobs. I was holding this card..." and cupped his hands and held them inward. "...close to my chest."

Eyes darted again, "Ravi?"

"Yes."

The next hour was used to share the advances they believed Franklin had made.

"We don't specifically know what Ravi accomplished that made him a suspect," Vinod reminded everyone. "Possibly he might be protecting only the formulas that he knew would be used against us."

"We should have inspected the package Franklin gave us, TC lamented, "But that doesn't matter now. "Let's take what we know. I'm sure our good friend would be wishing us success in this."

Home of Karl Johns. Austin, Texas.

Karl was stretched out on his couch watching cable TV. With fur the same pattern as a black and white Holstein, his seven-year-old cat laid on his owner's chest, purring.

"How'd it go while I was gone, Dr. Bob?"

Rubbing its neck, Karl mulled over what he seriously could do with finding out a bunch of drill heads bit the dust. And he had bored himself looking at the extra documentation sent by Worthington about the specific dos and don'ts for entering the tribal site. Now a beer coaster, the reference material was not as interesting as the drill bits.

For his part, Karl sent emails to a network of professional geoscientists overseas who had blogs and twitter, hoping they could give him something to report back. He also contacted Looks and Wren. She had a disdain for "oil barons," as she liked to call the oil giants, so he was sure to get feedback from her. His active calling list of friends and subject matter experts, spanned over thirty specialties, including climatology, paleomagnetism, and plate tectonics. They were part of his diverse work and play life style but still not as close as his inner circle forged in college.

Karl wanted to remain close to them after college and came up with the idea of a tattoo, the "glue" that would keep them together throughout their professional and personal lives. When back together as a group, conversations about their journeys wove back to who got their tat first or whose was better. Perrie and Karl were the first to get them. Others resisted for a while but ultimately even Jen got the tat by losing a bet that she was going to land a job with Halliburton. Wren and Looks faked their disappointment, thrilled Jen didn't go off to the dark side. After she was offered a job with Apache they held a dark party with black cake, dead flowers, and black balloons symbolizing the detrimental effect her company would have on her. Jen tried to convince them that she was part of the "new age" movement, to institutionalize big oil towards greener business philosophies, goals, and practices. Unconvincing, she settled for the title, "secret agent who will fail." Jen accepted the kidding, never telling them she actually turned down her dream job. Ending up with a small round circle split in two colors, green and blue, a closer look at Jen's tat on the back of her shoulder revealed a tiny gold dot. She would tell people that's where she was born.

All their designs were meant to symbolize Earth. Wren's tat was on her lower back below the waist line. Look's was on his shoulder, as was Peter's who had the smallest version on his lower hip. Perrie had the tattoo placed on her calf muscle, after landing her first graduate job in Hawaii. It wasn't until Peter saw Karl sleeping on the couch in Lloyd's trailer that he noticed the revised design with "mother" imprinted above the earth image.

Peter was back in town between consulting jobs so he and Karl planned to meet up to decipher the data sets taken in Mesa Verde. They lived within commuting time of each other. Since college Karl had gravitated towards Peter's domain, taking advantage of Peter's need of a pseudo partner to research ecological drainages.

Knocking on the door and ringing the doorbell, Peter yelled into the seam of the door, "Anybody home?"

"Come on in," Karl yelled back, followed to the front door by his cat, "Hey, what's up?"

"Everything's good. We were going to check out the maps?"

As Peter got set up at the dining table, they talked about the trip to the Mesa Verde.

"I'm not saying it was a waste of time or anything but I was surprised you didn't get Looks to go with you instead of me."

"I tried. You were my last choice."

"Thanks."

"You know he doesn't like airplanes."

"You mean he doesn't like to be sitting in them."

"Actually, he would have been psyched to see the cliffs up there."

"No doubt."

"Here," Karl directed after flattening the maps, "Look at these printouts. But I'm missing the color version. I didn't have time to pick it up. I reviewed these and marked the targets in yellow. Here's the docs I got from the DBA, and the detail from the inventory sets we recorded. Guess what? They don't sync up."

Peter studied them carefully. Dr. Bob jumped up on Peter's lap purring away.

"Hey, buddy," Peter cooed as he scratched the cat's ears, rechecking his own notes, "The coordinates sync to the baselines you took at the trailhead."

Karl handed over multiple pages, "But look at this. It came snail mail."

The document stated the results of the feds restoration efforts, including a listing of the artifacts by tribe and piece number, and a form letter explaining the activities and resources recently involved.

"Basically, the first list we had claimed all the artifacts were recovered. Supposedly, Mary Sullivan was involved in that effort. These guys, the team that put the relics back are saying everything wasn't recovered. There's about eight pieces that aren't checked off."

"Why wasn't the original inventory record amended?"

"Bureaucracy probably," Karl believed, "I got the first inventory list from the park rangers. Same access Worthington was given. That copy was stapled to these other docs and mailed to me. So somebody's got it manually reconciled in their office, just not in the database."

Karl read the letter again and summarized, "According to their version, the reconstruction team went back out to the site a year ago, per the restoration agreement almost three years since the robbery, so that's our tax dollars working hard. Not."

"Documentation is always the last thing to get done," Peter said, searching his laptop for the files and pulled up the waypoints recorded at the site.

"We flagged over thirty items to get triangulation on our four pieces. Of the eight pieces in question, what are the chances Worthington's pieces aren't there at all?"

"Maybe Lloyd was right...slim to none."

"It's too bad we can't convince the tribes to let the government permanently store these relics in a safe place," Peter said.

"Do you blame them? With the crap storm they've been through. There's no way they would allow us to permanently house their religious and cultural ancestry," Karl preached. "If they find out this site was put back in shambles it will spark a lawsuit. If that happens, we'll never see these pieces even if they do exist."

"You said there's supposed to be a tribe representative along for the ride," Peter remembered. "Maybe they played musical chairs up there and shoved pieces in the wrong places. Anyway, it's out of our hands."

"I'll have to let Worthington know the artifacts are doubtful. He's not going to be happy about it."

"Are you going to tell anyone else?"

"Not sure yet."

Peter's interpretation of the answer was yes. Karl didn't know how much effort to invest, but he always applied his conscience, rightsizing the underdog. It was only a question of whether he picked the proverbial scab, informing tribal leadership to let them take it on, or whether he opened a new wound with the Park Service to show how inept they were.

"Do you want to go out for some food?" Karl asked.

"I've got errands to run and will pick up the color topologies for you. I'll circle back here when I'm done. Did you figure out anything for Jen? I'm expecting her to call."

"Wren's busy with it. She'll do a deep dive. You know how she hates the oil companies. Looks will probably analyze what Wren turns up. I also sent some email to an international distribution."

"We'll wait and see then. On second thought, let's meet over at the Iron Cactus."

"Cool. See you at seven."

Karl went back to the couch deciding to take a nap.

"Jesus!"

He was woken out of a dream. Handing a Pueblo leader a sheet of paper, it had names of people who took spiritual relics from the burial sites.

The Indian leader looked at him sternly, "You cannot blame men without understanding their will."

"But they need to be punished," Karl pleaded.

A rattlesnake was next to the elder's feet and the hole beads on the tail were buzzing.

"Not without my—"

The answering machine had picked up after the phone rang three times: "Hi. This is Karl. Have you kissed the earth today? Please leave a message."

"Karl. Wren. Where are you?"

Disoriented, Karl searched for the remote handset and answered, "Nice going, Wren. I was ready to kick some ass."

"What?"

"You woke me. I was dreaming about an Indian dude. He was going to give me the answer to my problem. Crap. I'll never know what he was going to say! What's up? Did you find out anything?"

"No and maybe."

Karl rubbed his eyes picking out the sand, "No first."

"Nothing on the drill heads. At least there's nothing front facing. I searched some of the server content. You know, busted in on Jen's firm and some others. Man, they really should hire some IT folks to put up a wall."

"You're the lady with the keys."

"Yeah, like that gets me dates. Anyway, no news doesn't mean they're not emailing the snot out of it or typing letters to their lawyers to cover their evil deeds. But nothing yet. I left a sniffer on there to beep me when a key word shows up. The maybe is there's a blog out there. Somebody is bitching about the government funded effort to scam the consumers by underwriting the oil barons' losses."

Karl was skeptical, "That's seventies stuff, Wren. The oil barons have left the building."

"Not quite. According to a couple blogs they're back. There's some soft shit on a couple advocate sites. They claim the oil dudes are lowering their own import thresholds."

"A contrived oil shortage?"

"Greed, the root cause of everything worth stealing! Mind you this doesn't compare to what's hitting Nigeria."

"Hmm. Thanks for scrubbing out there. Oh, shoot! I've got to meet Peter five minutes ago. I'll give him the news."

"Yeah, yeah, story of my life. I can snag 'em but I can't reel 'em in."

"I'll pray for you. Oh! Did you get the actual source of blog?"

"Not yet."

"K. Gotta go."

"Later."

Looking for a parking spot, Karl saw Peter's car pulling in to a pay n' park. They walked into the building together.

"You look like you were sleeping. What'd you do, pass out?"

"Actually I did, but Wren broke the spell."

"I should probably call Jen," Peter stated. "She probably thinks we blew it off."

"Say hello for me. I've got to hit the men's room."

"Hello, Jen...It's Peter. I did get some news. Wren found out some stuff."

Peter repeated what Karl had told him and then filled gaps, "No, nothing on the drill heads. Not yet anyway, he answered and paused to listen. "Well, if you think that's worth it. I wouldn't take it that far."

Karl came back mouthing "hello" for Peter to pass on.

"Hold it. Karl says hello. I'll tell him. I'm assuming you're not committing crimes, but on second thought...no, don't tell me. K. uh...ya. yep. Got it. Bye."

"Well?"

"She says hi and can't wait to see you again," Peter recited.

"Cool. At least she *will* get a hug and kiss from me."

"Go for it."

"What is she going to do?" Karl asked.

"She says she thinks Doug, you know the engineer at Apache, she thinks he can get his hands on some actual detail that shows who took the drill heads."

"Awesome."

"I wonder why they want to take that risk? She's going to get her butt in a sling."

"She must be serious about this. There's evidence and she thinks it points to bigger and worse."

"I guess," Peter said, remaining neutral. "It feels like we're making something out of nothing."

"Oh, I don't know. You've got all this stuff happening around the world in broad daylight. Drill bits are being stolen. The country's running out of oil. Worthington's shopping for pottery. Sounds pretty normal to me."

Forces in Opposition

Day 152.

Office of Dr. Bud Worthington. Rice University. Houston, Texas.

AFTER RE-SORTING OLD mail into piles, Bud became distracted with other thoughts, staring out his office window. The sunlight illuminated from the fringes of clouds that straddled sky and horizon. The moving tree branches were mesmerizing to Bud as he tried to clear his mind. Through the window, the muffled traffic noise from the work commute was loud, but barely audible to a man who was trying to expose a world in peril.

Literally unknown to his peers, the professor was anxious about his new momentum to publicize the conclusions of his research. The earth was changing, evolving as it always had, but soon all geological events would align against the odds science had predicted, with their conceptual ignorance. The probabilities of a catastrophic forcing could not be rationalized away.

Hell, Bud thought to himself sipping leftover tea, *no scientist will readily accept a concept like this, let alone comprehend it on pure instinct. The whole world is up in arms when a black man is beaten. We go into frenzy when a celebrity is accosted. Global nations always at war, making victims of its citizens, too busy conquering for sake of greed. Does it matter if heads are deep in the sand as the worst scenario plays out?*

"And selfishly I've drawn in another young lad who is no more prepared to accept this responsibility than a soul drawn to Heaven for his atonement," he spoke, resting his chin on his bow tie.

The professor was startled when a female appeared at his office door, "Excuse me, sir. I'm about to leave for the evening. I was told you have your evening tea. It's ready for you," said the female.

"I apologize…I'd forgotten Margaret called in sick today and I thought she'd left. And, I've forgotten your name."

"I'm Mary Smith."

"The university assigned you from their resource pool to help out? I must say they trained you well."

"Yes, I'll bring you in a fresh pot immediately."

Picking up on his thoughts, Bud felt foolish sabotaging his progress, "By any measure, I can count my good fortune. By their simultaneous efforts, Karl is looking for the Holy Grail. Jude seems capable of providing expertise. And Franklin is willing to help."

He clasped his hands, as if in prayer. "Everybody is in motion with no barriers to fault their efforts."

The tea was brought and placed on the marble top of the antique wooden server.

"Ms. Smith, thank you. I won't be in need of you, so feel free to lock Margaret's desk as you leave. I'm sure she'll be coming in tomorrow. At least that's possible?"

"Yes, Dr. Worthington. She'll be here tomorrow from what I am told."

"Thank you again. Would you close my office door behind you?"

"My pleasure."

Bud ambled over, and upon satisfying his curiosity, poured a cup. It would be fun to tease Marge that indeed he remembered to take his pills after lunch. He went to the bookshelves, for a visual check of the multiple volumes scattered on the shelves minus one.

Sitting down again, Bud turned to shut it down. He felt warmer almost sweating.

Damn tea, he thought. His stomach acid burned and suddenly a sharp pain rose from his midsection. The sudden intenseness confounded him. Dr. Worthington attempted to stand, but dizziness overwhelmed his efforts.

Seconds later, ringing filled his ears. "Ms. Smith," Bud yelled out. "Please! Smith!" Bud repeated loudly.

He heard mumbled dialogue in the outer office. Bracing himself with the chair, he desperately tried to reach the window to call out. His arms weakened. Another attack, and this time with lethal pain. Loosening his grip, the victim slumped to the floor. He held his chest while regurgitation splattered on the tile. Bud's precious mind was racing as he looked at his bookcase. The black books that represented his life were no longer supreme. His brain was responding to reserve oxygen for its own survival. Muscle tissues contracted. Auditory capabilities diminished, overcome with sporadic amounts of breathe.

A flash of random thought about his father. Then anger for his inability to defend himself for the Packard award. The surge of cardiac pain froze his movement clenching his jaw shut. A wave of fear and regret. His research. Intentions lay barren. Lifting his head, he pushed with his feet sliding his hips to another spot on the floor, moving through the liquid waste. With fragile strength his body shook, as Bud slid one or two inches between bouts of failure eyeing the bookcase.

> The next wave of unpredictable but forceful earthly evolution was triggered as the pulse weakened, barely lingering. More extraordinary than other endless natural progressions, a half a billion tons of molten lava achieved crystallization. Superheated in seconds, basaltic liquefied and flowed under extreme pressure, poisoning anonymous crevasses of massive size. The sporadic surge was tremendously greater than the thousands of previous eruptions spanning millions of years. A pattern of undetected slip movements continued to shift massive blocks of earth. Unable to withstand the intensity of pyroclastic energy, the lithosphere fractured a two mile radius. In seconds, massive propulsions of iron, granite, and basalt rock thrust upwards, spearheading a surface breach, ripping a raw portal into the landscape. A prolonged shock wave, forceful enough to undulate the surrounding area, left the existing ecology torn and scarred.

The surface skin temperature rose, crested, and settled. Dr. Worthington's heart seized, no longer capable of fending off the ample drug stimulus. The beginning thread of temporal journey forced the body to release the soul.

Human thought transformed into the elegance of ethereal momentum. The struggle for survival ended, leaving the search for truth to others. Bud was dead.

Quietly positioning herself out of view, Ms. Smith had slipped back in to witness her effort. After locking the door and shutting off the lights, she crouched over the old man to check for a pulse. She was surprised the physical reaction was so vigorous for the elder male. Each death had peculiar acts.

"Crawling didn't do any good, did it?" she coldly scolded her victim.

Performing the rest of her tasks would be simple. A USB flash drive was inserted in the back of the PC. Automatically selecting the hard drive, an executable program began to extract all its contents, existing or deleted. Breaking the silence, heads on the hard drive crackled, downloading files.

The victim's face had discolored with a dark hue on the lips. The assailant pocketed the prescription drugs on the desk and made a call. She hadn't seen the meds earlier.

"Yes, patch me through…it's secure. Patch me through now!"

A second later she was connected, "I'm downloading the drive contents. The old man is dead."

After a pause, "He's been on some kind of medication. I grabbed it. You forgot to tell me?"

Another pause. She didn't wait for her handler to finish, "No, it's more than that. I would call it a fucking complication. How do I know there won't be traces…Yes. It looks like he had a heart attack, but…"

Another pause to listen.

"It better fucking not!" Smith growled as the call ended.

She was told, "…the drug doesn't leave a trace, no matter what the fucking complications."

With minutes remaining, she made quick visual inspection of the vast amount of literature lying around.

"What a pig," she mumbled as she checked the progress on the monitor, careful not to expose herself through the window.

When the status bar displayed one hundred percent, the intruder rechecked for a pulse confirming permanent death. She was very thorough retracing with a treated cloth, removing her DNA, eliminating her physical existence.

Backing out of the office, Mary Smith whispered, "Ciao" as the door clicked shut.

Using the same route she exploited earlier, she made one more call making sure her alibi was still waiting at the bar. She walked to the only exit that had a failed security camera.

Her subsequent movements evacuating the campus lacked any effort to obscure her presence. She was home free as she walked out the east doors of the Weiss School of Natural Science, moving between cars in the parking lot and onto the sidewalk. A few more yards and she got into a car. The student jutting between vehicles forty yards away was insignificant to her. Driving away, she sang to the CD oblivious to the same student running across the street and towards her car, stopping suddenly, and then turning back.

"Pass me those Doritos."

Jude reached through the seats, grabbed the bag and tossed it into Arthur's lap, "When did you start eating junk food?"

"When I realized I'd be sitting on my butt for two hours in the dark, watching the windows fog."

"Ya, that's probably a first for you. I told you this would be the highlight of your day."

"I'm not surprised you don't get bored with it," Arthur stated flatly, tossing the bag on to the dash accidentally bumping the Pringles can. It fell to the floor.

"Ya dill rod, Clarke. You bent the wire! We've probably missed something."

"Yeah, I'm sure the entire world just caved in and we weren't paying attention. It's almost six-thirty. Didn't you say our man was going to retire for the evening?"

As Jude reworked the connecting wire, he blasted Arthur, "Hey, you're the one that said let's stay! I've heard all this before. Like twenty times."

He checked the battery, adjusted the connector, and examined the locknuts, "Sometimes he hangs around. He works on his research from what I can tell. The way he talks about it, it's like his child."

"The tenured staff ignores him. Got that from a good source."

"They aren't the only ones," Jude commented, thinking about his uncle.

"Don't touch the can... Hey, look, there's Worthington at the window."

"Come in base, we have a visual," Arthur mocked. "Okay, you proved your point. Let's head out."

"K. Let me fix this to make sure it works so I don't have to tell Karl you trashed it."

Jude bent the pigtail antenna slightly and heard static then it went silent.

"Damn thing, there's no sig...there's one."

"...be impatient, I'm going in soon.... Yes, he's still here."

Both paused listening, waiting.

"What? Didn't you say...?"

"Shhh! Hold it..." Nothing else was broadcast.

Arthur insisted, "Didn't you say it picks up a wide area?"

"Yes, but it's pointed at his window!"

"Wasn't that female? That wasn't Olivary."

"Be quiet for a minute."

Arthur wiped the window clear of moisture, waiting for another transmission. Nothing.

"Olivary is usually gone by now," Jude advised. "That couldn't have been her. We should probably stick around until we actually see Bud."

Arthur nudged his partner, "The office lights just went out."

"Good, we can go around and see him drive off."

There was a quick burst of leading static. "...me through..."

"It's her!"

The clip fell off again. Jude quickly pressed it to the ground wire. A wave of static hit the transmission and drifted out, "The old man is dead... ucking complica...etter..not."

The words they heard were as clear as if said to their face.

Scaring Arthur, Jude suddenly opened the door bolting out of the car, leaving pieces of their surveillance material in his wake. Arthur got out watching the window. Abruptly he was overcome with the sense of eminent danger.

What if we're discovered!

He quickly got back in the car and huddled down. Moments later he was startled again when Jude banged on the window, "We've got to get in there, Clarke! The doors are locked! Where's my cell phone! We need to call nine-one-one!"

Jude ran off again, headed to other entrances, hoping some of them had not been secured. Since the breezeways were gated at night he used critical energy and time to reach the open part of the "U" shaped building.

"God damn it!" Out of breath and still unable to gain entry, he reversed direction towards their car, but jolted to a stop. In the distance, a female crossed the office parking lot.

Is this who I heard talking?

Transforming his energy from recovery to that of a stalker, the student tracked the stranger's movements as she walked down the block. For no other reason than desperation, Jude became more certain of the female's role.

I need to confront her!

The thought initiated a burst of aggression and he exploded with speed, but the gap in distance was too great. She had reached her vehicle. His heart pounding, Jude let up as the car drove away. With one option left, he jogged back to where he left Arthur but the locked car was empty.

"Jude!" Arthur yelled from the corner, "Wait!" as he ran to his roommate.

"I couldn't go inside. I need my cell phone! Unlock the car!!"

"*No!* We can't be implicated in this."

"What are you saying, Clarke? We've got to help him. He could be alive! He was *right*! Somebody *was* after him!"

Arthur stepped back ignoring Jude's frustration. From a distance their voices echoed. Distressed, Jude bear-hugged Arthur to get the keys.

"Let me go!" Arthur ordered and his roommate froze in place, shocked by the tone of Arthur's gut-level command. "Do you know what's going to happen when you make that call?"

Arthur demanded attention, "First, they'll have your name and number. Then lights and sirens. They get in the building and find him. The police will have you on the scene, and *you* have to explain how you *knew* Worthington was in the building."

Sweating from lapping the building, Jude relaxed his shoulders and looked at the ground as Arthur continued, circling him, backing his roommate up to the car, using his hands to accentuate his argument, "It won't end there! When they figure out *you* ran around, they'll find your *fingerprints* on all the doors, they'll ask what *we* are doing out here!"

As Jude's eyes darted to see if anybody was noticing the commotion, Arthur lowered his voice remaining terse, "We're students. Remember? We aren't supposed to be here right now. Doing this! And when you tell them we heard the woman? They'll be processing our asses and this whole thing blows up *in our faces*!"

Jude kicked the tree guard next to him and gritted his teeth.

"We need to get this right and figure it out," Arthur insisted. "But not here. There won't be any do-overs."

There was no comeback or protest. They both heard the pronouncement clearly. The old man is dead. The school would place them on detention if answers didn't come quickly. The media would swarm. Whoever did it would be watching and listening.

Jude wiped his eyes and face with the sleeve of his jacket. *Why did this happen? Bud was supposed to be paranoid for no reason.* He had no energy left to challenge his roommate's logic and later that night, suppressed the impulse to call anyone.

"You win. Let's get outta here."

Home of Jude Caine.
Houston, Texas.

WRETCHED WITH HIS decision not to report his mentor's death, Jude found it impossible to come to terms with the horrific event and its aftermath. Causing sleep deprivation, his dreams of the fateful evening replayed for second chances.

He could have gone to the campus police when he learned of Worthington's concerns. He could have told them he saw something in the window when he was "passing" by. He could have made an anonymous call from a pay phone. He didn't have to reveal the facts.

Convincing himself that Arthur bullied him, Jude knew his reaction would have been different if he were alone that night. He would have dialed 911. He would have given his name. He would have told them he was waiting in his car. But there were no second chances.

The entire campus worked through its grief of an old teacher passing on. The university homepage's active link, "We mourn the death of Dr. Bud Worthington" reported that "a mentor, a great teacher, and scientist lost his long battle with Crohn's disease. Paul Brewer was quoted saying kind words about his friend.

"I've been alongside Dr. Bud Worthington as a colleague and close friend. He believed discoveries in the natural sciences were unbounded. As a visionary, his preeminent research would have given him a place among the greatest scientists. His absence will impact the advocacy of a seminal work but we shouldn't let those efforts die with him."

The weather had turned with drenching rain. The muck of leaves choked the grates and alleys. Matching the gloom with a hangover, Jude woke in the afternoon, days after the incident and argued with his roommate. Again, they debated the decision of doing nothing. Jude's repetitive claims they needed to do something, remained as conflict between them.

The junior spent the rest of the evening and early morning hours consuming alcohol at a slow methodical pace to imbue his sensitivities before attending the events of the deceased. The front of his head still throbbed as the outside funeral procession gathered for the completion of Mass, attendees standing shoulder to shoulder. A thread of cigarette smoke reaching Jude reminded him of sitting in Worthington's office chairs, looking at the stacks of books. It odor wasn't so annoying now.

The eulogies were just words coming from the mouths of strangers telling less than the truth. They knew nothing of the precious truth about the professor's love for geology and teaching. About his struggles and obsession to complete his life's dream to share supreme knowledge. His paranoia, which turned on him, then failed him. *How could Worthington's death be blessed when it was murder?* Jude thought. To him, as the minister spoke of forgiveness, it seemed premature and all too inclusive.

Leaving to clear his mind, the third year student turned to squeeze through the standing crowd, certain his sweat carried the smell of alcohol. Two professors from the Earth Science department believed they were discrete with their conversation.

"...a good example of why they shouldn't offer tenure."

Jude stopped to listen, pretending his focus was elsewhere.

"He hadn't contributed for years. I don't know why they didn't force him out."

"I heard they offered him another assignment but he wouldn't take it. So they were stuck with him."

"Well this is one way to get out of a shitty deal. A win-win as far as I'm concerned."

The student made fists, gripping tightly until the tension reached his forearms. It was the only way to control frustration. Jude concluded his exit past them and out to the parking lot. He wasn't sure if he actually spoke the phrase "you suck" or was just thinking it as he passed the faculty members.

Arthur was remorseful. His coherent appeal to Jude to stand down seemed harsh now. At that moment, he was convinced they could be implicated. Much of his reaction was reflex from his upbringing, listening to countless dialogue between his uncles and aunts perfecting how a case should be litigated or how they would defend a client. When he was a teenager, the family of lawyers would drink their tonics and martinis mentoring him as if the answers and methods were family recipes.

"Arthur, very few will have the insights we are sharing."

One of his uncles always repeated the same thing somewhere between his fourth and seventh drink, "Go with your gut to cover your ass. There are no do-overs."

There were numerous news stories and press announcing the discovery of Dr. Bud Worthington's body in his office. Poor Ms. Olivary found him lying there, his rigor mortised hands and arms asymmetrical from each other. The unofficial COD was rumored to be massive heart failure due to old age complications.

The level of interest from the state, local, and campus officials was in step with any other unfortunate non-circumstantial passing of a noble and gracious human being. Cards, flowers, and letters flowed into the university administration. Students placed memorabilia outside Worthington's office window. The mosaic of colored wax that flowed from lit candles exacted a pseudo repair on the small cracks in the sidewalk. From the outset of the professor's death, campus life slowed down and stopped. Then restarted.

As the aftermath of Worthington's death passed, completely submerged by the future, every day activity found incremental progress, providing near instant closure for the bereaved professional community. Immediate changes were made to the student's curriculum, shifting the gap of teaching duties to a number of professors. The university began an aggressive search looking for a replacement to cover academic commitments.

Closure was incomplete for Jude. All that remained was the pressure to tell the truth.

Walking alone in one of his funks, he passed by Worthington's office, looking upward at the closed window. All his thoughts were smashing together, all played out to exhaustion. With the death virtually witnessed by them, he accepted the surge of guilt, a symptom of his silence while the killer remained at large.

"How often does a man like Worthington come knocking on your door," Jude had asked Arthur when he returned home.

"Once and maybe twice if you pay attention."

"Tell me something I don't know," Jude recalled thinking as he sat there staring at his plate of food. "Anyway, I called my parents."

Arthur showed intense concern fearing Jude had wavered from his agreement.

"Trust me, Clarke, if I had actually leaked anything you'd be watching my mom packing my underwear."

Jude had played the voice over and over. The voice raised in tone, his eyes focused, *I'm at the conclusion of this rather critical body of evidence and before I ask you to join me, would like you to be aware of the risk.*

"There's only one option that's being handed to us, Clarke."

An idea had surfaced between bouts of sober-less states of oblivion. Jude wasn't sure if the idea had been suppressed underneath personal remorse or behind the guilt from stiff reluctance to trust the professor and his proclaimed genius. The idea settled into a mind that was transitioning from grief and condemnation, to absolution and preservation. Maybe it was what Paul Brewer said about his friend. The research had to survive. They couldn't let it die. They had to own it. They had to take it.

Days later, Jude and Arthur continued to debate the mission of getting possession of the black books. The disagreements weren't about whether or not to do it. The challenge was how to do it and when. Certain they were the only ones who knew the existence of the volumes, more justification was touted by the two juniors as they became more comfortable with the idea of stealing the research from Worthington's office.

Adamant, Jude believed taking physical ownership of the research was the only way to protect it, explaining that he felt empowered as Worthington's emissary. Arthur seemed fearless. Whether thrust in his lap or deemed to be closer to his natural talent, his exposure to these raw unfiltered circumstances released energy, battling logic over emotion. He said he *was* supposed to be a part of this action.

Getting ownership of the black books was, as Arthur put it, "likely to cause the forfeiture of my future career, but I'm going with my gut."

"You think Olivary is going to leave us both in there at the same time?" Jude doubted, as they developed a plan the next day. "Wouldn't it be better if one of us stays outside the office?"

Standing again, Arthur paced the floor, "We should both present ourselves to her. We tell her there are some textbooks that you left in his office."

He thought for another second, "We can both enter the room and for a back-up plan, if she follows us in, we'll act like we can't find them."

"We need time! There's seven, remember?" Jude emphasized.

"Yes," Arthur agreed. "So, if Olivary does follow us in, I'll say I want to make an appointment with the new professor. She'll have to go back out to her desk."

"Like you said before, the only way is to take them out the window somehow. But we might be seen and throwing them to the ground is too noisy," Jude worried out loud.

"Umm...I took a precaution on that possibility and hear me out here," Arthur cleared his voice. "I've brought someone else in..."

Jude shoved his upper torso into the couch raising his arms in frustration, "You're kidding, right?"

"Jude, *you* even get that we can't be in two places at once, with Olivary in our faces."

Arthur kept Jude from interrupting, revising the plan, "Hear me out...so instead, we're going to walk out with one volume, and you claim Worthington borrowed it from you, the case studies from your uncle. With me out in the office, Avey will be...Yes, she needs to be outside the window and you're going to toss her the volumes."

Jude sighed, "Clarke. Avey? No way. She can't..." And then scrunched his face. "Is she really right for this?"

Arthur reminded him that Worthington's massive collection would be removed, assessed, and some of his work would be showcased in the Fondren Library, "This is the only chance to get all of them."

Squinting with an air of suspicion, Jude put his roommate on the spot, "You're dating her."

"True story," Arthur admitted, "But I didn't tell her everything. She's a big fan of Worthington and totally agreed that if it's just library stuff, we shouldn't let it get lost in some bureaucratic review."

Arthur's note to self was to remind Avey of what he just told Jude.

Jude cringed, "I hope we can count on her. And I even hate bringing it up, but with her leg and all, she needs to be spot on, Clarke."

"She will be."

"I think we'll need ten minutes or more to grab all the binders..." Jude continued, concentrating on efficiency. "...if I get lucky and remember all the locations."

"Well...," Arthur paused, "you said they're all the same height. You've seen five, right?"

"Bud talked about seven, pointing them out. The other two are in proximity to the ones I've seen. We'll just have to go with it."

More effort was spent figuring out what day and time. It drove Jude nuts but Arthur finally settled on a time of four-thirty after he spent an hour, debating Friday was the best day of the week.

"It's a win-win," Arthur concluded. "A majority of university staff will be departing for the weekend, leaving more parking spots and less foot traffic. And we can just show up at the last minute. Based on what you said, Ms. Olivary likes to leave by five-forty-five. That nails it!"

"Nice work, Bond."

During the next seventy-two hours nothing else was top of mind for Jude and Arthur, other than their plan to obtain the black books. Having slack time was hardly motivating. Nothing else was more compelling than getting their hands on the material.

Friday afternoon seemed to drag forever, as Jude sat in a study cube, in a building adjacent to Worthington's office. Arthur was still panicky because Olivary forced him to make an appointment.

He reminded Jude of the same detail again when he sent a text message, "I have 2 get 2 WO by qtr after. U can't B late!"

Jude was uneasy about the third resource and text back, "no worries about me. what about av??"

And Arthur's immediate reply, "np. she'll b in place under the window."

At the designated time, Arthur left his car, and walked the distance he had timed a day earlier. All the parking spots were taken adjacent to Worthington's window. *I hope somebody leaves!*

With a deep breath he ignored the knots in his stomach, entering into the office, "Hello, Ms. Olivary."

Looking up, she habitually reached for her appointment book, "Hi, Arthur. Now what can I do for you?"

Arthur opened his mouth to answer, but the secretary interrupted, "I was a bit confused as to what you needed. I'm wrapping up the schedule changes for the new professor and have to complete it before I leave."

"Well see, I wanted to stop by and let you know how bad we... I mean how bad I felt about Dr Worthington and everything."

"Well, thank you for saying that. I know you were close to Dr. Worthington as well as a number of other students and professors," Margaret replied glancing at the closed door to the vacant inner office. "He will be missed. I know I'm not at all settled with what happened."

Arthur nodded letting her continue.

"I still expect him to come through the door, kidding me about something or having an empty cup of tea to fill. I can't believe I wasn't here the very day he had his heart attack. The only day I've missed in a long time..." Her voice was emotive, "...and I feel like if I were here I could have helped *some way!* Did you hear my car got vandalized? I didn't think it was a big deal, but the detective seemed interested."

The secretary sat motionless as Arthur stood dumbfounded, not knowing exactly how to respond.

Where's Jude! he thought dismally, trying to fill the gap in their plan. "No I didn't. It was a real shock to campus. But maybe things will get back to normal."

"The detective assumes it was natural causes but he isn't ruling anything out yet."

He heard the outer doors slam shut, "...I think that's Jude."

Coming into the office without an introduction, Jude assumed they were on track, "I'm sorry I'm late. Did you tell Ms. Olivary what I needed?"

"Well...," Margaret hummed, "not exactly. Arthur and I were talking about Dr. Worthington."

"Jude, why don't you go ahead and explain it," Arthur asked.

"Okay," Jude improvised, wondering why Arthur didn't follow through with the plan, "See, I realized this morning that Dr. Worthington still had a book I loaned to him. My uncle called wanting it back. Arthur said he would let you know because I had to get to class."

Jude glanced at Arthur, "Right?"

"Well, I was about to mention it."

"So...," Jude took control again, "...since Dr. Worthington's library will be moved soon, I was hoping I could get in there and retrieve it?"

The secretary's body language was not positive, "Now, I know you boys were respected by Dr. Worthington and everything, but I've got to get this schedule out as I explained to Arthur."

Shaking her head, the secretary became concerned, "I can't help you and get my work done. Because of the new rules, we have to be out of here by five-thirty. Security does a walk through."

"Really?"

"Why the new rule?" Arthur pried.

"It's because of Dr. Worthington. They are making sure staff gets out of their offices because of liability reasons. I don't have a way to finish this work at home."

"Ms. Olivary?" Arthur injected speaking over the top of Jude, "We don't want to compromise your work. Jude can find it on his own. Would that be okay?"

"I'm concerned about his papers and personal items being gone through and rearranged, so I would want to be in there. If I can figure out how to get this table parameter to work and the tabs changed then..."

Arthur seized the new opportunity, "I'm pretty good with functionality. What application is it?"

"Word."

"Well, if it's not confidential information, I can help."

Manipulation is all we've got at this point, Jude thought as he watched Arthur try to worm his way in to save their plan.

"Right on time guys!" Olivary announced, catching up to them after locking the doors.

She thanked Arthur one more time for his help, not aware of any motive that took advantage of her. It was five-twenty-eight and the boys felt they had finessed a miracle. With Olivary out of sight, they banged knuckles, walking around the corner boasting to each other of the skill and quick wits that were needed to keep the plan from failing. In mid conversation Avey came out of the shadows, practically knocking them over. The three of them huddled in the rain mist.

"What happened in there? Where is the seventh book?" she whispered too loudly.

"Whoa! Shhh!" Jude demanded.

"You said you were going to give me seven! I waited and your arm suddenly pulled inside and the window was shut. I could see Olivary's face. She didn't look happy."

"Hold on!" Jude urged, grabbing her shoulders and moved her off to the side. "When I got in there, thanks to Clarke's tutoring, I started to locate the volumes," he explained and let Arthur interrupt.

"We're fortunate that she couldn't figure out Word tables!"

"Like we thought, she was real touchy with Worthington's stuff," Jude continued, looking to see if anybody was approaching them. "Anyway once I got the door to block her view, I grabbed the lowest books and gave them to you, right?"

"I took those and was waiting but a car came towards us, and you said to hide. Then I saw your arm hanging there with one volume. I had to run back and just barely caught it."

"I heard Olivary coming, and I was praying you were there. But I had to use the ladder to reach two books at once. I can't remember if I saw three, but it was freaking me out because I'm up there balancing and I can hear Arthur trying to keep her attention. Then, after I tossed that big one to you, she walks in."

"I thought we're caught!" Arthur admitted. "I started to say we had to get these books, as I followed Olivary into the office and there's Jude on the floor. He faked his ankle being hurt and how he had to open the window for fresh air. Genius!"

"We limped out of there! Can you believe that? It worked! Arthur said, looking at Avey. "We got all the books! I have the last one! We brought it out when Olivary escorted us out of the office."

Avey looked at it, "No. Jude said he had them all when he started flinging them out of the window. When the car came past, I was keeping track. You," she said pointing at Arthur, "told me earlier there would be seven. I only count five plus this one. The last one was like a huge binder! I almost fell on my butt catching it."

Jude rolled his eyes looking at his roommate.

"Don't look at me. I was trying to keep Olivary pinned down."

"Ya, that was a lot harder than catching books and dodging cars in the downpour," Avey declared.

"Where are the books now?"

"In the car."

When she opened the door and Jude recounted, he realized his mistake, "I saw the last three on the upper shelves but I got hung up with moving the ladder. I was thinking three and then had to settle for two," Jude explained. "We can't go back in there."

"We can't hang out here any longer either," Arthur instructed. "Let's regroup at the apartment. Avey, let me take you home," and looking at Jude, "I'll see you in a couple minutes."

Arthur and Avey walked across the street and eventually were out of view.

Jude got into his car, relieved it was over, "We pulled it off and no one suspects a thing!"

Day 122.

Rice University. Houston, Texas.

A S THOUSANDS OF students prepared to leave campus for summer break, no one had the slightest notion that a man's most guarded secret had vast consequences for the world. On a path of normalcy, the university approved funding to display a portion of Bud's book collection. The student committee sponsored a bronze plaque, to be located in the courtyard. No one had reasons to wonder if they could be doing more. Except for Jude and Arthur.

Jude stirred with regrets, having taken possession of a scientific treasure. The burden of ownership had become a source of agitation. The black books, volumes of untested research, held little value if nothing was accomplished with them. He wanted to get them to whoever could wield the power of their contents. Arthur wanted to maintain control of the black books. He reasoned passionately that they needed to understand the detail that Worthington captured so they could achieve his ultimate goal.

"There's too much here for us to do it justice," Jude claimed. "The research could be over our heads. You admitted that yourself."

Arthur wasn't to be moved, but listened intently to his roommate's justification.

"We need Peter and his group to front the information. We don't have credibility out there."

"If we lose control of the volumes," Arthur warned, "then we might as well have left them on the shelves. And nobody is familiar them."

"Let's call Peter and see what he thinks. If his group doesn't have time to figure it out, we'll do it ourselves. But I don't want to waste my whole summer if they can save us time and point the way."

With no agreement the students needed to complete other obligations. Arthur had to submit the financial statements for the fundraising committee. Jude had agreed to help the new professor who replaced Worthington.

"Olivary asked if I would do a favor for Professor Emery and draft a reading list for the freshman summer class. I couldn't turn her down."

"Clarke, where are you?"

"At the house. Why?"

"You won't believe this!"

Jude stood in the anteroom beyond Olivary's desk cupping his hand to keep his voice from echoing, "I'm down here helping Emery. He had a box with a bunch of Bud's office mail that never got opened. When he was cleaning up, there was other stuff that he didn't know what to do with. But get this. There's a camera hookup!"

"That's a stretch for Worthington."

"He says he found it on the bookshelves."

Out of breath running from the car, Jude bounded onto the porch and through the door. He found Arthur in the kitchen with his girlfriend, "Hey. Hi, Avey."

The glances between them were instant recognition that she was going to be a permanent part of whatever they did and didn't do.

"Well, let's figure it out together," Jude announced, with a big smile on his face and held out the webcam that he took. "The box of mail is out in the car. Emery said I could go through it whenever."

"This equipment doesn't help. The files are probably on his system," Arthur said.

"Way ahead of you. I told him that Worthington had a couple of Peter's copyrighted files on loan for a class project. His computer was sitting in the corner unplugged. I switched some cables from Emery's system. Thank God it booted. I went in using the safe mode and loaded a bunch of files to my flash drive," waving the device.

"Sweet," Arthur purred as he powered up his laptop on the kitchen table.

Avey remained quiet catching on to the real reason her friends were involved.

"There's a mix of file types. I wasn't sure what to pull," Jude admitted.

"That's okay. I have most of the file associations built in my system," Arthur answered. After selecting the contents on the thumb drive, an application loaded to view the single frames.

"Stop, that looks like two people," Jude indicated. But these are blurry. He had the camera pointed towards his computer.

"That was smart!" Arthur thought.

"Yes!" Jude replied. "Anyone would mess with his system first before searching his library. The camera must have been on all the time."

Arthur switched directions with the viewer, "I hope Emery pulled the plug in time. This has been cycling, writing over the top. I think I can search with the time stamp."

"April 2...," Jude reminded everyone.

"Are you kidding, it's stuck in my head too!"

The search parsed out a number of frames. Clicking through, deliberately slow, Avey was mesmerized seeing the reality of what Arthur told her when she first got involved.

"There he is!"

Single frames of still photos showed the lower half of Worthington at the window. Then an image of him drinking tea. Their eyes collectively focused, horrified with the next sequence of pictures. Gritty images showed a man crawling, staring upward at the camera. Three more single frames showed a dark image bending over the professor touching him. The lack of intervention was obvious.

"He crawled there so the person would expose themselves!" Arthur revealed.

"Her clothing! That's the lady that I chased!" Jude announced.

"It's hard to take even when you know what was coming," Arthur said, closing the files.

"You guys should have gone to the cops! You should go now!" Avey scolded. "It's risky hanging onto this!"

"Now you know how I felt," Jude shared.

"As bad as this is, no way!" Arthur disputed. "There'd be no black books. We can turn this evidence in anytime."

"What's the difference?" Avey commanded. "At least the police would have a lead."

"For one, "Arthur defended, "there's a chance–"

"Jude can say he found it in the box of mail. We leave it on the thumb drive," Avey interrupted. "The police start investigating and we still have the black books."

"I was going to say, there's a chance that whoever did this is still looking," Arthur responded and decided to tell them what was bugging him. "Jude told me the female he saw wasn't carrying anything, so we assume she didn't take anything because we have all the volumes. We're the only ones that know the research isn't on the computer. How long will it take for anyone else to figure that out?"

"That's why we need to involve Peter and his buddies," Jude insisted.

"Well, that's still an option, but I don't know if we can trust *them*. We'll share everything and nothing happens," Arthur claimed.

"Let's all compromise," Avey refereed. "I'm not totally convinced the police shouldn't be involved, but I know we'd be buried if we pulled them in. What if we share what we have with Peter, including the pictures and we keep everything in our possession. We don't have to hand them over."

"I'll send Peter an email," Jude offered, "and we can get on the phone with him over the weekend."

Sitting in a student break room, the undergraduates remained in lockstep during the call with Jude's uncle. Using the speakerphone, they shared what happened after spring break.

Keenly interested, Peter interrupted to get more detail. He had heard about the professor's death through contacts and asked about the funeral, "I know Karl was bummed out when he heard."

The moment came when Jude described what they were doing when the professor died.

"You think he was murdered?" Peter asked.

"No, we can *prove* he was murdered," Jude restated.

"That's hard to believe. And you didn't say anything to the police?"

Jude muted the phone to whisper, "He's getting upset. I can tell." Then he responded to Peter, "I was using the Pringles can listening to conversation."

"So no proof."

Jude had to explain the device, reminding him it was Karl's idea, "It doesn't come with the tape recorder attachment," Jude said sarcastically. "So if we go to the police it's circumstantial."

"Then, it's a crime the police know nothing about?"

"Exactly! But we would have lost our chance to get the research because the entire office would have been a crime scene. The local news said a university employee died. End of story."

"And you're not going to the police?"

"We've got more evidence to consider before we do that."

Peter rubbed his forehead. He was an expert working finite detail with specificity, not solving a legal and criminal snafu involving his nephew. Considering this was a waste of time he resisted, "I'm confused. What do you want me to do now that I have this incriminating information?"

The undergraduates continued to explain the additional evidence they had recently uncovered.

With more reluctance from Peter, Avey signaled she wanted to help make their case, "Peter, since all this has happened, why aren't you convinced to help us?"

"It's not me that has to be convinced. The consensus was Worthington was a bit of a flake. I'm not the only one who believed that back then. He had no support and some say he wasted the school's money."

He heard Jude cough in the background saying, "Bullshit."

Avey waved him off with her hand, "None of us have heard that since *we've* been here," she fired back. "But what I hear you saying is, even though Bud was murdered, that's not because of his research. So somebody randomly took his life."

Peter tensed up, "You guys said the photography is blurry. Unless you take it to the police it's not going to be validated. Like I said, it's not me that you should be coming to."

"There's nobody else we can trust without this blowing up in our faces," Jude pleaded.

"So," Peter responded, "you're proposing that you guys study everything you have from Worthington's office and bring those conclusions to who?"

Jude explained it again, "You, Karl, and the others and we'll make our case. If you think it's still bogus then we'll uh...we'll cross that road if we get there."

"And why us? Why not let the police handle it?"

"Because they'll take all the evidence and our statements and—"

"K. I got it," interrupted the uncle. "We've been going around in circles for an hour. Let me talk with Karl and I'll call you back tomorrow."

Arthur was perturbed after Peter hung up, "He doesn't get it. I'd say we're on our own."

"He drives me nuts sometimes too," Jude admitted. "If he gets the full story, Karl will push him to do it. He just doesn't like it when things aren't black and white. My mom tells stories of him when he was old enough to mow lawns. He had little schedules and went door to door asking for customers. Like he had his own bank account. She said he was a little adult."

The next day, Karl called and left a message. It was a complete jolt to Arthur and Jude as they listened to the message again:

> "Hey, Jude. Karl. I convinced Peter to give you a shot. No easy feat! We'll put you up in Austin for the summer if you can handle that. I've sent you an email with the details. Later."

"It's too bad we missed his call. That guy is awesome!" Arthur responded, psyched about their future. "I wonder how he convinced Peter?"

"Who knows?" Jude replied, looking at the other instructions in the email. "It's more than we could ask for, getting to stay in Austin and maybe even meet with everyone. It's like Peter rolled over. Anyway, we've got some quick decisions to make. How's Avey going to take you leaving?"

"I think she'll probably come with us," Arthur replied.

"What? No, I mean…she…her parents wouldn't go for it, would they?"

"You know when you took off for spring break? I was *with* Avey…and her parents."

"Jesus, Clarke!" Jude blurted. "Why didn't you say something? I know you're tight with her and everything, but—"

"I love her, Jude. She's cool and everything. But mostly because she's smarter than you."

Jude laughed, "That's not saying much. Her parents won't mind?"

"We were going to hang out together all summer anyway. The email says the house has three bedrooms. It doesn't sound too complicated."

"We got some calls to make. Can you get out of your lease?"

"Probably."

"What about getting it back for next year?"

"Not sure. I'll figure something out."

Jude thought that was a strange comment for somebody that was manic compulsive all year about commitments, grades, and dominance.

Jude, Arthur, and Avey accomplished three days of work, explanations, and closure to relocate three hours from the college. Before the physical work, they had to convince parents to buy-off on the revision of their summer plans. Jude's conversation with his mother was more about forcing himself on Peter than about wasting his time. She peppered him, but he fended off the assault.

"Are you sure he's okay with this. I can't believe he signed up for housing three of you. What are you going to do all summer? What about the summer internship you've always done."

"Peter and his buddies are going to let us research some stuff for them. No, I can't do that internship anymore. Remember, Worthington sponsored it. How much trouble could we get into?"

Right after his call, Jude talked to his uncle, "How come you agreed to have us down there? You seemed pretty against it."

Peter didn't share what he was thinking, deciding it was better to have Jude under his control, "This way, we can all take a good look at it. I think you guys can be persuaded to do the right thing."

Avey had to remind her parents they already approved of her hanging out with Arthur.

But they thought it was on the condition of attending summer school workshops on campus and related field trips, "Are Arthur's parents aware of his plans?"

"Yes, Mom."

"Is your semester going to go to waste? We spent good money this year. To throw it away wouldn't be right."

"Dad, we are going to be studying every day with Jude's older friends who are professional geologists. I'll get to apply everything I've learned this year."

Arthur balked about his parent's plans for him, keeping up the pressure until they relented in his favor. After hanging up, his mom had a smile on her face, "You know Arthur is not going to be a lawyer right?" she predicted again to her husband.

"Yes, I'm starting to let go of that. Are we really going to send him the funds? I could let his sister invite someone to Europe instead."

"I think he's earned it. He's top of his class in a field we know nothing about. He's so different from our other children. Did you know he has a girlfriend? He says he'll bring her to meet us at the end of the summer."

"Really?"

"Let's swing by Bud's office before we head out," Jude offered.

Huddling at the bottom of the office window, it was all that was needed for the dam to break. Eyes teared. This is how they wanted to remember Bud. Not any part of his funeral or his grave site, or what people thought about him.

Home of Peter Childs. Austin, Texas.

After arriving at Peter's vacant house late evening, the group decided to bed down in sleeping bags on the couch and floor. Ten minutes of silence relieved every one of their consciousness.

The next morning, Peter quietly observed the collapsed travelers and grabbed his workout gear, leaving a note behind:

Hi. Great! You're all here. I went to work out. PS. My neighbor across the street is very nosey. Just ignore her.

Mrs. Beal wasn't going to let him go without an update. A widow, she filled her days staring out her front window, sometimes through binoculars. Out of respect to her loneliness, Peter put up with her countless attempts to tattle, including the incident she was crossing the street to report.

"Hi, Peter. I wanted to tell you three kids were sneaking around your house late last night. I think two boys and a girl. I was going to leave you a note, but then you drove up."

"One's my nephew and his friends. I gave them a key."

Avoiding an interrogation, Peter thanked her for watching the house.

"Are they staying long?"

"A couple weeks is all," Peter responded, slipping into the driver's seat and starting the car, "I'll introduce them to you soon. I'm sorry but I have to go. Thanks again."

He left her no chance to tell him about the UPS delivery that he missed. Annoyed, Mrs. Beal returned to her house to watch the other neighbors. Having taken the delivery slip, she would have a reason to meddle in his affairs again.

Early afternoon, the students met Karl at their summer residence, a two-story with yard and landscape.

Jude greeted him first and as he completed introductions, Avey broke rank giving Karl a hug, "Thank you for making this possible Karl. You won't regret it!"

"Of course not! I'm looking forward to it!"

Karl finished the walk through, "It's all yours then. Did all your stuff arrive at Peter's?"

"We have the load with us to unpack," explained Jude. "When's the big meeting?"

"I think everybody chimed in for the beginning of next month. It will be a quick week-end."

"Great. That gives us enough time to dive deep into the black books!" Avey exclaimed.

"Peter and I want to go over some stuff tonight at his house. I heard you have unusual information about Worthington's death."

"That's a major understatement," Jude replied.

"Nothing is what it seems these days. But let's concentrate on the research."

Arthur couldn't help himself, "Karl, what's Peter's hang-up about all this? Obviously you support what we're trying to do."

"He's trying to get his arms around it all. There are other issues that we'll talk about."

"And you're not...freaking out about any of it, like the death?"

"I care about the circumstances of his death in case it puts us at risk. But no I'm not worried."

"Do you think Bud's research is really that good?" Jude tested.

"There's the catch. What was he trying to uncover? No one seems to know," Karl answered. "I'm going to bolt. See you guys later."

That evening the discussion turned serious, as the group gathered around a large coffee table Avey sat between her college mates.

Jude didn't hesitate to get to the main issue, "Let me bounce a couple things off you guys and test the water."

"Go for it."

"Like we said, there's proof Bud was murdered and we've all agreed to set that aside for now and concentrate on what Bud created. I owe it to him to move his research in the direction that he would have."

Avey wanted her feelings heard, "I know I came into this late, but as we were driving out, I really thought about Bud's contribution. The volumes aren't a bunch of scrap books from a hobby. They're a chronological path of unique research. It's like a diary. What they lack in presentation is made up for by the way he challenged the current science. We want to find out the truth."

Peter forced his issue. If he could get the police involved, the students would be forced to hand everything over and all this would go away, "Go back to basics. Let's assume Bud was killed for his research. We gather those facts and take it to law enforcement. Get that out of the way first and then you can concentrate on whatever you want. It shouldn't be more complicated than that."

Arthur quickly responded, "When we're forced to explain what we know, we'll become targets of the investigation."

"How do you figure?" Peter asked.

"Simple logic. If it was murder, it wasn't a random act. Nothing was removed from his office, because we have it. So, the person that did it had motive. Maybe that person..."

"It's a she," Jude added.

"...Maybe she was hired."

"Oh come on!" Peter challenged. "The point is she or other people might consider tracking us down."

"Geeze," Peter replied. "It's not like some gruesome conspiracy!"

Arthur continued, "If we go to the police, it will be at our expense. We'll end up spending the summer defending our reputations."

"So instead, we keep all this so-called 'evidence'?" Peter questioned. "Eventually somebody needs to know."

Avey pleaded, "We're on the *same* team right? Doesn't it make sense to put ourselves first before others and find out the truth ourselves? We're asking that you trust us before you trust somebody else."

"That's where we disagree. It's not a matter of trust," Peter corrected. "It's about spending time on something you know nothing about. I don't have all summer to waste. I've got clients that need attention."

Peter looked at Karl, waiting for comments from him. Privately, he was glad to have someone else battling Peter.

"You guys know where I stand. Since we have the black books, I can't see you totally walking away, especially since Jude studied them. Peter, we should at least share what we have been up to."

Jude thought all along Peter was hiding something.

Peter crossed his arms defensively and his jaw tightened, "But don't jump to conclusions."

They listened intently to Peter's explanation of Jen's discovery with her friends at Apache.

"She's still figuring things out?" Avey wondered.

"Yes."

Karl shared what they had learned from their trip to Mesa Verde explaining the documentation errors when they attempted to map their data, "We're still not to the bottom of what differences there are and why. There's no obvious connection between the drill bits and the artifacts. The de facto link might be Worthington's death. That's why I think it's worth digging deeper."

And he surprised everyone, even Peter, when he showed the package he received, "Look familiar?"

The three students were astonished seeing another black book in Karl's hands.

"I got this in the mail a week ago from Worthington. It's probably the last piece of mail he sent."

Arthur got up to get everyone drinks. Coming back into the room he had a peculiar look on his face, "Karl, did you tell Bud the results of your trip?"

"When we got back, I sent him an email

"What did you say?"

"That I went out to the site and mapped the pieces and I would have more detail in a week or two."

"The site. By name?"

"I'm not sure. Why?"

He repeated what Jude and Avey already knew and took another angle with it, "I've been thinking the woman probably took information from the computer. If that's true, then *they* may have your email."

Peter interrupted saying, "Why would they bother in the first—" and Arthur talked over him, "Because Bud told Jude he never put any of the documentation on his computer. If they didn't get what they wanted, it must be compelling enough to keep trying."

Karl directed the new implications towards Peter, "It's a timing thing. It's in our favor if the black books are still a secret. They become more valuable depending upon who becomes aware of their existence. We get a couple at bats because we control them. Then it gets tougher because the other side will be waking up."

Peter was convinced it was all speculation they were relying upon, "Go back for a second. Arthur, you expect further attempts? It didn't go any further than Worthington's office and according to all these assumptions, no one could possibly know about the research."

"True, but like Karl said, we might be ahead of them *by accident*. There are records of Jude meeting with Bud. Olivary was very close to Bud and she wouldn't hesitate to share any information."

Peter continued to pick at their logic, "Anyone reviewing the calendar wouldn't know what or who they're looking for. There's nothing proving those meetings were critical to anyone."

"I wouldn't be too sure about that," Jude replied back. "Olivary scheduled time for Bud to work on his research. She scheduled all my time. We involved because we're linked to him. We wouldn't know if somebody is asking her questions."

"That was my motive to come down here," Arthur shared. "I dumped the lease so no one would know where I went except for my parents."

"Again, you guys are jumping to conclusions!" Peter insisted. "If no one knows about the information Worthington had, *and* they can't find it because there's nothing on the computer, then its over. There's no reason anyone would keep searching. Get the evidence to the police, we'll put all this behind us and you don't have to sacrifice your summer. Go have fun!"

While all the students treated that as a smokescreen, Karl was convinced of a lethal threat, "If anyone is anxious to get their hands on Worthington's research, they could contact the parents with some scam. If Worthington was killed, these guys aren't going to be road blocks."

Jude decided to throw more fuel on the fire surprising everybody, "We have another advantage...I got her license number. I figured if we ever got traction, it could be the hammer."

Peter tried to dampen the effect, "You all make it sound like the second coming, turning it into something suspicious and dangerous," then switched gears. He grabbed on the idea that they might lose interest if they had to work with the research day after day, "I think you're going to find out it's a waste of time. What Karl and I have doesn't affect you guys."

The majority vote determined they would meet the following evening. Avey watched the group of men interact for a while then went outside to wait for the boys. In the late evening, Arthur went to her room to say goodnight before heading to bed.

"I was watching you guys talk. Are you okay with everything now?" Avey asked.

"It's better. Peter strikes me as a consensus builder, if it goes in his direction. If not, he doesn't want to hear the facts. I'm with Karl."

"Me too. And Jen sounds passionate about what she's found. Her and that Doug guy. Karl told me her and Peter are kind of a couple. Maybe she'll convince Peter," Avey hoped.

"It'll take the whole group! Remember I was telling you about Wren. Jude calls her the computer ladybug. There's Perrie, who is working with mid-reef or waves. Can't remember. Then there's this guy they call Looks."

"What's his real name?"

"According to Jude, Robert Straw. He's an extreme sports dude."

"Just like you except for the fear of falling."

"No, that's fear of *failing*! Well, I'm tired," Arthur segued into his real motive, "but it would be very relaxing to stay here with you," Arthur hinted.

During the house tour, Avey had called dibs on a room, deliberately setting a boundary. She deflected her boyfriend's body language and subtle offer, wrapping her arms around his shoulders, "You think you're going to stay here tonight but I'm not offering...," guiding Arthur to the door.

"You're kicking me out?"

With a kiss, she gently shoved Arthur out the bedroom door, "Yep."

None of the students could get to sleep. Jude got up, to sit on the couch with one of the black books. Brushing his hand over the leather binder, he remembered his first impressions of Bud's work, "What an idiot I was," he softly spoke. He looked up through the ceiling, "Hard to believe we're in charge."

Summer Residence of the students. Austin, Texas

The students wanted their exploration of Worthington's research to be their best work. The next morning, they tested strategies that defend their arguments. They had to overcome Peter's objections. Avey's idea to categorize the information with spreadsheets and filters.

"Having this information at our fingertips will give us more control over Peter," she voiced as she flipped pages of the black book, "Bud's research is full of statistical data so they must be the backbone of his research if he took this public, right?"

The boys nodded.

"Then why did he send Karl for that artifact?" she asked them, "What role does it play?

"You know Peter wants that separate," Arthur instructed.

"That's one item that needs more attention. Maybe I'll get to use my expertise," Avey said.

Jude rejected the notion with humor, "I don't want to disappoint you, but we're in not Egypt."

"There are cultural similarities."

"Don't quit your day job," Jude teased back.

For the first half of the day, they continued to capture information in a spreadsheet with filters, a virtual index by subject matter and then Avey would combine their inputs.

Arthur pulled another volume out of the box. Bringing it over to the table he flipped through the pages, finding a loose sheet in the center of the book, "Here is a page that isn't attached. It's addressed to you, Jude!"

Handwritten by Dr. Worthington, the document kept the students gave them clarity of purpose:

Dear Jude,

> *I don't know precisely when you may find this note but when it's discovered I hope the circumstances are in our favor. I hope you are still willing to apply yourself in favor of the research. There is another very dear friend that has risked a career to resolve the sub_x equations so you are not alone in that endeavor. I would not wager that my life was wasted on this entire effort and cannot think of better minds to answer..."*

When Jude had passed the letter around that afternoon, Peter didn't agree that it proved the complicated nature of his death, believing instead it proved Worthington had gotten more paranoid in his old age.

Karl's interpretation was more positive, "People assumed Bud had gotten lazy and was sucking down scotch on the university's dime. He was. But Rice missed a great opportunity to gain from his commitment to ideals."

Although the letter boosted the energy for the second meeting, Peter's abrupt disagreements were stronger than before, as he attacked every piece of information that was submitted for discussion. While he had passionate concerns for Jude's autonomy, he was also on the hook as a surrogate guardian, mandated by his sister. While everyone attempted to speak as contemporaries, Peter was less objective.

He repeated that the research wasn't as unique as everyone thought, "If Worthington was going to communicate something big, then these books would have to be real thing. Nobody I know has been preaching his theories, but you have to assume geology professionals are monitoring and reporting much of the same evidence. It's not like science wouldn't be collecting data and taking the pulse. It's not like truth isn't being told. Geologically, it's told every day by someone or by some event. Just in smaller, more concise chunks!"

Karl attempted taking an opposing view, "Everything about Worthington's dedication and his field trips is evidence of a holistic fabric joining geoscience and religion. I think it's a timing thing and not chunky science like Peter says."

That got a laugh from everyone including Peter, while Karl continued, "From what these guys have shared of his research, it implies it's event-based but the conjoined elements of science and adding some kind of spiritual nucleus turns the argument into a 'when', not 'what' challenge.

"Science and math aside, what makes the addition of religion the centerpiece for time measurement?" Peter challenged.

"On the basis that all religions are primarily record holders of man's descent through time. Every piece of information has a time stamp relating the chronological order," Karl stated. "Bibles don't just list information, they organize it. And these past cultures evolved with stories, rituals, and rules."

Arthur started laughing, "I'm agnostic, so I would have to discount the relevance of religion, assuming the information was erroneous, misinterpreted, or falsified. And since I have a natural bias towards math, I think it's the 'what' over the 'when.'"

Jude wanted to move on, thinking they had drained about as much as they could out of the subject, "There's a first. Clarke agrees with Peter. Avey is recording the comments and we'll try and answer those questions later."

Finishing her review, Avey ended the session, "Okay, that should be it for now."

Karl leaned over to Jude, "I'm hooking up with Looks just to get a fresh perspective. I'll need to borrow the volume that has the math models."

After getting back to their house, Arthur and Avey went for a walk to clear their heads. Avoiding the third wheel role, Jude went to his room and reread the letter. The teacher wrote of the fondness he had for Jude and made comparisons to an earlier student whom he respected very much. Lying in bed, Jude was overwhelmed with the stack of scientific journalism. *But why did he do it?* The answer came to him with focused examination. It was courage and leadership. *I know I'm not that strong.*

None of the house sitters fell asleep easily the second night, unsettled about the efficacy of *their* commitment. This was to be their job, their choice for the summer. The students were not aware of the impact of their pleadings.

All the adults had new pressure from sources beyond their control. Jude's mom had left Peter another phone message, expecting a status report. Arthur didn't know his parents were taking some heat from his aunts and uncles. No children in their families were allowed to have that kind of freedom although his mom secretly enjoyed the commotion. Avey's folks wondered if their daughter made a rash decision that would put her heart and emotions at risk. Peter was the lone hold out in *his* circle of friends and felt pressure to give in. Karl remained imperious to any bias. Jen had launched a small campaign of her own with Doug in tow. Perrie and Looks would soon be joining the venture and the shear weight of their logic would cause more reaction and conflict.

Mixed with the distraction of night sounds, Avey was exhausted the next morning, drained by replaying the new information in her dreams. The gift she received from Arthur at breakfast was salve for her fatigue.

She was intrigued with the miniature camcorder on a strap, "This is awesome! Video, pictures, and music all in one. Where did you find it?"

"On the web. It got a design award."

They fought with the plastic packaging to get it unwrapped and attached the neck strap so she could model it.

"And I thought I was going to get a pretty necklace," Avey teased.

"You're too rough for real jewelry," Arthur joked

Yawning, Avey swung her leg around the bottom foot rest of the swivel seat and her apparatus hit the metal.

"How's your leg doing?"

"It's fine. Really."

"I noticed when you were sitting on the couch last night, Peter glanced over at it a couple times."

"That's pretty normal. People stare and their eyes go up and down."

"And the next thought they have is, glad it's not me," Arthur said, mocking haughtiness.

"Did you think that when *you* first saw me?"

"I don't remember really. If I looked down it was only to make sure you didn't trip."

She backhanded his chest.

Arthur coughed, choking on his toast, "Actually, I didn't know. The first time I saw you, it was at the semester fundraiser. You were standing behind the literature table."

Arthur leaned into Avey and kissed each part as he named them, "I do remember your eyes and your nose and your lips."

He paused thinking how he would word his question, "Do you ever think back to before the accident?"

"Sometimes. It's still seems weird that it happened. Years ago, just hearing the word handicap would upset me. I do dream as though I have both legs. I never have any weird dreams about it."

Jude entered the kitchen sweating through his t-shirt.

"That's probably why I don't see it, because you don't. Hey, Jude, is it raining out there?"

"I was running and got into a pickup game. There's a nice court down off the boulevard. I see you got your gift."

"I love it," Avey cooed.

"You're lucky. Clarke never gave me anything except the policy sheet for rooming with him."

After grabbing a bowl of cereal, Jude went to get showered, "I'll hurry up, then let's divide and conquer."

Karl was about to give the math binder to his friend during connecting flights in Denver. Looks was arriving from a seminar on climate intrusions. Karl was returning from a lecture on natural landscapes at risk in the Southwest. For the two hours of layover, they discussed the single volume on the second-floor foyer.

"So you say not much traction on math side?" Looks repeated. "Are these pages it? What do you want me to do?"

"Guess. Literally. I went through it. Bud's relying on somebody but I can't tell who was leading who. There's got to be some research out there tying this down to his Gaia and all the other stuff."

Looks sampled a couple pages while Karl checked for messages, "So far so good. No one saying Peter pulled the plug and sent the kids packing."

"These *are* pretty amazing. I don't understand all of it, but I wouldn't treat this one section as bogus. It would be nice to have the supporting documentation."

"No kidding. Apparently Jude has blasted through the math with a sample he was given."

"Guess huh?"

"Crack it open and see if you can do anything with it. Jude shoved his stuff in the middle there with references, so you can browse with his links. I gotta figure it's a compass for somebody like you."

Looks saw the time, "We'd better head over to our gates."

"See you in a couple weeks."

"Sure enough, dude. Good times!"

Home of Peter Childs.

As summer days passed, the heirs of Dr. Bud Worthington's academic testament hoped their efforts to deeply understand the contents of the black books would pay off. Their debut with the rest of Peter's group had finally arrived. Looks stood in Peter's living room, waiting for his friends.

"Where are you going to crash?" Peter asked.

"Over at Karl's. Wren is staying there as well."

"That leaves Perrie over here."

"And Jen."

"She's not sure she'll be finished in time to make it here."

"She missed the spring trip to the park. Does the woman ever take a break?" Looks accused, watching Peter's grimace.

"Okay, stupid question. But she gave you a bunch of feedback from the oil fields. That's serious if it's true."

"What? The drills getting ripped off? That's not been proven."

"No, the dry wells. If we had more data, it might give us a pattern or reference points."

"I don't know Looks," Peter discounted, putting his negative spin on it. "Anyone can get goofed up out there. Who's to say the maps or coordinates are ever right. You know, guys with high school educations and software bugs."

"There is one constant...Jen did the work. I wouldn't count that out."

"Anybody home?" Wren yelled coming into the house, and gave big hugs to greet her friends.

"My God, Wren, you look great!" Looks exclaimed.

"Mr. Atkinson, God rest his soul, took off eighty pounds!"

"You look super!" agreed Peter.

"I didn't want to spring break with you guys because I hadn't hit my goal."

"We wouldn't have cared," Looks replied.

"I didn't know if I'd just put it back on and I didn't want to hear your shit the next time you saw me."

Looks put his arm around her, "Besides all that personal training, what's my gal been up to?"

"Well, the part of me that's still here has been pretty busy. Karl had me slinging hash around the internet."

"No kidding! Would you be surprised if I told you Karl handed me a stack of work?" Looks offered.

"He hasn't changed! He gets his agenda going and like a little mouse, visits all our houses and leaves turds."

"I almost think he believes none of us realize he's tapping the others," claimed Looks.

Wren picked up a can of soda and raised it, "God bless our little mouse."

"I guess we're putting you over at Karl's," Peter confirmed.

"I just came from there. He was on the phone. It looked like he was going to be awhile so I drove over. Where's Jude and his gang? I hear they've really stepped into it!"

Peter bit his lip, withholding sarcasm, "It's just hard to believe they want to keep a lid on it considering how they got involved. You heard about their potato chip can. Can you believe it?"

"Excuse me. Like that's not in our DNA?"

Eventually Perrie arrived, happy to see the group, "I sure missed you guys. Has it been a full year already? I can't wait to see Jen. When is she coming?"

"Late tonight," Peter answered.

After the students appeared, Karl coaxed everyone to mingle.

Avey started talking with Wren and Perrie because the men cliqued up for their own discussion, "Arthur and I heard some of the stories of how you guys all got together. But Perrie, you've got an oceanographer's background or something, right? Everyone else is land based except for Wren and you."

"My forte is volcanic riffs and now big wave research. Back then, Scripps University allowed certain majors to project share with peers from Rice. Peter and Jen were in my class the first year. We worked virtually together for two semesters."

"Awesome. Probably a lot of effort to stay connected to each other."

"For graduation, I drove over from San Diego and I got to meet the rest of the gang. Wren, we sure got blasted that night."

"Ouch. It was wicked. Haven't done rum and coke since."

"Wren, you've lost so much weight. You really look great! Do you feel different and everything?"

"I'm not as tired, but what's really changed is I'm not getting mind controlled from the commercials and stuff. Like I've turned it off in my head and it doesn't matter anymore."

"Really!"

"The explosion of food commercials is constant and when you're fat, they come at you twenty-four hours a day. Like I wasn't hungry, but, hey, dig in."

"So you turned it off like a light switch?" Perrie asked.

"Like I took control of the switch. Thank God food just doesn't show up your at door! I wouldn't have a chance."

Avey was hesitant but wanted to share her experience, "When you said that about controlling the switch I was thinking of my leg and everything."

Wren put her arms around Avey and Perrie, intending to blunt the seriousness and giggled, "Okay, girls, we're bonding!"

"That 'switch.' I could have easily let my parent's baby me for the rest of my life but didn't, since it was my destiny. But I'm glad I was in high school."

"Why?" both women asked.

"Because maybe as a kid, I would have been too protected from everything and held back. In high school, I was already running track and had a chance for a scholarship.

"So what was your accident?" Perrie asked.

"We went camping in Yellowstone. The weather was rainy and I was coming out of a grocery store in Colter Bay. I had my earbuds in and singing to myself, enjoying the rain. This driver was backing up one of those huge motor homes and I felt it hit me from behind, like someone was pushing me."

Perrie's eyes started to water.

"It happened so fast, knocking me down flat."

"He didn't see you in the mirrors! How could he miss seeing you?"

"I was at the back but the vehicle was turning. My one leg got pinned and the other one I moved like doing scissors."

Wren hugged Avey from the side, "Oh dear goodness! Where were your folks?"

"They came out when everybody was around the bus. I was underneath and I think I blacked out. I remember the crushing and grinding from being between the tire and the pavement."

Avey accepted the napkins that were passed around, wiping her eyes, "Did I wreck our moment?"

Wren hugged the younger girl again, "You don't kid around when you bond girl!"

Looks moved closer to join in after losing his round, "Everyone looks teary eyed."

"Oh, we're just talking. Avey was saying she lost something and couldn't find it," Wren covered discreetly.

"That can be corrected. I'll get going on the paperwork. What are we missing?"

It was innocent male sarcasm. There was pause.

Then Avey couldn't hold back, "My leg."

The women started laughing so hard, Perrie had to hold Wren from falling on the floor. Look's face got so red and he didn't know what to say or do. He just stood there. The uproar attracted everyone wondering what they missed.

"It's a first!" yelled Perrie. "It's a first!

Perpetually in good spirit Looks defended his record, "It was a set up!"

"First time Looks didn't have a come back! Nice work, girl!" Wren celebrated.

Perrie gave Avey a high five. Still everybody else was confused.

Wren was still laughing, "I guess it sucks to be you, Looks!"

Arthur came around and hugged Avey from the back, "Way to get on everyone's good side."

Looks went back to Karl and Peter who were at the table chatting with Jude.

"Worthington basically kept recruiting and the wheel stopped on Jude and Arthur," said Karl. What did he call it? Oh yeah." He changed his body position, imitating his old mentor, "You're likely to move beyond novitiate and will start to enjoy the work as an apprentice."

"He actually said that?"

"Ya, I was sitting on the work bench brushing out the cavities of a decayed seed pot and asked him when I could start finding them instead of cleaning them."

"I never got involved with him," Peter stated proudly.

Karl explained his interest, "He was collecting all the time and once he got you stirred up, it was very seductive. The physical science version of 'Looking for Mr. Goodbar,' was 'Looking for Mr. Goodbar's pottery.' He's probably the reason I went off and did all the trippy stuff."

When they laughed Peter slipped his dig in, "His work for all we know has no purpose now."

"Well, he never gave up, even when Rice pulled the funding. He tried to cover it with his own money," Karl defended.

The group merged together wondering when they would get started.

Sitting next to Looks, Avey carefully studied everyone, "It just hit me. You all remind me of the *Goonies*."

"We don't use inhalers," Looks responded.

"Ya, all we got were these crummy tattoos!" Perrie added.

Arthur bolted from his chair, "Hey, I heard something about that! What's the story?"

Everyone flashed their tat if they could and shared their own perception of who forced who into it and why they did it. Karl ended up fending off the general claim that he goaded everybody into getting one.

Encouraging everyone to get settled again Karl kicked off their meeting, "It sounded like everyone has introduced themselves. As you know, Dr. Worthington met his fate, God bless him. Some of us believe he was actually murdered because he was ready to flash some heavy stuff. You all got a call from me with that detail so we're not going down the sympathy road. We're all here to try and figure out if the research is any good because of two important facts. First, no one else will bother and second I personally had to beg each and every one of you!"

"Yeah," Perrie dared, "don't you have anything better to do?"

"At this point, no!"

Karl glanced at Peter, "Suffice it to say we're not all up to speed on what's going on, so I asked Looks to do a deep dive and develop some eye candy. Jude is going to intro the model calculations."

"Uh, Clarke and I pretty much spent our last semester at school getting involved with what Worthington called the black books."

"Who did the work?"

"Good question, Perrie. I don't have the exact answer, but I think Bud did most of it with help."

Karl intervened, "Maybe everyone here and a large part of the student body were tapped by Worthington." He motioned Jude to continue.

"Okay, so we got this and other binders and learned off them," Jude explained. "We loaned Looks the one that has the mathematical models."

After Jude told the group about his encounter with the sub_x equations, Looks initiated a keystroke to display the first image on the wall-mounted screen.

"Do we have to look at you flying through the air again?" Karl complained feigning disappointment.

"I just wanted to see it on Peter's new screen. Not too bad."

Another key stroke and the first model illustration came up. The colored photo was of Earth taken from the Apollo-8 flight, "I wanted to start here in case anyone forgot what we're affectionately standing on."

"Yea! That's our baby!" yelled Perrie.

"Leaving this perspective behind, this next shot shows the earth, still physically intact and three-dimensional. However, I sculpted away the atmosphere and bodies of water. These pics show the entire globe with each hemisphere minus all the liquid."

"Nice, but who says we're heading for a drought?"

"Not a prediction, Peter. Just a simplification to sort out the relevant mathematical dynamics. In order to get at the binder calculations, I stripped away everything except rock."

"Cool. It's a dried grape," Jude observed.

"More or less."

Peter was edgy, "What's our takeaway? We can distill it all down with a composite model, but Earth is still a functioning planet with all its ecosystems."

"Is it?" Looks disagreed. "If you consider everything, and I mean *everything* we've taken out of her, it's not difficult to imagine the weaknesses we've created. Over centuries geological stress points have changed radically."

"Sure, it's one giant rock, but there's no scientific evidence—"

"Peter. Whoa. It's just a vision, a starting place," Looks emphasized. "Let's not sweat the details yet."

Arthur watched as Peter tightened, then sighed, "Okay, I didn't mean to take us off track."

"You didn't. We're all facing a difficult challenge. Let me throw something out to the group."

The presentation showed the mid-ocean reef maps and the current geological hot spots.

"Think of it this way. The population walks around on earth's surface and they look up at the sky thinking this is all beautiful and permanent," Looks theorized. "But it's like Peter said, it's a piece of rock, *but* it's constantly under extreme dynamics, orbiting the sun at sixty-seven thousand miles per hour. We make a full rotation at about a thousand miles per hour at the midsection. And don't forget the thirteen miles of atmosphere that surrounds us, the pretty blue color above us, is a thin coating. The only thing tangible is under our feet at just roughly twenty-six thousand miles of circumference. Not bulletproof or permanent."

Looks tried to get a read from everybody, "Thoughts?" he asked, then became sarcastic, "Am I being too conservative with the evidence?"

Karl attempted a truce, "Well, it's like nailing jello to the wall. It needs some simulation work."

"Simulation of what?" Peter challenged.

Karl intervened again, "Nothing too specific. We're still working the kinks out of the math."

Looks took offense immediately, "So far I think I'm dead on. No pun intended. It's not a big leap considering other anomalies like the five-hundred meter crack in Africa."

Then Peter went right to the argument, "Okay. Then what science are you guys aligning to because I don't know it."

"Hey, that's cool. We might have overworked it," Karl conceded hoping to disarm Peter, but Looks had the last say.

"Oh, I don't know about that. It's a little more serious than peeing in your pool."

Karl took over again, "Let's take a break and then Wren's can share her stuff."

When everybody got up to stretch, Avey followed Wren to the backyard. "That was intense! Are those three always at odds?"

"Sort of. You have to understand Looks. He's like our visionary. You know, always a step ahead. And some of his stuff comes at you pretty iffy but usually ends up near target."

Wren sipped her drink, "But he's susceptible to the piddlely stuff you and I don't think about."

"Like what?"

"He's still a little messed up from when Rodney Dangerfield died before Joe Cocker."

Avey started laughing, "But seriously, when we confront Peter with facts, he seems oblivious to reality. Arthur and I think Bud was going to predict some huge forcing."

"Well, that's for us to figure out right?"

Karl fended off Jude, who had the same reaction to his uncle's reluctance, "Itty bitty steps. We'll get there."

After moments, Wren hollered, "Does anybody want to see what I have?" as she hooked up her laptop and waited for the group to reassemble.

"Dudes, let's get moving. The week-end is all we've got," Karl reminded them and pointed his finger at Wren.

"Okay, so our man Karl gave me a call the other day and begged me to start chasing down RRS feeds, blogs, and tweets. I started looking for leads on those annoying drill bits that were snatched up. Apparently, there's a government agency potentially involved called the National Energy Technology Laboratory. NETL. Don't know if they're friend or foe."

"How did you get all that?" Avey asked.

"The less you know, the fewer of us end up in the hoosegow. Let's call it a weakness in instant messaging. Never leave home with it."

Karl choked on his beer, laughing, "You always crack me up, Wren."

During freshman year, Wren and Karl first met at the university student center. Trying to get his laptop booted after it shut down, it kept blue screening. After removing the battery and reseating the hard drive, she had the laptop working again. Karl learned she was a CS major involved with the early science of security and encryption. She took her first job with Netscape during the Internet boom, and eventually went on her own.

Her passion for exposing security flaws in the browser evolved towards becoming a security analyst.

"Also, there was a blog out there chipping away at the non-contrite oil barons. I put some time and energy on that but haven't come up with anything useful. Whoever set it up closed the backdoors and duck taped 'em."

Avey sort of raised her hand, "What's relevant about the blog?"

"There's a number of posted articles going after the oil industry, raising up speculation that they and our government are in bed together. If that's true, the taxpayers are going to get it in the ass again. Could be the Peak Oil dudes. But like I said, the blog entries stopped."

The group discussion shifted to the multiple volumes. Karl wanted everyone to know more about them, "There's seven of them," he said. "Hey, Arthur, how many have you guys scrubbed?"

"Over half of them. Avey has a subject index."

"Have you guys noticed anything peculiar?" Karl prompted.

Avey was quick to answer, "Bud collected a lot of data about the extraction of material from the earth like oil, minerals, and gas. He also has a comprehensive list of earthquakes, volcanoes, and sinkholes."

"Back then, I probably clipped some of those articles for him," Karl reminisced. "Other than the math model, are the black books anything but an archive of natural disasters?"

"I think they are!" Arthur interjected. "He has statistics, probably from the students."

"We're not completely done there," Jude offered.

Wren was genuinely impressed of the undergrads efforts, "Karl told me you three went in and took the books before they shut his office down. Pretty head ups!"

"We thought we missed one. Turned out Karl had it."

"Worthington gave it to you? Why?" Perrie questioned.

"Got it right after Peter and I got back from Mesa Verde. Jude?"

"I didn't know. Maybe because he suddenly got suspicious."

Peter came out of a trance, detached from the conversation since Jen called. After leaving his cell phone on the counter, he slipped out the back doors and went through the metal gate to the hill. Reserving this spot for cooling off after a workout, its new purpose was to create distance, increase the degrees of separation from his friends.

The gap had been increasing on its own. With Karl leading, they were all mesmerized. It was bad enough with his friends, but Jude was mixed up in it, energized, feeding off of it. His sister wasn't cool with her son taking off for the summer. Their money was tight and they wanted Jude to enroll in cheaper classes for the summer semester. She asked Peter if he could push to get this "project" done and ship Jude back. She wouldn't take any monetary handouts for reasons obvious to her, making Peter aware of them.

"That's nice of you, Peter, but what if we can't pay you back for awhile? Never? I don't think so. Bill wouldn't hear of it. Twenty thousand dollars doesn't grow out of the ground. If consulting fell off you'd be at risk. I just wouldn't do that to you."

That was about the only way Peter could easily extend his help to the family without getting criticized. But Peter sensed he didn't have any effect on Jude.

He seems to be more interested hanging out with Looks. Or is Karl his favorite?

Jen adds another layer, Peter thought, certain her arrival would cause a flurry of energy around the whole oil versus Earth thing. He *was* her close friend all the way through adolescence. The slipstream of emotional attachment between them bogged down in adulthood and decoupled their relationship. He saw it begin to erode during college. Back then, Jen hid her emotions when she spoke to Peter, limiting what she shared.

"How's your mom?"

"Fine."

"Is she staying busy?"

"I guess. That's a long story."

They went out together many times. But when they started getting serious Peter felt everyone else had a fresh start with her compared to him. He told her he had a window into her and as much as he wanted to look beyond it, for some reason it was a barrier.

She was blunt and frustrated with Peter, "Figure it out and get back to me."

Peter leaned back on the grass. *I guess I never did that.* And he could never compete with Karl. Not even when Jen was involved. *Karl is the MacGyver of Earth sciences.*

Charismatic and quirky, Karl always dismantled the truth, stepping on it, checking out its resiliency. Worthington took him in and enjoyed watching his favorite student take a field problem or book research and twist it to make something functional out of it. Consulting work became a rigid frame Peter fused himself to. Smart as he was, he was never clever like Karl.

Peter's intolerance of the group's efforts, to solve Worthington's hoax, was like a cleaver separating him from the mirage that all his friends had accepted. Everyone else drank the proverbial kool-aid and saw that all the activity was connected somehow by something. None of it touched him except by association.

Worthington mentoring Jude? Why would anybody kill Worthington for his so called black books? Why would Jude and Arthur waste all that time babysitting Worthington? None of this affected Peter directly. *Did they have to steal the books? Chasing a woman down the street?* None of it touches. Nothing. *All a waste of energy.*

Below him, the noise of bristling trees mixed with the languished hum of the day's commute. Peter didn't see any way around his deference, other than to harden his will to compensate for everyone's gross errors of judgment. His friends were freely allowing every piece of information to become an absolute purpose, so as a friend he had to resist even more.

Karl and Wren would be working their ideologies of covert survival and gaming theory and he would be forced to question their motives. Jude, Arthur, and Avey were immature and he would have to challenge their integrity. Looks and Perrie were forever devoted to discovery and he would be forced to ignore their relevance.

What am I? The designated asshole?

Peter headed back to the house determined to refit the plan. If he was subtle about it, they would eventually see the problem for what it was. Nothing.

He pet Wren's shoulder as he went by, "Have you seen Karl?"

"He's out front. Jen tried to reach you. She's talking to him."

Approaching him, Karl signaled the call was ending, spreading his forefinger and thumb narrowly, "Yes. He's standing right here. I'll tell him. Yep, love you too. Bye."

"What'd Jen say? She can't make it now?"

"How'd you know? Her flight got delayed twice and she would have missed her connection. She's heading home and said for us to call her when we're finished."

"Damn."

Karl made a face, "What? Suddenly you miss her?"

"It's complicated."

Peter got his back slapped, "No doubt. Where have you been anyway?"

"Just took a walk."

"I know you're worried about Jude and everything. But maybe just roll with it."

"Maybe."

They walked into the house. A number of separate discussions were going on.

"Where we at? Any more from the books?" queried Karl.

"Avey has been trying to figure out if there is a correlation between when Bud sent Karl on his field trip and the blog shutting down."

"A bit of a reach isn't it?" Peter nagged.

Jude defended Avey, "I think she's right. There could be a person of interest in there somewhere. Bud said someone was helping him with the calculations."

To avoid more arguments Karl announced that it was time to pack it up, "Let's give everyone time to relax before dinner."

Looks hugged Avey goodbye whispering in a Chicano accent, "We don't need no stinkin' goonies."

NEADE. Undisclosed location near the Pentagon.

"Yes, I was told the target was compromised. We moved the hard drive contents up to priority one."

Colton liked what he heard over the speaker phone, putting it on mute for a second. Angela had the data from Dr. Bud Worthington's office sent to a DARON analyst.

"These guys are gold. Nothing like Wolmit," the executive bragged.

Colton's mood was optimistic even though an accidental death made it tougher to keep NEADE's operational independence intact, "So have you completed the analysis?"

"Yes, we expressed the material but let me go over it on the phone if you don't mind."

Colton was anxious to hear, "Go."

The chief data forensic analyst discussed the method of the analysis and their findings using the keyword list provided by Angela, "Overall, we didn't see much data survive to be analyzed. I don't know the root cause of the corruption. The remaining data was in the normal proportions typically associated with a standard client and application suite. That translates to email, with inserts. Even some of that was corrupt. The rest of the drive had information that was purposely deleted with a commercial scrubber. Clean from a forensics point of view. No chance of retrieval."

"No other unique files or text documents?"

"Not matching the keyword list."

"Angela, you have the list?"

She opened her folder and slid a copy to her boss, looking him straight in the eye. As Colton inspected the content, she studied his reactions. She had another version in her possession. The copy she gave him could be misconstrued as a draft if need be. It had phrases and single words directly related to samplings pulled off Dr. Franklin's system. It also contained over a hundred words and phrases that would have been utilized if Dr. Worthington had illegal research in his possession relating to NETL or NEADE.

Colton rubbed his chin, "You said inserts? You mean attachments?"

"We think they were documents," the expert shared. "We see the header signatures but nothing else, and pictures. Pictures of what we assumed to be artifacts."

"Four pieces of stone?"

"Yes, sir."

Angela was surprised when asked if that confirmed the original was from Worthington, "The only way to tell would be a timestamp. We'd have to review the other sets."

Another action item was assigned to them.

"We were able to pull all the current email. It's in the packet that was expressed to your office."

Withholding the earlier conversation he had with the same analyst, ordering him to send the other information as classified, Colton ended the call, "Fine. Thanks for your help."

He swiveled in his chair, "Let's think about this for a minute. Here's this Indian, supposedly sending to Worthington who won't let Millard in the door and there's nothing on his drive."

"He kept it offline then," Angela concluded.

"I think he was paranoid and took the time to cover his tracks. Like he feared for his life."

"Maybe."

She didn't realize Colton was fishing for a better answer.

Angela booked a flight that evening and vowed this time to close off loose ends. A few days later, to satisfy Colton's agenda, she called from her cell at Rice University.

"Angela, the analyst packet has an email from a Karl Johns. He referred to some artifacts hunting. I've sent you copies. Find out anything you can about him, pronto."

"Okay."

"There was also an appointment file. A couple names showed up consistently. I've shipped that off to you as well."

"Understood."

"What have you got for me?"

"They've cleared out Worthington's office. It's in safe storage. I've got the location."

"Let me know as soon as you find anything out about the email."

"Yes, sir."

Call ended.

The standard protocol of announcing meeting participants was not an arbitrary omission by Colton. Angela's partner was in the room.

"You know I like Angela a lot. She doesn't bitch about things like you do. But she was holding back. Is that something you know about?"

Presuming his boss was fishing, Jason negated the impression and deflected the criticism, thinking instead of Angela's dedication.

During a checkpoint with Angela days later, she could tell her boss was fired up about something. His cadence was different and his phrasing overtly harsh. He was hung over or someone's screw up crossed his path.

"What have you got?"

"I researched the email and met with one of the university professors. He pointed out that artifacts like these are usually protected and have restrictive covenants by the American Pueblo Council. With some help, I found Worthington had applied to go dig these up."

"These guys were helpful because?"

"I posed as a new intern at the university."

"So where are these...?"

"Stones. On government land—Mesa Verde National Park. There was a request for data and the requestor was Karl Johns."

"What was he sent?"

"The site inventory."

"Ship all that information to me."

"Yes. What are you thinking?"

"That we need to get our hands on those items."

"They're in protected status."

"Fuck 'em."

Angela took a deep breath. It would be disastrous to withhold information from Colton, "Also, I found out a bit more from the appointment book."

"You fill Smith in. I need to collect a favor and line this out."

Barely catching the last sentence, she immediately speed-dialed Jason, "Hey, give me a call when you've got time."

"Yes, you'll have the specific ground coordinates. The information will be sent by 0500 hours."

"We'll checkpoint with you at the site."

"On an as needed basis only."

"We can't be responsible for the condition of the package."

Colton disregarded the exception, "Do your job."

Home of Peter Childs. Austin, Texas.

All next day, the group of geologists ferried back and forth between the three houses. Karl's virtual connections were consumed by Wren. To avoid ad hoc discussions that might cause friction, Peter's house remained central to share major findings, with updates scheduled at eleven and seven. Jude's team included Perrie so more effort could be applied to untangle the meaning of the evidence in the binders.

The morning meeting took just under two hours to get through and ended abruptly. The effort to share new information was tempered with the group's waning interest. Culled from the volumes, Avey and Arthur showed examples of political debauchery with foreign oil over the last ten years. Peter was encouraged with their opinion.

"Worthington was a major packrat. He had pages and pages of articles and websites. We're still researching the web for more current information. Much of it probably had value at one point but is no longer relevant."

Jude was next, having explored one of the last volumes, "It was more like a diary of Bud's exploits in Arizona and New Mexico. His detail of the Acoma area. You went there, didn't you, Karl?"

"Yup. He got permission from the local Pueblo council to bring students from college. It was more like a kick-off to help some of the indigent communities. Worthington was hoping if he gave a little, he'd get a little."

"There are pictures of him with some of his students and some of the Pueblo community."

"Probably those who benefited from *our* hard labor."

When the photos were discovered, Jude was amazed at how vibrant Bud looked in his younger days. There were notes in the columns, sometimes with dates, names, and locations.

"We got caught up looking at the pictures. I'm still going through the text for more clues."

The rest of the meeting time was used by Looks to flash his revised interpretation of the perplexing math computations, "Suffice it to say, maybe I was a little rash the other day with the raisin image," Looks offered. "There's still some upside."

"What?" Perrie asked.

"That I don't understand the model, yet. I'll keep playing with it."

The mood was somber when the college students returned to their house. Perrie had to catch-up on her business email so it was back to the three of them. Avey looked up from her laptop having the feeling of being back in the campus library. The sounds of frequent page turning, keyboard clatter, spontaneous grunts and sighs. The humming sound of the laptop fan. But a new feeling washed over her. A nervousness. A consciousness of suspended disbelief. It was difficult to keep believing in their mission. They had two volumes left and hours of work stored on the laptop. But nothing had really been resolved. And Peter only seemed more agitated. Her search index was the only milestone of their accomplishments.

Suddenly she became critical of that approach, "This sorting tool would be impressive if we had to regurgitate all of Bud's facts on a test, but I think we're failing. I know it is what it is, but it seems like we're wasting our time."

Jude was more upbeat about their achievements, "I vote we keep at it until our review is complete. Looks may not have gotten anywhere trying to pull the geo-puzzle together, so we've just got to put our heads down and keep moving forward."

Arthur's frustration was slightly different, "If I'm going to blow off an entire summer, I want something out of it. We have to complete our initial reviews. But let's try and force our hand."

Avey was confused, "Like how?"

"Try and find something in our favor with the resources that no one else has—the black books. Forget about trying to find the huge secret. We know there were others involved. We're pretty sure there's another group working against us, so let's cancel the effect by trying to find out who's on our side. I'll finish off my stuff and then grab one of the remaining volumes."

Arthur looked at Avey, "The index is important. It's like the 'mini me' of the volumes."

"Just think," she confessed, "if we suddenly found the secret, the whole thing would get out and people would be like debating. It'd be a nightmare, like how the news takes a sound bite and spins it one way or other."

Jude glanced at Arthur, "Why don't we go to the *National Inquirer* and blow the lid off this. Could you imagine the headlines? 'Goonies mess with science, blow up Earth.'"

The mood lightened taking them off course.

"Goonies grow up and mess up!" joked Arthur.

"Hey, I only said the group *reminded* me of the goonies."

Arthur was apologetic, "I wasn't fair. I should give you credit. How about, 'One leg woman discovers new Grand Canyon.'"

Avey slowly walked towards Arthur and then tackled him. They went over the couch backwards landing halfway on the floor.

"That's two points for a reversal," Jude announced. "And a deduction of one point for illegal use of a prosthesis. You tried to take his nads out."

They got back to work after deciding what they needed to have in front of the team that evening. Using the index, Arthur accepted the task to extract any detail from the volumes that could identify unknown persons. Jude continued to review the Acoma archive. Avey picked up where Perrie left off.

"Guys, this is interesting," Jude reported. "Worthington has hand written notes to the side of the photos. He was really into the religion side of it. Here's what one says:

Spiritual guidance from Acoma Pueblo is implicitly manifest to the natural workings of the earth. And another, *Historical research lends itself to relate physical science to the spiritual values of their architecture and pottery. Must keep working the connection.*

Jude flipped through pages as he spoke, "He practically asked me to go to the Acoma Pueblo. Here's a picture of an Indian with Worthington."

"Indian? That's Native American," Avey corrected and was ignored.

"He's got some scribble, 'This is the...'I can't pronounce it...'tcraikatsi'?[57] Here's a photo of a site."

The photograph was attached by the corner with glue that had yellowed.

"Early scrapbooking sucked."

Placing the book on the coffee table, Jude knelt on the floor and Avey shimmied up next to him, "When was this taken?"

"I don't know. Worthington looks a little younger. Here's another photo of a site and a glossy of a couple stones. Is the image clear enough for you to make out the scribing?"

"No, I can't tell if they're stone or plastic."

"I'm serious!" said Jude.

"I'm kidding! The perspective is too far away. Besides, it looks like a cheap studio shot. Flip through the pages. Maybe there's some better close ups."

The search did not yield a better photograph, but Avey was still curious, "The books I've reviewed haven't had any pottery or anything like this. Arthur, look in the spreadsheet and filter for pottery, artifact, or relic. Have I listed anything?"

"Nope."

"Let's try something else."

Avey went to the kitchen and came back with a steak knife. Before Jude could react, she placed the blade flat and sawed through the anchor points of the site photo. Lifting the edges of the picture, she found writing on back.

"What's it say?"

"Need complete map. Still no success"

"Hmm. Okay," Jude said and placed the photo in the crease of the page. "I'll keep going through this. I'll let you know if I find something else."

---

[57] White, "New Material From Acoma," 305. Head of the group.

"False alarm then? Obviously not as good as what I showed you guys," Arthur jested.

"Ya, right, Professor Clarke. So you lucked out with the last volume, reading it backwards."

Everyone went back to their own sections until a watch alarm went off.

"Let's pack it up. I gave us twenty minutes to get over there."

The last group meeting was almost déjà vu. Everybody showed up, but unlike the first day, the energy was sucked out of them. Sluggish and fatigued, Looks had dark circles under his eyes. Peter's hair was uncombed. Perrie was wearing sweats and Wren was snacking.

Nervous about the progress, Karl reminded the group of their goals, "And, it's seven-thirty. Our last face to face. Okay. Dudes from college, what have you got?"

Arthur decided to go first, "I was scanning Avey's index attempting to find anything that jumped out to give us clues of other people that Bud involved. Nothing was in the volumes as..." and Wren perked up when Arthur used his bending fingers to illustrate a quote-unquote, "...*attached* within. There was a bunch of loose documentation in the back. A brochure from the lab you mentioned yesterday—the National Energy one. And a couple business cards. They're up for bid."

"Mine!" Wren shouted, "I can definitely use a backdoor key," she cooed.

"We're guessing Bud could have other connections worth locating," Arthur concluded.

"Good job guys! Did you have any luck with the other stuff?"

"Not as good as mine," Arthur bragged, as Jude began his update.

"In the book I finished there were a lot of pictures. One was like a commercial glossy of stones and a couple more of a dig site. Avey got the idea to look on the back. Bud had written some notes. But it feels like a dead end."

"Pass them around," Perrie suggested.

"I didn't bring them with me. They're like the ones Karl talked about earlier."

"That was short and not so sweet," Karl confessed. "Anyone else?"

Looks rubbed his eyes, "On our side, we're still bogged down in the calculations."

Karl was anxious, "This meeting can't be a complete washout. What has my Wren got?"

"Like I said, I was skimming the surface," she replied. "There's some possibilities, but I'm not going to compromise your home connections. When I get back, I'll be able to cover myself going in and I should know something more."

"Are you going to go after NETL?"

"That's one target. I can do some checking with the business cards I just got."

Karl didn't look over at Peter, presuming his smugness, "We all take off in waves tomorrow. If everybody doesn't mind, let's just hang out. Maybe something will pop up."

Jude and Arthur went over to Looks and reported the status of their assignment, "There's nothing in the volumes about the math other than what Bud shared with me."

"I've extrapolated as much as possible and all I've done is identify the false positives," Looks declared. "I still can't envision the extent of what Bud was doing or waiting for. It looks like the models are incomplete, as you said, Jude. It's a very thin blueprint."

"No kidding!" Jude commiserated. "We need the keys."

"Or more thought," Looks interjected, "...to see beyond it."

Later that evening, the girls left for salads convincing themselves to eat healthy. Karl split to go look at the glossy photos. After Jude left with Arthur, it was much later when Peter went over to the shelf where he stored his watch, wallet, and cell phone. He had missed a call. The message left him stunned:

> Peter. Karl. I'm following my intuition. I'm catching a plane tonight and going back to Mesa Verde. I think the photos Jude talked about are similar to the same pieces Worthington had us map there. Just a hunch. This time I'm armed against the damn dust. Keep this quiet until I get back.

"It's all hype. He always takes it off in a random direction," Peter complained to himself. It pissed him off at first, but at least he didn't have to make that trip again.

For his part, Karl was tired of accommodating Peter all week, putting up with his resistance. He needed to get on track with what his intuition led him to do and act on it.

From his view, everybody else missed it –Worthington must have been signaling something. *Obviously placed there before his death, a government brochure and business cards were there for a reason!* And Arthur's suspicions were as telling. If somebody did have the contents of Worthington's hard drive, and his emails were examined, then they would know what Worthington was looking for. And who was helping him. It might be too late already.

He couldn't wait for the approval any longer. From the government or Peter. He needed to recover the artifacts. If they even existed, that would jump-start the team again.

Instead of asking Peter and having to defend himself, Karl left Jude a message. He ended the message with the suggestion that Peter didn't need to know what they were about to do.

Jude and Arthur carried out the instructions verbatim, loading the SUV with Karl's spare lap top, and his four gear bags.

"My friends won't mind if I borrow it. Drive it over to get my stuff, then leave it parked at Wal-Mart at Cedar Park, on the west side as close to the building as possible."

The final day, Peter informed the group of Karl's surprise departure keeping the details to himself. He was surprised Jude didn't seem interested. With the reality of dispersing, the group gathered for an assortment of goodbyes. Wren gave Perrie and Avey big hugs and handed Avey her plastic business card.

"Call me if you get the wide eyes again. Anytime, okay?"

"You bet."

Looks tempted Jude to travel to Idaho for an "awesome bridge jump." He brought enough gear for the both of them.

"I'd like to, but I better not. We're all pretty tight, and it would goof up the flow of the group right now."

"I figured, but I wanted you to know you're always welcome."

Arthur was singled out by everyone. "You take care of Avey for us."

"Of course."

In moments, the cars had driven off and it was down to a head count of three students who were determined to uncover any truth they could find in support of Bud's lethal sacrifice.

Day 84.

Residence of Dr. Kenneth Millard. Richmond, Virginia.

RAIN PELTED THE balcony glass, blurring the image moving about in the apartment. The third day of wet weather was a coincidence to his isolation. There was nothing of value outside Kenneth Millard's apartment to pull him away from the dread he conjured. He imagined his passions were curses or made to be, having been manipulated by Colton. His quivering lips pulled down, the wine and pills allowed him to wallow deep in the abscess.

Kenneth's voice was rancid and bloodshot eyes were swelling with drug-induced tears that had been uncontrollable for hours, "How did I? How did I get myself in this?"

Kenneth Millard moved along the wall, his oily fingertips brushed across the canvases of his collection. Again he pushed back his sweat-soaked hair.

After the wine glass broke on the tile floor splattering its contents, he sunk to his knees, whimpering softly, "Everything I earned he corrupted. My talent. My character. He's stolen my self-worth. Twisted it! I didn't start the lies."

The façade of a partnership with Willis Colton was evident to Kenneth early on. Believing he could get the upper hand, he had been out maneuvered leaving a sullen ego, his weaknesses perverse. For many minutes he didn't move. The contortion in Kenneth's face let tears fall, leaving stains on his pants. His physiological being was sufficiently drugged with a simultaneous mixture of an old Valium, two tabs of Librium, and a prior medication of Lexipro. The fear and failure had remained unresolved for months, making residence in his soul over time, pulling deep from adolescent behavior. It had become easier to medicate than deal with a piercing reality.

The road trips came to a halt after he met with Worthington. Colton demanded he not represent NETL. By then, Caroline had called off the engagement. She was frustrated with a man lamenting about his career and was tired of his frailty, his incapacity to stand up to others who bullied him into submission.

They used to lay in bed on mornings and Kenneth quizzed her, flaunting his intellect for the arts. Playing the surrogate, as his mother, it was a nuance Caroline put up with. The thin attention she gave was always returned in kind with dinners, shows, and jewelry. The forbearance waned after Kenneth began obsessing about Colton. It became impossible to lay there and hear him complain and scheme. Fighting with him only served to intensify the underlying blames about the choices and failures he conjured.

Encountering difficulty as he tried to recall the combination, Kenneth attempted to retrieve the hand gun he kept in a floor safe. Shaking, he got it on the sixth try. Wiping his nose with the back of his hand, he thought of his mother's dedication to his upbringing, determined to move the Millard generation a few rungs higher. She had repeated her promise many times, "As much as I love your father, I can't allow you to follow in his footsteps."

Her pregnancy was an error in judgment between a young historian and an older construction laborer with handsome features. She began her career at the Museum of Fine Arts in Houston, having access to collections unsurpassed in Texas, including works of Picasso, a variety of Renaissance and Baroque pieces.

Her marriage was endured with an imbalance between parental roles. While the father labored day and night jobs, the mother raised the son. Living in a house with nine hundred square feet, the family survived on poverty level income. All remaining resources escaping debt maintenance were trickled into personal aesthetics for their only child.

Grace started the training early, bringing Kenneth to her work after hours to view the art pieces before they went in front of public view. From pottery to oils, mother and son appreciated art and art culture twice a week. Week-end trips to other museums were common throughout his upbringing. Reaching through vanity, hoping for wealth, she tried to raise him up to a higher class of living. At times, Grace would have to undo what the son learned from the father, the latter having been instructed from the start not to refer to his child as "Kenny."

After decades of enduring the social lethargy of the father, she was diagnosed with cervix cancer. More of her personal time was redirected away from her Kenneth and towards her husband until death.

It was all these memories that escalated his condition. Thirty-six hours ago, Kenneth took a verbal beating from Colton. He was reprimanded for failing and misleading NETL about his professional capabilities. The accusation was accurate, since no one in the industry trusted him at this point. Not wanting to hear indignant banter from Colton, he could have hung up. He wanted to. But he persevered through the verbal torture, glad his contract was terminated. And on his turn he would not hold back. He could make his own threats and reveal the plan he had to expose his boss. But his motives were short-circuited and he became sick to his stomach when he heard Colton take his revenge.

Shocked, Kenneth pleaded when Colton completed his threat finishing with, "I warned you your fuckups were going to bite you in the ass."

He couldn't fathom being framed for murder.

Colton wasn't bluffing, willing to put him in the cross hairs, "I've got you with Worthington and apparently he called GTS after you left. You read what happened to him."

Crude as it was, Colton was torturing Millard to crush him. It served the purpose of finishing out an investigation that Sterling insisted upon. And then he could throw Kenneth to the side.

"You should have done your job. Now you've compromised a government operation, and we have credible information of your suspicious links to a terrorist cell."

After contacting his lawyer, Kenneth began to consume pills. The explanation he heard from his attorney was ludicrous.

"You're telling me you can't take my case because of what?"

"He's labeled you a terrorist. And although that maybe completely false, your case will have to be settled under the Patriot Act, which guarantees you court appointed representation.

"I'm not a terrorist! He's lying! I've got my own evidence!"

"I made some calls. He's got the ball rolling in his favor. Under this act, a Grand Jury precludes the defense council to enter evidence. So my hands as your counsel are tied. Under the act, they can literally hold you under suspicion, claiming domestic terrorism."

"And you say I should turn myself in? On what fucking charge?"

"Again, and I checked into it myself. The records are sealed. You must have really pissed someone off. Get to a federal marshal as soon as possible."

"And you can't protect my rights?"

"If they invoke any charge of murder, and realize they've held prisoners for a lot less, judicial review is every six months. That means you can sit in an orange jump suit for a year before an appeal to the U.S. Court of Appeals in Washington."

"He can't do this!"

"You're telling me it's bogus, right? Your best and only path is to turn yourself in. Going with court appointed representation your case will look more favorable."

It only took a few hours to sink in. Colton said it on the phone. Kenneth was the prime suspect for Worthington's death. He couldn't let Colton take him down. He had to trap Colton the same way. Even if it sacrificed his own honor.

After steering himself to his bedroom, he fell onto the bed looking at the ceiling and then to the crumpled paper. His focus was finite. Masquerading in his addiction, a complex configuration of depression, fear, hate, and revenge had flourished, dominating his soul. His ultimate motive, expressed as words on paper, was the only way to end the pain.

He tucked the paper inside the envelope, "All the messengers end up getting fucked. If Worthington had a story, he died with it. Why should any of us pay for Colton's cruelty?"

His feelings of cowardice were shunted by the drugged conviction to end the downslide of his reputation. The ringing phone didn't shake Kenneth from his trance. It was ignored. Nothing immediate could conquer his resolve but he wondered if time would dilute his courage. A lump in his throat formed bringing the heart of the matter to thoughts of his mother. She hadn't raised him to end up taking a life. He set the gun and envelope down to wipe his eyes.

The gut of suppressed emotion was morose mixed with selfishness. Embedded throughout childhood, his mother's influence left Kenneth vulnerable against the pure vitality of maleness. On this day he could not retreat from the negative energy consuming his body to resist the destructiveness of others. Barely able to sit up, Ken slouched over. Buried deep, a thread of tenacity gave him hope. *I'll be free of him for good.*

> The submarine levels at the base of the ocean floor too were victims of a conjured nature. At some point the cause and effect of lystric slope failure of flank instability, and the shifting tonnage of grabens and horsts blocks, were all root causes. Immediate and persistent, the energy from volcanic activity was transformed simultaneously to fluid. Dispersed across a hundred square mile area, the new energy lifted seemingly impervious and indestructible solid matter. In minutes, the exposed lateral bedrock near the epicenter was pulverized into ocean debris. Betraying itself, the underwater crevasse merged shut, leaving the synchronic consequence of a tsunami for mankind to suffer through.

The next act was defiant. The perverse echo was gone in a split second, as the frail human energy in the room was upended and unburdened. The rain could be heard again, hitting the glass door. The next day, the answering machine picked up again, "Kenneth! Are you there? It's Bryan. We decided to help you. Please contact us as soon as possible."

The NEADE boss got a call from Jason. He was looking for the green light to go in. No one had heard from Millard for three days since Colton set his snare. Jason's report was new information to Colton. He accepted it with no remorse or credit, even when he left a message to Angela, telling her of the death. He accelerated the federal investigation, limiting the jurisdiction of city law enforcement. Specific information was classified with military protocol, evidence was removed from the apartment, and the mandatory county autopsy was ignored. In less than ten hours

Dr. Kenneth Millard's corpse lay in state awaiting further arrangements from his attorney of record.

"It really surprises me," Colton sneered to Angela. "He was up to something, but I thought Ken was too much of a pussy to take the easy way out."

Angela ignored her boss' callousness. She never bet Millard would meet Colton's standards. Few did and they remained wary.

"I wish that Punjab scientist would do himself in. He's become a fucking pain in my ass. I've got a mercy lawyer breathing down my neck to cut him loose."

"Oh, ah I thought Franklin was out of anyone's reach?"

"*Was* is right, although it's not completely played out. It's the same group of piney ass lawyers who have been hanging around the Iraq war prisoners. I'll know who leaked soon enough. We need to avoid getting inventoried anyway. Guantanamo is going through another round of body counts to shut down. In the meantime, let's see what we can snag from the hook in Austin. The college snots you located at Rice are tied in somehow. Get packed and head out there. Update me once you've had a chance to look around."

Angela flipped her cell closed. It appeared everything Colton touched was turning against him. A political backlash was already in motion because of one death. She presumed others' interpretation of leadership failures would be harsher. If she could have read Colton's mind, he was closing ranks. He had to be aware his support base would start planning exit strategies if they got a whiff of Millard's suicide. He had to feel the pressure.

The bosses liked solutions, not problems. Between her and Jason, they had reached a pinnacle of competence and trust. Angela counted how many errors had been committed. Aware Colton was anchored tightly with vested interests, she wondered how long he could repelled the impact of random accidents and miscalculation. *His skillful use of arrogance is double-edged. He had to be feeling the pressure.*

Jason sensed an erosion of leadership, increasingly dissatisfied since joining the team. He wondered why Angela was slow to believe they were effectively censured. He tried to convince her they were advocates of Colton's actions. How could Worthington's death be a mission vetted for the sake of national security? Millard's suicide was just another unfortunate circumstance in defending the nation's future? For him, the ethical fog had cleared and he insisted these were Colton's gross errors of judgment, not victories on the way to winning the war against science.

Who would be the next victims? he thought upon learning Angela was tracking college students. *Is he going to march on them too?*

Two additional incidents were consuming Colton's energy. A yelling match with his aide James Hyatt and he was up against the wall with the scientist he held in captivity. Without the correct calculations, NEADE would suffer a setback.

"That fucker better crack," Colton cursed through his lips as he made the last call to the lieutenant in charge of Franklin.

"Give him access to his lawyer *after* my people show up."

His second and third calls were respectively to a legal agency in Miami and to Jason Smith to give him travel orders.

As soon as he was tapped, Jason immediately texted Angela, "on my next assignment."

His temper boiled as he finished his message, "call me."

Angela saw her partner's text and pulled out her second cell phone, like that of Jason's, whose connection minutes were purchased with cash. Angela insisted the unsecured line of communication was by necessity.

"I'm here. What's up?"

"Colton's a maniac! He's been keeping Dr. Franklin bottled up like a war criminal. I had no idea he was in Cuba! Those dungeons are full of enemy combatants!"

Angela moved her cell farther from her ear to dampen the yelling and gave her side of the story, "I thought he parked him in one of the civil lockups here. I didn't know either."

She didn't share her revelation that it took major juice to get anyone into the Bay.

"You should have told me. Now I've got to sit on his bullshit train with a bunch of lawyers! Millard's body isn't even underground yet!"

"I heard about that from him as an fyi. Colton didn't spend two seconds on it," Angela reported, hoping to extract more information about Millard's death. "How did you find out?"

"I got in there and saw everything. I mean everything. I did a secure call to Colton and he calls in the feds to make sure it got shut down."

"Normal for him."

"The place was wiped clean. Erased phone messages, that sort of thing."

"You didn't, did you?"

"Hell no. I'm not that stupid."

"Was local enforcement in on it?"

"They didn't know what hit them. Colton slammed them with CIA statutes. They were more than happy to back down."

"We'll never know why Millard took his life," she concluded, caring only to know if any loose ends remained.

"I guess not," Jason paused and intentionally he changed conversation.

"Hyatt will shit his pants when I tell him Colton locked up a government civilian in a war camp."

"That's risky."

"He can be trusted. We've traded enough information to have a neutral spot to cover each other's back. He doesn't want to go down for any of this either. He thinks Colton will hang himself."

"These are one-off failures, Jason. They can be fixed by those above Colton."

"Colton is jerking *us* around. You can't separate his screw-ups from us or the future of NEADE."

Exactly what she didn't want to hear.

"Will Hyatt take Dr. Franklin's situation up to the top?" she quizzed.

"I doubt Colton kept him in the loop, so James could be blamed for not having a pulse on it. My guess is he'll leak it to cover his ass."

Angela rubbed her forehead feeling stress. Too many players with too many new loyalties. The mistakes needed to be shielded from public opinion or they would eventually fuel the centrists in Congress. NEADE would suffer and go into lockdown. It would be harder to operate independently. Research could stop.

"I'll touch base when I get back from the Bay. You've got it easy," Jason claimed.

"Hanging with the college brats? I doubt it."

"Back to Houston then?"

"No, they fled to Austin. Colton took what I gave him and did what he always does...beats it until it gives. Maybe they'll cough up what they've got and we can all go back to our desk jobs."

"You always get the fluff assignments. The golden child," Jason claimed. "I'm gone."

"Good luck. To us."

Angela said it on the pretense of being a good partner, reassuring Jason's trust of her. Collecting her flight information online, she got packed and checked one more time for messages. Before leaving she made one call on the untraceable cell to plant a seed that would eliminate another risk to NEADE's future.

U.S. Naval Station.
Guantanamo Bay, Cuba.

ANY HOURS LATER, after making flight connections in Florida, Angela's partner received security clearance for him and a legal team to enter the military facility in Cuba. A preliminary meeting between Colton's people and the defendant's attorney of record set the stage for the series of tactical delays. On the leeward side of the base in the bachelor quarters, Jason was on a twenty-four seven time clock waiting for the call. Benjamin Chapman representing the prisoner, waited at a nearby hotel at the mercy of the same schedule.

The late hour update given to TC and Navin did not dampen their spirits. They were coached earlier that an interview with Franklin was likely, but further progress was contingent upon that face to face dialogue.

Four months of perseverance weighed in to free an innocent man. No one deserved more credit than Navin. He felt personally responsible, embarrassed for not discovering the formula error and had become more assertive and desperate to find a way to discover Franklin's true fate. Taking the lead from TC, who had stood up to Franklin's boss, Navin believed Shepard had made a crucial error exposing his inability to force a solution from them. He took advantage by bargaining the data model for the whereabouts of Franklin.

Shepard was asked to come to a meeting on the pretense to review a proposed redesign of their methodology. His demeanor was rigid when the conversation started, "So what is the real purpose of this meeting?"

"We want to reconcile with you," replied Navin.

The boss sensed the strategy Colton gave him was effective after all, "Have you rethought your position?"

"Actually, yes," TC agreed. "We have, but it will cost you something in return."

Shepard was immediately repulsed, "This is clearly out of line. You have no right..."

"Excuse us, but we have made progress on the model."

"Prove it."

"First, we want to set some terms."

Shepard delivered the threat as he was coached, "You'll give me the proof under a court order anyway!"

Navin took the lead, "Please consider our offer, Mr. Shepard." His manner was calming. "Time is important to both of us. In less than an hour, you can be updating your boss. A court order will surely impede our memories."

Shepard's scowl deepened.

"All we ask is for a little knowledge in return."

"What?"

"Where is Dr. Franklin?"

"I don't know."

Navin stepped on TC's foot signaling him to stand, "We are dedicated to finishing the model that Dr. Franklin developed. You can benefit in that knowledge or not."

"How do I know you're not bluffing?"

TC pulled a paper report from his folder, "This is evidence of our commitment."

Shepard quickly thumbed through it, "I cannot guarantee anything."

"Then we would be at an impasse. Please take us seriously."

The manager walked out of the room leaving the two men inert, looking at each other for validation. Two days later, the manager passed them a copy of a flight schedule with a manifest dated the same day Franklin disappeared. Underneath a column titled, "Non-Military Personnel," there was a single name blacked out. The destination was Guantanamo

Bay. Shepard had come to terms that possession of a working formula outweighed leaking Franklin's location.

"God damn it!" It was five a.m. Jason couldn't sleep anticipating the call. His energy was bound up, sitting for eighteen hours. Colton's legal team brought the agent up to speed on their tactics when they checked in. There was Brogan Tyler, Colton's hand-picked senior partner from Tyler-Ash, including his two associates specializing in human rights cases involving military detention, and a court reporter. They were getting paid to play hardball.

"They don't give a crap about anybody else. Just their games to force a confession," he complained, throwing cold water on his face. "Screw it!"

Breaking the plastic ring on the bar handle, the agent opened two mini bottles of scotch. He was in a serious mood to deal with his disappointments. The NEADE assignment looked good on paper, but its value had spoiled quickly. From the start, most of the crap Colton threw his way was typical bullshit from a control junkie. Admiring the testosterone flares from Colton, Jason knew he had lingered too long. Conflicting with Colton's bravado and sinewy persona was an imbalanced ego. And he could crush an opponent without effort. Jason tilted his head back to finish the second mini bottle. He knew this gig wasn't going to be much of an esteem builder.

The phone rang.

Shit. Jason swallowed anyway. "Hello..."

The empty bottle was tossed towards the garbage can and the tight bank off the wall shattered it, "I'll be down in ten minutes."

Reaching the lobby, Brogan boasted of his strategy, "Colton doesn't want this guy to walk yet. We expect a fight over it, but we've got paperwork to bury the defense."

"I guess anything is fair game," Jason commented.

"There's no such thing as a fair fight," Brogan grunted.

None of them had seen the Guantanamo Bay military facility before. Massive in size, the prison spanned six hundred acres with a commensurate boundary of security fencing and warwire, designed to slow down anyone who attempted to cross the perimeter in any direction. The facility was adequately fortified to manage its occupants, in opposition to the political will to mothball it. NEADE's legal team cleared three gates before getting out of their vehicle to enter the foyer hosted by military guards. After security and wand scanning, the group was escorted to another building.

Ben Chapman was already on site having endured the same inspections. With his legal experience from Amnesty International, Franklin's lawyer expected the full brunt of resistance to get the case adjudicated. Of utmost consideration was evaluating the physical and mental condition of his client. Although Chapman made qualified demands to have immediate contact with his client, a face to face visit was purposely delayed. He presumed it was a defensive tactic to clean up their detainee, with a complete physical and if necessary, massage documentation.

Late in the day after sitting alone in an empty gym, Ben saw a man in a fresh orange jumpsuit entering from the end of the room, waist-chained with hands and feet restricted. The prisoner shuffled towards him with a military escort. The doorways on opposite sides were guarded. On the plane and in his hotel, Ben studied the snapshot he was given—a picture of Franklin with his folks. The man walking towards him was indeed Franklin but Ben was astonished with his physical appearance. Typically a shower, haircut, nail trim, and a meal did not fix or gloss over signature effects of long-term isolation and debility. Ben reached to his shirt pocket and glanced at the photos.

"Extraordinary!" he said quietly to himself.

"Dr. Ravichandran Franklin, I'm Benjamin Chapman."

He gestured for his client to sit down across the table, the only option allowed. Seated, the prisoner tilted his chair back; his chains scrapped against the metal frame. The guard had moved within hearing distance gaining a vantage point to see the middle space between them.

"Please, may I call you Franklin?"

Only a nod was given.

"I am required to sit across from you. And I cannot give you anything without explicit approval," Ben said reviewing his notepad making check marks. "Before we get started, I want you to know that I am astonished at your physical appearance."

The lawyer paused, wanting to place his hand on his client's arm as a sign of affirmation, but knew better from experience that physical contact sometimes triggered unwanted consequences, "Franklin, your parents delegated me to represent your legal rights. You have the option of revoking this action thus subordinating their wishes. Before we proceed, do you understand this?"

Another nod.

"Do you want to revoke the privilege of my representation and have it reassigned to another person or legal entity?"

Franklin shook his head. Ben cleared his throat.

"Good. I want to proceed with personal and legal interests. First, there is a letter that your parents wrote."

The guard placed one non-descript envelope in front of Franklin removing them from the larger mailer, "It has been opened and inspected," he said with authority.

"Unfortunately," Ben advised, "you cannot take the letter back to your cell. You may read it at any time while I'm with you, and at the end of our meeting I've been given permission to collect it and save it for you."

Franklin bowed his head, raised his cupped hands slowly, and sneezed. And sneezed again.

The offer of a clean handkerchief was ignored

The prisoner placed his hands on top of the envelope as if to feel and savor the energy coming from within. He did not remove the contents even though Ben remained silent encouragement to do so.

"Secondly, in light of what's happened and happening now, I'd like to have audible evidence that you have in no way been physically or mentally tortured. Can you answer?"

Silence.

Ben noticed his client's concentration—his gentle hands brushed across the envelope surface with his fingers together.

"I can understand if that's comforting for you."

From case experience, Ben had seen prisoners exhibit the condition many times in a variety of ways, from the extremes of frenetic dialogue to complete silence. There was no better or worse state of being. It would pose a barrier of sorts if the captive could and would not, or was incapable of responding verbally. The lawyer's prime concern was that it signaled a man void of trust.

The men sat there motionless for twenty minutes. The handwritten letter remained unread and after guiding the envelope to his chest, it was laid back down carefully. Bearing witness, Ben assumed his client was denying himself the tangible evidence of home to avoid building hope.

When he became disinterested the lawyer was certain the effect of isolation was worse than believed, "Franklin, I want to tell you what will happen now. My objective is to get your physical release secured as soon as practical. There are no hard obstacles in our way that can't be dealt with. I have twenty years of representing clients such as you that have been unduly detained with or without cause. I will work to reestablish your inalienable rights as guaranteed by the United States constitution."

The scientist appeared to listen, but did not show any reflexive gesture or respond in any way. Ben did not tell his client that later in the evening he would probably encounter heavy resistance. He did not dare voice his opinion about the incredibly unfortunate circumstance that gaining freedom came down to paper work and intense negotiation.

Ben looked at his watch, "It's time for me to go."

He reached, looking at the guard for approval, and retrieved the letter to store in his briefcase, "I'll be back in the morning. Please take care of yourself."

Franklin's lawyer spent the rest of afternoon reviewing the official records of his client's physical and mental health. After eating dinner in the officers' mess hall, Ben returned to the assigned briefing room and worked on other material. He knew they would make him wait again, for no reason other than to frustrate him. Ignoring their game was the best defense.

Whatever the motive was to tip the legal scales, the delay tactic was fraught with risk. Ben knew when a prisoner was given a perception of hope, through physical contact with a positive authority figure, the fragile captive becomes extremely vulnerable and volatile. As a rule, Ben knew every minute his client had to endure since their meeting, was a minute working against both of them. In most cases the ending was terminal either physically or mentally. Ben never hyped expectations he could deliver his clients the freedom they deserved. It was extremely important to lay out the procedures and give explicit signals that freedom was close but never put a clock to it. Looking at his watch, he hoped the government would end their stalemate.

Hours later, an officer came to the door and upon hearing the click of the handle, Ben sat up quickly waking from a labored nap.

"Sir, please follow me."

The lawyer stood up slowly rubbing his neck, trying to straighten. His clothes were wrinkled and damp from sweat. *How could it be two a.m. already?* "Please wait just a moment. I've got to collect my things."

He scrambled to stack his work papers in order and get them back into his leather brief.

In a few minutes Ben followed the lanky officer, broadening his stride to keep up. In the maze of empty hallways with office doors, the officer stopped suddenly, pivoted to the left, and opened the conference room door, CA-11. Everyone stood up to complete formal introductions, and with a great deal of arrogance, a lengthy and thorough explanation was given for the requirements of military oversight afforded their prisoner at Guantanamo Bay.

Ben was moved to agitation, "We've got an innocent American citizen who has been incarcerated within purview of the military for almost six months. Let's hope they've done their job. Please let's get down to business."

Required reviews started out slow on purpose. After ensuring the power of attorney was proper and all relevant documents were legitimate, the delay tactics still didn't recede. Yet another sticking point was "discovered" three hours into the discussions concerning the scope of authority to release Dr. Franklin. Ben's insistence that he had obtained the legal right to represent and counsel his client was subordinated by their concern whether he had the proper authority to *physically* recover such a prisoner.

"Your guys put him in here post haste and managed to keep a tight lid on it. Reverse engineer it or I'll pursue torture allegations."

Brogan Tyler positioned again for control, not interested in idle threats, "I'll attend to it and sooner if your client can share germane and relevant information with us concerning his involvement to deliberately share classified studies and operations with unauthorized personnel."

Jason was perturbed witnessing the legal brawl. The plan was to squeeze something out that was valuable. He rejected that proposal in the hotel lobby, but was ignored and scolded by Brogan, "That's on a recommendation from your boss. You best stay with the team on this."

With the imposing impasse it was decided parties should take a half hour break. As Brogan hoped, the long walk to his conference room gave Chapman's temper time to simmer. After his escort left, Ben threw his brief on the table. With momentum, it slid off and buckled opened on the floor spreading its contents.

"God damn!" he mouthed loudly thinking of his challenges. Getting Franklin to confess, let alone getting him to talk seemed impossible.

As he stooped over to collect the papers and folders spread across the tiles his demeanor changed instantly, "Extraordinary!" he said softly.

Beyond the thirty minutes, the lawyer was led back to CA-11. Brogan refreshed memories and laid out his plan to extract a plea for freedom, "The sooner your client gives it up, the sooner he'll be attended to."

Ben pushed his chair back and stretched his legs across the edge of the table, in deference to those who thought he was in the crosshairs and clarified his intent, "The sooner part. And you attending to my client. That's what I expect you to deliver."

Tyler was bemused, his raucousness held below the surface.

"What I mean is," Ben continued. "You should have him processed and in the front office in forty minutes."

Remaining silent, Brogan cocked his head in disbelief as Ben revealed his own demands, "It's six-fifteen. At seven, my call will halt the publication of an interview I did with James Risen of the *New York Times*. He snagged a Pulitzer Prize for discovering the government was secretly eavesdropping on innocent folk."

Tyler squinted, grinding his back teeth.

"Surprisingly, the paper is still hungry for Bay victims. Before I came down to manage this snafu. I gave them a bio on Dr. Franklin. Oh! The article became more interesting to include your managing partners' involvement with Enron."

Brogan angered and tried to deflect the perceived ploy, "That's sticking your pecker out, Mr. Chapman. We're trying to work within boundaries here. You can't be thinking you actually have control here."

"You're right. You're the one raping my client over and over."

"You're underestimating my influence Mr. Chapman. And my..." his tone became bitter, "...God damn patience!"

"Now your boss...is it Colton? He's been in the back office cooking up this shit. I'm sure he's going to like NEADE showing up in column one. As a matter of fact, I think we're planning to run a picture of him too."

Having to suddenly weigh the risk of legal and political scandal, the color of Brogan's skin changed to light crimson.

The senior attorney walked to the door, "Give me ten minutes with my team."

Ben concealed his smirk as he left.

Colton's attorney was livid and his acrimonious energy burst, "Who the fuck told him about Willis and NEADE?"

Everybody shook their heads.

"Get that fucking guard in here!"

The officer validated that procedure was followed to precision during the prisoner interview, "No, sir, at no time did the prisoner speak."

More questions were proposed, asking about physical contact.

"His lawyer never touched him, sir. I put the inspected letter in front of him and the detainee."

"Who has it now?"

The door slammed open to the room harboring Franklin's lawyer. The guard, followed by the group of lawyers, grabbed the brief and shook out the contents on top of the table. Hands pawed through the papers until the enveloped letter was seized. Exiting, the document was inspected by everyone in CA-11. After the soldier in command was berated, the legal meeting resumed with Franklin's lawyer in attendance.

"I don't know what or how you did it, but we'll find out. You have our word your client is free to go."

Ben tossed a writ of habeas corpus on the table. The additional contents guaranteed Dr. R. Franklin's release at eight a.m.

"Are you kidding?"

"Sign it."

Still disgusted, Brogan did, throwing the pen on the table. The agreements stipulated Franklin was to be given back pay during his absence, a healthy severance package, and restriction of his right to pursue legal course against individuals but not against the federal government. It maintained balanced confidential non-disclosures between parties.

"You're lucky I care more about my client's credibility than Colton's, otherwise I'd hang him out to dry," Ben assured.

It was six fifty-five.

"What about the call? We need to get you to a secure landline."

"Actually, I mixed it up being tired and all. It was *if* I called, run the article. If you're really itching to read it I'm sure we can get it bylined in the *Bay Gazette*."

"You son of bitch!"

Ben knew there was no unfettered signal available for a cell phone or landline and he enjoyed playing with their egos. They could have boxed him in for hours even if he had such an article on tap. As it was, it would take them days and weeks to sort out the leak and it would be risky if they broached the subject with any major newspaper.

The signature was costly. Tyler knew a brutal discussion would ensue when the decisions came to light. Ben packed his brief and followed the guard out into the hallway and back through the maze.

Once affirmative status was given that Franklin would be meeting him in the main offices Ben went to the men's room and went limp against the wall, mentally and emotionally fatigued. After a minute, he reached into his underwear and pulled out a sweat soaked envelope looking at what Franklin had etched on it. *That was some kick-ass handwriting.*

The words, NEADE and COLTON were tore in pieces and flushed down the toilet. Before he left the bathroom Ben washed his face, looking at himself in the mirror, "You should have gone into high stakes poker you idiot."

Seeing Franklin approaching him, Ben waved Franklin forward and they walked out. There was complete silence as they traveled back through the three gates and to the outside boundary of the forty-five square miles of military prison. While the scientist enjoyed the wind blowing through the open windows, Ben focused his blurry eyes on driving. He was startled when Franklin finally spoke asking for a cell phone.

"You had me going there. I didn't know I was dealing with a pencil lead snorting junkie. We're damn lucky I keep spare envelopes in my brief."

The smile on Franklin's face, looking into the midmorning sun, was growing as his freedom engulfed him. He was living again.

Handing his cell over to his passenger, a voice answered the outbound call, "Hello? Yes! My good friend. It's Franklin."

"Oh blessed Shiva!" TC was ecstatic.

"Please though. Tell me who was hired to get me out of prison?"

"His name is Benjamin Chapman. He's there! No?"

"Yes, my brother," Franklin sang, elated, "I will see you soon."

In his native dialect TC shared devastating news, "Ravi, we've been told a Bud Worthington has died."

His eyes swelled with tears. Who told you?" Franklin asked, bewildered. *How could they know my involvement with him?*

"I got an anonymous email."

After a few words of encouragement Franklin ended the call and set the cell on the seat.

"Is everything okay?" Ben wondered.

"I have apparently lost a dear friend."

As he gazed across the shifting landscape, Franklin's thoughts turned to his mathematical model and Worthington. Unknowingly, Colton had provided his prisoner with the gift of isolation, allowing him to realize what Worthington was trying to teach him.

In his deep contemplation, exercising the equations, he remembered what Worthington had lectured him about – the instruction for the first Proteaceae seed. With his head down for two years, he had been trapped in his own lab, missing the changes happening below his feet.

His brutal isolation provided him clarity and purpose. Why was the new wave of velocity present? How was the density of the earth changing? Had anyone bothered to notice? Some one in the oil fields must be seeing the effects of this!

His thoughts turned to the time the professor scolded him, "My young man, don't allow your tendencies of mathematical prowess to overrule the pure logic of simple congruence."

Then his thoughts turned from Worthington to revenge.

Day 63.

Mesa Verde National Park, Colorado.

371400N 1082847W

SINCE LLOYD SAW Karl and his friend, the growing season was on the lagging end with the last of tomatoes and squash. Duke came checking on his master in the garden and suddenly took off again.

"Those squirrels get the best him," he said out loud, groaning as he stood up to head to the trailer. Something was lying in the grass just off the path.

With familiarity, Lloyd changed his stride in the direction of the mound of fur, "Well, I'll be. Duke! What's wrong, boy?"

Lloyd dropped reaching the dog's head, "Duke, what's wrong?"

He wasn't alone. From his peripheral view, he saw an image, just before his shoulder stung. He cocked his head more, "You dirty pot licker, you shot my do—" he stuttered, trying to raise and reach.

As his eyelids flickered and his body slumped to prone position, the caretaker raged at the man who had come within reach. His brain was quickly going to sleep as the soldier laid him gently on the ground.

A second and third man dressed in camouflage approached the shooter, "Did he get hurt? We don't want him having stories to tell."

"No, sir," said the shooter, removing his dart.

Two men carefully hoisted the body and moved it inside to the couch. With all three men out front, they ran down the path towards the road. Activating his mike, the lead radioed the chopper, "Resident is secure. We'll be at point yankee-echo in five minutes. Standby."

"Roger, will standby."

Reaching the chopper, the lead ranger looked at his watch. The drug induced sleep would last another forty-five to sixty minutes. The pilot lifted off towards coordinates charted days ago. Cutting across the carbon blue sky, the blade rotations pushed slapping tones into the dense air. Sound waves reverberated off the canyon walls that lay ahead. The combined narrowness and height of the rock outcropping made it impossible to land directly at their target site, so as planned the men dropped lines and rappelled to the brush below. At normal pace, they had a ten minute hike to reach their destination.

The military chopper swung south on orders to drift beyond line of sight. With medium packs and weapons ready, the recon team was in a jog to reach the ancient site. On a condition of silence they split up and approached from three sides. Advancing on mike clicks they all met at the place Karl, Peter, and Lloyd stood months ago. Appearing to be ground litter, two sets of digital photos were taken and the material was secured in evidence bags.

The lead compared a GPS coordinate against information printed on a laminated card and took additional readings with his device as he moved to pinpoint the exact location of the buried artifacts. While one man positioned for offensive surveillance, the third soldier opened his pack and spliced together the handle of a sensing unit, then snap-connected a digital display to the housing. The device provided the functionality of sensitive ultrasound typically used for land minds. The signal measured the density of images and according to a recheck of coordinates, recorded one of the artifacts they had been briefed about. A sawzall was deployed to cut a deep pattern at a measured depth. For archeologists, this process would be sacrilegious. For thieves, it was how work got done.

With pry tools from two sides, the earthen clay slab was lifted to ground level. The dirt block revealed a relic that did not match the digital printout. After expanding the perimeter and rechecking for buried mass, the cut and extraction process was repeated finding a larger pot wrapped in cloth. The lead looked at his watch again and nervously translated a message to the pilot, expecting the status to be brokered to his client.

"At the site, negative on the gem."

"We'll be at pickup point alpha papa in twenty minutes."

Quickly, the two pieces were secured in cases and placed in the backpack. After filling the ground cavities with compost of needles and loose rock, the remaining loose dirt was tamped down and line cuts were brushed over. After reaching the soldiers were picked up at the extraction point, the craft circled back to the left and out between the massive rock walls of the steep mountain range. Mission over.

"Sir," the pilot reported on mike to the command lead, "on recon, I spotted a dust trail coming towards yankee echo."

"Not in scope. This is a bump and run."

"Right, sir."

On their way back, a recap was transmitted to their superior. And when the results were reported, the news did not give Willis Colton the closure he expected. Their bounty was nothing like the evidence Wolmit or the DARON analyst had provided.

Karl spotted the helicopter going in towards the canyon just as he was retrying the lock combination, "So much for security."

Passing through the gate, he pulled in under junipers and waited. If they tried to get a visual it would be towards the sun. With the helicopter gone, Karl drove the road to the property line where they had been greeted by Duke. Stooping low, he kept his eye on the horizon and moved swiftly across the edge of the parking lot, then flanked the trailer. Expecting to hear Duke, he saw the dog lying on the ground.

Duke had caught Karl's scent and lay whining not able to get upright.

"Where's Lloyd, huh?"

Finding no signs of blood on the dog, Karl continued his search for the owner. Entering the trailer, there was a sigh of relief locating his friend. Finding a normal pulse, he placed a glass of water, some aspirin, and Pepto Bismol on the coffee table waiting for Lloyd to gain consciousness.

"Lloyd, are you ok?"

After blinking, he tried swallowing, which triggered a cough spell. Taking hold of his rescuer's arm and leg, his mind picked up where it left off, "You bast—"

"Lloyd, its Karl!"

The victim eased up and slumped back down, "I'm what? Where's Duke? He's shot!"

"No, no, he's okay."

Doctoring the patient for dehydration and a headache, his memory improved, "Man, they jumped me. I couldn't do anything. It stung!"

"What stung?"

"Like a wasp. Something got me in the shoulder."

Coaxing Lloyd to remove his shirt they found a small puncture, "They drugged you and Duke."

Clearing his voice, Lloyd stood, hearing Duke whining at the door. Still dizzy, the old man convinced Karl he would feel better outside. Sharing his own ailments, Duke greeted his master.

"That's a good boy. Hold up now. That's good."

"I looked around the property and inside your trailer when you were out. Nothing is out of order."

"That's good. I don't have many tools to fix stuff. What'd they come for?"

The chopper landed an hour later at its base. The mission commander stood next to Willis Colton whose grimace was triggered from someone else's failure. The commandoes lined up across from their superior officer.

"You're telling me your men didn't screw up."

"That's correct."

"They told you they don't have the items I wanted."

"They followed the coordinates you provided. You were briefed earlier – we aren't pit diggers. We could only secure what was targeted. If it wasn't—"

Colton's temper flared, "I don't give a goddamn what was or wasn't."

He yelled above the chopper blades spinning down. His demands were palpable, "I need those pieces. You needed to locate them. Give me the recon!"

The lead ranger recited his log, "We went in at 1400 and managed the occupants. We made the target area and secured the cargo at the exact coordinates."

The first lieutenant motioned for the cases to be opened. Looking down, Colton revived his anger, "You men pulled up worthless crap. You have the photos. What does it take?"

Putting his hand up to halt all conversation, Colton opened his cell and hit an auto number, mistakenly quick Ken Millard. Quickly terminating the connection, he redialed.

"I've got to get that asshole off my cell...you've got twenty-four hours to figure out why these men came up empty on your data."

Colton paused listening to an explanation, but interrupted, "Let me help you pull your head out of your ass. Get the records off the drive and go over them again."

Again a pause.

"You guys are killing me. Straighten it out. Twenty-four hours."

Colton's attention shifted back to the soldiers, "Anything else?"

"Yes, sir. We found these at the site."

The ranger held baggies with blue flags in them.

"What are they?"

"We don't know. Maybe evidence?"

"Maybe."

Colton reached in his coat pocket and handed the commander his card, "Call this number. Ask for the lab director. They'll take it from there. And send me your field log."

Turning, Colton strode over to his limo and was ushered inside. The vehicle drove across the base, where he boarded a jet.

Karl stared at Lloyd as they ate lunch, "I think they came for the relics that we mapped out when Peter and I were here. Do you remember?"

"Of course I remember. I'm not senile!"

"Well, if they went up to the site, they probably dug up the artifacts that we mapped. Did you get a look at them?"

"I remember a man in camouflage. Then I started feeling dizzy."

"I'm glad I got here for you, but I'm too late to make a difference."

"Whadda mean?"

"I came back to actually dig up those pieces. They hold significance for the research."

"Did you get those DBA papers that you were waiting on?"

"No, but the artifacts suddenly became important enough to take without permission. And now, nobody will see them again, let alone trace them. I'm guessing it was our government this time and not some greedy thief. What's the difference? They're gone."

Lloyd got a grin on his face, "Those dirty buggers came up empty."

"Who's to say?"

"Go in the cupboard and grab the keys on the hook."

Slowly, Karl and Lloyd made it over to the shed. As Lloyd instructed, the four-wheeler was backed out and the middle floor boards pulled up to uncover a root cellar.

"Go down and you'll find a burlap sack. Careful, it has pottery in it."

Karl climbed down to retrieve the Native treasure. The sack contained a few ancient pots and three stones wrapped in period linen. Upon careful inspection Karl realized the glossy photo was an example that Worthington might have borrowed from his friend, Paul Brewer.

"Lloyd! How did you get your hands on these? I think these are the ones Worthington had sent me for."

"That's who?"

"A professor I work...worked with," Karl wiped his brow. "Every bit as feisty as you. Peter and I figured out the pieces had been misplaced!"

"Well, I guess I told a good lie, but that's what I did. Let's get something to drink and I'll tell you why."

Putting everything back in place, the artifacts of interest were carried into the trailer. Lloyd explained how he was caretaker when the robbers had made off with the relics. But when caught, he had heard claims that the pieces were left hidden on the trail.

"It occurred to me that they would have ditched them, so when Mary first went up there to inspect the area, I took a walk down in that draw that I told you was full of snakes."

"On the hike that night, you said the thieves came from the hiking trail and crossed over but got caught."

"That's where I ran into their loot. I never let on what I found down there."

"Why didn't you hand the evidence over to Mary?"

"Those idiots would have put them back in the ground and sure enough somebody would have come back again. I figured they were valuable. I just hadn't gotten around to telling anyone."

Karl became concerned, privy to Lloyd's secret, "Those dudes are going to be pissed. They probably accessed the same records we did."

Then his paranoia kicked in, "You know, I think we better get the hell out of here."

"Well, I can't up and leave, at least without explaining."

"No, not a good idea, and we don't want anyone to report you're missing either. The army dudes are probably going to bug the line and keep an eye on you somehow. Tell you what…"

Karl laid out an exit plan for Lloyd and provided him a phone number on the back his business card. They rehearsed the plan again before Lloyd called Mary and told her his daughter was diagnosed with a rare form of leukemia.

"Oh my gosh!" Mary blurted.

Listening next to Lloyd's ear, Karl heard her response, "You've got to get going. Don't worry now. I'll take care of Duke!"

Lloyd had to convince her, with Karl whispering to him, that Duke was going with him.

"Are you sure? That sounds like a bother. Make it easy on yourself."

Karl emphasized the importance of their decision, "You won't be coming back! Tell her your daughters have never met your best friend. She'll fall for that."

Mary agreed to come get Lloyd and Duke in the morning.

After hanging up, Karl continued to coach Lloyd, "And remember, grab only your letters if you want and some favorite trophies. We don't want anyone to suspect you're going to be gone a long time."

Lloyd looked around realizing he had some hard choices to make, "Maybe some of the fire crew will pack it up for me when they come next summer," he wished.

"Get down to Albuquerque and like I've written down, board your flight. Don't tell Mary where you're really going.

"Yep, and I call, ah—"

"Wren. After you land in Denver, call this number. She'll come get you. Remember Lloyd, do not call your daughters until you get to her house. She'll have a secure line. You don't want to worry them at this point."

"My hell no, they think I lead a boring life."

Karl swept his hand across Lloyd's back, "No kidding! Okay. I've still got some daylight left. I'm going to leave with the pottery. None of this happened, right? If anyone shows up again it'll take them a while to put their finger on where you are. I'll be check pointing with Wren so stay on course."

Lloyd nodded, "I guess we've come clean on this one for good."

"Ya we have."

Karl took a step forward and hugged Lloyd, "You've saved the day, maybe the world!"

Lloyd's wide grin showed the tooth that had a shiny piece of metal in it. As they walked down to the car Duke came along side bugging the younger man to throw the ball. After a couple throws Karl went to the driver's side and opened the door.

"I'll call Wren as soon as I get to a landline."

"Alright. I know."

Lloyd's eyes glanced down to the seat, noticing a mask with a respirator, "That work okay against that dust?"

Karl sensed Lloyd wasn't as feeble as he seemed, "You bet it did!"

Old Ebitt's Grill. Washington, D.C.

"**S**ON-OF-A-BITCH."

In the restaurant booth, Jason dipped in his seat sensitive to patrons hearing Colton share his anger. His aide leaked the Millard death to Richard Sterling, the ranking member of the committee.

It wasn't a revelation. Colton expected they were getting daily feeds from Hyatt but so far was successful neutralizing the effect, "Hyatt may have their undivided attention, especially when he hands them ammunition, but I've got ammunition too."

What pissed Colton off was the context of the leak. The steps to close off the problem were in place but rumors persisted. He supposed there was an unofficial statement floating around that exploited the facts. And Colton had no reason to think Hyatt would share the memo with his agent.

"You never know if these things have legs or not," Hyatt told Jason in confidence, "but the incident we spoke of has triggered the first shoe to drop in a larger movement to recalculate leadership at NEADE."

"Colton's bulletproof," Jason claimed, meaning it as an absolute.

"Maybe not. The memo says and I quote, '...lack of direct evidence, withstanding executive ability, failed to contain risk. The response to extenuating circumstances will ultimately need to be investigated.'"

"What are they referring to? What are they saying?"

"The suicide. It'll force a panel review upstairs. The byline is some people have been calling for Colton's removal before NEADE was retrofitted. They believe the demise of Dr. Millard might impair NEADE's capacity to deliver. All in all, Colton's tenure is anywhere from shaky to fully screwed."

In a rear booth Colton continued his rant during an early breakfast, "He knew goddamn well we buttoned up the problem."

Jason motioned for his boss to keep his voice lower, but was waved off. He was still boiling from his self-negligence, having barely salvaged a key aspect of Franklin's incarceration, "Was there any mention of the scientist's cell phone?" Colton asked.

"No, we put a line through it on the property form and no one questioned it. I don't think they even checked the contents of the envelope."

"If it's brought up, stall and let me know. I can retrieve it."

Colton realized the significance of the cell phone and had it expressed to him personally, compliments of a military flight. Wolmit was able to get into the phone call list by reprogramming code sets. Three calls occurred on consecutive days at different times.

"Find a cord and leave it on twenty-four seven. And monitor it."

"So far, a couple misdials, but it didn't pan out."

Colton was sure somebody might call the number looking for Franklin. Given he was unable to coerce from Franklin, it was the only thing left to exploit. According to the guards, the prisoner never changed his mode of silence nor his eating habits. They reported the literature on his papers was always scratched out, except for a drawing that sometimes appeared on the bottom of the page.

"I'll fax it to you," responded the officer. "It's a picture of a small plant coming out of the ground. You know, like a seedling."

It angered Colton when he studied it, and he carried the mood to breakfast in front of Jason, "And how the hell did my legal team end up getting screwed in the ass?"

"Brogan took the reins. The wheels fell off when Chapman disclosed he knew about you and NEADE."

"I saw the report. We got our dicks stepped on. But Franklin will still fall into place."

Jason perked up, wondering what the spin was going to be this time.

"He'll feel compelled to help his lab rats."

"He doesn't officially work for NEADE, right?"

"No. But *their* asses are on the line. He'll save his team."

Jason decided to dig for more information. All he knew was NEADE was trying to develop a solution for proactive catastrophic planning and was guessing at all the other dynamics. His boss could ignore him or answer it anyway he liked, "They're working on what? Protecting who against what?"

"Look. You guys just do your jobs, you and Angela. There's shit in the wind here."

Colton left money on the table and they walked out, "Believe me you don't want it on you. NEADE has a partnership with the private sector and its geology experts and all the crap that goes with it. A model is being developed to enable predictions. There are new energy sources that will be tapped and the U.S. needs to be first. You remember the race to the moon right?"

"Sure."

"Same deal. We're trying to accelerate the solution."

Jason attempted to push once more, "And NEADE is under the gun because...?"

"When the shit hits the fan and we get fucked in the ass by all those piss-ant countries in the desert, China and Russia included. Ya got it?"

"Sure."

Jason got the message that time. No more handouts. He wondered if Hyatt was right. Maybe his boss hadn't misplayed his cards.

There was so much more eating at Colton. At the surface, hard evidence gathered from Worthington's computer confirmed a breach from NEADE but a suspect remained at large. And the artifacts remained a mystery. From these seemingly unrelated events, the thin layer of frustration ran with deeper roots.

The radical solution for predicting earth's behavior had morphed into something else. On the way to managing the enormous financial, political, and public makeover for the oil industry, another path had opened up. It surprised everyone – NEADE ingenuity discovered a new energy source. While one research team remained committed to predicting Earth's geological forcings, a new team was dispatched to identify the value of a new geological substance. The smartest and most creative, employed and controlled by NEADE, were to master the discovery.

But they stumbled. At first, field operations secured evidence from oil drills and contained operations. But these were random failures in America's oil fields. No one could predict when or where the substance would appear.   The research team predicting seismic activity would have provided clues as to the location of the substance. But they were deadlocked, having their lead scientist taken from them. NEADE's success wasn't supposed to be teetering on a single set of physics calculations.

And it got worse. The U.S. controlled oil reserves had been at a state of incalculable risk. But the oil industry was fat again. NEADE gave the oil conglomerates the power to bargain with foreign adversaries. Gave them unprecedented monetary control over supply and demand. Gave them an army of field agents who controlled the public image of oil. Armed them with propaganda to extinguish scientific opposition. Big oil was supposed to be satisfied.

But the new discovery was leaked. Waved in front of big oil. Before the properties of the substance were defined and before the dynamics of the source were understood. Although a pure accident, they said the new substance was a sign of providence. They proclaimed it was like just like oil, remaining out of reach for thousands of years. And suddenly, a new era was borne. This time it was theirs for the taking. When they heard the energy components were off the charts, they were instantly tired of managing a finite resource with global risk. They wanted the new energy source that was rumored to be infinite in supply. Their impetuous visions conjured a future were they could squander relentlessly.

Colton was keenly aware he was in the cross hairs. The model of seismic prediction wasn't complete. A rare substance was barely understood. The oil men were impatient. Yet, no one cared about the grime realities of protecting national secrets. No one cared that innocent people had been killed.

But Colton understood the essence of power. The new discovery could recalibrate world dominance and there would be an *instant* new world order. NEADE needed to control its own destiny. Nothing could be dismissed. Even the slightest provocation would be investigated, analyzed, and reported. Anything impeding NEADE's success would be tracked, circled, and taken out. The leaks to the NEADE leadership had seriously eroded Colton's support base but hadn't wiped out his acts of resourcefulness. He had been tested all his life. With a handful of gut-wrenching near misses during his CIA service, everything else was white noise.

The NEADE boss launched another team, with written assurances that a parallel effort could overtake Franklin's men, matching the research footprint in fifteen days. Housing the replacement team on a separate floor, Colton reminded the new lead they had to remain as a shadow, "You tell me when and I'll pull the plug on Shepard and his team."

And he played out another hunch with the contents of Worthington's computer, "Take these computations and compare them to your work. Let me know if there's an absolute match."

A strong minority of his superiors and NETL congressional appointees became outraged with the mishap concerning the death of Dr. Kenneth Millard. Timing his revenge, his strongest deflector, Senator Bolen fueled the fire.

Colton blunted the attack immediately, voicing his position with Sterling and Royce during their meeting at the Pentagon, "Off record, Bolen doesn't have a fucking clue what it takes to nail it."

Sterling didn't want the discussion to turn polemical, "Deliver the answers our patrons have asked for. Then the noise goes away."

Image obsessed, Royce nodded in agreement as was expected.

Colton was offended, "On record, Bolen's a fucking idiot. I'll hand this live round to him and it'll take his head off. The answers aren't on some fucking hors d'oeuvre tray."

Sterling became reactive, "*Our* patrons are concerned more about the ultimate prize. Make sure all the *other items* don't overshadow your accomplishments in the lab. And keep in mind your brethren are managing to keep the focus on climate. Without that deflection, you would be at Bolen's mercy."

"If there's new blood to be spilled, it's not going to be mine. He'll go down."

Sterling firmed his eyes on Colton. His warning ended the challenge, "Don't confuse your value with your virtues."

Colton's frustration was perverse. The solution to *all* his challenges channeled back to one person. Still one man knew more than anyone else. Colton had that person where he wanted him. And was forced to let him go.

But he never allowed anger to blind opportunity. Lab reports confirmed DNA profiling evidence on two of the ground markers found by the army recon team. The FBI databases and local files had no matches. Based on tests for amelogenin, all that could be confirmed was the blood belonged to a male. Weighing that information, Colton turned to follow the long lead that went in his favor when two other agents in Austin reported in.

"There's a large group. They appear to be in and out of the residences. We could go in," offered the agent, "to collect DNA for a complete identification, instead of relying on line of sight information."

"Angela is on her way down there. Do a memory dump with her. She'll make the recommendation back to me."

Colton wanted her to confirm the risk. It was another way to test her loyalty.

Summer residence of the students. Austin, Texas.

Avey suspicions grew from frustration. Their routines had become sloppy. The sizzle of excitement and hype of new discovery was completely played out, leaving them with mundane tasks of going over familiar detail. When she stored the volumes in a secure place, her teammates complained of the additional effort to lay everything back out. She asked that they keep the house locked all the time and the blinds closed, but when she returned from her runs, the front door would be unlocked.

And this time, she saw the black books and notes scattered on the tables. Their laptops were unsecured with files open. Her agitation with her teammates intensified as she went looking for them. The antique convertible sports car stored in the garage became an excuse to conquer the tedium.

"You guys! Do you know the front door was unlocked? Anybody could have walked in and ripped us off!" "We thought you'd be right back."

Avey became angrier, "Right. You know when I go for a run it takes at least thirty minutes!"

Jude tried to settle her down but the joke fell flat, "Well, we just got here, so whoever showed up would have only had a couple minutes to steal us blind."

Avey glared, waving the hardcopy of an email, "Do you know we're being watched?"

"How do you know?"

"I couldn't prove it at first. It seemed there was more traffic on this street than when we got here. I've seen men sitting in cars."

"Probably salesmen."

Avey raised her voice a notch glaring at Jude, feeling her emotions sweeping logic away, "Have you joined the stupid parade? We can't be careless anymore. It feels like we're going to get caught!"

Her eyes swelled up and she started to walk out. Arthur jumped over the car door frame and ran to put his arm around her, "Hey, he didn't mean anything by it," he reassured, looking back at Jude. "He's just a slob. We'll do a better job."

Avey wiped her eyes, "Maybe I need to go home. This is getting serious."

"What do you mean?" Arthur asked.

"I didn't tell you guys but I sent Wren some of the license numbers. That's why I go out a lot. She didn't match any the first time, so I figured I worried for nothing. The third search showed a couple of the cars – owned by the rental companies."

She pushed the paper into Arthur's hand, "That means something doesn't it?"

Jude got out of the car and attempted to smooth it over, "Okay. I believe you. What does Wren think?"

"You know her. She and Karl would force us to relocate and we'd all be in camo."

Arthur and Jude's laughter was infectious.

Wiping tears she shared what mattered to her, "It's different than when we got here. We already know somebody is running around after what happened to Bud. And now there are people watching us. And we're on our own when you think about it. We could be put in jail and no one would know."

The boys knew they would have to change their behaviors even if the threat wasn't real.

"Why didn't you tell me?" Arthur asked.

"Because I was playing a hunch. Just like you guys taking a chance watching Bud. Look what happened there!"

Late, after they had eaten dinner with little conversation, Jude left to join a pickup game.

"Hey, can we talk about the cars and stuff," Arthur asked.

"I guess," Avey replied, still looking at her book.

"Are there other things bothering you? I mean, I see you stretch, you go out, you come back perspiring. You're training again?"

"I'm trying. It's not coming along."

"You've tried it before. Is it worse?"

"It's different. It's a lot of things. Maybe I'm madder at my lack of progress than scared about being watched."

Arthur squeezed her hand, "Maybe we bit off more than we could chew."

"You mean I did. You seem perfectly fine with everything."

"This is the easiest summer I've ever had. I admire you for trying."

Avey leaned in and kissed Arthur, "I just can't give up on it without trying. I want this piece of titanium to be more than just a place to put another shoe."

Arthur smiled.

She leaned back into Arthur so they could hug, "It's not me, but it's always going to define me. We just need a break."

"You mean quit for a while?" Arthur tested.

"No. Some help to figure this out."

"Good. I was hoping you weren't going to leave."

"I'm not that much of a baby."

"If you want to make some progress, why don't you use that thing to kick Jude's ass when he gets out of line?"

Jen thought she better call Doug, knowing her news would be trivial. More buttons could have been pushed if she had been able to join the group in Austin. Like always, Karl absorbed a problem and had the will to figure it out. Peter was more self-absorbed. *They haven't changed*, she reminisced, driving from work. Karl had been appealing to her when they met at college. *Should I try again with Karl? He's such a renegade. Makes Peter look like Mr. Rogers*, Jen giggled.

Kate answered when Jen called after the dinner hour, "Hi, Kate. I was hoping Doug was home. I promised him an update on a project I'm working on. Is he available?"

"Sure. Hold on."

"Hey Jen," Doug spoke.

"I owe you an update on Peter."

Doug lowered his voice, "First, remember we were talking about the field tests going on? New software is going to report back all drilling information from the field within a forty-eight hour cycle. More eyes keeping track of what we do. Like always, they're ramming it in before training is completed. Are you aware of it?"

"Yes. I saw it too. We're not planning any changes on our bore tools that I know of."

"So, anything on those drill heads from your friends?"

"Not really. Still looking at it. I don't know if I can do any more with that. But my guys met and there were rumors floating around about big oil being in bed with the feds somehow. But that in itself isn't unusual."

"Randy found out from one of the executive secretaries the big wigs were meeting in Washington to defend higher costs at the pump. But all that seems obvious given the price swings because of supply and demand. Other than that it's been kind of quiet. It's like everybody pulled in their horns."

"Seems that way. Maybe we jumped the gun."

"If there's a cover-up, they're doin' a damn good job. We'll have to wait for the next big wave I guess," Doug replied.

"And your job? It's okay and everything?" Jen asked, worried about his future.

"Apache hasn't kicked me out yet. All normal."

"If something pops up promise you'll give me a shout."

"Sure enough. Take care, Jen."

"Night."

When Jen hung up she had a knot in her stomach. Everything couldn't be normal.

Home of Wren Kennedy. Denver, Colorado.

Forced to get involved with Lloyd was a mixed blessing for Wren. In an empty house her work and life balance was finely tuned to – one. Her world of one. Her work with keyboards, computers, screens, and robust connections was her life. If a technique failed, she improved it. If it was effective, she practiced it. If nothing would work, she invented a solution. If there was code to be written she would miss meals. If a new technology needed to be learned sleep was gladly postponed. In her world of one she rarely made room. Unless it held promise.

When Avey called asking for information on the cars circling the neighborhood, it was a hunch Wren could get into. A simple pass-through to her buddy at the nine-one-one call center took all of five minutes. Wren listened to Avey because it had potential.

Since the meeting with Peter and the team, she worked the puzzle she was handed because it intrigued her. Her progress, or the promise of more, was from persistence and luck. Anticipating results coming in small doses, she enjoyed the hunt more than the capture. Her addiction to hacking was metered by the dynamics of information technology and the intrusion of time.

Inevitability, even the most complex barriers in the virtual web were mastered by the poseurs. The only way to stay sharp, to keep an edge, to stay in front, was by doing. Times at bat and finesse. Odds went up, sometimes exponentially when she exhausted all the angles. It was a one-player mantra. Others could try to keep up, but they had to match her resilience and cunning. It was her routine, her world.

But there was a new disruption and interruption.

Karl had involved her with a temporary visitor. And she would have kept saying no. In her world, his request to house Lloyd and his dog was flagrant intrusiveness. Nothing could change her mind.

A dart? Military helicopter? Army men? And *Karl managed to keep something away from their greedy little hands!* She wrestled with the terms but only for a minute. This man was a hero. His dog was a hero. They were survivors. She wanted to hear the story first hand. She made room in her world, but it wasn't much to look at.

To a spectator, parts of the house had junk piled high spreading out into the living room stopping short of the kitchen. The moveable carts with servers on the bottom and monitors and keyboards on top, were connected to power strips and surge protection on the floor, competing with stacks of manuals and books. Seating was limited to a single couch, lounger, and dining chairs.

At the airport, Wren matched the description Karl gave her, "Look for a grandfather, slightly humped over, hat tilted to the side, and a shiny tooth grin. Make sure to speak up."

She approached the stranger and introduced herself, "Lloyd?"

"Are you Wendy?"

"No, I'm Wren," she giggled.

"Oh. Okay. Did Karl send you? Gene's boy?"

"Karl did. Yes. He did."

"Where are we going?"

Driving back to the house, Wren was tense, "Ah, Lloyd? I just wanted you to know you're more than welcome, but I'm kind of a...a pack rat. The house is...it's a lot messy."

Standing outside the tutor style house when Wren unlocked the door, Duke charged ahead, sniffing around.

"You know my daughters are nice girls and they keep a good house, but they're basically what I've heard called clean freaks. When I visit, I have to walk on egg shells and have to—"

Wren put her arm around Lloyd, "Thank you! Welcome home."

And he did make himself at home, not showing any apprehension even when he called his daughters. He stuck to the story that he was visiting some friends that he knew. He said he would be looking forward to spending time with them soon.

"Once their spouses get wind of my plans to stay with them, they won't bother to find me," Lloyd predicted.

All three residents settled in, though their life habits could not be completely united. Their diets didn't match exactly, but everybody liked to eat a late breakfast and an early dinner. Lloyd enjoyed stretching out in the lounger, fast asleep. Wren would still be sleeping when he woke early. The dog needed short walks to the park but no one threw a good ball.

Every evening, Wren surfed podcasts and blogs or followed twitter. Lloyd always tried to lure her away earlier and have a random conversation. This time, the bounty of mint chip ice cream he dished for her had turned to soup. This time, Wren had to blunt his purpose, "Lloyd, I really have to get on this stuff. Isn't there a game on or a paperback to read?"

Searching the blogs for news of oil getting their due was a good use of time while Wren waited patiently for her other bot to return.[58] Her expertise and knowledge of illicit cybercrime already paid off and gave her the edge to secretly move one of her bots to a computer in the NETL call center. Although her foray into government-secured domains was explicitly illegal and considered malicious, Wren justified the achievement by her own standards. She wasn't going to sell what she was stealing, like the cybercriminals who were motivated by profit.

---

[58] Hyperdictionary. "Bot." http://www.hyperdictionary.com/search.aspx?define=bot. © 2000–2007 HYPERDICTIONARY.COM. Any type of autonomous software that operates as an agent for a user or a program or simulates a human activity. On the Internet, the most popular bots are programs (called spiders or crawlers) used for searching.

Her methods were a mix of elegance and crude tactics. She always tested for the easiest way to penetrate someone's virtual fortress. The first bounce up to the NETL firewall proved the government organization could blunt intruders from entering through the front door with spam. Checking the back door, pinging different web and server ports, she found nothing unlocked. Searching other angles, Wren couldn't find the contractor award schedule; that information had detail of the equipment purchases and types of connectivity. Not out of tricks, she decided to make contact with the human side of NETL. Often that was the weakest link of all impenetrable organizations.

Earlier, Wren initiated a game of pretexting or phishing. To accomplish this, she attacked the fleshy part of the network – the call center. All high-powered organizations invested in them to filter public requests for technical support. But first, she had to masquerade as a victim just to find the call center. Then she hoped to exploit whoever was willing to help, to create a virtual door she could walk through.

After browsing to the NETL website, she connected to a "live chat" session. An icon of an agent's smiling face and text bar popped up with the ever-present timed delay, "Please wait for the next available agent."

Minutes passed before Wren was allowed to type her first message.

Panicked: I'm hoping you can help me this evening. I've got big problems!

N. Paul: Hi. We'll be with you momentarily. Please describe your issue.

Panicked: I've lost my cheat sheet and my boss is absolutely no help either. I need to get a file to NETL and there's a deadline. I think there's a direct line that I can speak to someone, but I don't know the number.

N. Paul: What type of technical problem do you have?

Panicked: I think I'm supposed to load a file. All I know is I have to get this research in for my boss who has left on business travel.

N. Paul: We can assist if you are having actual problems with the connection. Have you started the file transfer with GeoLab?

Out of the mouth of babes! Wren wrote down the information.

Panicked: I'm not sure. I just got trained and the previous admin left me a list, but I can't find it.

Apologetic and willing to provide excellent customer service, the operator gave Wren the direct support line to deep support.

N. Paul: I don't have the ability to help you with this type of problem. You'll need to call the toll-free number I have provided. It is the direct contact for our support desk. Is there anything else I can do for you this evening?

Panicked: No, but thank you very much.

On plan, at exactly twenty-five minutes before the universal work shift change, Wren called the NETL call center. The gender of the agent answering her call was critical. A woman would want too much information and might blow her off. Men liked helping stranded females.

Andrew: "Hello, this is Andrew with NETL. How may I help you?"

Armed with her remote-control program on a generic laptop, Wren started the conversation complaining.

Wren: "It's for my boss, Dr. Kenneth Millard," she said, using the information from the business cards Worthington had.

The support agent attempted to politely interrupt.

"And do you think he'll care how much effort this takes? I've tried it over and over. Live chat said they couldn't help. I'll get blamed again for the same problem that he caused."

Wren invoked four elements in her favor, all based on call center efficiency and performance measures. First, on a Friday before six pm, the call agent had to assume there was a genuine customer on the line. Second, the exact reason for the call had not been logged by anyone. All Andrew knew was an emotionally-charged woman was blabbering about her boss. Third, every new call was logged to measure support success. A call this late could make or break the monetary incentive dangled in front of them. Fourth, it was minutes before the shift change. Usually agents were not allowed to transfer an open call to the arriving shift.

Andrew: "I'm sorry to hear that. May I have your name?"

Wren: "Flustered! It's been a crazy day and—"

Andrew: "Who am I talking with?"

Wren: "I'm sorry. I'm Suzie. It's just that I've tried this thing over and over."

Andrew: "What exactly are you attempting to do?"

Wren: "I'm trying to up or down the file. He told me to get this file to you. Whatever it's called, I need to get it to you."

Andrew retrieved the call log passed from their offshore team in Singapore.

Andrew: "Miss, you can't give us a file directly. It has to upload to another server."

Wren: "So I have to call someone—"

Andrew: "No. You've got the right place. What are you using to connect to us?"

Wren: "A computer."

Andrew: "I mean, do you know the application you are using that isn't working?

Wren: "Oh! Yes, GeoLab."

The scam needed to appear creditable to the NETL support engineer. Wren began to lay down her snare. "Dr. Millard told me he was done with this research and to send it by GeoLab. He was in a hurry and told me to call you. I keep trying and nothing works."

The call center representative could push her back to live chat for any reason. He looked at the clock making sure he had sufficient time to connect to her computer and troubleshoot virtually. Activating remote client connectivity over their broadband connection, Andrew logged on explaining she would see the cursor moving and screens changing as he reviewed the system.

Wren: "I told Dr. Millard we should load everything required of us, according to the rules," Wren added.

Andrew: "That's good. I'm glad to hear that you did. Do you know how to run the application?"

Wren: "I don't really know it. He said I would get trained and of course at the last minute—"

Andrew: "Okay. That's fine. I need to—"

Wren: "You can help though, right? If I don't do this I know he won't hesitate to fire me."

Andrew: "Yes, Suzie. I need to figure out what's giving you trouble. Give me a minute."

Both parties were compliant to each other's wishes. Experienced with many clients, Andrew launched a routine inspection. He had quit complaining to his boss that novice users would stop escalating to the help desk if the software team designed user friendly software.

This was another critical moment. The caller remained silent aware of the reaction, anticipating the support lead would become suspicious. She could see his cursor moving to check all the obvious places that would tell him the computer was setup correctly.

Andrew: "Suzie?"

Wren: "Have you figured out the problem? I swear I need to find other work. This is much too complicated for my—"

Andrew: "Hold on, please," the agent interrupted. "You don't have our software app installed."

Wren: "Software what?"

Andrew: "Application."

Wren: "I don't? I thought we did!"

Andrew: "Suzie, usually these computers are preloaded. Your laptop isn't even our standard model. You say you work for a Dr. Kenneth Millard?"

Wren: "Are you kidding? I'm so embarrassed! Dr. Millard said everything was ready to go. What do I do now? Is he even in your system?"

Andrew: "He is. I already checked that at the top of the call. But this isn't the laptop we assigned to him."

Wren deliberately kept her energy peaked, "I told him that he needed to let me learn how to do it on *his* laptop. He insisted he had to leave early and took his equipment."

Andrew: "Suzie—"

Wren: "We started loading something called the startup CD around four this afternoon. I couldn't watch it having to take calls and help Dr. Millard prepare—"

Andrew: "Suzie...? Do you have the CD set?"

Wren: "I can't get to them now. Dr. Millard is very sensitive-minded. He locked them up."

Andrew: "Do you mean security-minded?" the gentleman corrected.

Wren: "Yes, that's what I meant. I just knew we should have used his computer."

Andrew: "Also, did you know that Dr. Millard's account is marked inactive."

Surprised, Wren held her breath hoping the red flag wouldn't crash her scam.

Wren: "Are you sure? He didn't say anything to me."

Andrew: "It could be for any number of reasons."

Wren looked at her clock. Time was still in her favor if the call agent wasn't scared off. He looked at his watch noticing the connection was robust enough to handle a big download. Recognizing Millard's account was granted executive support status, he filled his cheeks with air and slowly blew out.

Wren: "Is everything okay? Can you still help me?"

Andrew: "I'm going to quickly download the application, and then we'll pull the file across."

Wren wanted to keep him focused on her as much as possible. So she started talking to him about her new dog.

When Andrew originally took control of her PC, it had triggered a bot to be sent across to his computer. To avoid hitting threshold alarms that would signal a virtual threat, the software code was pushed over a few metered bytes at a time. When the NETL agent started the file download, transferring the GeoLab application, the foreign bot had silently installed itself on his computer and had begun to take information.

In bot form, Wren's remote control program was capable of interrogating the LAN and DNS properties stored in the call agent's computer registry. Consulting for other clients, she had dropped it in this far before, proving to them that an intruder could invade their systems. For business use the bot was harmless. This time the bot was armed and collected the valid domain internet protocol addresses, returning them disguised as a single data packet. After the bot sent the encrypted contents back to Wren's laptop, it deleted its encrypted code via the recycle bin, and terminated itself permanently. The bounty of code was automatically pushed from one computer to another using file sharing protocols running in the background, invisible on the active link and to the call agent who could see her desktop.

Wren remained impatient badgering the call agent with anything she could think off to keep him multi-tasking. She didn't want him doing other things, like sounding the alarm. Monitoring from another laptop at her side, Wren saw evidence the bot had successfully completed its task. In a race against Andrew, the bot had won.

Andrew: "Okay. I've got the application download showing complete on my side," Andrew announced. He paused. "Suzie?...Suzie?... Miss, are you there?"

The NETL call agent finished off the call log and leaned back in his chair to greet his teammate that had just checked in, "Hey, I just saved you twenty minutes on a code thirty-two."

"Somebody in big trouble?"

"More like somebody was drinking their lunch."

The support ticket was logged to client KM-004561-NETL and a comment was added that the reinstall was completed on a non-standard device. Everything seemed normal. If there were any irregularities, the firewall would have alarmed. The transaction presented no risk to the center's security. And if anything out of the ordinary was noticed, the call log noted the caller's phone number. All had been completed by the book.

"Sweet."

Wren methodically labeled the cash and carry cell phone with the date, time, and number she called and placed it in cardboard box labeled "USED", with the other cells she would re-purpose.

The illegal data, the electronic keys given to every device on the network, held the first and second quad of the IP address. She embedded the numeric sets into two other bots that were set loose by eleven that evening.

Until Duke came up behind and pushed his wet nose into her elbow, Wren was entirely consumed with her hobby, "Duke! You scared me!" She took his head in her lap and rubbed his ears, "How come you're still up? Oh," Wren said flatly. "Let me get my coat."

There was no sense waking the owner. She could be down the street and back faster than Lloyd could get his eyes adjusted to the dark. Doing his business, she and Duke returned to the front door. She thought it must be a drag to be confined in a house compared to his surroundings just weeks ago.

"I'll give you a good walk in the morning....when I wake up that is."

Wren had a good night with big wins. She would sleep well even if one bot hadn't pinged back. It just meant there was no activity to report. Her own firewall would protect her. Monitoring alarms would page if something tried to follow her bots home.

Austin, Texas.

NGELA HATED HER new detail, but she couldn't ignore how Colton managed to snake around to find the students. And she couldn't ignore them because once again Colton assumed there was a connection to Worthington. *That was closed business* she thought.

The two agents assigned to her were as crude as their boss, skirting the boundaries of conduct while challenging their own ineptitude. She had instructed them to send their digital logs to her. And told them, she would forward those files on to NEADE. More than once they sent the batches straight to Colton, forgetting to copy her.

Then she learned they put surveillance activities at risk by not rotating cars and failed to change time of day surveillance of their suspects to avoid detection. And the two agents felt compelled to bust her down.

"Look, guys," Angela said, staring at her men in the parking lot at Denny's. Mike Timms was at the wheel and Bill Landry was shotgun picking his teeth. "If it happens again, you might as well head home. I'll make the phone call to have your mommies pick you up at the airport because you won't be employed."

The driver looked at his partner, and then sneered, "Angela's hot. Do you think she'd go out with me?"

"She's no good for you. Go after that gimp. She's your type, all athletic."

"Oh, good catch."

They drove off ignoring Angela's rant, "We report to Colton as far as we're concerned," snorted Timms.

"Asses."

She couldn't allow them to run over the top of her. They had no clue what was at stake and the moronic crap they pulled was just that. She wanted to clear the information before Colton saw it. She needed her agents' whereabouts and daily pattern of their surveillance targets. But that's not the way it was being played so Angela decided to judge the students' depth of involvement for herself.

That morning, Angela hung in at the Starbucks near Ellers Park. If everything held true, her mark would be arriving within the hour. Time passed. The agent began to think the weather was too inclement, that her target passed on working out or that Timms or Landry had screwed with the detail.

Photos showed a woman in running tights and tank or zipper tops. The hat was always the same color, with the swoosh on the front. Angela stood up and gazed out the front. The muffled traffic noise mixed with sounds of water, plied against the road over and over by tires.

"Damn it. Where are you?" Angela asked herself in a low tone, moving to the other end of the window.

Through the crowd, she noticed a woman at the counter fitting the description of her runner. The influx of customers had concealed Avey's arrival.

"Will that be all?"

"Yes. Coffee is all. Thank you."

Angela waited for her at the pick-up counter, "Excuse me. Do you study at Rice?"

Waiting for a reply, the woman stranger looked at Avey and saw her eyes concentrating, connecting dots. Timms and Landry had been made during the sloppy execution of their duties.

"Avey. I've got to talk to you quickly. You must trust me!" the stranger demanded in a whisper.

Avey stepped back but did not continue the retreat, biting her lip, *"You're* watching us!" She noticed the sudden attention of a stranger in line, "I mean, you've seen us perform, right?"

As if they were acquaintances Angela continued the syncopated dialogue, "Yes, I'm looking forward to it. Do you have a minute? I'd like to get the schedule."

Angela motioned to the table she had vacated. Slowly, as Avey moved to the chair, the college student discretely reached down her front and activated her video recorder.

"I'm listening," she said softly, lowering her zipper as she sat, hoping the lens and microphone would provide evidence of the encounter.

"What are you and your friends up to?" Angela inquired.

"I could ask you the same thing."

Angela took in a breath. *Why can't anybody just stand down!* Her eyes darted to watch the traffic, "You know about the surveillance."

"Your guys aren't that good."

"Tell me about it."

Lowering her head to blow on her drink Avey adjusted her zipper again.

"You and your group... you've got to stop doing whatever it is," the stranger demanded.

"Why?" Avey asked.

"It's federal business. I can tell you it's getting a lot of attention. You're making me and my boss very nervous."

"What's your name?" Avey pried.

"Sorry. This isn't show and tell time. Figure I'm giving you a break."

With her fears materializing into something tangible, the interrogation suddenly seemed ludicrous to the college student, "It's a free country. We're not doing anything illegal."

"*Avey*, it's out of control. You could be prosecuted. Why not hand over what your have?"

"We don't have anything that belongs to the government."

"Look, my boss is a prick and wouldn't be happy to see us together. I'm sticking my neck out giving you a chance. Your group needs to end it."

Angela looked out the window again evaluating her next move. *They don't know how much shit they're in.* She wanted to drill deeper, and then saw Timms drive by. The female agent stood suddenly giving Avey a final warning before disappearing through the front door, "Make the right decision, for your own good!"

Avey's sweat turned her shivering cold. Fumbling to turn off the camcorder, she waited to use the public phone convinced her cell phone was compromised. Starting to punch the phone buttons, she fought the urge to blurt out everything. Too many people might overhear. *Settle. Just ask for a ride home.*

Driving back, Arthur and Jude listened to Avey's recount of what happened.

"You must have been freaking out! I can't believe you actually sat down and talked. What did she look like?" Jude asked excitedly.

Avey dangled her digital camcorder from her neck, "I know what you're thinking, Jude. No. She's not Bud's killer. I think she's an agent, like FBI or CIA, because she did say *federal business*. I'll play the video when we get home. It may not be any good. It was inside my jacket."

"That's proof we're on to something if they're warning us," Jude concluded.

"I think what it *does* mean," Arthur corrected, "is they don't have a clue what *we're* doing. This woman didn't explicitly mention the volumes or anything, right?"

"She just said stop doing *it*. Dead give away they don't know much."

Jude took it one step farther, "But we don't know *why* she wanted to help us."

After running in to the house, Avey booted up her laptop. The video clip cut off the image above the chin and the audio was muffled. They could barely make out portions of the conversation.

"Damn it!" Avey yelled. "I guess it's better than nothing."

Jude lay back on his chair, "Wow. We'll have to get this to everybody."

"We shouldn't use our phones or maybe not even email," Avey insisted.

"Karl is on business. Let's over to Peter's and wait till he gets home."

Fatigued from his second trip to Mesa Verde, Karl concentrated on piecing the puzzle together. Bud's death, Lloyd attacked, and the artifacts. Certain his possession of them had consequences, he drove from the airport towards his hometown.

Early that morning, in the Albuquerque airport, Karl cleared his unique cargo by getting a pre-inspection to avoid exposing the relics in public. Some of his clothes were sacrificed so his roller bag could be carry-on. With the suitcase in the back seat, Karl was smug with his idea to get ahead of whatever force was building against them. But when he thought about the conversation with Peter before take-off, his agitation surfaced.

"What gives? Why did you leave? You need to take a paranoia shot?"

"That's an understatement. Lloyd was attacked."

"Come on!"

"He was drugged with a dart. I saw the military leave the area."

"That doesn't make any sense. What's going on?"

"They hit the dig site where we were. But Lloyd screwed them good. He had the pieces all along. Long story but he lied to us when we were there. I pulled him out of there. Wren will have him for the time being."

"Whoa. You could go to the police."

"I don't think so, partner. Whoever is behind this is breaking the law with the law. I've got the stones and I need Avey to make a trip with me to get them examined. She'll keep Paul Brewer honest."

"The possession of artifacts makes you an accomplice."

"I've got Worthington's paper trail to protect me for a while. We may not be able to hang on to them very long. I've got to take advantage of our lead. These could be the keys to Worthington's research. We've got to figure out what they mean."

Peter didn't want to give Karl the other news that Avey was contacted. It would just incite him to build on his theories of nothing. He was really perturbed when Karl brought it up instead. It meant Jude and the others were going behind his back, making plans.

"Add Avey's encounter. It's not speculation anymore. We made some choices."

"No. I'm serious," Peter responded defensively, "We should think carefully about taking this on."

"It's only a matter of time before we get locked down. I don't want these guys up my tail pipe."

"Your what? This isn't a game! You're carrying stolen property and you don't want somebody chasing you? You really need to get a grip. You need to stop this."

Karl nervously scratched his head, "Goddamn it!" He got stares from a passerby and lowered his voice. "We're on to something here and our government wants to hitch a ride. No worse! They're trying to take our ride. The *next step* is get to the pueblo. We've got to make contact with the tribal leadership."

"Are you kidding? There's nothing they would know. We can't barge in there suddenly holding their property! Return the pieces to the feds and walk away. You're getting sucked into it."

"There's a connection!" Karl wiped his forehead. "In fact, it's all connected."

"Assumptions piled on speculation," Peter accused, exasperated with the quantum leaps Karl always took.

"Peter, someone has to go to there and open up communication before I get there with the stones. It can't be a bunch of college students walking around. What's it going to take to get you on board?"

Peter remained unwilling to go, but he struck a compromise that would shut it down for good.

Karl bargained to pull his friend in all the way, "You can't straddle it. I'll agree to hand over the relics to the Pueblo, but you have to be there."

"I don't do Spanish."

"Jen does."

That meant Karl had Jen in his pocket too.

"Damn it!" Peter said under his voice, angry about getting put in the middle again. The feelings, all the crap from college bubbled back—when he had to turn down those guys when they wanted to go into business together. And the major hassle when Karl was dating Jen. He hated being manipulated. Standing up to all of them wouldn't stop them. And he lost all control if he wasn't there. The waste of energy trying to convince Jude to stay put wouldn't compare to his sister's temper. She was expecting Jude to come home. There was no way to stop Jude and no way to tell his sister they were neck deep in something no one understood.

The gear Jude had gathered for Karl, allowed his partner to avoid returning home. His only stop would be at the house sitters to pick up Avey. After meeting with Brewer, they would head west and make contact with Peter at a designated time.

In the afternoon Peter was to pick up Jude and Arthur, who were told to pack their vehicle at the back of the house.

Waiting for the boys to finish, Peter assessed his involvement. Caught in the middle at first, his deal with Karl might ultimately solve his dilemma. Karl had managed to push him and others to another level. And to continue to resist him would affect Jude's loyalty. Instead, it was more useful to have Karl's plan stand on its own and let it self-implode. And with the relics getting returned to the tribe, all the hype and speculation would erode Karl's influence and everyone would be forced to acknowledge the truth – Worthington had nothing and never did. Peter didn't want to be involved. But he liked his odds of finally getting his way.

Office of Willard Colton. NEADE Headquarters.

Close to noon that same day, Colton sat in his office and replayed Angela's message left the previous night, providing status of the stakeout in Austin. He listened to her assessment of the people they were tailing and the risk she claimed to understand. A portion of her message lingered in his mind as he spread out written logs and summaries. Her recommendation that the surveillance was a dead end bothered him.

Colton was already familiar with the detail of demographics and sheets of thumbnail photos sent by Timms and Landry. Mindful of his own executive role, he had not assigned the project review to a deputy assistant. Habits were hard to break. He craved the intimate details to drive his own conclusions. A slave to the drama of pure discovery, he placed a loupe on the desk. According to their initial reports, there were four males and one female. More recent information from Angela indicated the younger subjects stayed at a separate residence.

Determined to give it all a thorough scrub, Colton continued reading chronological details of visits to stores, movements between houses, and information from other surveillance devices. Normally, the minutiae would have been compiled and analyzed by subordinates, generating an executive summary. Instead the stack of paper held the interest of a seasoned veteran who used to be the source of similar detail.

On an enlargement of a more recent photo of the young girl, there was a red circle drawn around her leg, with the word "gimp" penned there. The virtual copies Angela sent, noted house addresses, phone and tax records numbers.

He studied the forms. Sensing familiarity with one of the names, Colton turned on his desk light pushing pages aside grabbing the loupe. Hunched over the tiny digital images, the detail left no doubt. Colton was suddenly tormented, "Fuck me."

The open FedEx package on the corner of his desk was put back in play as he hit the speed dial for Angela. Upon getting connected, he started talking without hesitation when he heard her voice, "Your targets are deeply involved. Not like you thought. I need you to get set up to enter the premises of a Peter Childs and a Karl Johns. Pronto!"

Angela felt her ability to influence and control plunge, "Catch me up. What's changed?"

"I think these bastards have been at the dig site for the pieces. I need their DNA," Colton ordered, glancing at the blue flags hanging out of the FedEx envelope. "This is high value at this point."

The half-empty folder became a punching bag as the executive slammed his hand upon it, harder each time, between the words of his curse, "God Damn it!" Pissed, he couldn't accept the omission. His error. The link was staring at him all this time. They were in it neck deep. College kids with something they shouldn't have. The only ones to know what Worthington had. What Franklin has. They must have figured out the research together. NEADE owned it.

"Fucking geeks. Not on my watch."

Smoldering, he stared at the small digital image of his chance acquaintance on the flight from Sun Valley. Calls were made to provision documents for seizure and arrest.

After briefing with Colton, Angela calculated she had about two hours before they executed warrants. She kept to the task of informing her two agents of their priority assignment to enter the private residences. They were told to stay out of the area and move in on her signal.

Agents Timms and Landry jerked her around again not paying attention so she repeated herself, "You heard me...right? Eighteen-hundred you get a call from me on Childs."

"Sure," Timms replied, rolling his eyes purposely.

"Roger that," quipped Landry. "The houses are so far off target. She needs to take a Midol."

As soon as Angela left, they renewed their plan of picking up the tail on MA-002 in spite of their orders, "She's not the boss of us," Timms taunted. "We'll end up in the same place, plan or no plan. She'll be there watching for the other one while we getting the heavy lifting done."

During the short team meeting Angela did not relay the terms of the operation as Colton had laid them out.

"Detain them as soon as possible," he directed.

"Are you sure we want to take that step?"

"The inside link into NETL was compromised when Millard screwed up. These idiots are about to open up another wound. I've got the FBI signing off on NSL's. They have something. I want it." [59]

The pounding rain drowned out the engine noise as Karl accelerated, merging into another segment of rush hour traffic. A blast of a horn didn't faze his concentration. The plan he concocted was a novelty from a book he had read long ago. With his activist friends, he studied many how-to books on passive warfare, explaining how to thwart a government circumventing the law. How to resist a government that manipulates to dominate. How common every day people protect themselves against a government out of control.

There were many examples exposing the wasteland of government. Japanese interment camps. Agent Orange in Vietnam. The training of foreign armies. Too many examples to deny the truth. Too many examples to ignore the audacity. The books explained why citizens should arm themselves with civil disobedience. Why innocent citizens should resist exploitation or physical capture. Karl was energized. He would not be inert. He would not be a victim.

It seemed obvious that someone would be following him from the airport. They came close enough, going after the artifacts. They almost stole Worthington's black books. He wanted to be on the offensive. Trained to avoid being the victim. Trained to be defiant.

He traced the city block of the Cedar Park Mall counterclockwise, passing the entry to Wal-Mart. The logic was each successive left turn reduced the probability that anyone following him would be able to make every light. Karl counted on gaining at least five minutes per each of the four left turns and upon pulling into Wal-Mart, would net an additional fifteen minutes of lead time.

Parking on the east side of the lot, he was ready to confront a car pulling up along side with men rushing to detain him. It didn't materialize. No one drove up to his car. Placing his luggage in a cart he sprinted to the front doors. No one chased him. Entering the store Karl maintained his pace towards house wares. Waiting moments to have the aisle to himself, the transfer of the wrapped bundles to a new storage bin was completed. He tipped the bin upward, securing the lid against the front of the cart,

---

[59] National Security Letters allowing broad and specific surveillance on suspected terrorists.

placing another bin behind it. The empty suitcase was shoved underneath the cart with the name tag visible.

Standing upright, Karl noticed two people at the end of the aisle blocking the byways. His impulse was to use the cart as a battering ram. It was a false alarm. They had been waiting for a clerk to catch up to them. The would-be civil disobedient looked left, right, and behind on the way to checkout. There was no terse broadcast over the sound system for customers to lie on the floor for their safety. Only the announcement of a price drop on stereos.

Conversing with the cashier about the gold stars on her vest diluted any interest in his luggage other than proving it belonged to him. The bar codes were accessible for scanning so there was no reason to fuss with the bins.

Karl nervously fumbled with the lids for no reason, "I finally got around to emptying out the suit case."

The clerk laughed, "Your stuff is probably too old by now to be useful."

Then she paused before pressing the key to finish the transaction. Karl assumed she triggered an alarm. She stared at the items in his cart. In seconds he was going to bolt, "I was just thinking. There are bins with locking covers. You seem to be having trouble with your lids."

Another false alarm. Karl relaxed nodding with his acceptance, "I'm okay. Thanks."

Exiting on the opposite side of the store Karl located his second car. Nobody approached him as he beeped his locks open. The car started and he drove to the exit. Nobody swerved in front of him to block his path. His plan to disrupt and subvert went flawlessly. *Even if no one was paying attention*, he thought.

"...Do you copy? God damn those guys!"

Angela had not gotten a response and it was past go time. Then her radio picked up intercom that sounded like Timms and Landry talking, but she could only hear Bill:

Bill: Did you see him?

Mike: No. He has to be out there.

Bill: *Mike*, he's not out here. I'm watching his car.

Mike: He didn't get by me, *Bill*.

Angela tried to break into their conversation but they continued to dis each other, "Agents Timms and Landry."

Bill: Are you saying I screwed up? You were watching chicks again right?

"Jesus. Those idiots," Angela mumbled. She clicked the mike a couple times and repeated their names.

Bill: Ya, we're here.

"Your mike is open. I can hear your conversation."

Bill: The fucking button gets stuck.

"We're supposed to be on a green light to pick up the subjects. What's your twenty?"

Mike: That stupid bitch. Can't she tell we're in hot pursuit?

Bill: Wal-Mart.

"Report to planned location. Do you copy?" Angela waited in silence.

When Mike got back to their car, they sat there trying to figure out their screw-up.

"We lost him. The GPS says his car is still here. And the other transponder hasn't gone off."

"We better get over to her highness before she shits her pants."

Bill: Ya, be there in a few.

Protocol barred them from doing anything else. They would need direct approval to pursue outside the physical area of the operation. Even if their suspect bolted on them, he wasn't a criminal as far as they were told.

Twenty minutes of travel brought the three agents together, a block from Peter Child's residence.

"What the hell do you think you're doing?" Angela yelled. "You're supposed to be executing on my plan. It's 1845 hundred. I've got a checkpoint call with Colton in an hour and he wants this deal in the books."

"We almost had Karl Johns."

"That's bullshit. You guys were screwing around."

"While you were getting your nails done, we were tailing him from the airport. We put GPS on his car when we got here a couple weeks ago."

Angela was shocked but she forced her face to show complacency. She responded with, "So what. Your gig was here."

It occurred to her if they tagged the suspects' cars, a tracking unit could have been mounted on her vehicle. She took Timms straight on, "Then how did he give you the slip?"

"He had another ride or something. And the bug at his house hasn't responded so he hasn't gone back there."

The agency approved device was set to send an alert to Timm's cell phone if it was activated by movement.

"You placed equipment in the house?"

"Sure, Colton said do it when we could. Planted it after Johns was heading out."

The tingle on the back of her neck increased. Angela's mind raced with speculation. *Were they tracking me? Did they just accidentally leak their pact with Colton?* Testing her hunch, she watched their facial expressions as she spoke, "If Colton wants to shake this down on his own with you two bozos then let's call him."

Landry looked at the ground when his partner responded, "Hey, don't get your undies in a bunch. Colton told us before we came down here to install bugs. We thought we could get the suspect nailed and get back here before we ran out of time. Bottom line. It didn't work out. You beatin' us over the head is for nothin'."

The two agents tried to hit one out of the park and swung and missed, she thought. They didn't have a suspect in their back seat and at the moment they didn't know where he went.

"Okay, let's get this over with. I want the list on all the tracking equipment and logs before 2200. Got it?"

Her order reset the chain of command but she knew Colton still ruled.

As the agents deployed, they entered the residence of MA-004 through the back door. Out of sync, they were too late to apprehend the group Avey had jokingly called the goonies. MA-004 had a three-hour jump on them. MA-002 had managed to pick up a passenger and was heading out of the area as well.

The suspects had initiated their own brand of civil disobedience. Before Peter met Jude and Arthur, he made his phone calls from the mall to Jen, Perrie, and Looks. Perrie was the most surprised but promised support in anyway she could.

Looks was anticipating the call, "As a group, we're off the diving platform Peter. Let's make it count."

The tougher call was to Jen. Peter did not have and really didn't want to take time to explain everything he was feeling over the last month. While on the phone with her, background noise complicated the dialogue. He was bumbling, trying to update her at the same time building up to the question.

"Peter, it's me. You *can* ask me."

"I'm doing that Jen. I don't mind saying it scares the shit out of me. I need your help. I'm heading to the Acoma Pueblo right now. I need a translator to speak with the tribe. I've put all my jobs on hold. This is it, for a couple weeks."

Jen could hear Peter swallow over the phone, "I'm asking, Jen. And I'm figuring it out at the same time."

Those words resonated with Jen. The background noise became more effluent and distinct. Foot traffic and voices reverberated off the tile and stucco walls. Jen was transfixed for seconds.

"Jen?"

"Yes, Peter."

"Can you do it?"

"I'm saying yes. I will."

She had already told Karl she would help, but to have Peter ask her was soul connecting.

He quickly went through the details of whom, what, and when, apologizing for the lack of time, "We won't be able to talk again until we get there. See you at the airport."

"I'll see you soon."

Karl called Wren from a gas station. They knew each other's habits and patterns so well, the dialogue was robotic. Karl wanted items expressed to him. Wren told him of her success with her IP search with the bots.

"Sweet. You'll do some deep mining now?"

"Into the DR sites first. There's mucho grey fiber in the land of cost-cutting." [60]

"Okay. You've got our comm backs too. I might need a reroute or file upload."

"No problemo. I'm going turn up my other site so that'll be cake. Hey, by the way, Lloyd's still here."

---

[60] Optic fiber laid and left dormant, but connected to leverage disaster recovery objectives.

"Let's get through this next wave. Then he can go back to retirement."

"K. Later." Karl replied and then returned to the car.

Avey had unzipped the luggage and was studying one of the stones, "How's Wren?"

"She's cool. We need to checkpoint with her in four hours. You ready to go?"

"Sure, got my reading right here," pointing the stones.

Angela's email to her boss that evening would report that two male targets were missing. She dreaded the eventual phone call.

"It's not like you to get this sloppy. What's your take?"

Angela avoided details, "That they left town and took evidence with them. We probably got too close to them."

The favorite agent couldn't tell if Colton knew she was stating an actual fact. Then she was handed an absolute bomb.

"You might have tipped them off according to what I heard."

Shit. What does he know? Timms! "How so?"

"Timms says you were tailing the female pretty close, like in the same room with her."

Jesus!

"I was. I wanted to get a good look at her."

"She has a limp or something?"

"A prosthesis on her right." *Son of a bitch. He's checking me out!*

"I've ordered tails on them. We're moving on this fiasco."

Wanting to ditch his men, Angela knew it was Colton's call to make and she smartly avoided asking. If he didn't trust her, she didn't want to confirm it.

"Angela, I don't want more distractions for the committee. There's an internal breach that I'm dealing with but this operation can't be leaked out."

"Understood."

It pissed her off. She left messages using both cell phones, and then went down to the garage to inspect her car.

Colton had more evidence to question his favorite agent's motives but couldn't afford to dump her. NEADE was reaching thresholds that required discrete action.

It's moving towards zero-sum at this point, he thought and considered the consequences. *Angela was frustrated, reached her level of incompetence, or somehow turned.*

Faults and Convergence

Day 56.
Residence of Dr. Paul Brewer.
Houston, Texas.

"DO YOU KNOW, since I've been at Rice I've never seen Dr. Brewer. Have you ever met him?" Avey hoped.

"A couple times with Worthington, about halfway through my studies. Most the time his health was so bad he worked from a home office. I think he's on a retainer from the university."

Near the university grounds, their car drove through an adjoining neighborhood.

"If we focus on what Paul can teach us, maybe we can publish Bud's work and you know, use the revenue to build his program back up. The university will come running back with a huge stipend of some kind. Here's Paul's house."

They pulled into Brewer's driveway, a two-tire track with grass in the middle. His small front yard rose steeply from the sidewalk. Avey noticed assortments of rocks, a variety of sizes lying around, some fit neatly against the open corners of the porch and stair rail.

"Quite a collection."

The doorbell ringing was answered by a chubby man, thick in the face and hands. His diabetic condition swelled tissue and had ruined good eyesight over the duration of the disease.

"Are you Karl?"

"Yes, sir. I called you two days ago. You said to come by."

"Yes, I did. Who is this with you?"

"Avey Barnes. She's a student here, majoring in hieroglyphics. You've studied Egyptian and Mayan works as well, right, Avey?"

"Yes. Referred to as Maya writings, classified within Mesoamerican including ancient Zapotec."

"Sounds like you've been paying attention," Paul complemented. "Good to hear. There's room for another expert. I've been pushed aside years ago. Come in, come in."

The hallways were scattered with more rocks and stone. With small talk, Paul recalled how Bud used to talk up things about Karl this and Karl that.

"He said you kinda took off on your own after school," Paul looked at his subject for recognition. "I remember Bud was a little ticked off, having put a lot of energy into you, but said you couldn't be house broken."

While Avey laughed at her friend's expense, Karl picked up his bag again, anxious about their needs.

"Now, young man, you say you have something to show me?"

"Yes, sir. Ah…in the hallway here?"

"Of course not! Let's take your things to my lab."

They followed Paul across the creaky floor and waited for him to jiggle the door open to the cellar. The basement air was diffused with earthen odors.

"Can you get that light switch?"

Avey turned on the single light illuminating the upper stair well.

"Follow me."

A staggered single step at a time, Paul made his way slowly down the narrow staircase. In the void of speech, the shuffling of feet was eerie, like marching into a concealed malevolence. When Paul suddenly stopped to get his bearings at the bottom of the stairs, his guests bumped into each other. The old man stalked forward, waving his hand in the dark searching for the discolored cord. Each successive clicking of a light chain led to the dim hibernated workspace. The lights broadcast over the room's contents as dust particles danced around their heads. The assortment of wood and metal shelving provided permanent residence for rocks and other earthly objects of past interest and inspection. Small cartons with other artifacts were scattered about, not moved for years. All impregnated with years of past service, a long work bench on the opposite side displayed hand tools, small scrapers, picks, and small brushes.

Karl coughed, clearing his throat, "Do you get down here much Paul?" He wiped his finger on his pants after dragging it along a shelf edge.

"Can't say I do. My heart's bad. And I can't take this dust anymore. Someone's got to clear it out. I can't do it."

The intense odors of decaying dirt and clay surrounded the intruders. Sedentary for years, rocks under the lamps had lichen and moss etchings. The elderly man's breathing was still taxed from coming down the stairs.

"Are you okay?"

"Yes..." his voice cracking. Dr. Brewer expelled a deep and elongated cough.

Karl second guessed his decision to employ the professor's help. While Paul got his breath, he anticipated more delay, "This shouldn't take long if we all pitch in. Here, I'll clear a spot."

Avoiding more airborne dust, the younger male carefully moved junk to the side. The three pieces were removed from the bag and laid on the table. Taking the lead to unwrap them ceremoniously, Paul edged his visitors to either side. He reached across the bench, pointing. Avey was quick to place her hand on a brush hanging on the peg board.

"No, flip on that radio. I always have it on when I'm down here."

Vivaldi seeped out.

"The pieces were stored in period material," Karl pointed out.

The extra wrapping was removed in the car, with certainty that the spectacle of modern day cloth protecting the ancient relics would not be appreciated.

"Yes. And the linen is still very tangible. It's in good shape."

Karl was encouraged Paul hadn't completely lost familiarity with his art. As if he was the first to do so, he worked each artifact loose, free of the linen.

"Can't see worth a damn." Taking his handkerchief out, Paul wiped his glasses and face, reaching up an unsteady hand to pull a swivel light with a magnifier under his face. The brighter light reflected on his moist skin showing the redness of dermatitis.

"My hell!" Paul froze, his vision affixed through the magnifying glass. A tremble in his body turned into a shooting pain to his upper chest. He stepped back waving Karl off, stooping and cradling his chest. Reaching into his pants, he shook out Dan Shen pills from a vial and slipped them under his tongue. Karl grabbed a chair and positioned it behind Paul, persuading him to sit down.

"Just hold your horses. This angina comes and goes. More so now. I'm on Digoxin as well." He steadied himself against the bench and after minutes slowly turned to face the discoveries again.

"Nasty thing that happened to Bud. He said he was so close when I had dinner with him days before his untimely death. He didn't tell many folks. But I knew. He kept saying he had the "El Santo Cáliz". He affectionately called it the Holy Grail. I wanted to believe in him. So many times he came back and each time he thought he had another piece of the puzzle, dangling the next story or clue in front of me."

Paul cleared his throat taking breathes between his opinions, "He was so patient with them. With those Indians. He once told me he was convinced the oldest one had psychic capacities. That was too much really. So much time has passed. And now look. The pieces are suddenly in my reach."

The convergence of energy towards the artifacts precluded all the distractions of the cellar.

"Have you seen these before?" Karl asked.

"Bud had old pictures out of some books. I gave him a few to show around. From another culture as an examples. I couldn't say these matched or even if they are similar. I never told Bud this, but I always assumed these pieces didn't exist anymore."

Putting on latex, Paul examined each one delicately, rotating the pieces. The three stones were compatible in overall dimensions.

"We'll weigh these separately for accuracy, but it's obvious there's extraordinary atomic variances between them."

Setting the blocks in a line, it only took seconds for Paul to make his preliminary assessments, "This one is quartz. That one granite, probably older stone than the first. And this one I don't know."

On each block, a distinctive deep groove pattern was vertically etched on three quarters of the surface with another unique marking at the top, "I'm not sure about the groove patterns. They seem to be intentional, obviously no eroding."

Karl qualified Brewer's observation, "Agreed. None of these stones are indigenous to the area that they came from. We believe sister tribes trekked the material in for these creations."

Avey was excited to have these specimens lying in front of her. She moved her hand to point to one of the carvings and Paul gently blocked her, "Your skin oil will damage the patina."

She put gloves on from the box dispenser and resumed her analysis, "These independent marks at the top on each stone are symbols. Are the patterns consistent with any design you've seen?"

"I don't know. Bud got me excited about these decades ago and I went and bought books. I've had no reason to stay current."

Karl wanted a faster examination. A more complex design had been cut into the face on the opposite side, "The other sides might be more compelling."

Avey flipped over one stone as Paul rushed to tenderly handle the remaining two, sharing his opinion, "These designs in themselves are interesting, but I'd have to get some books from my library to compare."

Pushing the magnifying glass away, the professor suddenly hedged, "I'd have to get back down here and prep these. They've got debris and particles that need to be removed very carefully. It's way too early to draw conclusions from assumptions."

Karl avoided looking at Avey who was signaling him with facial expressions. Their urgency was being challenged.

"Dr. Brewer. When I called, I said we had these pieces and hoped you could shed some light on their unique purpose, but we've got to take them back to the reservation."

The professor's eyes dimmed. He coughed and struggled to clear his throat, pulling off his gloves. Transformed, they were standing in a dirty cellar, permanent housing for a bunch of moldy rocks. It was a stand off. Avey moved to his side.

"Dr. Brewer, please! I don't know if we can get these back for you, but think about Bud. He died without seeing them. You have. And you can help us take it one step further."

He shuffled back and sat down on the chair trying to resolve old promises, "It's been a long fight you know. The whole university thought he was way off. You know...quixotic. I stuck with him because of friendship, but he promised me I'd have whatever came out of it."

The handkerchief came out again wiping sweat off and covered a bout of indigestion, "They denied his application. You know, Bud had an overabundance of pride. He was shifting funds here and there, trying to keep his trips to the pueblo and where ever they took him. I think the board knew what was going on for years. He wasn't stealing their money. But the hubris of his actions, they forged extreme arrogance towards his idealistic approaches, not to mention when he started teaching that system approach, ge...gehey...something."

"Gaia," Karl corrected.

"That's it. That was the nail in the coffin for his project. Then he just took it deep. Never brought it to the board again. Sounded too apocalyptic in ways that damaged his reputation. Even that Franklin feller took off."

As he spoke, Paul's sweat soaked through portions of his shirt. Mixing in the stilted air, it smelled sour, "Most of the board thought him to be discursive and too risky to allocate research funds to. He never gave up though."

Avey listened intently, but was anxious to concentrate on the artifacts they arrived with, "It's probably not the perfect outcome Dr. Brewer. Karl and I are desperate for your knowledge. There's no time."

"Avey can clean up the faces. She's learned it from your guys, Paul. Will you let her do it and we can go upstairs take a breather and come back down?"

He relented at first but knew it was beyond him to fuss with his dreams at this point, "Use the small picks and the scale brushes. Only remove the actual dirt casings. Be careful to not scrape below the natural patina."

The retired professor stood up slowly bracing himself and ambled towards the stairs with his guest. From upstairs bookshelves they pulled down as many references as they could find on the subject matter.

Paul was more interested in Karl's career than scanning pages, "So what did you do with yourself after school?"

"It's not as straight forward as some of my friends, but it's been fun," Karl admitted and shared some of his stories about his college transfers and experiences with his perpetual job choices.

Walking into the living room Avey reappeared two hours later, "I think I'm ready to have them inspected. Did you find any leads from the books?"

"Possibly."

Karl opened the few books they took to the cellar as Paul inspected the tailings from the cleaning, "For a beginning student of the trade, good decent recovery work," he admired. "You've paid attention in class."

As all three compared the tangible evidence to literature, Karl played out a hunch, "What if these stones are segments of a larger design?"

He rearranged the rocks, first in row and then gently twisted them in another pattern. Two of them side by side, equaled the length of one placed perpendicular at either end of the conjoined stones.

"The pattern changes depending on the combination."

Avey picked up the concept easily. Shifting the stones in place, she explained her idea of using just the front side with the complex pattern, in combination with the four sides of each stone, "There are sixteen permutations each, the parallel edges are aligned together, combining two bricks and rotating the third stone to the top or bottom."

Demonstrating her strategy, she showed how the bricks could be clustered like what Karl did, "There are sixteen more sequences, when you rotate the perpendicular stone to get a different pattern. Let's chart them as combinations of three, using letters ABC. This one is AB with C on top with the one edge, C_1," and she twisted the perpendicular stone, "and this is AB C_2."

Moving stone C to the bottom, she showed how the pattern changed, "This is AB with C_1 and C_2 on the opposite ends of AB. We do a rub for each."

Karl reached in his brief for paper and charcoal sticks. The first of the paper tracings were completed, labeled at the top, and handed to Paul for follow up, "See if any of these map to the book illustrations."

Once Karl and Avey got in sync, each of the forty-eight drawings took under two minutes each: sliding the stones in place, checking the orientation of each block to the sides of the adjoining block, and then smudging the image on parchment. Avey took digital images of every stone combination, then of the composite drawing.

"I'll get these to Wren when we get to the hotel."

Eventually, the group moved upstairs, sitting at the kitchen table to finish comparing the set of prints to the literature from Paul's library. Swapping papers and page flipping yielded nothing similar.

Avey stood up stretching her back then forward touching the floor, "I've practically memorized the images I've seen in the books. I don't see a match."

"Might be so," agreed Brewer. "These books were somewhat complete at the time of publication, but who knows what updates have been made."

Karl looked at his watch, "We've got to hit the road, Paul. I was hoping to identify the pattern to derive some meaning. Now we'll have to rely on the tribe that much more."

The visit and chance of discovery had reached a conclusion. Back in the cellar, Paul watched as the stones were wrapped and then asked Avey to turn off the radio. A part of his dream ended, coming true in a way he hadn't predicted. He had cherished the vision of him and Bud showing off their discovery, publishing their findings. The stories they told each other at their mutual dinners ripened with age especially the predictions of ignoring their pompous colleagues. All of it surfaced for the last time.

The strings to the lights were pulled as they passed under them and the door to the cellar was wedged shut. Apologies were expressed to Dr. Brewer for the way things turned out.

"No, no. It's nobody's fault. Just a couple old birds sitting too long on the same wire."

Paul took Avey's arm, extending it to place a small tool kit in her hands, "You deserve these. Make them famous."

Accepting the gift, Avey hugged the old man, "Whatever we can do, and we'll try and get these back."

As Paul peered outside from his door he shared one last hope as the guests moved out on the porch and down the sidewalk towards the car, "If not these, then the others maybe."

He closed the door, resigning the rest of his evening to just the memory of the day's extraordinary event. A hard knock on the door startled him, hearing his name called from the porch. Lacking pure agility, Avey had run back up the porch stairs, "Professor! Dr. Brewer! What did you say?"

Exchanging information, she hugged the professor again and returned to the car.

"What was that all about?"

"These stones aren't the only pieces Bud was after!" She stared at the linen wrapped objects in the back seat, "According to Paul, all Bud knew was these were like the starter pieces."

Anxious to reach their next destination, Karl privately considered reneging on his agreement with Peter, "Were not going to solve it here. Let's get something to eat, check in with Peter, and then hit the road."

Avey smiled and stared out the window as familiar territory passed by, "As much as I'd like to, I know we don't have time to see the campus. Do you remember Ashby Boulevard with the street lamps in the middle?"

"Sure."

"Arthur and I used to walk that whole thing after a rain storm. The smell in the air was fantastic. It always brought us back to childhood memories."

Avey paused thinking about the stories they had shared, "I'd like to do that again some day."

NEADE Offices.

Three days after the interrogation, Angela was still stinging, expecting Colton to ship her out to New Mexico. Running a sanctioned operation from her office, she finished debriefing four CIA field agents who had been detailed to tail the pedestrian suspects. Surprisingly, Jason was not assigned to the team. She hadn't heard from him for over a week.

Feeling negative energy from the agents, their tone was defensive and belligerent when she explained their roles in the kick-off conference call.

"The mission is to provision surveillance on four, possibly six private citizens. The profile packets you were given are real-time and accurate. Expect the trigger from myself or Willis Colton. There's national interest in the artifacts the suspects may or may not have in their possession. Take all precautions to secure those assets intact."

No one questioned the orders to pursue and observe, nor did anyone challenge on record, the motive of the ranking official who had authority over their bosses. Angela could visualize their eyes rolling and imagine their comments as they went on mute. The culpable reality was these agents were worthy of shrapnel and military honor. They were field NOCs from the CIA.[61] After the meeting Angela got three phone calls privately asking the same thing, "How the fuck did we get assigned to this shit job?"

She knew two of the agents from training but couldn't risk giving them more detail, fearing it would come back to bite her. Angela knew Colton was moving the dial, not her or her partner. Somehow he always managed to turn it up. It might be bullshit to other agents but she was smart enough to know Colton was on to something, "This is the front end to something bigger related to national security," she told the agents. "There's nothing else I can share."

---

[61] Non-official cover.

Following the trip to the Bay, Jason had been out of pocket with the hangover of political and legal fallout. The legal agreements that secured Franklin's release had to be processed and the whole matter was thoroughly reviewed with a broader legal team. Brogan was compelled to lord over everyone to satisfy his bruised ego. Privately described by one of his peers as, "taking the whole broom handle up the ass," the incident had career implications. No one had yet discovered the source of the disclosure that identified Colton and pegged him to NEADE. Brogan complained to Colton that the leak undermined his capability. Colton pushed back that he *thought* he'd sent the right team.

"Willis, I warned you going in that it wasn't a lock."

"Sounds like you brought a knife to a gunfight."

"That bastard didn't know what he was saying, but he had it," Brogan muttered with the last sip of scotch going in his mouth. "The lid won't go back on. You know that."

The exposure was lethal to both of them.

"I'll see you around, Willis."

Getting free of the Bay fiasco, Jason was assigned detailing Franklin on a permanent basis. The handoff would be complete after a meeting with the temporary place holder, a desk agent whose monotone review of the surveillance logs was like a sleep aid. Stuck with compliance work, Jason wondered if Colton had been tipped off about him and Angela. Or maybe he was being spanked for his role at the prison.

"I'm told Mr. Colton wants to get this guy for some reason."

Jason appeared courteous to his peer, but wanted to respond differently to the agent's scoop, "Thanks for the heads up."

Ya think, genius? Were you told Colton gives a shit about this guy's freedom? Were you told you're just holding the leash for Willis until he comes by and kicks the crap out of our guy? Do you know he wants to shoot him in the fucking head since he didn't cough it up? Did you know the world is about to cave? And we've got big oil leading us around by our balls?

But the agent thoughts didn't compromise his new responsibilities, "What about this log entry here?"

"Dr. Franklin booked a ticket. And I doubled checked. He made the flight and returned the next day."

"Did you observe any of this?"

"I had training to complete, so I ran it. It all checked out."

The agent didn't recognize the significance of the trip Franklin went on. If protocol was maintained, the handoff would have discussed the details of where the scientist went, who he saw, or what he did. Jason would have an IPD-113 in the file, documenting that the agent in charge was absent for this and other log entries. Instead, Jason thanked the agent for his help and waited for him to leave. He had bigger omissions to think about.

He opened up his desk drawer and read anew Millard's suicide note he found on the dresser. The single page he held was taken impulsively before other agents entered the bedroom where Millard lay dead. Then the agent re-read the second one – the other paper he found in an envelope under the quilt.

At the time, Jason thought his boss would appreciate the discretion. Two notes for a single suicide. Back then he stuffed the pages into his breast pocket with the intention to hand over the evidence at the team briefing. Minutes before walking into the meeting, he double-backed and went into the copy room. His heart was racing from the ignition of insubordination. Would he or anyone else ever see the evidence again? It could only have supreme value if there was no knowledge of its existence.

The first will wasn't symbolic of self-pity and anger. It wasn't a declaration of reconciliation to his bereaved parent survivor, to console or punish. Less of a suicide note, intended to be the last written evidence of a struggling soul, the page qualified as a confession and indictment of a government out of control. The diatribe outlined the encounters with his employer, NETL and the incredible pressure mounting to hide the truth behind the facade of the lies, policy of deceit, and manipulation of scientific facts. All admissions pointing to Millard.

The crumpled paper in an envelope, found on the bed was a personal declaration by a victim. This document listed others commissioned to hide, modify, and revise the truth. It pointed to the main architect of record in the narrative, "I, Willis Colton, a CIA officer…" Further down the page, a confession, "Under my leadership, people of conscience like Dr. Millard, Dr. Worthington, and other geologists paid the price for unknowingly opposing a massive secretive operational mission that serves the interests of oil for the sake of its own financial survival."

Jason concealed the opposing letters and delayed calling Angela, trying to determine his set of actions or how to explain it to her. His two suspicions were immediately haunting. Although both notes were typed, the one lying on the dresser was on NETL letterhead with a signature. The document tangled in the sheets was unsigned. Jason held cards that could be played once.

But the wills could be misplayed easily, failing to corroborate with the one individual whom Millard apparently trusted. With no one's knowledge, a large file box of evidence was being held by the shipper. They had placed the delivery ticket on the door of Millard's chosen recipient indicating the attempted delivery.

Convinced he was ready with a proposed plan of action, Jason returned Angela's call that evening. Portions of their dialogue began as reassurances their bond was still intact. His partner stressed the obvious. Their careers were inextricably knotted at the same point and still connected to a singular fixture having power and authority over them. Familiar with Jason's behavior, Angela pressed him knowing he was holding out.

"I can't give you all the detail now," Jason hesitated. "I've held on to some information but I'll pull you in when the time is right."

"What is it?"

Mentally he relented, "Millard had a suicide note."

Then he paused, "No. Two suicide notes. And they don't add up. One was in plain sight, the other between the sheets. It was too late to protect the crime scene when everyone entered. Wet boot tracks were all over. Millard didn't commit suicide."

It was easy to say it. He wanted to *say* it all, but didn't.

"I need to sort it out first. It may be nothing. I don't want you—"

"Hey, we're partners. You can always trust me."

"I know. Just need to do a little more digging."

For the travelers destined for the Acoma Pueblo, the highway signs showed they were 172 miles outside of Albuquerque. The first checkpoint with Karl was at eight-thirty that evening. By the plan, Peter's group would arrive near the Acoma Pueblo in advance of Karl, by three or four days, and try to locate anyone who knew of Worthington and his visits. Karl and Avey would show up as soon as possible with the artifacts. Kicked up by their vehicle, sand dust was still airborne by the time the next vehicle blew through it from either direction. Looking across the high desert scenery the aggregate heat waves distorted the distant landscape. In the trailing SUV, the occupant's forward line of sight was enabled by a high power monocular while the passengers in Peter's car were focused on other activities.

"Jude, if I didn't know better, I'd think you were Looks," Peter claimed. "You've had your nose buried in that map for two hours."

"Naw, just looking at the area. You never know."

"Know what?"

"When the opportunity is going to come around."

Peter took it to mean there was no more detail forthcoming, "You even sound like him."

Then he quizzed Arthur, "Did you find any of pictures in Worthington's albums worth showing around in town?"

"I've got a couple of Worthington that might work. When is Jen arriving at in Albuquerque?"

"She'll be there at nine-thirty."

"It'll be nice to meet her."

Jude couldn't resist, "Peter would like to meet her too."

The comment got ignored, but Arthur and Jude jabbed at each other with adolescent pride. Peter pulled into a gas station once he made the turn-off to the airport.

"You guys fill the tank. I'll wait for the call."

Arthur was confused, "You're calling Karl right?"

"No, he's calling me."

"And he knows the number to the pay phone," Arthur teased sarcastically.

"Actually, he does," Peter confirmed and walked over to the wall mount on the C-store building and the phone rang on the minute.

"Karl's one paranoid dude," Arthur admitted.

In their second loop waiting for Jen to come out of the terminal, Jude spotted her coming through the glass doors with luggage, "We'll get her bags."

Jen hugged Peter over the console as she climbed into her seat, "Hi Jude. Hi Arthur, good to finally meet you! Sorry I missed you guys at the group meeting. It's hard to believe what happened to Worthington. Really sad! I'd sure like to see his work."

Arthur held up the one in his lap, "We've got a few in the car. Karl and Avey have the rest."

"Splitting them up? Sounds like something Karl would do," Jen replied.

"Let's get going," Peter prompted. "Jen, I need your credit card."

"Sure. Have you already run out of money?" she joked.

"No, we need it for the rental. They won't have your numbers...yet."

When they boarded the shuttle to the rental center, Peter clarified he was switching vehicles as a precaution, "When Karl made the suggestion it seemed more reasonable than the other paranoid things he does."

The ten p.m. transit bus was mostly vacant allowing them to discuss detail; their conversations masked by the drone of the transit engine.

"So did Karl or Avey turn up anything with the artifacts?"

"I think she already figured them out," Jude boasted. "We'll have images sent to us. She took shots of the stones and some rubbings."

"We're going to use those as well as the photos?" Jen wondered.

Peter repeated their plan, "Wren will send them, but we won't disclose them until we have identified someone who knows Worthington. We don't want people thinking we're moving black market product."

While the boys were unloading the SUV, Jen whispered to Peter as she finished signing the rental contract waiting for the agent to return from a phone call, "This isn't like you. You don't think we should go to the police?"

"Believe me. I want to. The waves just keep coming. You know Karl, treating it like a conspiracy."

"Not hard to take that leap. A murder and Karl's friend drugged."

"There's no official proof on Bud's death, and how do you know...let me guess. Karl filled you in on Mesa Verde."

"Yep."

"Well, the deal he and I signed up for is once we find anybody that knows the professor, the pieces he got from the Pueblo dig site are handed over. It'll be risky enough defending why we have them in the first place."

"This will be fun!" Jen mocked, and then pouted. "Oh, I just remembered. We don't have enough assets between us to buy a jury."

She looked over at the boys across the exit lanes, "Jude and Arthur look like they're ready to go."

Slowly they walked towards the car, "It's not just them. You're all revved up with the drill bits."

"Drill bits, not guns. What about Jude and Arthur? Does your sister know?"

"Only that we're on a summer dig. That's all."

Jen gave Peter a kiss on the cheek, "Including Spanish lessons."

Everyone had enough of the air conditioned car, snacks, and Arthur's game of "Geologist Jeopardy." Repeating all the group discussion Jen missed, Peter didn't waste time participating and was glad when the three passengers finished with all their speculation as they drove the remaining three hundred miles.

Jude announced his plans as they reached the lobby of the only local casino, "I'm wiped. How about we score a breakfast and hit the sack until evening. Then we can walk around, play detective, and see what gives."

Except for the meal, everybody had a different take on the plan of attack. It was decided Peter and Jen would team up and work the casino property. Jude and Arthur would venture off the main streets and show pictures to people in the small community.

Jen coached them on how to approach individuals and the respectful way to ask for information.

"You two look like trouble if you hang too close together. One of you takes the lead with the other one following a yard or two behind. Approach your person slowly, to give them a chance to size you up."

Jude confessed he could only order Mexican food in Spanish. Arthur put his arm around him, having accomplished four years of Spanish and travel abroad, "I'll you cover you ese." [62]

Peter stood, tired of sitting, "I need to walk around for a while. Anybody interested?"

"I'll tag along. You might need an interpreter."

After they walked away, Jude gave Arthur an elbow, "Check that out! I told you what happened in college."

"Ya. Wait until Karl shows up."

"He's already spoken for."

"By who?"

"This chick named Avey."

"Nice try, Jude."

Home of Wren Kennedy.

"Do you need some help packing up?" Lloyd asked, ready for his breakfast.

Wren shifted the boxes away from the door, "Maybe later. It looks a little cleaner, doesn't it? You know your way around. I'll be gone for a couple hours. You can fix your favorite, just use the fan."

---

[62] Slang, meaning close friend.

Wren learned that fried spam stunk up the house.

"Sure. Duke and I will get a walk in, too. Okay, Duke?" he offered as the dog licked his hand.

"Cool. See you later."

Heading to her favorite restaurant, Wren was meeting with Looks. She broke the news to Lloyd that she was moving and told him it was time to visit his daughters.

Saying to Lloyd, "I got a great job offer I couldn't say no to!" she really wanted to tell him the truth and not a lie. He was entitled to know more after saving their collective asses with the artifacts. Between her and Karl, she decided they better bump up their game and take precautions. Lloyd became the odd man out.

For years, Wren had been buying up "dot bomb" infrastructure with pennies on the dollar. With ample funds, she converted a warehouse space into a mini data center. It was always her dream to retrofit an area and set it up the way it was meant to be done. No shortcuts on power, no skimping on fault tolerance, no blind eye to security. Her fort. She always wanted a reason to turn it up. This seemed as good as any. She was heading into deep waters and her puny setup at home didn't have much punch or teeth.

With more persistence and luck, her real challenge was to figure out how to bust down the NETL virtual firewall and come and go as she pleased undetected. Waiting for the bots to return information, she was counting on the certified quads stolen from the call center computer. With them, it was a virtual hall pass to sneak around without the fear of detection. The domain addresses she took from Andrew at the call center were in consecutive numerical order meaning NETL had a brother organization. And the second address was classified as "Class A" meaning the brother was bigger and because of its higher security level, probably had secrets worth poaching.

The prize her bots were hunting for was the location of the NETL disaster recovery site. Like corporations, federal agencies had redundant operations to maintain business continuity in case of a disaster. From experience, a DR site was likely unprotected. Consulting, she proved her clients cut corners because support and services fees were huge. Between workforce reductions and work going to offshore, no one on the IT staffs was perfect. The virtual gates to a DR site might look closed, but not locked as tight as the main data centers. With a set of instructions, she sent the search bots to scale the firewall looking for mothballed unprotected ports. She expected to have news from the bots when she returned from her meeting.

The waitress greeted Wren with a hug, "You look so good!" she chirped with a customer smile.

"I'm still on the wagon, Pam. I hope skinny food is still on the menu."

"Always for you. I saw your friend. I put him in the back corner."

She came up behind Looks, hugging him, "Caught you red-handed."

"Hi, Wren. That's something I'm sure you never want to hear."

Wren lowered her voice, "Do you have the answers yet? Should I be building a bunker?"

The patio was near empty after the early morning rush from the business crowd. Looks loved understating the premise, "Nothing too important."

He paused when table service was given, then shared his progress, "I'm suffering. I feel like there's something to the model and I can't break the code. I can tell things are in motion."

"How?"

"Because the model calls out an unknown third exponential. The standard measure uses two factors. This model puts another into play like a variable on steroids."

"No one has announced new and improved oil or something? Is there another source?"

Looks stared at her, expecting the epiphany any second.

"Oh! You think I'm going to find it. Hey, my line is in the water. It's a matter of time and luck."

"We need bites fast," Looks urged.

Sky City Casino. Near Acoma Pueblo.

On their first full day, Jude and Arthur had tag-teamed with Peter and Jen and ventured out again. Walking on and off the main drag to side streets, they felt the expanding heat and their lack of progress. Only a few residents on the back streets were willing to say they didn't recognize the people in the photos.

"It's your hairstyle, Jude. They look at you like the tourist who is nosey. *Un Fuereño!*" blurted Arthur.[63]

---

[63] Outsider who is male gender.

"You sounded impressive trying to answer them back in English, explaining you didn't understand what they were saying."

That started another round of complaints from Arthur, "I panicked, okay! But not on the last one. You need to stop crowding them, getting into their faces. Jen would give you low marks for that move."

"I couldn't hear what they said, so I had to move closer."

More practice on unsuspecting residents resulted in more rejection. Finally giving up, they went to find their partners.

"We hit the wall," Arthur reported when they caught up to Peter. "What about you guys?"

"I'll bet they wouldn't give the answer even if we paid them," responded Peter.

"It's been so long since Worthington was here. I watched their faces as they said no or smiled at us. There's probably no one familiar with him," Jen guessed.

Peter looked at the photo image of the two Native Americans standing next to a younger Worthington, "That's it! Worthington was throwing money around. If they recognize Karl they'll remember he was part of the money train."

Jude ignored the dig against Worthington, dabbing the sweat from his eyes with his t-shirt, "I recognized I got thirsty out there," he said. "I went through a liter of water. The heat takes getting used to."

"Let's take a break," Peter offered believing they were spinning wheels. "I've got a call with Karl in two hours and then we'll regroup. That puts us back out here about seven-thirty. There will be a shift change in the casinos by then."

After dinner, they combed through the casino, splitting off individually to walk around. The evening personnel showed the same resilience, with the same negative results.

Jen decided she had enough, "I've got to hit the lady's room. There's Jude and Arthur over by the bar. It's time to enjoy ourselves a little bit."

The noise of the casino drowned out the men's conversation of their lack of success, waiting for Jen to get back.

"Look at us break the fun barrier," Jude said mocking the excitement he wasn't having.

"Are we even in the right town?" Arthur worried.

"Wouldn't that be the shits," Jude answered. "We waste two days and find out Bud was fifty miles from here."

"You guys said it was the pueblo," Peter blamed.

"Actually," Arthur corrected for accuracy, "Karl did. Acoma Pueblo, Acomita, Sky City. Same thing. We're all just tired of being ignored."

Arthur saw Jen on her return weaving her way through the crowd quickly, "Here comes Jen. She's on fire."

Both Jude and Peter turned to watch her dodge a larger group standing next to a blinking one-dollar pay out. She side stepped more people walking abreast and zigzagged through another crowd on the main path approaching the bar. Short of breath she stood composing her thoughts.

"Here's your drink," Peter offered and pushed it to her.

Jen slid next to Arthur, shoving him as she sat down, "Maybe our plan is working! I entered the restroom and as I walked in, three workers were talking, but went silent the second they saw my reflection in the mirror. I think the word's spreading."

"Maybe they're afraid of women from Texas," Jude joked.

"They definitely recognized me. I didn't hear their whole conversation. When I got in there they were watching my every move."

"How do you know they weren't just having a private chick conversation?" Jude joked again.

"They *stopped* talking in *Spanish*," Jen evoked seriously. "Why would they if I couldn't understand them? So they must know me. They started whispering as I left, so I paused before the door shut. One of them said, '*Ella está con el viejo profesor de la tierra.*'"

"Meaning?"

"She's with the old Earth teacher," Arthur translated.

Peter relieved that there was a possibility they could dump the stones, "You sure couldn't tell by the expressions we got today. I guess we wait for Karl and Avey to get here in about six hours. I told him we struck out. Maybe they'll feel safer talking to him."

Less than four hours from rejoining their friends, their exploration with Paul Brewer wasn't a complete waste of time. With Karl driving, Avey continued to study the stones with a loupe, turning the stones over and over with her latex covered hands.

"Karl, do you have any more light parchment or onion skin?"

"Inside the brief, left side."

Avey scooted herself sideways, laying two stones on the console between them, "This is interesting. On the more complex side, the larger grooves have little embedded ridges that are intermittent. When I was picking at these in Brewer's basement, I thought they were arbitrary imperfections."

She took out her carpenter's pencil and shaved the tip with a razor blade. Laying the paper across the top, she gently forced it down into the subset of deeper grooves and carefully traced the imbedded ridges housed within the groove pattern. It left a unique design on the parchment. She did the same for the remaining blocks and compared the patterns side by side, "The inner groove has a distinct blueprint."

She held the sheet up for Karl, "It's not precision work, but they do form a unique pattern that terminates at both ends of the stone."

"No one in the tribe would have time on their hands just to be creative. Good find!" Karl complemented. Sitting back, Avey absorbed all her work she accomplished with the stones and the black books, "Jude said Bud used to quote Einstein all the time. The one I remember, 'Science without religion is lame. Religion without science is blind.' Bud was counting on both ideologies."

Looking out the small bathroom window at the moon, Jason flirted with his thoughts. His mind was spinning with the implied strategies of the deceased and the largess of political and global manipulation. Clearly resolute, the fabricated confession could be invincible from the grave. *The will on the bed automatically cancels the first one as a forgery. Millard didn't have the guts to kill himself.*

The agent felt he comprehended the extraordinary struggle that beset the scientist who sought revenge. What the agent understood better was the insidious nature of Colton's remark during his own debrief of Guantanamo, "...when the shit hits the fan and we get fucked in the ass by all those piss-ant countries..."

With Angela's help, can we effectively derail our leadership? He was certain James Hyatt was in position to carry out his threats. No longer standing alone with the detonator, Jason was certain of the path he wanted to take.

Day 49.

Sky City Casino.
Near Acoma Pueblo.

WHEN AVEY AND Karl reached their destination in the late afternoon, heat and fatigue forced them to their rooms. Arthur got the most of the sparse attention, but ultimately was blunted by Avey's insistence that she would give him the welcome he deserved after she rested and got cleaned up. Now that she had him close in proximity, her sleep was muddled thinking about Karl and Bud.

Refreshed, she dodged the obvious when Arthur came to her room. She reminded him of his promise of celibacy, "I still love you, Arthur."

"A lot of good that does me!" he said disagreeing.

"If you can find someone better than me, go for it," she teased, placing his hand on her breast to seduce him. "I'm sure we can satisfy each other without actually doing it. Clinton figured it out with his lawyers. You come from a family of lawyers."

Karl had finished updating the team, tired of waiting for Avey and Arthur. They fumbled their answers when they strolled in.

Jen retold her encounter in the bathroom encouraging Karl, "You just need to walk around and flash the picture of Worthington and with you doing it. Somebody will step up."

Agreeing with her, Karl split from the group. He was surprised at his jealous reaction to what he witnessed at dinner. Jen was sitting with Peter, filling in his sentences. And Peter butted in and tried to correct her a couple times. They were obviously on a rebound. As Karl walked alone, thoughts of them in college crept back, leaving him unaware of the superficial attention. When he stopped to ask questions, engaging a small group of people in the casino, an older teen waited until his mark was out of sight and then exchanged information with the same group. After Karl exited through a side entry, the teenager followed. When the same young man passed him front on, the exchanged glances provided Alejandro with proof that this *was* Dr. Worthington's assistant over a decade ago. The seventeen year-old had changed as well and was still of no interest to Karl who looked up at the bleached sky, feeling the cold draft from an approaching storm.

Waiting to cross traffic Alejandro circled and stood next to his subject, "Do you remember me?"

The noise from passing vehicles was deafening, "I'm sorry…" Karl looked at the unfamiliar face, and he refocused. "You said what?"

"You're Karl, aren't you? You came with Dr. Worthington to this town years ago. Your friends have been asking about my grandfather."

"Holy…" Karl pulled the photo out from his shirt pocket, "…shit! You're the kid! How did you find me? I mean who told you to find me?"

They stepped back away from the curb, reminiscing for three signal changes. Karl was still fazed. The offspring from the Acoma Pueblo told of his eavesdropping when his aunt was talking to her coworkers.

"You guys have really kicked up some bad history."

"Unbelievable. Then you actually remember us! I still remember you coming up and saying your grandfather wanted to meet Worthington. Oh! Why are they all upset?"

Alejandro rolled his eyes, "I heard my aunt say it'll stir up a lot of old stuff. She's crazy."

"And you say you're going to college?"

"Saving for it. I'm here for the summer to work."

"Let's go meet the group. They're not going to believe this!"

Quick with introductions, Jude and Avey were equally stunned, peppering Alejandro for his version of the past. Avoiding the trappings of adult civility, no question was out of bounds. Arthur observed more than talked, celebrating his girlfriend's return with tequila shots. Karl tried to get them focused on what they should do next and gave up; their stories and laughter reminded him of his past.

"Look, guys, I'm going to head back. You all staying?"

Feeling out of place, Avey whispered to Arthur and disappeared with Karl. Strolling back, she and Karl both sensed the energy shifting in their favor, "We created a huge vibe. Are you going to tell Peter?"

"Maybe. He won't hesitate to jettison everything."

They split off to their rooms a full two hours before Jude and Arthur came back to their room.

"Alejandro was cool," Arthur managed to say without slurring.

"Sounds like his aunt is buzz kill. I hope she doesn't put him in lockdown," Jude replied wishing for the best.

Searching their pockets, they found their room card and fussed with the lock entry. They weren't the last ones in the group to go to sleep.

The aunt continued to grill her nephew after learning he made direct contact with the strangers. She repeated how upset everyone in the family would be and how the whole town would know it was her own nephew that broke the silence, "Of all people..."

Alejandro wagged his head. Eating warm tapas tasted good so he put up with her rant.

"Your grandfather must not know any of this. All these stories are behind us. There's no sense bringing them up again," his aunt insisted.

"Why?"

"My father was criticized by some. He told the professor sacred information. Acoma people were upset. Back then you didn't share with anyone outside of the Pueblo. You know others just steal our culture and our pride with it."

She put more tapas on the plate, "This Karl. Didn't he say Worthington passed away?"

"*Killed,*" the boy repeated.

The aunt ignored the implied obligation with insistence, "Whatever happened to him doesn't matter to us. Not now. He was regarded by your grandfather. Not by others. Whatever was there can't be brought back."

Alejandro resisted, but his aunt would not budge, "You think you are right, Alejandro. In your mind the professor did good things, but you were a kid then. Everything was fun and exciting for a boy of your age. There were conversations that didn't include you. Many tribe members didn't like the professor. To them, he looked like the white man of many centuries—the ones who promised and just took from the Acoma. Your grandfather was younger too, willing to take chances."

Alejandro was woken by Sueto begging to be fed. He didn't remember getting to the couch. The bits and pieces of his aunt's scolding monologue flickered through his mental dullness. *Why would his grandfather make up stories? He couldn't have been trying to rip-off the professor.* That would be even more reason to talk to him.

His instability was tested as the dog cut in front of him, anxious to eat, "Okay. Okay."

"Alejandro!" his aunt yelled out. "Please make sure to let him out today. If you take off, he'll need water. Better yet, take him with you. He needs to get out."

She was leaving for work and gave him a list of chores, "Everybody helps out!"

"I know. I know."

"You shouldn't drink so much. You spoil your day off," she reprimanded.

The mature German shorthair with small brown spots and a large colored saddle spot in the middle of his back was orphaned by Alejandro three years ago when his parents moved near Denver. His father finished his MBA and was suddenly marketable as a Native American. Alejandro had been coming back each summer but as he became older and acclimated to his new surroundings, the summers spent in the area were not as exciting. Sueto was unaware that his playmate was to be a high school senior in the fall. The daily outings to play commando all over town stopped years ago and hikes with his grandfather ceased when the professor was unable to continue his field trips with students.

Alejandro got to work, washing the pots, vacuuming, and doing laundry. There was ample motivation to clear his schedule so he could meet with his new friends. Expecting his aunt to get upset again, he would point to the extra work he did in the house. And he justified his whole summer had been dedicated to the mundane. The teenager didn't want to miss the only opportunity to do *something* before he was back in school full time.

"Come here, boy!" Jude coaxed Sueto when they got seated on the restaurant patio. After checking new scents, the dog circled back to Jude and allowed his ears to be rubbed.

"Down," ordered Alejandro.

Sueto dropped to the ground quickly, spread out. Even his legs were splayed outward to the best of his ability to get low to the ground. With his neck was extended, his head lay flat against the stone pavers. He didn't move but continued to look up through his eyebrows at his master. Arthur choked on his beer watching the display of unusual physical compliance.

"What kind of command is that? Your dog is completely flat!"

"I taught him the move when we played in the desert as youngsters. Between fake bombs and attacks, we would stay low and then charge to the next rock pile. He used to race ahead of me and circle back, but I think that part's forgotten."

"My god, that's funny! I think that's sums up how my parents raised me!" Arthur joked.

"Here," Alejandro commanded Sueto and the dog quietly rested underneath his master's chair.

The discussion began to center on the impasse – getting the grandfather involved. Karl thought on it all night. He had to get some traction before the stones were given away.

"He's up there in Sky City?"

"We see him on Saturdays and sometimes during the week. Someone walks him down. Then he gets a good meal, because my aunt insists on it. She won't let him stay up there because she thinks he would die from starvation."

"Whoa! Does he want to die?" Jude wondered.

"My aunt says it's probably his time. She thinks he is cleansing his soul before taking the Spirit path."

"So he's off limits," Karl concluded out of respect.

"Yes and no. My aunt doesn't want him to know you're here because it'll stir up all the old stuff. But I think it would be good for him," Alejandro explained, remembering parts of the conversation.

"So," Karl interrupted, "would you be in trouble if we spoke to your grandfather? I don't want the whole tribe coming down on us, let alone your aunt."

Alejandro shook his head no and didn't believe his own answer, guessing he could handle the fallout, "I'd have to tell him what's going on and see if he's willing. It'll have to wait till I see him day after tomorrow."

Karl stayed this time to make sure other information didn't slip out. The students compared hobbies, talked about the desert and the weather.

Then they got Karl to tell stories of when he was leading renovation projects in the area, slugging down tequila with the other workers in the evenings. He admitted their daytime was a blur of work hauling gravel, fixing roads, and doing building repairs as they sweat out the alcohol. He and Alejandro speculated why Worthington never took Karl with him to the mountains but was so accepting of Alejandro's participation.

"We weren't at the dig sites or doing actual archeology work here because Worthington made wanted us to build trust with the community," Karl shared.

"I know the professor had many conversations with my grandfather but they stopped," Alejandro replied.

"He did run out of money. And university support," Karl confirmed for Alejandro. "Maybe your grandfather gave up on him. I hope we can reopen that door."

Before Alejandro left the restaurant he pled his commitment, "I'll figure out how to bring the news to him."

"Okay. We did our part," Jude declared to the three of them. "Are you going to tell him about the stones?"

Karl looked in the direction of the Sky City finishing his beer, "Not until he delivers."

The aunt was busy preparing the more generous evening meal unaware of her nephew's motives. He knew the extra dishes were for her father.

"Go over to Little Acoma and pick up your grandfather at the corner store. Mr. Thomas' is bringing him down, but he doesn't have time to drive him over here."

It was the break he was hoping for. With his aunt hovering Alejandro hadn't figured how he would leak the news, "No sweat. When?"

"I'd leave now. It's forty-five minutes." She thought for a second, "It's not like you not to complain."

"I'm bored," he feigned.

His two thoughts persisted as he drove: *Is grandfather too senile to remember the professor,* and *would he trust a man who returned after thirteen years?* Nervous, the favorite grandson waited several minutes in the parking lot. His new friends expected to meet the elder and maybe that was possible. Convincing his grandfather to help the strangers would take a miracle.

The past two summers, Alejandro saw age take control of his grandfather. The elder still recognized him by sight, but related to him as a young boy. Every weekend the old man would sit in their living room and gaze out past the small front yard and beyond to the store across the street. The desert and ancient cities were miles beyond. Alejandro doubted the thoughts of his living ancestor went much farther than the sidewalk. When the daughter invited family over for dinner she begged them to be respectful. It embarrassed Alejandro to hear the comments from those not even bothering to keep their voices down. There was no respect at the modern home for a sacred being:

"He's just an old man with old dreams."

"Why don't we put him in a nursing home where he can't hurt himself?"

"When I talk with him, he speaks Spanish. Who can understand it?"

Mr. Thomas' pulled along side Alejandro's car. In the front seat Amado sat up straight looking alert. Today he wore a straw hat with a leather strap on the brow and fake turquoise clip holding small raptor feathers displayed in front. The grandfather looked proud as he climbed out of the car using his carved cane made of dried and enameled bull cock. The deep crevasses encasing his leathery hands and face were more like mappings of history.

His teeth, worn and translucent, showed as a smile appeared. He recognized his grandson, *"Soldadito, ¿Dónde está mi hija?"* [64]

Encouraged by his parents and aunts to be bilingual, Alejandro replied in Spanish aware it appealed to his mentor. He knew little of the native dialect his grandfather spoke in private, but was proud they could converse with each other, "She's home cooking. She wanted me to come get you."

He let the elderly native settle to his surroundings as they drove slowly out of the parking lot. This would be one time when he drove under the speed limit to get home. Speaking about familiar topics like the weather and his dog, to get a conversation going, the nephew planned to reveal his chance meeting with his new friends.

On the verge of spilling the news, his heart's desire to expose another fate was stronger, "When are you going to die, Grandfather?"

"Not today. Soon."

"Is it what you want for yourself?"

---

[64] "Where is my daughter?"

"It's for the twin great spirits. They are in here and here always," he replied pointing to his head and his chest.

"Dad's worried about you and so are the others. But I don't think they respect the old ways."

"Do you?"

"I guess so. You learned it, but no one else had to."

"I can teach you."

"I think it's hard for anyone to understand."

The trip was more than half over. Alejandro had not revealed the homecoming with the strangers, but the elder interrupted, "Where is Sueto?"

"Home."

"You will need him."

Alejandro was puzzled thinking his grandfather slipped away from the present and old memories were flowing in. *Damn. I blew it!*

His grandfather floated away. They were suddenly on two different wave lengths. Missing the opportunity to engage his oldest elder when his wits were about him, the grandson stepped on the gas. Disappointed, the driver ignored the view of the Chuska mountains that hid the past from the future.

"What is he like?"

The boy thought the old man had really lost it but his impatience had to be tempered with respect, "He's still the same."

"How can that be? I haven't heard of him for many years."

It was twenty miles to home. Alejandro increased the car's speed and turned up the radio. He ignored his grandfather, unwilling to play into his sense of bewilderment.

"*Soldadito,*" the elder emphasized. Then he asked his nephew again, "What is the man Karl like after many years?"

"Karl?"

Erratically braking, Alejandro swerved over in the right lane, then to the shoulder, "Grandfather! You know about Karl!!"

The sense of magic was overwhelming, wiping out all of Alejandro's regrets about his only true mentor. The elder wasn't senile or half-witted as the others had said. It would be a sweet retribution watching all the aunts and uncles fumbling over excuses for their years of foul discourse.

"I met him, Grandfather. He and others! They want to meet you! Will you do it?"

"Cálmate y dime." [65]

Alejandro explained everything he knew of his new friends and of his aunt's resistance, "She told me not to tell, that you don't need to get mixed up in this again."

"We'll find our way. Her thinking is different."

On the way home, the two conspired on a plan to get time with the geologist. Alejandro was joyous with the aspect of his grandfather's apparent gifts of spirit, those that even he had disrespected moments ago. The proportions of the conversation had become entirely mystical, "Grandfather? Can you say how you knew of Karl?"

As his only grandson, the relationship had been sneered at by others but Alejandro knew he was worthy of the sacred knowledge his grandfather might share if imposed upon. With eyes ahead, the driver waited for the answer perhaps no living person had ever heard.

He wasn't sure he translated the question correctly in Spanish, "You said, when you were meditating, a friend visited you with his words?"

The old man nodded.

"Was it a vision?"

"No. It was Senor Thomas'."

Alejandro exploded with laughter slamming his hand on the top of the steering wheel, having been duped by his own indulgence. Amused by the hysterics, the smiling elder continued looking out the window thinking of his plan that he had held close for decades.

Jammed together in a hotel room, Peter and Jen sat in chairs at the table. Avey and Arthur lay on the spare twin bed and Karl was propped up against the vanity counter. Sitting on the carpet, Jude was disgusted by Peter's behavior. They all heard Karl repeat the phone message Alejandro left. The Acoma leader agreed to meet. Jude was sure Peter was questioning the plan again just to bug him. It took twenty minutes to decide if the stones should be brought along.

"We don't know if this guy has recollection of anything. I don't want to show up with them and risk having them taken," Karl requested.

Peter was exasperated, "We agreed to do just that. You're practically in Worthington's shoeprints. The old man will remember, and then you say, 'here are your stones' and we're out of here."

---

[65] "Calm down and tell me."

"Exactly my point," Karl defended. "I need time to make sure the dude's for real."

Jude almost lost it, "And Peter, there's no debate. We're not *all* going."

Karl reiterated the plan they thought they agreed on an hour ago, "Jen and I are going to the church. I'm agreeing to that."

Peter sensed his argument was swinging in his favor. He didn't want Karl to slip out of the noose of his own making. He pushed Karl one more time to take the stones.

Karl restated to his advantage, "I told you the stones would be handed over when it becomes *necessary*. Who knows if Alejandro's grandfather is even going to tell us anything. We'll go in there with an open slate. They said Jen could interpret so what's your problem? You've got someone in there *you* trust."

The words came out and Karl winced, "You get what I mean, right?"

Tempers didn't flair but they were simmering. Peter stared at Jen, then at Jude, stating his case, "Nothing would make me happier than getting this wrapped up. For all we know there's a warrant out for our arrest for these stones. I think this meeting will prove what I've been saying all along."

The comment wasn't lost on Karl. He regretted talking Peter into coming along. To avoid a major blowup Karl relented. The stones were to be shown to the elder.

The Church of Holy Saints.

Jen and Karl climbed the ten church steps bordered by iron handrail and entered the small foyer. Like other places of worship, this one had its own personality, its own pure energy.

"There must be over fifty candles in here."

The glow bounced off the walls and wooden floor that was shaved smooth by a hand plane.

"Our churches are too orthodox, too sterile. In here, you can smell the wood and the dust," Karl bragged.

The guests looked towards the alter and slowly approached the old man sitting in the front pew with another gentleman.

A few yards adjacent to the occupants, Jen leaned into Karl and whispered, "What stinks?"

Karl was too focused to bother with any distraction, "Eh, *Hola señor*."

"Karl, *Ud. ha venido por el pedimento de un pequeño soldado*."

Karl waited for Jen to translate, "You have arrived at the, huh, pleadings of a little soldier."

"That must be what he calls Alejandro," Karl replied softly to Jen.

The elder motioned for them to sit on the same pew. Jen brought over the wooden stool from the pulpit and set it down across from the men, "I am Amado," the other gentleman translated for the words of the elder. "And I am Mr. Thomas'."

The visitors introduced themselves, confused why they insisted that Jen be included.

"Tell him we appreciate being here and being in his presence."

Mr. Thomas' translated to his partner. And he added, "I've been with Amado since we were boys," and with his full attention on Jen, "You are here to understand there is no mistake when I translate."

Nods were given and the Spanish dialogue began to flow from Amado to Mr. Thomas' and then to English. They explained their role in the Pueblo and how they were chosen as young men to do certain things. Then Amado shared the history with his friend, Bud Worthington, and his sadness when they were no longer connected, "by our words."

Karl told of his involvement with Bud and trips back to Mesa Verde. It was the first time Jen had heard all the detail, realizing the commitment of these men. Prompting Karl to slow down, Jen repeated words and phrases in Spanish to aid Mr. Thomas'.

Karl, at times, spoke too fast or the terminology was unfamiliar, "We have brought sacred works that belong to your tribe. Would you like to look at them?"

The elder's excitement was bound by the teaching he was given. As the artifacts were removed from the canvas bag, Jen watched his peering eyes examine the linen. Surrounded by an old face, his gaze was young and sharp. His chant became audible but not understood by the visitors.

"He is asking that his voice be accepted and has strength to carry the message of this gift," Mr. Thomas' explained.

Slowly, all the stones were exposed again and studied.

"He knows these pieces have been mishandled but they are purified by the will he expresses."

Karl got a chill after hearing Mr. Thomas' translation. He feared he and others might have unintentionally mishandled the artifacts.

The elder wrapped the stones gently and set them in front of his guests, "These are for your journey."

With Mr. Thomas' help, Jen confirmed the stones were theirs to use, for what purpose she didn't know. Surprised and pleased, Karl wondered out loud what they would do with them or how they should proceed. It was an awkward conversation. Mr. Thomas' did not translate any of those comments to Amado. Instead the elder continued.

"He says he watches you and Worthington with respect."

"Uh?" Karl mumbled, thinking about Peter's reaction to the mandate that the stones remain in their possession, "Tell him Dr. Worthington passed away a few months ago and I am the only one left. I guess I take his place."

"He says he knows that," Jen replied perplexed.

"Alejandro must have told him," Karl said, then spoke to the elder. "My purpose here is to carry out Dr. Worthington's bequest to finish the research and I hope to discover the purpose of these artifacts."

Jen metered the answer jabbing Karl to slow down.

"...I—ask that you—allow us to—continue," And she nudged again to speed up a little, "what you and he started."

At that point, the elder and Mr. Thomas' began to speak rapidly trusting Karl with their legacy. Jen asked Mr. Thomas' to repeat specific words because the context of the information was critical to their success. Amado revealed the history of the stones telling of the migration, as he had done so with the professor. Karl and Jen learned the stones were carved by a main tribe and then concealed from foreign attackers who had weapons.

Mr. Thomas' translated the councils of the Pueblo sent a small group of the parent tribe to search for other dwellings in other regions, "It was to protect the gifts of our sacred beginnings."

They learned the important artifacts were continuously relocated because of the wave of conquerors from other lands. Over generations the ceremonies eventually died out in form but were still handed down by word. Then Mr. Thomas' explained the creation of a sanctuary.

Jen interrupted Mr. Thomas' for clarification, "Estás diciendo *cueva*?" Jen asked.[66]

Then she repeated for her partner, "He's saying a cave, but I think he means something like domain."

"Ask if he means city. Like Sky City?"

---

[66] "Are you saying cave?"

The elder waved his hand, "*Una cuidad escondida dentro de otra ciudad. La cuidad sagrada.*" [67]

Giving her a headache, the candle vapor and odor of the elder's clothing had overtaken Jen. She respectfully nodded to the elder, "*Perdónenme un momento. Me siento mal. Necesito ir afuera.*" [68]

"Before you leave what did he say?"

"It's confusing to me. Something like a city inside a city. A sacred city. I've got to get some fresh air."

A priest came out briefly to replace the smoldering candles. Showing no reluctance with Jen's absence, the elder spoke quickly. As if rehearsed, Mr. Thomas' translated at the same pace.

"You must journey with little soldier. He will lead the way."

"What are we looking for?"

"More here..." The elder touched the center of Karl's chest. "...than can be easily seen. Earth does not reveal herself all at once."

"Like messages or something?" Karl quizzed Mr. Thomas', looking at Amado.

"It was passed to me as a child like the one before me. My ancestors had wisdom beyond my time," Mr. Thomas' said.

"Did Bud know this?"

"Yes. He searched many times without the gifts you have now."

"We think there are people watching us. Should we come to you if we find, um...it?"

The elder reached across and placed his hand on Karl's heart, "Much will be seen by you now. But a burning will close your eyes."

Karl was and looked confused with the additional insight.

"You and another are no strangers to me. Do not weaken," Amado's friend warned in English.

The youngest man in the room was humbled with the instructions, even though the message was perplexing. The Indian chanted again and stopped and gave a warning. As Karl looked up, Jen was standing inside the doorway gazing at the beauty of the church scenery. Refracted strands of color coated the exposed roof beams. She approached slowly and recognized the meeting had concluded without her. Amado and Mr. Thomas' thanked their new explorers and a prayer was recited to honor their quest.

---

[67] "City hidden within a city. A sacred city."

[68] "Pardon me, I'm ill. I need to go outside."

When they reached the stairs, Jen's temper flared, "So did the good ole boys figure it out? I could hardly bear the stench of the old guy mixed with the candle fumes. I don't know how you stayed in there."

"What?"

"I could see you two leaning into each other. Did you suddenly get Spanish skills?" She didn't wait for an answer, "Oh, I get it. Amado was kind enough to speak English?"

"Not from what I could tell. Mr. Thomas' continued to translate."

Karl didn't hesitate to share what she missed excluding the warnings he was given. He didn't know what to think of the final instruction: "The one who leaves the path will suffer."

"Remember when he explained the reason for splitting the tribes?"

Jen nodded.

"The Mayans along with Incas were wiped out by plague before the Europeans conquered them. It's like the universities are more interested in cultures that completely died away so they could steal their bounty instead of embracing living ones."

"Why would he trust Worthington?"

"Not Worthington as the professor, but as the messenger. Amado seems to see some or all of the future."

"I wouldn't say they were rehearsed," Jen shared, "But to totally accept their stories at face value. It's a bit of a leap."

"Of faith," Karl completed.

"As soon as I said it, I knew you'd do that. What I mean is we have the same puzzle Worthington had. We still have more questions than answers."

"But that's just it. We have Amado guiding us. Would you rather have the stones accidentally discovered twenty years from now and no one to talk to? Avey made a couple calls before we went to see Brewer. The reply to her email documents the genealogy of the tribe. She was told it was probable the cache of artifacts stored in the Mesa Verde region could have evolved from around here. And the history of Pueblo migrations is speculative because the Conquistadors and priests had huge gaps of time between their visits to these areas to establish territories. So there were periods of months and years where the invaders had no idea what was going on. The elder basically told us the same history."

"Lot's of tribes split off though. And the stories become exaggerated memories."

Karl ignored the blinking "Don't Walk" sign forcing Jen to keep up, "Yes, but Amado is practically an eyewitness. And unbelievably," Karl patted the bag, "we still have the evidence."

"He's apparently at odds with his extended family and with the Pueblo so don't count on group hugs. Maybe he's been banned and the best answer is to hand them over, like Peter wants."

Karl stopped Jen before they rounded the corner to go into the casino where the rest of the team was waiting, "Let me guess. Peter has been working you over."

"He's got his doubts and he shared them."

"Aside from Jude and me..." Karl looked into Jen's eyes, "...what does Peter really think?"

Jen took a deep breath, "That you're the renegade and this is too personal for you. You know he thinks it's going in the wrong direction and we should—"

"Go to the police, right?"

"Basically."

"And you? What's you're take? Did you go to the cops when you found drill heads missing? Did your friend Doug contact law enforcement to complain about his injuries that you said were mysterious? Are your issues that much different than mine?"

"Karl, I'm struggling with it too! What does Amado and his stones have to do with my drill heads? I don't have a clue or even if that would make sense! I mean Bud's death got us here. But how Doug's accident could be pointing us in the right direction when I'm standing in New Mexico? I don't know. I guess that's where Peter puts the round peg into the square hole. And anyway, as far as I know the drill head deal is over. Doug says its business as usual."

"If we walk away from this, we'll be back to nothing. The math says keep going. We've got Bud's research, Amado's stones, and his idea about this other city, and Alejandro to guide us. And we have three students with more spine than a lot of people their age. It almost feels like the old group is trying to crash my car into the wall. "

"Don't think that I'm not in your corner, Karl. Somehow, I've gotten in the middle again between you and Peter."

Karl and Jen walked into the casino lounge finding Peter and Avey.
"Where's the rest?"

"The college studs are out on the town."

Karl took a deep breath of conviction, "We leave tomorrow for the mountains. Hope they can drag their butts across the desert."

Peter tensed up immediately, "Did I miss the overthrow and inauguration of a dictatorship? Oh! And I see you have the stones. Why am I not surprised?"

"It is what it is, Peter."

"He's telling the truth," Jen added as if it would calm Peter.

"Alejandro's grandfather gave us permission to explore the area. Why should we waste our time sitting around?"

"He gave *us* permission? Who gave *him* permission? I guess you had to be there."

"Ask Jen."

Jen bristled at the role of playing referee, "This isn't my gig. You guys need to work it out solo."

With Jen and Avey as bystanders, the debate raged on. Both men were resilient in their stance for or against doing anything further.

"We quit now and we won't have enough proof to...", Karl protested, appealing to those in the room, but was interrupted.

"Proof? We're at the same spot that Worthington got to and a lot of good it did him!" Peter alleged.

"Jen can tell you. The elder was straight up. We're not at the same point. Everybody has chipped in and..."

"It's a fairy tale. The old man is stuck in time, exactly why Worthington failed to discover anything. You should have forced him to take the stones. That was our deal."

"Well, it's not your call to shut it down. You can hit the road if you want. I'm done talking about it."

After Karl said his goodnights, Peter continued, "He pisses me off! What the old man said or claims to know doesn't prove anything. Karl is brainwashed by these people."

Sitting in the empty Keno section, Jen scolded her friend, "Go talk to him and have it out. I swear you two are worse than women."

Peter went to Karl's room finding him sorting gear and confronted him, claiming he had been misunderstood earlier, "I don't get it. You decide to go and everybody is just supposed to follow?"

"It's a choice you'll have to make on your own."

"And anyway you don't have any clues where this city is," Peter argued.

"Alejandro will guide us. It turned out Amado took Alejandro on trips up there with Worthington. They quit going years ago, but he says Alejandro knows the way."

"I don't get it. The whole time I thought we had a deal. I agreed to the meetings after Worthington passed away. I helped find the stones. I drove all the way out here. And some freakin' stray gets to you and you're off on another crusade."

"I pushed for the group to get together. You still don't think Bud was murdered. You didn't find the stones. Lloyd did. And you drove out here because I thought we were a team. Instead you just keep hassling me. I don't get that."

"It's because I can't trust you. You agreed if we ran into whoever knew Worthington, and this guy does, then the stones get turned over to the Pueblo. Let them protect the artifacts. Now, we're just risking our necks."

"The elder didn't want to take the pieces. He handed them back. He's counting on us to find the Holy Grail. This is what Bud was after his whole life."

Peter continued his assault, "Holy Grail! Now Brewer and the elder are sucking you in. According to everyone else, it's a goddamn fairy tale! A hoax! It always was!"

Karl became vexed, "You don't want to see it! They can't manage their own destiny. We're the bridge Peter. The only ones to show up. The only ones who can look into the past on their behalf."

Their voices rose with each response, echoing through the room.

"The bridge to where from where? You keep convincing us there's a master plan against people, against us, against you. You put you there. We didn't. When will you stop? When one of us gets hurt?"

Karl stopped packing and faced Peter. The dam was going to break and he felt his adrenaline surge, "Christ! You're so goddamn selfish!"

With his jaw tightened, Peter wanted to scream his friend for being the self-appointed crusader. Scream at him for being a fool that followed Worthington. Attack him for stealing Jude from underneath him. He wanted to attack him for stealing Jen's heart when it was his, "You don't listen to anybody. You never had to. We're all supposed to sit back and let you lead? Ya, I have an answer. Fuck this shit. But I can't leave. I'm stuck here with all this bullshit."

"Yeah right. We're better off without all your baggage. Make it easy on the rest of us."

Silence. Peter pinched his brow with two fingers, his voice stressed, "That's right. Just push everyone aside when they get in your way. I thought you were doing it because you're a loner, but now I know you're just an asshole. You don't know the first thing about—"

"You're not mad at me!" Karl yelled back. "You're pissed because Jen is here to stay, and you can't convince her otherwise. You've probably worked over Jude too. Just stay outta my way."

Very early morning, everybody was still confused having heard rumors about the blowup. Standing near the vehicles, it was obvious Karl and Jude had a pact because most of the gear belonged to them. Seeing two full mountaineering packs, smaller day packs, and four metal boxes, it was unsettling for Jen.

"Are we going for weeks? I don't have that much to take."

Karl cited a rough itinerary and punch list, vetting everyone's gear by himself, "I'm bringing some of the standard equipment I always carry on the road. We have to cover our bases depending on what we run into."

Concerned Alejandro had not shown yet, Karl answered questions in short replies avoiding direct eye contact.

Jen ran back to her room to grab more clothing. Coming down the hallway she was shocked to see Peter in the foyer, carrying his stuff, "Peter! You didn't answer your phone. I left you a message."

"I got it," he said blankly.

"You're not going from what I hear."

"Karl said that? Well, I am. I can't leave Jude," he stated flatly.

Walking out together, he told her this was the last leg of the trip for him. After today, when they made it back to town, he would be leaving. Everyone else perceived the riff. The sting of Karl and Peter's disagreement was apparent as the men continued to ignore each other as the vehicles were loaded. Even Jude knew not to make light of it.

As two vehicles drove off without incident, eyes surveyed them from adjacent parking lots and buildings. Karl was in the lead vehicle with Alejandro and Jude. Peter chose the tailing vehicle when choices were made.

Staring out the window, he remained quiet when Jen tried to engage him, "You must have said some harsh things to Karl."

"Nothing he wasn't asking for."

Near Canyon De Chelly National Monument, Arizona.

360453N 1090812W

D RIVING TOWARD A destination that no one was familiar with, Avey and Arthur both felt they got the worst of the deal. Ignoring Peter, they asked Jen what she thought about the elder and if she thought they were wasting their time.

"Amado was very kind. I was getting lightheaded in there from all the fumes and having to concentrate on their dialogue. Their Spanish accent is difficult to listen to. But afterwards I thought about what he told us and I realized when he speaks, you *feel* his words."

"Is he telling the truth or do you think it's all a hoax?" Avey asked, trying to pin her down on purpose.

"I don't know why he would tell lies. He seemed lucid to me. He and Mr. Thomas'. They come off like they represent Mother Nature or something. It's weird!"

Peter continued to look at the passing scenery, transparent enough to conceal his seething. Embedding itself, the episode with Karl had consumed him as he replayed the words and the facial expressions. His jaw tightened and released. His brow stiffened. All he could think of was how things were twisted by Karl and how everyone fell in line. It would only be a couple more hours and he could convince Jude to leave with him. Those thoughts evaporated as the others' conversation seeped in, "...must have been up in your room. I told everyone Wren called and left a message. That business card that we gave her. She was searching on that guy and found out he died or something."

"Who was it? When?"

"She didn't say. It's spooky. We don't know how long Worthington had it tucked in the pages."

The two cars passed "Milkwater", west of the closest state highway over 130 miles from Sky City. The trip continued just before reaching "White Clay", stopping at a gravel parking lot. Leaping over Arthur's lap, Sueto was the first one to touch the ground, sniffing around as everyone unloaded the cars.

Alejandro pointed out the trail head, but instructed they would be splitting off the two lane trail to save time, "I know the road makes switchbacks that we can avoid. We'll be in Navajo and Apache land."

"Your grandfather hauled you all this way as a kid?" Avey asked, fascinated their guide was very young when he made his first trip.

"There was a mule for gear and I would sit on top as we made our way."

Water, food, and radios were distributed and then lightweight containers were strapped to some of the packs.

Karl had never seen this area, "Hard to believe Worthington was here years ago!"

"He didn't carry much, except for water, trail mix, cigarettes, and his pills," Alejandro recalled.

Nobody complained about the hike. Not even Peter. It was a relief from being cooped up in a hotel, or stuck walking the pavement. The animosity that infected the group was silenced by the beauty of their surroundings.

Solid footing on the widened trail became challenging on muddy sections where sparse use of four-wheelers and ATVs had gutted the surface. Climbing out of the short canyons where arroyos were shielded from the raising temperatures, the hikers felt the heat transfer from the ground as the clouds doled out shade sparingly. Sharing in the excitement of discovery from the past to the present, Karl and the nephew obliged the other hikers when they asked questions. Jude studied the sky and peaks, asking about the mesa. Others talked about the landscape, reservation boundaries, and landmarks. Most of the dialogue bypassed Peter until he heard Alejandro say they were near the last mile, approaching "*la cuidad sagrada.*"[69]

Arriving at the unnatural boundary, the fenced perimeter was a gauntlet of tumble weeds and paper trash. Much of the fence was discolored with rust. The swing gate was eroded in an open position with the encircling chain held together with a padlock.

"The government doesn't protect this site anymore?" asked Karl.

Alejandro was apathetic in his response, "Everything of value had been looted long before the fence showed up. I was told by my grandfather the Acoma begged for protection, but it arrived years too late."

Entering through the gate, their footwear became coated with bronze sand and rock dust. As the group made its way into the center of the abandoned adobes, sporadic wind picked up the soot and created dust devils that trailed off towards the rising complex.

Avey elbowed Jude, "Look a little familiar?" she hinted, reminding him of the photo album.

"This would have been the area of ceremony," Alejandro shared, rotating in a circle raising his arms out from his sides.

Scattered, the only implement to survive time were portions of the ladders. His eyes saw the advanced desecration of a place he revered as a boy. His mental vision made the deterioration around them whole. He pictured the serene settings he was taught as a child, his thoughts mending and rendering as he looked up at the cascade of structure that was melded into the natural rock. Rotted and decomposed beams lay solid and new across the roofed terraces. Eroded walls and built-in staircases were semi-smooth coated with native plaster, their imperfect curves and edges, grey and white against the natural hue of ancient granite. Each horno and sambullo door with wood dowel was pristine but in reality leveled to the base, completely disintegrated. Cisterns flowed with reservoir water stored at the top of the Mesa. For real they sat idle, leaking tainted water, in disrepair waiting for the next storm to flood them beyond capacity. In his mind, Alejandro sat on the lap of his grandfather as he was told about the village and his grandfather's role as a young leader.

Remaining silent out of respect for their youngest companion, no one moved for minutes, taking in the dramatic view of the historic site topping out at nearly 1000 feet. Unique in its placement, the terraced adobes took advantage of the natural break in the Mesa at different levels. Midway

---

[69] A sacred city.

and higher, the mountain jutted back making way for plateaus of low grasses and soil. Instead of a continuous facade of single dwellings, the site was a footprint of adobes in rows, positioned like giant stairs, anchored to the successive levels of the plateau. Proceeding upward to the peak tops, sets of horizontal row of dwellings were supported by the structures underneath.

"Alejandro, how many times did Worthington explore here?"

"Many times. He was accompanied by my uncles back when they respected Grandfather. They brought the professor here so he could collect information about the historic and religious significance of this village. I heard them say it never turned out to be much."

Avey nudged Arthur whispering, "I'll bet those are the individuals in the other photo with Worthington."

"What's happened to all the ladders and framing?"

Alejandro was totally matriculated into modern society, but his voice sounded disgruntled for he was taught to feel the rawness of the prejudices and carry the remorse of his elders, "Used for fuel by the thieves to keep warm while they partied and ransacked the place, burning anything that could burn."

Jude remembered the old photographs he saw in the black books, "Sorry to say this, but this place has really been hosed."

Office of Willard Colton.

"There's not much I can do about that fucking piss-ant," Colton surmised privately after berating Hyatt in his own office.

Colton's language had the force of conviction to destroy a career. Acquiring power from Sterling and the popularity within the NEADE executive committee, Hyatt was just out of Colton's reach and they both knew it. Colton knew Hyatt spoon-fed the latest escalation to bait the committee and when he approached his aide, it was to make him aware of the newly discovered blog that was assumed to be superficially linked to Dr. Franklin. He wanted to start legal proceedings against the scientist, but Hyatt resisted.

Colton attacked, not accustomed to debate with subordinates, "It's a breach of his contract leaking classified information. Idiots get fired in the private sector all the time. We need to nail his ass!"

It was infuriating to hear the explanation of legal requirements. He didn't care if a board of review afforded all government employees a right to a hearing.

"It's not a light switch Willis. We'll have to go by the book."

Blasting him for dragging his ass, Colton launched into other failings his aide had precipitated, among them the leak of classified information to Jason.

"He's not my problem, Willis. He's your guy right?" Hyatt said coolly. While he didn't expect Jason to backtrack to his boss with their private discussion, it served him well at this moment.

On his way out of the building, Colton made calls to insure other activities were under his absolute control. He hadn't planned on leaving Washington, but he needed some room to breathe.

Day 47.

Entering la cuidad sagrada.

360453N 1090812W

"IT'S THREE ALREADY. Let's move over to the shade and decide how to go about this," Karl announced.

Sueto appreciated the water being drained from Jen's camel pack. As soon as he finished, his nose was on the ground following small lizard tracks, minutes old. While the wind cooled them, the group tried to figure out what they should be looking for.

"When I sat with your grandfather," Karl dictated, "Mr. Thomas' said the path was, 'seen by many, but no one had walked it for many lives.' Jen. He was telling you something about beauty?"

"Yes, he said, *La belleza vive en la piedra*."[70]

"Alejandro, does that make any sense? The beauty lives in the rock?"

"It's been a long time since Grandfather spoke of it. Everybody in town stopped listening to him after a while. It was the professor's dedication that must have convinced my grandfather that Worthington was sent to revive the beliefs of the ancestors."

Jude was impatient, "If your grandfather was told the answers, how come he never found the stuff himself?"

---

[70]   "Beauty dwells in the rock."

421

"The story was passed from elder to elder by the head of the clan. It's possible some of the details of the story were translated wrong or forgotten."

Hearing the discussion Peter thought it was good news.

Jen remembered Mr. Thomas" explanation, "No one knew the exact location, so they could not betray their faith during times when invaders came for gold."

"I'll shut up," Jude promised.

Avey repeated the phrase and snapped her fingers, "Karl, pull out the smudges. The beauty in the rock could be our drawings."

Karl pulled them from the pack and unfolded some of them.

"It looks like art to me," Arthur admitted. "Maybe these symbols are here somewhere."

"All symbols in Pueblo art have a spiritual meaning," Alejandro verified.

"Let's split up," Karl directed. "Look for anything like these symbols. You all have the images on your PDAs. Alejandro and I will use the originals. Everyone go to channel eight. Watch out for snakes and stuff."

The college students took the north side. Jen voted for the middle, leaving Karl and Alejandro to the south.

"Acid rain's probably taken its toll by now," Peter happily doubted their plan of attack as he walked with Jen.

Climbing up stone steps to the next level, she wondered why he remained so defiant. The promise of discovery was greater with the younger team.

Moving a damaged ladder in place, Jude scrambled up a carved out water chute forty feet from the ground, "If you guys follow, be careful. They're slick with algae from the storms. It's kinda permanent," he exclaimed when he surveyed the stains on his shoes.

When they caught up to him, Arthur surveyed the structures, "Look's like some scribble way over there." Then he miked to Karl, who was ascending a stone stairwell, coaxing Sueto to follow.

"To your left and up two flights."

The hand wave was affirmative. In minutes the radio toned, "You're right. It's symbols, but not as detailed compared our drawing. We'll keep looking."

Jude went up two more levels, "I found something."

At his location, a wall drawing covered the remaining surface of crumbling façade.

"What do you think they drew it with?" Arthur asked.

"Probably plant or animal products," Avey answered. "It's not as faded because it's on the north side of the wall. Less direct light."

"No, I meant what did they use, a paint brush?"

"Probably air brush or spray can," Avey joked.

Jude looked towards the gate below, across the foothills and basin. The anvil cloud shapes forming from the plenum of warm air were coming towards them. He voiced his concern to Karl.

"Thanks. Let me know if you see any lightning."

Jen radioed to say they found a drawing as well, not exactly matching the images they had. More feedback from the teams confirmed many wall sketches had survived the dynamics of nature but no exact matches. Sometimes hidden, the wall art was getting more elaborate as they climbed higher. A century plus of sand and other erosion had accumulated in corners and at the base of many walls. Some piles became steps to reach the top edges of a higher wall. The climbers took advantage of the decay and other props to reach two-thirds of the way to the highest row of dwellings. Jude looked at the gain recorded on his altimeter.

"You wouldn't guess we've come up over six hundred and twenty-five feet."

Arthur studied the network of chutes below them, "No wonder no one died of thirst. There are cisterns all over the place."

"Mucky green ones," Jude added.

Avey wiped the inside of a stone tank with her finger, looking at the residue, "Mother Nature definitely keeps these at full strength."

Karl came back on the air waves, "Everybody, Alejandro just remembered some of his grandfather's teachings. It's Ocatc. It's part of a sacred deity. Three of them."

"Sweet. We have three stones," Avey responded.

Jude relayed her question, "Are we looking for the image of a face or something like that?"

"I'll put him on," Karl offered handing the radio to his partner.

"No, it's the patterns. All the symbols have spiritual meaning. Ocatc, God of the three Gods, was the strongest or the purist, I can't remember. But they were portrayed with a symbol, not the image of a being."

"Hold on, guys," Karl asked and laid some of the drawings on the ground.

"Do any of these look familiar?" he asked the boy.

"Not really. I was only seven or eight. That was long ago. I just remembered Ocatc because Grandfather was always talking about it."

Karl radioed everyone telling them maybe it was a false alarm.

Peter looked at his watch certain they had reached a dead end, "Let's keep moving up so we can finish and get on with our lives."

To reach the highest domicile, Jude stacked the remnants of a ladder against an inside wall, then scaled it to the last section, climbing onto a thick multi-layered span of rock material that fused the acres of natural stone to the mesa bedrock. With inspection Jude could not detect any erosion or deterioration. From where he stood on the head wall, the peaks ranged from two to four hundred feet higher. Their shadows reached the steel fence perimeter at the base of the ancient Pueblo village.

"Hey, guys, this section looks pretty good for being centuries old."

"No tread or skateboard skids yet?" Arthur asked sarcastically.

Avey moved with surprising agility between the smaller huts and the outside facing walls just below Jude.

"The artwork on these walls has survived pretty well," she reported. "Jude, tell Karl we're at the highest section of adobes."

Having done so, Jude persuaded his companions to stay put while he explored higher, climbing up one of the main chutes. He dumped his pack at their feet, preparing to scramble up the steep angle, "Here's the radio. I'll be back in a few. Those guys aren't going to show up for awhile."

Arthur and Avey found a shady spot that afforded views across the valley floors. The sun had passed its zenith, coloring clouds as they changed shape, draping an isolated valley many miles in every direction. Soaked through with sweat, they enjoyed the cool air.

"What do you think Avey? Are we wasting our time?"

She leaned into his body tucking her thumb in his back pocket, "This is freaking me out a bit."

"Really?"

"Think about it. We're sitting on an ancient foundation in eighty-five degrees, sweating to death. There are lizards, scorpions, and snakes hiding from us until dark and you haven't even bothered to kiss me and tell me you'll keep me safe."

Arthur caught on to her bit, "That's because I've been consumed with Jude's comfort. He's been out of his element, you know. He's completely reliant on me for direction."

Laughing they kissed and kissed passionately again. Hearing Jude approaching, Avey adjusted her shirt, and combed her hair with fingers, "We better see what everyone is up to."

The whole group came together near the top of the head wall and to the center of the massive complex. Karl and Alejandro were tired from helping Sueto manage through some of the difficult sections. Water and fruit were welcomed nutrition. Jude got comments for the stains on his hands and clothes.

"Don't worry," he said, pointing to the clouds. "Maybe I'll get rinsed off."

"Do we want to call it quits for today?" Avey tempted the group.

"Karl, what do you think? Have we made any progress beyond Bud's efforts?" Arthur quizzed.

Karl remained cautious of Peter's mood, "I think so. The symbols on the stones mean something. I still don't know exactly what we're looking for, just like the last pillagers that came through here."

"Is that meant to be funny or pathetic?" Arthur tested, looking at Alejandro emphatically.

A smile came across Jen's face, sitting next to Alejandro, watching his reaction. She had no connection to this place but she wanted to somehow acknowledge the elder's wisdom, believable or not, that now belonged to a younger man, "We need to get serious and figure it out," Jen suddenly voiced. "We need to focus our energies on this."

She placed her hand on Alejandro's back, sweeping across his shoulder blades, "We've got Alejandro and his memories. If we leave, the opportunity may not come to us again."

Karl felt Jen had finally let her passion guide her regardless of Peter's will.

Jude stood up in support of the renewed effort, "Bud even climbed all over with less than what we have. We can do this!"

Cloud cover above them had merged, transforming the light blue sky to orange hues. Narrow golden rays coated the walls of the adobe bending at right angles, widening and shrinking on broad and narrow stone faces.

From the valley floor a massive oblique shadow crept towards the gated village.

Nobody disagreed with the new plan, but Peter insisted they put boundaries around their decision to forge on, "We can't hang here all night without heat and extra food," he submitted. "Let's give it a couple hours, then head down."

Avey couldn't resist, tired of placating him, "If you're in a hurry, we could meet you at the cars."

Peter signaled his frustration with the thought of wasting more time, "All I'm saying is we're going to lose daylight. There's no reason you guys couldn't come back."

Karl came to his defense, "Peter's right. Whatever we can solve can be used later. We don't have a death wish to finish."

The explorers started to examine all the walls that had the most complex art drawings. As they worked across from the east to the west side, at the highest levels, they narrowed the count to fifteen murals on as many walls worth closer inspection, spanning over 100 yards. Avey convinced them the drawings were related somehow to the tracings, "as far as I know, that's the only thing we have going for us."

The new agreement was they would vote on a potential match, comparing the paper images of the stones to those on the walls.

Nobody could suggest what they would do if they discovered any relevance even though Peter pushed for an outcome. He wanted it to be an absolute that would signal completion hoping if Karl resisted the group would harness him in, "If nothing matches, we pack it in."

"I hear you, Peter," Arthur confirmed but went no further with his affirmation, when Jude elbowed him.

"What are you doing?" Jude complained.

"Just balancing it out a little," Arthur noted, trying to soften the conflict between old friends.

To Peter's amazement, three walls were done and crossed off. It was faster than even he expected. Another wall was similar and some of the symbolic elements were identified as repeats. Jen immediately claimed it was an exact copy of one of the stones. Everyone's focus intensified. Letting the process work, Peter remained neutral not reacting with his usual displeasure. He sensed most of the group was beginning to fatigue, possibly looking forward to leaving the site. Rushing their deliberations about the mural that matched the drawings, the debate was about whether the artwork was a replica or a part of an unidentified larger schematic. To make sense of it, the walls were hypothetically numbered to keep every one straight on the ones which were being discussed. When compared, the artwork on the seventh, eighth, and ninth walls varied in complexity.

Sueto laid down, satisfied with just watching and listening as everyone moved to the walls farther away. Even Avey seemed to have dull allegiance to any progress.

Karl attempted to qualify a couple quick decisions, but there was instant disagreement, "Did we try it by matching the reverse side of the papers?"

"No need to," replied Avey. "On this wall, number seven, the drawing doesn't have the vertical blocking or slashes. Neither does this wall, number nine. The one in the middle has that funny shape like a pair of band aids, same shapes as number four did. That's it."

Jen used her handheld to scroll through single images, then reviewed the combined images while the others managed with the paper versions, "What wall are you standing in front of Avey?"

"Let's see, it should be nine, like I said."

"And I said a drawing matched wall four, right?"

"Yep."

"Karl, give me the single smudges for each of the stones. No combos."

After he collected and handed them over, Jen turned to Peter, "Let's take a walk to the other end. You guys stay put for a second."

There was no sign of reluctance from Peter until they got out of earshot.

"Ten," Jen spoke.

"Does this have a purpose or did you just want to hear me scream in private?"

"Yes and not really."

While walking along the stable portions of rock Jen counted the walls when they passed them, "There's fifteen walls with drawings correct?"

"And?"

"The one that matched was the fourth one in...eleven."

They had to climb down a hill of scree, walk across the roof, and boot climb up a short wall.

"If you do the math, a match should be on the twelfth wall, coming up."

"Figuring on what basis?"

"Alejandro said there are three deities. We have three stones with three designs. The match is on every fourth wall, with splits of three between them."

"No way," Peter rejected. "The Indians weren't that smart."

"Really? Hand-made stone structures lasting hundreds of years, a water system, and complex art. I guess math wouldn't be in their top ten."

Jen held up the drawing with her arm extended, looking beyond to the wall in front of them, "This is the third wall as a comparison. Nope."

She held up the next singular drawing rotating it. No match. She held up the third drawing and rotated it until it aligned.

"No go, huh?"

"It's this one. I was just eliminating the other two. You have the radio. Tell them the sixth, seventh, or eighth wall should map to something. And it's probably the main one, like a center of all this. What did Alejandro call it? Ocatac?"

"Crap. We'll never get out of here."

"Did you have plans tonight?"

"Yes. Leaving town and taking Jude with me."

Peter radioed the message hearing hoots in the background. They started back.

"Hang in there, Peter. Karl needs you. Regardless of what you think, he's in line first."

"Heard that one before."

Jen planted her feet so she could stop Peter's forward progress, turning him around by grabbing his jacket. Pulling him closer, she kissed his mouth, "There's time for us later. Let's give this thing what it needs."

Peter's immediate reluctance melted. It didn't feel like he was being played but maybe he was just a victim of circumstances. Sueto went out to greet them as they came up to the group studying the wall in fading light.

Avey had matched the three individual smudges that mirrored the wall's art. "You were right, Jen, but with a quirky twist. Look!"

Showing the drawing to the group – the collage of the three stones, two side by side with the third over the top, was the combination of design that had eluded them.

"When we smudged them in Brewer's basement, there were a multitude of combinations. Out of forty-eight, this one is it. Except the top drawing is upside down, probably exactly how you matched it before you radioed us, and the left side is reversed. I put a flashlight on it from behind while I compared. Whoever did this was genius."

"And, a section of these drawings are under the surface, with all this dirt blowing around," Jude said, showing the small trench he dug and cleaned the wall. "This lower border is unique to the drawing Avey has. We keep seeing part of the image that was repeated on all the walls."

Jen quickly preempted Peter's impatience, "Cool. So what now?"

Jude had completed his inspection, "Don't know exactly. There's three walls with art on them. This wall is solid. It's not like there's a door knob."

Karl came over from his examination with a flashlight, "It's kicking our asses. It's got seams, but all flat, nothing pitched or angled that would allow shifting."

Relieved, Peter took a deep breath and exhaled slowly.

Karl voiced his defeat, "Sorry, guys. I don't see any thing else other than the symbols matching. Maybe the murals are the last attempt to honor the Pueblo Gods. Like each smaller stone block is the thumb nail of the painted wall."

Jude couldn't resist asking if that meant the Acoma invented the first wallet sized photos.

Nobody responded but Karl who was becoming remorseful, "I have no idea how old they are. I don't know what else we can do. For bringing you all this way, I promise you dinner and endless drinks on me."

Alejandro was keenly disappointed, recognizing his grandfather's exaggerated claims, "He hung on the story long enough. Whatever the truth really was, I guess it changed from person to person."

"The heritage is real," Jude insisted. "These drawings are real. The stones are real. If we could just break the code!"

"I don't think there is a code," Karl relented, aware of its effect on his own mentor.

Jude didn't want to give up, "We have three walls with drawings that match the stones. Let's dig down and see if there's something a couple feet lower. You know there's been a lot accumulation over decades. I'll take the wall to the left. Clarke and Avey can do one."

The wind had transitioned from warm to refreshing bursts of cool breezes. Signaling the nightly storm, there would be a severe breach in the plenum of air rising from the basin. Dampened with sweat, each individual pawed through their gear, pulling out warm clothing and head lamps for the hike out. Oblivious to his master's regrets, Sueto had his nose down tracking another lizard when it flushed from its hiding spot. Shooting through the group, the dog took the shortest path, to head it off in the direction of the wall that had been examined. Karl brushed the sand off his gear from the dog's quick invasion and handed out lights that pulsated when twisted on.

"Here, clip these on so we don't lose anybody. I'll give you guys fifteen minutes. The storm is going to be on us pretty quick."

No one paid attention to the dog except Peter. Back and forth in one direction then another, he watched the dog sniff for the lizard. Then he went full tilt after it flushed from underneath a small rock. It looked as if both would hit the wall in their path. Instead the dog pulled up at the boundary and started digging.

"Alejandro, Sueto thinks he's going to excavate the lizard. He'll be here all night."

He walked over to the wall to pull the dog away, "Hey, guys! Come here!" he yelled.

Surrounded by loose clay and gravel, the conical hole dug at the base of the wall was six inches deep exposing a narrow shaft.

Karl came over first, followed by the others. He shined his light placing his hand at the opening, "It's not a snake hole."

"It's a tunnel isn't it?" Alejandro appealed.

"The air flow is a good indicator. Let's give it a shot."

Karl ran back to his pack, barely glancing at Peter. Both men knew what the new discovery meant. With a small scoop shovel, the lizard's escape route was made wider and then debris was removed to reestablish the air duct that was exposed minutes ago. Energy levels were taxed, but the younger individuals who were summoned back, were on knees scooping dirt as Karl carved the hole wider. Jude punched the bottom of the hole with a stick and cool air arrived in volume.

"Oooh! That feels good," Avey cooed, leaning forward at the hip, with her whole leg tucked and the other splayed out. It mattered that her thighs ached from the hike. She strained to get the small pack swung around to dump it out and twist back. And Arthur and Jude hustled to get the granular soil loose. With a single trowel between them, one used his conjoined fingers to sweep the material into the pack while the other gouged the earth. Their hands and finger tips felt the pending blisters and the abrasive quality of the miniscule rock shards. It mattered that their physical toil hurt, but they were working as a team. It mattered that their muscles were exhausted even if exhilaration masked the feat.

It all mattered. They didn't care who was fighting who or why there was disbelief and suspended loyalty. They didn't care that the rain began splattering against the decayed plaster finishes of the existing walls and starting to interfere with their progress. They didn't care if the hole had to be one foot or ten foot deep. All of their energy mattered now. To track Worthington. To steal the black books. To learn the contents of the black books. To meet Alejandro and his grandfather. To get to the top of the mesa. To find the truth.

Jude reached his arm down, fully extended, "The wall still goes the entire length."

While more debate about the existence of a cave took the form of what-ifs, Karl stood up and walked towards Peter, "Let's talk."

Reaching a structural corner out of earshot, Karl leaned up against the wall, "Maybe you're still pissed off but you know there's gotta be something behind the wall."

Peter's jaw jut forward. His mannerism was of dejection and self-pride. He shook his head, moving to the more obvious issue, "Did you see that it's probably going to downpour?"

"Yep. I'm going to send Alejandro back down before it hits. He can lead you and Jen back."

"I'm staying. So is Jen."

"I'm saying you were right. You called me on it. You can leave."

"What about Jude, Arthur, and Avey? Who's got their back?"

Karl thought he yielded, "Take them."

"You know damn well they'll want to stay. And I'm responsible for Jude, not you."

Karl got a faint sniff of Peter's resentment and reiterated his own, "Maybe you don't but these kids actually cared about Bud. He was ostracized and the board practically shut him down. He was moving funds here and there just to keep searching for this, giving funds to the tribe. It's real. It needs to be discovered. His stuff needs to go public somehow."

Peter didn't want to waste time again hearing about Karl's motives, "I get it, Karl. You're the de facto replacement. You'll make it all happen. What I don't get is *why* is it you?"

Karl pushed off the wall and shifted his weight forward, ready for what, he wasn't sure.

Peter continued the verbal assault, "You've got money, you go off and try this, dabble in that. Everyone else has to make a living. Then this whole thing ramps and you're like what? The poster child for the Acoma! The whole world is being monitored by thousands of experts and we're suddenly the only ones saving it?"

"Wren and Looks are on board. You've seen their stuff."

"When the fuck haven't they been?"

Along with the increasing rain, a mixture of resentment and latent anger had resurfaced. A small gust of wind blew into the doorway lifting the thin layer of the remaining dust into the air. Both men listened for a moment hearing the yells from the group.

Following audible stomps Jude appeared in the doorway, "Hey, guys. I don't want to bust your love fest, but we've got the hole dug. We're at the bottom edge and there's a cave or something. We have to decide which side of the wall we're going to be on. The storm looks bad."

Pausing a couple seconds until Jude left, Peter was still indignant, "We're not going to solve it here. I'm sticking around for Jude's sake. When we get back don't count on me. Period!" he stated with permanence.

"Fine by me. You'll be missed."

People change. Karl realized he didn't like Peter and maybe it was a fluke they ever got along. Pelted by light rain coming in at an angle they walked back to the group. Given by the last golden rays, a partial rainbow embracing the back ridge went unnoticed.

Karl took Alejandro aside, "You need to go down and let your grandfather know what we found and our exact location."

"I want to stay and help."

"I know. But if something happens to us, you'll be our way out. There's no one else I trust to get down quickly and make it back. You know this area better than anyone."

His disappointment for the right reasons was refreshing to Karl.

"You're not going to miss the most important part if we find something. Handing it over to your grandfather."

They spoke for minutes then hugged.

"Sueto. Let's go."

Jen saw that he was leaving, "Alejandro, thank you! Your grandfather is going to proud of you!"

Avey and Arthur said they'd see him in a little while. Jude looked up from his position, shoulder high in the vertical crater and nodded to his friend. Their glances confirmed the bond that had been developing since they met.

Watching until he was out of sight, his attention turned back to the task of getting the hole large enough to survey beyond the wall. In turns with Arthur, they lowered the depth beyond the bottom edge of the wall, clearing the dirt levy from underneath the barrier. Jude cut in foot holes for climbing out. With the storm blackening the sky, they enhanced their vision with flash lights.

"How is it, Jude?" Avey said peering into the hole, "It looks creepy."

"Don't remind me."

With no notice, Jude grabbed Avey's arms, pulling her down. He screamed, "The ground is moving!" he cried out. "Something's got my leg. It's biting me!"

Avey screamed as well and blurted out something but she was so frightened the words mumbled together.

Jude started laughing, "Oh my God! Was that you trying to save me?"

She snatched her composure back and pushed herself off Jude's chest, "You dork! I thought you were really...hurt!"

With a swing, loamy soil flew when she hit Jude with the makeshift bucket.

Everyone else who had come running was perturbed with Jude, especially Peter, "It's bad enough with the weather! Stop screwing around!"

Passing Jen, Karl walked back to the gear that had been moved to the nearest overhang and started re-sorting to take only needed items, "He's working on asshole right now, moving up from being a jerk. Tell everybody to make their way in here and we'll get set up."

Three static bursts on his radio was a positive update from Alejandro. They had switched to parallel channels different from the others.

Gathered, Karl assigned caving gear and specific duties to each member, then separated them into teams of two, "We can leave the rest here and collect it on the way out."

"If we get out," Jude whispered to Avey just before she elbowed him in the gut. "Oh! That one hurt. Owww. You win."

"Is everyone okay with the arrangements? No complaints? Before you get in the hole, turn on your blinks. They last about twelve hours."

The first helmeted crew emerged out of stone structure headed straight for the hole. The following team waited for a wave or hoot before following.

Karl planned that if the preceding team didn't signal that meant they were in trouble. He deliberately made sure the instructions were understood, assuming Peter would appreciate the attention to risk. Switching their headlights on at the sump, Karl and Jude saw the collection of drainage at the bottom.

He looked off angle at Jude to avoid the glare, raising his voice to be heard above the wind, "Peter's going to see this and freak. Pass back that we need to cover the hole with the tarp."

Karl hunched down and attempted to slide under the wall. With his length, he couldn't completely lay flat, so guided his feet under the wall, allowing his hips to lower. Jutting forward, he was able to lie on his back and shimmy underneath the barrier. Jude watched his partner's supine body half disappear and then with more wiggling, the hole had consumed him. One second. Five seconds. Fifteen seconds. Thirty seconds! Quickly, Jude adjusted his beam, lighting the entire bottom of the passage. Rain pelted the hole with more intensity as he dared himself not to panic. Indecisive, he looked back at the group about ready to signal for help. Finally, a hand thrust back with an "ok" sign.

On his back. Karl's headlight shot straight up as he pressed upwards after he had breached the wall on the opposite side. With forearms, he lifted his upper torso, quickly engaging the flood lamp in his free hand. Not breathing, he checked the patch sensor on his vest to see if it detected fatal air, then exhaled and welcomed the oxygen. A full breath eased tensions as the explorer sat in the undercut established as a portal into a sanctified Earth. The more sensitive detection gauge indicated no alarms for dangerous thresholds of atmospheric imbalances. At first stoic, he shivered with a sense of fright. *It had to be hundreds of years since light had penetrated the sacred cave.*

His mind calmed when his ocular senses, strained from darkness, articulated a large cavern with more artwork. He easily imagined early craftsmen etching their scripts on the wall. Convincing himself nothing evil could be resident, Karl activated his timer. Kneeling in a trench that was tiered on the inward side as broad steps leading to a level floor, he thrust his arm under the wall signaling, an "ok". Muffled scrape sounds came from the opposite side as a pack and metal container were dropped from his partner.

Another lamp was positioned to compliment the one pointed towards the back of the room. Flooded with thoughts of Dr. Bud Worthington, Karl looked up to the partially illuminated ceiling of fifteen feet at its apex. In retrospect, if they had stopped searching earlier, he would have followed Bud's failed path. He cleared another pack with feelings of jubilation.

Relieved, Jude continued to lower supplies into the hole. When his share was done he jumped in and hooted. Before going under the wall he paused, talking with Arthur and reminded him to lower all his gear before they got in. His nerves sensitized, Jude squirmed completely under the wall and as he lifted his head, peered inside of the cavern with similar awe. Against the dark orange strata, their personal red strobe flashers were backlit by waterproof flood lamps.

"When everybody gets here, it'll qualify for a rave. This is amazing!"

Both men expected to see two additional entryways from lateral directions.

"Karl. The two other walls with images? Were they bogus?"

"It's just a big puzzle I guess. We're lucky the dog dug in the right place."

The gear and remaining members all made it inside within a half hour. The last team fixed the tarp over the hole, spanned underneath by an eroded ladder pole, and slid into place by Peter who crouched to anchor the tarp for the worsening conditions.

Huddled together, kneeling or sitting, heads bobbed in different directions to warrant off freakish suspicions. Pupils, dilated from their adrenaline, pulsated when vision was impacted by glare. Hushed comments reverberated off the walls. Everyone started to whisper so gently that the enunciations were overemphasized with their lips and hands.

"I can't believe I'm here. This is scary and serene at the same time," Avey shared.

"Yes!" Jen nodded. "I don't know if I'm frightened or excited. It's cold though." She let her breath out to confirm she could see it and leaned into Peter for warmth.

"I'd have to say I'm awestruck," Peter admitted, looking at Karl who started to unwrap the stones from the cloth, laying them in the middle of the group. He had bragged earlier the stones were their official good luck charms.

Karl glimpsed upward, smiled, and pulled out the smudge depicted on the outside of the entry wall and the single line tracings Avey had completed in the car, "Okay, first no one is getting dizzy, right?" Karl asked and rechecked the carbon monoxide detector. No one spoke. "We have to keep in mind that the air supply may be tainted or insufficient. You all have masks and a fifteen minute canister.

Karl looked at everyone, "Hey, it's serious, but you can smile." Then he continued, "The drawings look like a close match to the artwork on the entryways on the back wall over there. Likely there's multiple paths leading to another place. I doubt the channels are weaponized. Pueblo tribes used spears and stuff, but I don't know what kind of weaponry they would incorporate in a place like this to protect it. The front wall was the big stopper. And somehow these stones figure into it. Any thoughts?"

Everyone had suggestions about using caution, moving very slowly, staying with their assigned partner, and what they should do if someone were injured.

Karl continued his instructions, "Remember the buddy system and keep checking with each other. We'll use the same routine. Do not take other routes when we retreat. We come back out the same way we went in, unless we're blocked."

"It's amazing the natives could carve out a place like this," Jen uttered.

"Centuries of laborers," Karl replied matter-of-factly. "This could have been a prayer room or for ceremony."

Arthur studied the paper drawings, "Karl, the drawing Avey did with a dark line embedded into the rest of the pattern. It looks like a maze."

"Good catch. I'll reposition the light on the back wall showing the other entrances. Let's move that way and check it out. Oh, and hooting is banned."

Giggling bounced off the surfaces.

The rear team marked the passageway to the outside with a reflective patch adhered to the wall. The lead team moved with personal lights scanning in all directions forward. As Avey took pictures of the walls that were basked in light, they all shuffled towards the multiple passages. Karl was encouraged that the three paper smudges matched the decoration encircling the three archways. The immediate conclusion everyone repeated was each stone should be taken down that segment of the tunnel.

Avey asked for the lights to remain still and she recorded the three images and proposed an idea, "Unless anyone's strongly against it, let's each take a path."

"I'm concerned," Peter replied. "If we split up and run into trouble, that's going to create problems for getting us out."

Karl showed patience, withstanding Peter's earlier personal accusations, "I agree, but I'm also concerned for time."

"Do we have to finish it all tonight? I realize everybody is pumped, but can we call it a day and come back?" Peter tested.

Karl looked at his watch. It was ten after ten.

"What if we walk out of here and for any number of reasons we can't make it back," he guessed.

Peter was going to interrupt, but Karl out-whispered him, "We've also exposed the entry point. We've got to fill it in as well. And it's probably raining like a mother out there. We're dry. We've got lights and snacks."

"Okay, okay. It was just a suggestion."

Ignoring Peter's obvious motives, Karl tapped Jude on the arm, "How about we go down this route, check it out, return and the next group can go, then the next."

"Works for me," Jen answered, "Then we have the manpower if something happens."

All were positive with that option except Peter, miffed again with the occupants' optimism. Avey handed them the proper stone and the first team started into the middle shaft, half crouched. The remaining cavers gathered at the first portal quietly watching and listening. Peering into the middle tunnel, the light beams were partially blocked out. In places, the tunnel width narrowed to less than three feet, forcing the explorers to turn their upper torsos parallel to the wall.

In her softest voice, Avey shared her fears. "I hope to God there's not a booby trap."

As the sedentary group heard the echo of helmets chafing against the rock, all realized their inactivity allowed exhaustion to seep inward. Jen sunk to her knees leaning back against Peter. The remaining members switched off their headlamps letting the beams of the flood lamps reflect on them.

Silent, Jen's thoughts wandered as her eyes studied the art forms. Her back muscles were temperate and began to feel warmth from her lifelong friend. As he repositioned himself to support more of her weight, the simple care embodied a hint of seduction.

Jen thoughts shifted to them as a couple. *Maybe this trip is a restart of our relationship.* She couldn't chance asking him or even bring up the subject in front of the group. She embraced the joining of their bodies and the aspect of protection.

Tired, she could easily meld into his, "I could go to sleep right here."

Nothing. She moved her hand blindly on his thigh gently squeezing his leg. Waiting for a subtle reciprocation, she whispered, "Peter—"

"Shhh. I hear something."

The scratching sounds and thuds that had completely disappeared resounded as thin beams of light blinded Arthur, "They're coming back," he reported. Their teammates' shared bulk reached the threshold.

"The paper map was accurate enough to guide us to an alcove," Jude boasted his claim, "It's a dead end. But we're sure it's a doorway!"

Karl explained their shared optimism from the examination in the tunnel, "We think we understand what the Acoma did to protect this internal domain. These guys weren't a warring tribe on the offensive. They were typically defenders, so they would have developed complicated systems to defeat or confuse."

Jude butted in, "It's a maze! There are other paths. We didn't go down them, just stayed on the pencil line." He patted Avey on the back.

Karl lowered his voice after Jude's outburst, "So far, everything is based on the triad deity. All three stones represent the complete design on the walls outside and the maze on the inside. Imagine if anyone had shown up without the stones or just one of them. They would have had a difficult or impossible time proceeding. At the end of the tunnel, there's a wall that has a built-in receptacle that will probably accept one of these stones."

Karl explained further, "This is probably why their weights are different. Paul Brewer measured almost a pound variance between this one and the others."

Peter wasn't buying into the theories and answered back, "Don't you think it's strange, that if someone were to eventually retrieve whatever is on the other side of those walls, it is completely dependent upon three pieces of rock that could have disappeared or even broke?"

Karl didn't hesitate debunking Peter's guesses, "The whole world skipped over this place and ignored Amado's stories. He said they found another safe haven to preserve the stones. Other than the completely random thief in Mesa Verde, the pieces were secure. If it's all a big accident then I'm definitely okay with getting lucky."

"You guys have nothing to fight about," Jude demanded, trying to stop the argument. He wasn't going to let their rivalry displace the extraordinary journey that began with Bud's invitation to discover an unknown past and future. "It was me and Clarke who pulled *you* in so you're here as a favor," he directed at Peter. "And nobody gave a shit about what Bud was doing, except Amado. So if anyone got *lucky*, it was him."

When Peter was about to answer, Jen laid down her terms, "If you guys are going to keep at each other, take it outside," she demanded.

Peter backed off. Even he was fatigued with the conflict.

Reminded to anchor the reflective patches so they were visible from two directions, Arthur and Avey got their lights situated and started down the left hand maze.

"And put them at each intersection," Karl insisted.

"Just stay on your drawing and you'll be fine," Jude reminded them.

Karl had handed his CO_2 gauge to Arthur, "There were no problems for us, but keep watching it."

Concern grew for the second team because they were fourteen minutes longer than the first pair, but apprehension quickly dissolved when similar noise came from the tunnel as they returned.

"What a trip! A little scary, but awesome!" were Arthur's first words.

"It's the same deal you described. A carve out in the wall. Avey had a mirror, so we bounced our light into it. There's a round ball or the top of a knob in there about half the length of the stone. Did you guy's hear Avey scream?

"We thought it was you," Jude teased.

Arthur continued, ignoring his friend, "We saw a snake. I don't know what kind it was, going down another route. We tried the radio, but just got static bursts."

Entirely confident, Jude turned to the remaining pair, "You guys want me to take this?"

Jen took the paper map from him, "We're consenting adults and we're going solo. No kids allowed."

Peter prepared his gear, and then stepped into the doorway, waiting for Jen, "If anything happens, make sure you tell them it wasn't my idea."

"No, we'll give you all the credit," Jude assured making fun of Peter's fear of interment. "Here's lies Mr. Childs. A good geologist, who got sucked in by his friends."

With it taking an additional seven minutes beyond Avey and Arthur's round trip, Karl was getting ready to go down the passage for an improvised rescue.

"Hold it!" Jude cautioned. "Listen."

Muted voices funneled back through the right hand maze. Louder thumping and scrapes could be heard, and then Jen emerged with Peter yards behind her.

"Damn. That scared me. I didn't know I'd be phobic down there. My sweat was sweating."

Jude reported the data points on his altimeter device, "At the end of our maze it was cooler, but the air we let in at the entrance was warmer. It's gone up six degrees in this section. The rest isn't going to warm up unless we knock down the front wall."

"Is everyone ready to return?" Karl prompted, anxious to work the next problem. The group huddled again. Acclimated to their surroundings the experience remained surreal, with their senses still at a disadvantage. Light beams cutting through the absolute darkness caused their eyes to continually adjust to harsh intensities. Hearing was difficult because low sounds deadened against the oblique surfaces while higher tones reverberated. Their skin was clammy with humidity from their own body vapor. To the nose, mixed odors of their own sweat was sour and there was a faint whiff of what Jude identified as "new asphalt."

"We all know our routes. I've separated out the essential gear so we avoid jamming ourselves. Jude and I will take two of the containers and you guys can have one each."

"Why bother?" questioned Peter. "It will slow us down."

"Because it'll save us time if they're needed," Karl insisted. "We've been in here ninety minutes already, give or take a century traveling back in time. Let's get positioned at the end of the routes and start tinkering with the stones to see if anything happens."

Arthur returned from checking out their main exit, "The rain is still coming down hard and there's water collecting on our side now. The hole is not blocked but I could hear the tarp flapping."

"After thirty minutes, whether we figure it out or not, the teams come back out," Karl announced.

Home of Alejandro's Aunt. Acoma Pueblo.

After the late shift, the daughter was not happy walking into her home, "He's stunk up the house! Father!"

Amado had boiled herbs and roots on the stove then mashed them in a modern day bowl. A skunk odor permeated the air.

Finding the elder in the back bedroom, the daughter was not respectful of the trance she disrupted, "Father! I've told you not to cook those roots in the house. It takes days to get rid of the smell!"

His eyes slowly opened, "*No saludarías a tus antepasados si aparecieran?*" [71]

She ignored his placation taking the raw mash and headed to the back yard to dump the stew. Resuming his meditation in the darkened bedroom, Amado pushed out all interference to be at full strength. Sitting with knees pulled to chest, his preparation instructed his soul to release and allow spirit animals to commit deeds. Many before him had not achieved this gift nor had he ever shared his ability to do so.

"He will be the death of me!" she confided to her brother calling him after dinner, complaining of their father's behavior. They exchanged memories of Mother yelling at her stubborn husband and pleading that he needed to take his concoctions "out to the desert so Mother Earth could scold him as well."

Upset he brewed the mixture, she knew it was a sign he was delving into his old ways, but for reasons she didn't understand.

"Did Alejandro tell you?" she asked her brother. "About the old earth professor? A group of strangers is looking for Father. He's been acting strange and up to his old tricks. Alejandro must have taken him to get the roots!"

As the explorers exited the great room, the pulsating red blinks clipped to the jackets began to fill the tunnels. Each team shuffled towards another protected sanctity of unknown value or risk. Most proficient of the teams, Karl and Jude reached the wall first. The six by six foot barricade was semi-smooth, very cold, and damp to the touch. Three feet high from the ground and centered, was a tooled arch extending over a narrow shaft, believed to be a primitive locking device. While Karl examined the wall for detail, Jude carefully aligned the block key to the shaft and inserted it into the small well no more than an inch then flipped the stone and repeated the process.

"The seams are perfected by smoothing," Karl reported. "It looks like they were stuccoed with fine-grained cement."

"So they were probably separate blocks at one time?"

---

[71] "Would you not greet your ancestors if they were to appear?"

"Yes. Then were precision fit by sanding the edges. You'd need a heavy maul to crack them, but with compression of the enormous weight, the segments would still need to be chiseled out."

With trial and error Jude thought he had discovered the best way to insert the stone, "I hope the others are just as careful. I don't know if we're going to lose these once they're inserted."

"Go for it."

The stone was positioned, with the symbol facing them, the deeper pattern towards the back. The grooves were the mechanical edges that aligned to the cylinder, much like the metal key on a tumbler lock.

"The Egyptians have nothing on these guys," Karl quipped.

The stone sunk halfway and settled.

"Can you lift it back out?"

Upon doing so, Jude let the stone settle back into slot and grabbed the block to apply force to twist it.

"It doesn't rotate," he reported, trying again in both directions. "But when it drops in you can hear something. Listen."

Straining to remain absolutely still, holding their breath, they heard other sounds.

"Maybe the sides of the walls share the release," Karl thought.

A couple double arm thrusts on the opposite sides of the wall cracked the seam. Karl inserted the edge of his scraper into the hairline fracture to remove the residue from the margin. They were anxious with only four minutes left before heading back to their take off point.

"Did you hear that? I wasn't even touching the stone," Karl whispered, placing his ear tight to the ancient jamb. I think the others are having an effect."

Avey and Arthur were in position working the key more aggressively. Arthur believed he understood the mechanism, comparing it to bank vaults that had connecting internal rods and locks that pinned the vault door shut. Applying force on their lock failed because Jen and Peter were slow to do anything with their stone. On the moment they jiggled their key into place, the interior bolts released on theirs and their partners' doors. Arthur and Avey heard the mechanism, and worked to rotate their door finding it was on a central pivot.

Avey offered her sneaker from the artificial limb to jam the rotating wall, "Hey, untie my shoe. I'm not getting locked in here."

Arthur wasn't sure he even wanted to go further. He took her shoe off hesitating.

"Don't worry. I won't stub my toe."

Calcified, the other teams' doors did not open. Jude and Karl heard muffled sounds again.

"Push on that side, then I'll do mine."

Jude sat on his butt, placing his feet flat against the wall and pushed. A scraping sound of rock surprised both men as the stone blockade shifted inward.

"You moved it!" Karl said loudly as he applied his shoulder to the wall. It rotated open, surrendering another length of tunnel. When Karl adjusted his headlamp he could see it emptied forty yards away into another room.

"We did it!"

Covering Jude's headlamp simultaneously, he reached up turning his off his light, "Someone else made it in there!"

A faint light danced across the end of their passage.

"Sweet."

Office of Willard Colton.

The military was a safe haven for Colton. For his idealism. Ruthlessly coached by his father, he was emboldened to take risks and deal with the consequences. Fully amplified with credentials and gut instinct, he rarely savored the jumping off spot he created, severing contact with his father. So much farther ahead and so far back, he left him. The call that came five years ago was not a sorrowful bridge of flooding remorse. It came at the time Colton was in Asia. His mother waited for a response to her devastating news about her mate. Her eyes sadden even more when his response was deflection, and not respect or love. Military allowed Colton to transform and shield himself from raw emotion. Every mission had its perks, but power was the addictive quality he sought for most. Power with authority. Authority mandating compliance. Consequences for resistance.

After setting resources in motion that afternoon, Colton felt he could easily crush Hyatt, even though their earlier showdown revealed a collapse of the political strengths the NEADE boss had relied upon. His own team would have to help void the indiscretions.

A bunch of pansy asses hiding behind Congressional appointments, Colton thought as he belted down two fingers of Bourbon, looking out at the maze of lighted city infrastructure. *Let's see what the college snots are really up to.*

With gear packed he headed to the rear plaza of the NEADE complex. Couriered to the heliport on campus he resumed travel on a military chopper to oversee the new mission. With an ETA of twenty-four hundred, there would be forty personnel actively deployed in a "search and rescue." Textbook for Colton, it was one way to exploit the sovereign rights of a Native reservation without due process.

With the heightened storm activity, a night search in the desert had low probability of drawing attention. Tracing the suspects to over the state line into Arizona, a senior mission commander reported the ongoing surveillance of their vehicles that were tagged with GPS devices. Early planning monitored the incoming weather pattern for hazardous conditions and a green light was given, ignoring a low pressure system that would bring in gusts of forty knots. Over military voice comm, Colton was excited about the prospects, "You say there's a perch at the top?"

"Yes, sir."

"On my go, we'll get some drops from there. Let's kick ass."

Inside la cuidad sagrada.

360453N 1090812W

Yelling out loud felt like breaking a code of conduct. Ignoring the two waves of static on his radio, excitement overwhelmed Karl as he and Jude scrambled down the rock tube that emptied into a final destination. Carved with blunt instruments, shale and rock dust lay scattered on the uneven floor of the polygon-shaped room; it was a miniature of the first room. Two of the three access tunnels were empty as four explorers crouched, concerned for the remaining team.

"Go up that other channel and see," Karl ordered.

When Arthur started to walk up the remaining chute, he saw Peter and Jen slowly moving towards him. With all accounted for Avey began taking pictures of the stationary object in front of them.

"In sixty or so feet," Karl interjected while coughing, "we just traveled forward in time by two or three hundred years."

Everybody got the logic that the room would be the youngest section of the maze system because it would have been the last section to be completed.

Karl studied the stone structure they had surrounded, "This massive coffin could date back farther. It was probably used elsewhere before being moved here."

"They didn't spend much time decorating it," Avey remarked.

"Probably to conceal the value of its contents. It's just a big rock," Karl theorized.

With the fine dust particles floating in the light beams, breathing the musty air in the antechamber was unpleasant. Hunched down, six gentiles surrounded the triangle segment of rock raised a few feet from the floor.

Arthur knelt to avoid scraping his helmet again, prompting a complaint, "I was having fun, but it sucks in here. Can we getting moving?"

Karl selected a brush from his pack and lightly skimmed the surface of the opaque tomb looking for more clues.

"It's obvious our keys go in the slots," Jude prompted. "This hole is grooved like our pieces."

"Just covering our bases. It might be booby-trapped," Karl cautioned.

"Crap," Peter blurted, knowing he'd have to retrace his steps, "We left our block in the door." He returned a couple minutes later.

Finished with the cursory examination, the teams shuffled to opposite corners and began to wiggle their stones into the slots.

Once fitted, Jude noticed the rock slid easily, "If we let go of these, we're probably not getting them back without some dynamite."

He let his go. With a sharp clunk sound, the top edge of his stone key was below the surface of the coffin. Avey dropped hers in and the same ratchet noise came from their corner.

"Come on, Peter, drop it," Jen encouraged.

"Hold on! Did anyone notice the passage relocks itself?"

"You didn't jam yours open?" Jude shot back.

"We did!" Arthur stated. Avey punched him for taking credit.

"Okay, so we didn't read the safety manual. We'll follow you out." Peter released his stone, but the sound was muted.

"You took too long, now it won't work," Arthur kidded.

Karl motioned for Jude to move to the opposite corner. On their knees, they hit the upper sides of the monument with their palms, leaving sweat prints on the surface. Applying more force, Karl shoved his shoulder into the side.

When he was satisfied nothing changed, he lay parallel to inspect the edges with light, "The lid is eight inches thick or so. If we team up with our combined weight, we might budge the corner that's caught."

The women shifted behind the men so they could exert group force.

"I've got a small drill if we have to get serious with it."

Karl's statement was followed by a grunt and the gashing of metal hitting the jammed corner. The force of Avey's titanium prosthesis sheared off a small section from the lid as she stood perpendicular to it. A stunned silence was preserved as Avey sat back down and reattached herself.

"Way to go, Avey!" Jude hooted, his voice booming in the small area.

"You said it was just a big rock," she said wistfully. "I didn't mean to scare everybody. That's just my game face."

The gap in the lid exposed the inside corner of the vault. Gripping the cracked end, the men were able to pivot the top, breaching the container. Protected for centuries, lights revealed the linen-wrapped pieces. As others peered over shoulders, each piece was laid on the ground and unwrapped for brief inspection. Wiping sweat from his face, Karl re-laced the superficial hand-woven material ready to instantly deflect any debate about his next decision, "I'm ready for the containers."

Avey listened to the echo noise between their short bursts of dialogue. She could hear clothing rubbing and helmets clacking. Their feet scuffed the ground as they repositioned from kneeling to squatting. She felt the raising temperature of six bodies dissipating moist heat.

"It's starting to feel good..." A new sound preempted her claim. "I hear dripping. Listen!"

Head lamps began searching like beams advertising across a sky. A thin funnel of water streamed along a precipice across the back edge of a small dihedral. Multiple cracks were servicing the flow that had reached the enormous depths of the dense rock. The floor of the cave had become slippery in places where access moisture mixed with the layer of dust.

"If rain made it in here it must be a flood outside," Peter worried, "How do we know this place won't fill up?"

"These don't look water logged, but there's always a first time," Jude replied.

With that penetrating fear, Karl worked diligently with a deliberate pace to protect the fragile relics. Minor rework was accomplished to fit the foam precisely to the perimeter of the stoneware. Jude inserted balloon liners into the hollow portions of the stoneware and filled them with porous foam. Faces dripping with perspiration watched the operation repeated to fill the remaining two cases.

As he looked again at the water accumulation, Karl waited a couple minutes for the foam to reach its proper flex. The exterior pottery surfaces were reinforced with a waterproof liner and nudged into position inside the containers. More spray foam was injected to negate small voids. Once the spray material had matured, the metal skinned boxes were closed and locking turn screws were tightened.

"Pretty slick, huh?" Karl declared, pleased with the efforts and doled out one case each to the other teams leaving two for himself and Jude.

"These can take a beating and they're waterproof."

"At least if the pottery breaks, it'll be contained," Arthur assumed out loud.

"Yes, but just the same, don't use it to protect yourself from Avey."

Satisfied everyone was ready, Karl and Jude retreated up their tunnel. To avoid the chance Karl would be assisting him, Peter guided Jen who was behind Arthur and Avey. As the only dissenter to their quest, Peter began to think of consequences. He wondered if his deep resentments were going to be challenged.

He had pictured a different outcome. He thought the black books would get boring and the students would give up. He thought the artifacts would be taken by the Acoma. He was surprised Amado was even alive let alone sane. And there were lots of opportunity to quit searching. Demoralized, he continued moving his feet forward inches at a time waiting for Avey and Arthur to swivel the wall, to enter back through the maze tunnel.

Milliseconds before a conscious reaction, Peter heard the abrupt scream. He heard the grind of his helmet and felt his head hitting the side of the tunnel. He realized Jen's body was propelled backward initiating the collision. The slippery floor compromised his footing as he caught the brunt of her mass. His senses reignited, Peter saw the root cause of the disruption in the three beams of agitated lights surrounded by a green glow. Avey was halfway through the scant opening struggling to free herself. Her arm had been yanked forward when she retrieved her sneaker.

Arthur reacted quickly pulling on her waist and slipped, causing the domino effect. Scrambling to his feet he tried to leap frog over Avey to attack the intruder in dark camo. Peter pivoted Jen back towards the anteroom and sprung forward as well. He slithered through the opposite channel that formed when the wall pivoted open. Arthur grabbed the attacker around the hips and failed again. Jabbed in the upper chest, he was thrown backward. With the attacker's strength, Avey was constricted, still squirming to free herself. Certain he could overpower the others, the enemy solider used her as a shield as he ordered them to the ground, but that and another command was ignored.

Alert to an opportunity, Peter rotated the wall crushing the attacker's shoulders, allowing Avey to lower her torso and fall through his legs. When he swung the student behind him, his foot planted on her prosthesis causing it to come loose as she fell back. Instantaneously, the invader turned to fend off a renewed effort from Arthur.

Peter forcefully raised the metal shaft from the ground into the soldier's groin area. When another blow connected to the soldier's head, he suddenly dropped. Sliding their assailant backwards into the tunnel, force was applied to close the entryway effectively ending the one man invasion. Out of breath, the gang held their sides checking for wounds.

"We're lucky there was only one!" Jen winced.

Arthur nodded, "Yeah but, why only one?"

"Probably the alpha. Tried to score on his own," Avey said between breathes laughing at herself trying to balance on one leg.

When they realized one container had been left in the chamber with its captive, the hesitation was fleeting.

"It doesn't matter! Go!" Peter urged as he stayed behind propping up Avey as she put her leg back on.

"I owe you, Peter. I'm sorry I—"

"I got it. Let's just get the hell outta here!"

With bruises and scrapes they filed back to the great room. Isolated from the brutal foray, Jude and Karl were alarmed when they heard Peter's voice.

"What's his problem now?" Jude complained, having just transported some of the gear and the first metal case to the other side of the wall. He was soaked from passing under the outside barrier that had become a dam.

All four survivors emptied into the cavern noticing the reflections of ripples above the point of entry.

"We got ambushed!"

Emotionally charged, their voices were no longer constrained. With the intrusion of many conversations, Peter explained their ordeal, "One guy. He had camo and night vision."

"He grabbed me!"

"Peter nailed him his junk, then his head," Arthur recounted, slapping Peter on the back.

"He's out cold, but he's locked in there now."

"In where we got the artifacts?" Karl asked.

"We shut the door on him. He can't get out. There's no keys remember?" Peter claimed.

"*That* door may be shut," Karl replied, "but I left ours open for Alejandro."

Jen noticed Jude was drenched, about to ask why and he obliged, "The tarp blew off. Short story, you'll be in the dunk tank in a minute."

He put his beam on Karl, "All clear out there."

One by one, the team lay prone in the water holding their breath resisting the cold and their physical exhaustion, to negotiate the deep pools of water on both sides.

"Keep your eyes closed because of the soot," Jude cautioned.

"It can't get worse. Might as well add swimming to the experience," Jen submitted when it was her turn. She quickly disappeared under the breach. Karl and Jude kept their eye on the maze entries as the others retreated.

"You go, Jude."

It was impossible to see an outline of him once the student went into the green brown water. In reverse order, Karl was alone in the cave as before. The original ecosystem, a bastion of sanctified caverns and channels had been permanently exploited by mortal disruption.

Lying on his chest, Karl struggled with the buoyancy to push the last carton through, and then his pack. To clear the path for his friend, Jude collected the articles from his exterior perch. Glancing back at the remaining lamp Karl got into position and with a rapid but forceful transition, he pushed through the hole coming up on the other side, standing in rib deep water. He quickly wiped his eyes to see Jude reaching for his arm. The strong wind gusts were carrying substantial amounts of rain.

"Any signs of others?"

"No."

He smiled. Avey must have been right, "Good."

As Jude was helping him up, Karl's expression changed, "He's got me!"

"Ya right. Psych!"

Losing his upward momentum, Karl lost his grip and completely submerged. No detail was possible looking into the murky pool. Unable to enter the hole, Jude saw his partner's body gyrate, trying to survive.

Jude thrust himself chest down on the ground and reached in probing. With his headlamp he could see blood streaks in the water. Without warning, Karl stood up gasping for air colliding with Jude.

"I'm okay. It's his blood!" Karl shouted, "He bashed his head into the wall when I jerked back. He had my throat!"

Scratch marks were visible on Karl's neck as he lightly massaged the front of his wind pipe.

Jude yelled for help as his partner submerged again to retrieve the victim, lifting the upper torso above the water, "We've got to pull him out so he doesn't drown."

With extraordinary effort, the soldier was extracted from the sump and carried over to the closest hovel.

"As soon as he comes to, he'll be right back at us," Jen feared. With a belt and spare cord they bound his hands and feet, covering him with a tarp to minimize exposure. Jude returned from an adjacent rooftop running to the group.

"I saw lights and I think I heard a helicopter above us. There are probably more of them on their way!"

Arthur decided to search the many pockets of their captive, setting the revolver to the side, not knowing how to remove the clip.

He found a small device with blinking LEDs that he unclipped from an inside vest pocket and inspected, "The amber is probably power. This one is...it's transmitting!"

"How do you know?" tested Peter.

"Because the logo says GPS tracker! It's been sending all along!"

"Raise your hand if anyone wants to give up!" Jude announced looking directly at Peter. "I'm not. These guys are going to have to earn these containers."

Amado's warnings had come true. Reluctantly, Karl pushed the group one last time, "We're all better off if you guys start heading down. I'll stay here with the soldier. He still has a pulse. I don't want an accidental death on my hands."

In the increasing wind and steady rain, a debate could have raged on about what their next move should have been. Peter could tell Jen wanted to keep possession of their metal box. *She'll get tired of dealing with it* he thought.

Karl yelled enforcing his request, "Peter! This is what you wanted! Take Jen and start down! Ditch your container if you think you're going to get caught. Arthur! You and Avey need to take a different route so you're not bunched up. These guys will have a harder time climbing around in their gear. You're a lot more mobile without a container."

Jude kneeled beside Karl whispering, "Should I hide ours?"

"It's not supposed to happen that way. Get your gear and switch cases with me."

"Why?"

"I'm not sure, but do it." Karl wanted to say more than he did. "If these guys take possession of *these* artifacts, we'll never see them again. The others are the diversion. Go!"

Jude went into the next adobe to collect his pack and other gear. He ran back to Karl after pretending to check on the unconscious soldier. Patting Karl on the shoulder, he headed south, running parallel to the head wall retracing steps back to area he, Arthur, and Avey ascended earlier that day.

Day 46.

Exiting la cuidad sagrada.

360453N 1090812W

SLOWING THEIR PROGRESS, Jen and Peter carried one of the larger containers as they descended over walls and down-climbed on decayed wooden supports. Peter insisted they should ditch the case, but Jen continued to resist, "No. We're going to carry this out all the way. This might be the only link to what Worthington was after. Besides, it belongs to Amado, Alejandro, and the Acoma."

After multiple vaults, catches, and scrambles, they paused leaning against a wall to rest, blocked from the wind. Fresh perspiration replaced the layer Jen wiped away from her face.

"Listen!" she whispered, trying to silence her own breathing.

Moving behind Peter she pointed to their left. A shadow scoured against an adjoining wall and then a green hue coated the ground in front of their resting spot. At their level, a back wall left them with no retreat. Holding very still, they prayed the consuming darkness would conceal them. In the intruder's favor, his vision gear showed detail of the darkened corners and in seconds he shone a powerful flashlight in their faces with a command.

"Drop to the ground slowly, face down, spread eagle."

Jen nudged Peter. He didn't see an opportunity to flee and instead lowered himself to his knees.

"Peter!" Jen murmured, wondering why he was just giving up.

She followed suit. Purposely, the beam blinded them while footsteps approached.

"Face down," the agent ordered and radioed his contact speaking quickly, "Check my twenty. I've got two suspects. Over."

Peter raised the container to his chest blocking the light so his eyes could readjust to the dark.

"On the ground I said. Put the box down."

Peering from behind the frame of the container he could see the human silhouette, his one arm extended holding the light. The other arm was bent at his side. He needed to bring the man closer.

"You want to take this?"

"Just hit the ground."

Peter heard one more step, "Take this before I drop it."

He pulled his arms in. Anticipating the solider was closer, he thrust the container outward praying it would block a bullet. As the metal box went airborne waist high, Peter lunged towards the agent at ground level. The collision of bodies was decisive, but did not give Peter the advantage he needed after they struggled to their feet. Leaning back, the civilian blocked the first elbow to his face with both arms but was knocked off balance by a scissor kick. The landing hurt. Fatigued, Peter didn't have the quick muscle to respond defensively. His thoughts scattered, he managed to roll away from his attacker. They should have surrendered outright, but maybe Jen was able to get away. Getting back to his feet, the shriek of gunfire froze him. At first, he thought he was hit. Simultaneously drawing his revolver, the agent was also bewildered. Above them, the echo cascaded over the site.

"What are you? An idiot? Hit the fucking ground before *you* get shot!"

Once the wrists were zip-tied, the agent reported the interference, "One male secured with case. One female roaming."

Concealed in one of the cisterns, the reverberation of the single shot halted Avey and Arthur. Neither sure of its source, they continued planning their route.

"I think you're right! It will save us some energy," Avey contemplated, tapping on her prosthesis.

"Let's stick to the main chute then. It's bigger and faster," Arthur agreed, pointing to one that had the steepest grade. With his legs spread, Arthur cradled Avey as she leaned back and grabbed the sides of the chute to gain momentum. The green biomaterial with fresh rain water propelled them so fast that Arthur had to brake with the sides of his legs. The segment of carved waterway got them half way down, ending in a cistern. Even with the wind gusting, the enormous splash was uncharacteristic. They didn't notice the agent above them as they ran across the small dirt plaza looking for another chute to continue their expedited retreat. Climbing in, the two pushed off and started to gain speed.

Arthur heard the sound of radio feedback, "Someone's behind us!"

The pursuer decided to follow determining it would be impossible to keep them in sight. The agent stepped on the chute, and misjudging the gooey surface, fell on his hip, barely able to recover his radio. Gaining distance the students mimicked the technique used at water parks, leaning back on shoulders and arching their backs to pick up speed. A wide turn put the riders on the lip of the chute, almost ejecting them.

"When we climb out, he'll see our water trail!" Avey whispered as they slid down the chute.

"Can you get your leg off?"

"Say when."

Coinciding with his order, they broke to a stop, in parallel to a rooftop a few feet lower. Arthur slammed the unit down on the stone chute, breaking off a huge chunk.

"This will get his attention. Hurry, throw some water out to this side!"

Arthur quickly jumped out sprinting over to the opposite side of the roof, and then ran back.

"Push off!"

They were out of sight when the tracker arrived at the damage area. Climbing out, he followed the tracks and jumped down off the roof in pursuit. The rouse wasn't discovered until he hit the ground, finding no wet spots.

"Lost two suspects," he radioed.

Still coursing downward, Arthur anticipated their entry into the last cistern. Stopping short of it, they climbed off the chute quietly and ran across the adobe structures to a remote section of fence. Wading in waist deep tumble weed, they followed the perimeter to the next mangled section they could fit through.

Looking back, Avey could see roaming lights throughout the mesa city, "Are we the only ones to get away?" Avey questioned.

The desecrated base of the mesa once reserved for sacred celebration and healing had become the center of command dominated by Colton's team to transact military business. Believing all suspects would be captured and proprietary evidence seized, Colton waited comfortably in a Humvee, listening to the field reports over the radio. Finally getting word of a capture, he left the vehicle to examine a metal case containing a sculpted clay vessel with binary colors of black and white patterns. Colton shook his head, disgusted with the worthlessness of his bounty.

"Where is he?"

Colton was led to the single captive of the night. Shock draped both the men when they recognized each other in dim light. Brief silence committed both of them to promises of retaliation.

"You've stepped way outside your circle, Mr. Childs."

Colton and another man continued to interrogate him. Ignoring Peter's claim of Native American sovereignty, the senior official lectured the civilian about forfeiture during a federal military operation.

"I can't say I'm impressed with your fortitude," Colton bullied. "Hanging your ass out for a couple clay ashtrays. You even talked your friends into it. Millard was right about you."

Minutes later, Jen showed up being led by another agent, "I'm sorry, Peter."

He had never seen her entirely spent. Her eyes and face wore exhaustion. Covered with mud and slime she sensed their critical failures. But they were together now. That's all she cared about.

"I really don't get this fucking shit!" Colton announced to his prisoners. "You wasted your whole careers on nothing, unless of course you know something I don't."

"It wasn't my idea," Peter deadpanned, looking away from Jen. "If I had my way a lot of us wouldn't be here."

"Guilt by association is a terrible stink to have on you," Colton reprimanded. "And not much of an excuse."

His words were trumped by a gruesome sight. Catching everyone off guard, splashing noise came from behind Peter and Jen. The body had reached the cistern with unbridled speed. A small metal carton trailed, bobbing in the pool of churned algae and rain water. Soldiers ran to the edge and lifted out the man wearing a head lamp. Both cuffed and yelling, Peter and Jen attempted to reach the cistern but were forcibly pulled away. They saw the diluted blood stain on the jacket.

"He's shot!" she screamed. "Someone shot Karl!"

Vital signs were taken immediately and a radio call was made. From the vehicle they were placed in, Peter and Jen strained to see what was happening, banging on the window.

"Is he dead?" Jen muttered, crying from exhaustion.

The chopper blades muted the dialogue outside their temporary holding cell.

Peter held her close, consoling her, "I don't know."

He could not resist thinking of all the warnings he threw down. But even a friend would not want this morbid consequence to have proved his point. In the streaks of spinning emergency lights, Jen saw more activity hoping to see some one familiar.

"Have you seen anyone else out there?" she asked barely audible.

"Not yet," Peter digressed, only to resume thinking of the multiple times he questioned the risks. He hoped he would see the rest of the team, but more so he worried about Jude. His body ached from being shoved forcibly into the cave walls. His forearms were bruised from fending off kicks. His swollen jaw and cheek bone were throbbing. The physical pain interfered with the thought of Jude harboring the last steel carton and the likely outcome of his futile resistance. With grief, Jen wiped intermittent tears trying to fall asleep while Peter stared out the window. *Where is Jude?*

After hearing a gunshot, Jude stopped moving, kneeling on the ground to switch on his head lamp. Diffusing the light with his hand, he took another compass reading and looked at the military device in his hand. He disallowed mental images to invade his objectives of escape and hoped the gunfire was a warning shot.

As the moon crested, with cloud cover fragmenting its refracted light, Jude let his eyes readjust to the foggy darkness. Rain was not a factor, but the wind gusts shooting across the mesa roared at times blocking out all other sounds. On roof edge, after checking below his position, Jude climbed back up to the head wall to avoid detection. Within yards he encountered a suspended rope swaying in the wind. Instinctively, he knew the rope was not bearing any weight although someone could have just descended before his arrival. Lowering himself back down Jude hid in the corner of another roof top to recalculate his escape route. The cistern next to him had filled up. The chutes were still flowing with storm water. If Karl was the bait and the others were captured, the attention would turn to him. Going down to the desert floor wasn't an option.

Jude decided to maintain his early course and travel up the main chute he had traversed in daylight. The top of the mesa had a potential route climbing off the backside. His daytime inspection was brief but he could manage it with his head lamp. If anything, he could climb down the other side about fifty feet and wait until dawn, only hours away.

Protecting his eyes from the rain mist, he knelt on the rim of the cistern and walked the perimeter to the lower end of a secondary chute. Distorting the sense of motion, Jude squinted through the fog mist at an image that seemed to be moving in his direction. He wanted it to be Karl but couldn't take the chance. Without pause, Jude jettisoned up the chute, crab crawling with one arm to lower his center of gravity, maximizing his forward progress. He held the container by its handle switching arms when fatigued. He ignored the commands to halt and only turned his head to check his distance from his adversary.

Euphoria. That's what he wanted to feel. He thought the agent fell and slipped down the chute when he heard a dull thud mixed with profanity. Reaching the main chute, more abrupt in grade, it became nearly impossible to straddle it without slipping. The athlete's agility was deployed flawlessly as he continued to climb upward until cresting the top of the chute with burning thighs and arms. Confirming what he heard earlier and surprised with its immense size, Jude saw the military helicopter, certain it was manned. Crouching down, he looked back expecting others to be following soon. The stronger wind gusts moved cloud fog across the upper mesa, allowing Jude to conceal himself at times. As he crept closer, going underneath the craft, an audible hum and the static-laden voice could be heard.

"Suspect is coming your way. Do you have a visual?"

The side door opened ejecting a helmeted soldier who jumped to the ground on the opposite side. Jude slid his body forward shielding the case from light reflection, watching the boots go away from the helicopter.

"Negative. Visibility intermittent. GPS says there's three of us in this soup. I'm on my way in your direction. He's up here somewhere."

There's no way I can walk off the mesa, Jude reconciled, impatient with his dilemma.

Between the two highest plateaus of sandstone crags, the main water trough extended across two-thirds of the lower levy shared with the helicopter. The ledge was only twenty-five yards away. Using cloud cover, the student stomach crawled past the partially disintegrated trough, to the edge of the cliff. Back to a crouching position, Jude strained his eyes, looking down and across the depths. He could see dark forms of rock, but everything was opaque. With the uplift of the wind current stronger at the edge of the plateau, the sweat soaked jacket dried quickly. The metal case tired his arms but he couldn't fail now. The exchange with Karl was understood. Peering over the edge, a single gust nearly took him off his feet.

Euphoria. Jude closed off images of capture to stay focused. Suddenly shadow was permanent and the stars were muted again. As the wind chattered the external liner of his jacket he considered his safety. Limited by cord length, Jude quickly tethered from the latches to secure the container to his torso, resting it on the front of his hips. He stood up, leaned at the waist bending his knees to test for clearance. A flat sounding knock triggered an impulse to turn around, but it would be fatal to his planned descent if he changed position to look. Knocking him off balance, another gust of wind pushed him forward. Euphoric feelings vanished. Hesitation cost him as the wind surged exponentially. The fog hid the details of his error.

The soldier that tried to follow Jude up the chute had gained a partial visual of his suspect and shuffled his feet silently to intercept. The helicopter afforded the soldier cover but he had to get around it aware his vision would be blocked for a fraction of time. The shortest distance was to go under the craft with a belly crawl but also too slow chancing detection. With radio silence, the pilot had also cleared the top of the plateau to the right of his partner. They would acquire the target in less than a minute. Both soldiers reached the ledge at the same time staring at each other in disbelief. It might have been a full ten seconds before the pilot palmed his flashlight shoving its beam straight down a foot away from the ledge, the light diffusing into the dark.

Two beams shot frantically into the dark plenum in front and below them becoming bright when hitting the ledges immediate at their feet and dull where the distant vertical slabs of the mesa formed peaks. The strobe effect from fast moving beams was mesmerizing. The first soldier yelled but went to his mike noting no reaction from the pilot and continued with loud profanity. Confused by the unnatural act, the pair was profoundly shocked.

"What the fuck happened! You did see him, right?"

"He fell!" was the audio response.

"I know I saw him in the fog. Then he was gone!"

Peering off the cliff face, the search lights failed to make connection with anything other than rock surface.

The wind had become stronger in ebb and flow gusts while the soldier replayed his approach, "I was right there...," and he pointed back to a place behind them, "...when I struck my boot. He must have heard me and panicked."

The pilot justified their actions, "We cornered him. It was that or give it up."

"There's no way he could have survived."

"Get aboard. They called in another injury below so we're it. Report this one as a suicide."

At the base of the mesa, military operations solidified. Sitting with him in the vehicle, the field operations lead briefed Colton, right after the chopper took off with the injured civilian, "We've still got eighteen men in the area. Of the two injured, one needs medical attention. And one agent unaccounted for."

"How badly injured?"

"I heard he's got a broken nose. Apparently he was ganged up on. I think he took it in the crotch a couple times."

"And the agent missing?"

"I'm not sure. We think a GPS is malfunctioning. It shows his position on the other side of the mesa."

"This weather fucked up the operation tonight. Score one for the Indians. We've got how many detained?"

"Three in hand—two male, one injured, and a female."

"The injured one, let me know his status pronto. Don't publish the sit-rep until you hear from me. Let me see it." [72]

The officer concealed his dismay again.

Colton reviewed the report, "That leaves three college students at large. What does the TC say?"

---

[72] Situation Report.

"The TC confirms it. Two males, one presumably dead, one female..."[73]

"We haven't officially recorded the death?"

"According to the pilots, the kid bit it. The other male and one handicapped female unaccounted for.

"You think they slipped through?"

"No, sir. We're still working it."

"I say you're shit out of luck there too."

Not having worked with Colton before the commissioned officer didn't like his superior's bravado, "I'm doing my job, sir. We don't have tangible evidence indicating they've left the area."

Colton recalibrated the soldier, "I can't afford your job to get in my way. Have the team stand down until the weather clears. Run scans on outbound traffic against this profile," handing a document to his man, "and have your team set up accommodations for our guests at the casino. We can start interrogations after they sit there for a while. Ignore their first amendment rights until they start crying."

The officer was duly concerned, "For the record, we've got what we came for. Why not just cut these people loose."

Colton didn't like the insinuation and restated the premise firmly, "The record will show these people were trespassing on federal land with intent to steal for profit. As transgressors, they attacked and injured federal agents. Some of them are evading arrest and leaving the scene of a crime. I think their asses can be cooking on a chair for a couple hours without screwing with their rights."

The officer wasn't going to pick a fight now. He could always register his official complaints away from the purview of this commander, "Understood. Yes Sir."

"And release the Indian kid. Let him find his way back."

"Sir?"

"Do it."

The look was confirmation of Colton's biting authority. The soldier made a mental note of another deed that would likely have ramifications. Colton turned music back on when the man left. Tapping, licking, and smoothing, he lit a cigar waiting for mission closure.

Savoring the moment of the elongated sidebar of events, Colton anticipated how this would play out in Washington. He could easily convince the leadership to focus on the progress of the NEADE research,

---

[73] Tactical Officer.

diminishing the antics of James Hyatt. His team would need to shift back with regular duty, and push hard to close off old and new rumors. Angela came to mind. A sharp agent. A favorite. *Not much rope left.*

Barely enough for Arthur and Avey to follow the trail, the moonlight shone through the thin boundaries and tight voids of gray clouds. They saw how spectacular the top of the mesa looked, but fatigue silenced their energy to appreciate its natural beauty. Walking quietly, they finally reached the main switchback, now covered with tire tracks. Unbalanced, Avey found it difficult to negotiate the high and low sections of washouts and mud puddles on the narrow road so Arthur stayed abreast of her to add needed support. She didn't resist his help after the fourth episode of tripping that sent her sprawling to the muddy ground. When spooked by abrupt sounds, they moved off into the scrub oak, juniper, and grasses. Moisture from the ground cover soaked their already damp clothing.

"I'm too tired to shiver," she said, offsetting more of her weight to Arthur. "But thanks for keeping me warm."

"No worries. Do you think anyone got ahead of us? I've been watching for foot tracks but another vehicle could have come through wiping them out."

"I think we would have heard or seen it."

"Shhh! You're about to get your wish!"

They hurried off the road to conceal themselves and waited for the headlights of a military vehicle to break the deadlock of night. Cabin lights revealed a driver and passenger through the windows as it past them. When the glow of the tail lights was in the distance, the hikers followed the vehicle with renewed energy. They were a few miles from the main forest service road where they left their cars almost twenty four hours ago.

"I'm positive is saw Alejandro in that jeep!" Avey repeated.

Near Canyon De Chelly National Monument, Arizona.

360453N 1090812W

"**Y**OU'RE CALLING FROM where? How did you get there? That's three hours from here! Alejandro, what have you done!"

"Please, I'm sorry. I'll explain, but I really need you to pick me up."

"Your father will not be happy," she promised hanging up.

Tired, the aunt finished her shift abruptly, "Lucy! I've got to punch out. I won't be helping you with the tables. Alejandro is stranded out near Milkwater! That's almost to White Clay on forest road!"

"My goodness! What's he doing way out there? It's almost two."

Alejandro handed the cell back to the officer.

"Sorry, kid. I'd get my head taken off if I took you any farther."

The teenager understood the message of revenge. Watching the military taillights jog off in the opposite direction, he anticipated the impending anger his aunt would deliver. In the cool night, a few drops of rain lingered with the air, fresh with odors of wet dirt and hard surface road. The darkness surrounded him as a blanket. Regardless of his ordeal, he was wired thinking of the beliefs his grandfather held to. The pleasant feeling would soon be replaced with accusations and verbal abuse. He would have to bite his lip to avoid reacting to his aunt's yelling. The less information he had to give up the better. Alejandro rationalized his expected punishment. *At least Grandfather will be happy.*

Stretched to the limits of their vitality, Arthur and Avey continued their painful steps on the road ending where they left the cars. Approaching the junction, wary of any offense to detain them, they could see a pull off for vehicles and at first thought they had made an error.

"I'm sure this is the place we started from. We didn't take a wrong turn," Arthur whispered.

Avey wasn't sure they weren't lost, "Well, where are the cars?"

"Maybe they got towed. Let's sneak over there and check it out."

The remainder of the storm tailed off to the west and cooler desert air prevailed along the ground. Fully draped in moonlight, they crept to the border of the gravel. When a figure suddenly appeared from behind a tree, the short burst from Arthur triggered Avey's scream.

"Alejandro! You scared me!" Arthur scolded.

"They dumped me and said they wouldn't take me further. I hid, not sure it was you guys. What about the others?"

"Don't know. We were hoping they were ahead of us like you, but I guess they could still be up there."

Alejandro explained his treatment, meeting the one in charge and about the vehicle that dropped him, "That guy is a real asshole. At least the dude that gave me a ride let me call my aunt. She's on her way, but I'll warn you, she's pissed. Did you find anything in the cave?"

Excitedly, Avey told what they discovered and that it might have fallen in the hands of the military.

"Did you hear the gunshot?" she asked.

On the return trip, Highway 264 was completely abandoned except for a coyote darting out to chase a mouse. The aunt abruptly slammed on the brakes, waking Avey. Her adrenaline perk lasted until they reached Gallup.

Upset, the daughter of Amado continued to repeat herself in Spanish assuming the dialogue was entirely confidential to her nephew, "I warned you about this and you decided to go behind my back. Your father will be more than disappointed! If I have my way, he'll come get you."

Still a simmering pot of anger, she complained about Alejandro's friends, "You tell me you're stuck. Then I see these two! And you tell me you did nothing wrong?"

Alejandro tried to defend his actions, but his answers remained subordinated against the wrath of his aunt, "You left me no choice. Again, who are they?"

He repeated their names, unsuccessfully fending off more minutes of heated conversation. With their destination framed only by yellow dashes of passing lane, Arthur was relieved to hear the reluctant adult yield, wondering if any of them had eaten. The car pulled into the driveway and Alejandro spelled out the rules to them after the aunt went into the house to warm up leftovers.

"She says you can eat here, but you must leave after. I'm sorry about this."

"I understand," Arthur deadpanned.

After their appetites were calmed, the two students agreed with Alejandro they could not return to their motel and instead would hide in the same church Karl and Jen visited.

"Grandfather will know what to do or I'll get to Mr. Thomas' and he can help us."

Emboldened, Arthur and Avey walked the darkest streets to reach the old sanctuary. The door of the church whined as it was pulled open far enough to accept the only ones who escaped.

"They might find us, but she told me hers are throw aways. She'll have her guard up," Avey assured as Arthur texted Wren.

Waiting for minutes, no reply came. Their body clocks signaled fatigue-laden sleep and ignored the hardness of the pews. Avey tried to cope with the raw abrasions to the lateral sides of her stump, feigning muscle soreness when Arthur quizzed her.

"Let's hope Alejandro can summon more help. We're going to need it!" she said, to put his attention somewhere else.

Day 45.
Warehouse district.
Denver, Colorado.

TAKING HIM TO the airport, Wren's parting with Lloyd was
bittersweet. When they dropped Duke off with handlers at the
cargo area, Lloyd showed the emotion of being separated from
his mate.

"See you, sweetie," Wren whispered, rubbing the dog's head and ears.

The two walked arm in arm to get breakfast just outside security
check-in. As Lloyd continued to push his breakfast around with a fork,
Wren focused him on the prospect of being with his daughters. Close to
departure time, they had to part.

"I'm going to miss you, Lloyd. Thanks for the help moving out."

"You'll be busy on that new job huh?"

"Pretty busy."

The intercom announced the first call. They hugged each other with
kisses on the check.

Wren reached in her purse, "Lloyd, here's a credit card."

He thumbed the card studying it, "No, I don't need your money."

`"It's fake, but it has my number on it. Call if you need me, okay?"

"I will. Don't worry. I won't tell them where you are."

Wren was startled, "Oh. You mean tell your daughters?"

"No. Those guys that gave me and Karl hell. I'm counting on you," the old man replied, with a grin showing the shiny tooth.

With her guest out of the way, the apartment lease was terminated by a letter. Wren vacated her prior domain, leaving no physical, financial, or electronic trace. And no one knew about the second site, spacious with no power limitations. With incoming two-twenty voltage, racks held power conditioners and uninterruptible power supplies. The architecture of the network and firewall rivaled the best commercial data centers. The servers and switches on the rack mounts were fully redundant with high availability, mirrored drives. The warehouse with a loft was the only thing left in her world of one.

She always wanted to turn up the site, believing mothballing it until consulting business picked up. It was a good reason to celebrate. Instead she was nervous. The game she entered without invitation was forcing her to do it. It wasn't target practice on clients. It was deep hacking in no mans land. Her fears, like those of her peers, were built on paranoia. It was a self-absorbing fear that no matter how good she was, how bullet proof her systems were, someone else out there could be better, quicker, and sharper. Her assessment of risk was analogous to underground miners who were always the first to know something was going terribly wrong, and the first to die.

Every data signal, every virtual noise, any missteps could set off undetectable alarms. The illegal penetration into NETL was so deep that the virtual path could close in nanoseconds. Then a network trace back to her firewall could instantaneously transmit her virtual location. If she was lucky, maybe countermeasures could shut the trace down but her bot would be stranded. But she was nervous for another reason.

Relying on her skills as a security specialist and as an intruder, she got her first nudge of another kind of threat. Sitting at the console flipping through screen images, she got her first inkling that her bot could be in trouble. The bot she had sitting for weeks never sent an alarm until now. The bot that nobody was aware of and sitting quietly, suddenly burped. But the alarm sent by her bot wasn't signaling blog activity. It was a threat alarm. Somebody was piggybacking on her bot and they had been there for a while. Self-absorbed with a strategy of retreat, her thoughts of her team drifted away.

"Jesus. He's coming this way!" Jason exclaimed.

To make up for the gaps in the surveillance record, he had tailed Dr. Ravichandran Franklin. Colton would be down his throat if he didn't have any news on the scientist and regardless of the hidden divisiveness between them, he couldn't afford to create any reason to doubt his commitment.

Separated by sixty yards of pavement and traffic, Franklin had crossed the street walking towards the vehicle. Jason turned on the engine, flipped down the visor to shield his physical profile and pulled out into traffic, watching his suspect in the side mirrors as he was forced to go straight instead of turning.

"Shit!" Jason gunned it around the next block and came back through an alley to the street where he last saw his suspect, "Lost him."

Cruising slowly, scanning both sides of the street, the agent passed multiple store fronts and warehouse entry doors. He spotted a man casually walking to every adjacent door and testing whether it would open, "Got him."

Jason pulled around to park at a safe distance. Satisfied with his vantage point, he thumbed through the classified report documenting bank account, credit card, and phone records. *He's not even trying to conceal what he's doing! What's he up to?*

Anyone who hung it all out, who had been treated like he had, meant there was a payback coming. Jason called on his cell and had a trace run on the address of the warehouse Franklin stood in front of, looking at a sheet of paper.

"No hurry. I'm just sitting here."

Jason dug out his cell and texted, "Call me."

On the fringe of becoming a conspirator, after breaking the code of conduct, he was ready to tell Angela about the suicide notes and his plan to use them and Hyatt to shut Colton down. He would need a substantial buffer for having withheld information. It would take an audience with Sterling to insulate them from Colton's reach.

Going on dark, the agent watched the scientist on the opposite side of the street, contemplating whether he should move the car again.

Getting his attention to answer, the cell phone buzzed. It was Angela, "Hey, were have you been?"

"I've been assigned to monitor Colton's Desert Storm operation," she replied.

Jason laughed, "Lucky you. I called because I'm ready to share something."

As he watched Franklin go slowly door by door, he explained what he did when he entered Millard's apartment, what he did with the suicide notes. He shared his hunches. That Millard was actually planning to kill their boss. His last message on the phone was from Colton agreeing to a meeting. That the will found on the bed was Millard's amateur effort to frame Colton as a suicide, although his own prints would have implicated him. That the will on the bed and the one on the dresser meant Millard's death was assisted. That the rush to close the crime scene destroyed all the forensic evidence, but he thought he had located an eye witness.

"The mail service box was sitting outside Millard's door when we walked in. It occurred to me the delivery service might give us time boundaries."

The revelation caused a stir of emotions that were held tight, "Did you find out anything?" his partner asked.

"Yes, but nothing solid though. But think about it. Colton probably snuffed Millard."

"Have you actually contacted Hyatt?" Angela wondered.

"Not yet, but I think it's a good move to pull him in."

"Do you have the documents with you?"

"Yes. I'll let you read them when we hook up."

Angela had already seen them. When Jason had tipped her off weeks ago, it didn't take long to locate them in his desk drawer, sandwiched between other papers. Angela knew Jason. She studied his traits when they met. She observed his personal manner. A locked desk would provoke someone, so he kept his work area open and accessible. As such, no one would bother looking there. Recently they were missing so she presumed he took them.

"I'll look you up when I get back then," Jason reassured.

"Sure. Good work! I think you've nailed it."

When the call ended Jason took a deep breath feeling more relaxed than he had in weeks. With the shared determination of Angela Gates and James Hyatt, the pressure could shift against Willis Colton and they could get out of the whirlwind of federal incompetence. Reflected headlights of passing vehicles bounced off metal surfaces and vehicle engine sounds wavered loud and soft. Franklin had inadvertently escaped again.

Shit, where'd he go now?

Jason took a moment to think of his pursuit. He could drive around again or get out and back track. There was still no call back on the address. Or maybe just be still for ten more minutes and wrap it up. The records would show he put his field work in. There was nothing immediately risky about the scientist that he couldn't manage later. His eyes drifted to the two wills that could prove Millard's intent.

As the knock on the glass window took his breathe away, Jason's hand instinctively moved to his service piece on his right hip. Surprised and confused, he pushed the button to power the window down,.

"How did you know I was...You were...?" he began asking. His instincts betrayed him.

Day 43.
Acoma Pueblo.
345347N 1073452W

WAITING FOR HIS grandfather to wake up, Alejandro's mood was combative. He was at the mercy of his aunt who had pounced on her brother again, complaining about the two men she was responsible for.

"It's not just Alejandro, its Father! The two of them are like children! I keep telling Alejandro he has to be the adult. And I told you about the friends he brought home. I swear there is nothing sacred about my rules!"

Signaling it was his turn, she handed the phone to her nephew. Stretching the cord into the kitchen pantry, the young decedent from the Acoma tribe expected his father's reaction to be more explosive, knowing he got every ounce of displeasure the sister could deliver in twenty-five minutes.

Instead, the son of the elder was soothing, explaining how his son should respect his aunt's wishes, "She is the only caregiver to the remaining parent and she agreed to give room and board to you as well. Your adventure had your aunt very worried. Did you apologize?"

"Yes, right away, but she screamed at me. I think she was more scared for Grandfather. Did she tell you she thought he was dead in the bedroom?"

"I heard that. And that he is practicing his medicine for so-called spirit journeys. He would always stink up the house."

"She got down on him for that."

"She says you are enabling your grandfather and that you brought strangers to her home. She wants to send you back to keep the two of you out of mischief."

"Arthur and Avey are my friends! They made the discovery. They discovered an inner city! *Una cuidad escondida dentro de otra ciudad!*" [74]

"That's a myth Alejandro. My father has always *believed* there was a hidden city. Probably they found the same old ruins like everyone else."

"I was there! The sacred Ocatc was drawn on the walls. We found a cave!"

"I do not doubt what you saw or did, just that it doesn't mean as much as you think. I'm going to arrive there this weekend and we'll sort out whether you can stay. From your aunt's view, the people you have been with should not be contacted again."

He didn't want his dad or aunt to know he was already helping two of the college students that were in trouble. The boy kept silent about his efforts to contact Mr. Thomas'.

"You've got to speak to Grandfather and he'll tell you everything. About the city and how he knew Karl was here all along."

"Alejandro, you know he's living in the past. Nobody loves him more than I do, but we have to face reality that his mind is feeble, not what is was. I'm asking you to cool it until I get there and we can patch things over with my sister."

Alejandro stared out of the pantry down the hallway focusing on the room the elder was sleeping in, "I guess."

"I trust your judgment, but stay clear of the whole thing until I get there. We'll see what can be done."

Alejandro wanted to resist more. The aunt was in hearing distance.

"Yes, sir. I'll see you soon. Love you too."

That same morning, a diverse group of leaders from the Acoma Reservation gathered at the Highway District offices. Of the thirteen people in the room the federal government was a minority of three. The governing council of the Acoma Pueblo was represented by Governor Pasqual and others. The Pueblo lawyer Daniel Sanchez, remained forceful trying to hold ground against the invaders. Their voices charged with emotion, they could not get objections validated about jurisdiction, protected sites,

---

[74] A city hidden within a city.

or the crimes against Native Americans. Forty-five minutes passed with animosity reaching peaks where the two sides stood as enemies.

After letting the three federal representatives battle the residents to verbal fatigue, a rule of law was announced, causing an abrupt silence in the war of words, "I have the authority to declare marshal law," Colton announced, holding his cell phone in the air. "If anyone wants to challenge me I'll make the call."

The governor was about to complain but was cautioned with an arm placed on his shoulder and a whisper from Sanchez explaining an encampment on their sovereign land could last over a year. Silence preceded subordination.

"I thought so. You're smart people. You get it. I want a private discussion with you and you," Colton ordered, directing his comments to Pasqual and Sanchez, waiting for them to lead the team to a vacant room.

Once sequestered, Colton scolded the Acoma leaders about their priorities, "You think it's about jurisdiction. Bullshit. The issue is about information. I want these citizens interrogated by our military," demanded the NEADE chief. "I don't give a shit if they're guilty or not. I need information. When I'm done, you can haul their asses in for a confession after that and I want the Goddamn notes."

There was no honor, no saving grace. The Native men had made no progress against the government, knowing this when they sat down in an empty room without their people. Sanchez stood firm on the precedence of the Native Americans Graves and Protection Act, "You have taken our sacred pieces. We have the right to take them back and will file an injunction with the Secretary of the Interior."

When the Native lawyer stepped forward to hand the document to Colton, a federal agent intervened and reviewed them, nodding to Colton.

"When I'm done with them," he replied with conviction.

Starting a detailed analysis of her injured bot, Wren isolated the software files, dragging the bot to a quarantined area. A healthy bot could push and pull data through the I/O ports of a firewall and usually returned after it sent the information it was programmed to collect. Being very careful not to corrupt the data code, she looked at the encrypted wrapper that piggybacked a ride home. It wasn't a botnet, so it wasn't an attempt to flood her domain. The code wasn't hers and somehow connected to the bot as if riding on the underside, hidden from view. Her bot used the same digital signatures as the federal government. It would have been impossible to identify hers as an intruder. How could she have a hijacker on board? *No one was this good!*

Her second bot was still functioning. When she punched out code to it, the response was normal. Feedback indicated the NEADE firewall wasn't aware of it. This was proof that the government didn't hammer the first bot. *When and how was my bot victimized?* She could disable the intruder and be done with it, except that abrupt action would kill the messenger and take away the ability to trace where the Trojan came from.

She had to sacrifice her bot and keep the intruder breathing in virtual space, so it could be autopsied alive for clues. It took her all night to pry off the hijacker and analyze the invasive code, while it was living and breathing, sending and receiving. Eyes tired and mind numb with redundant surveillance of her own fortress, Wren had omitted her daily conventions of tracking text alerts. Two of them came the prior evening to her unlisted cells. Retrieving the correct phone, she listened to the strained voice of the first message:

> Clarke. 3:30am. I'll text again. Trouble. A & I HIDING. others may be evading the military. Found pottery. Feds were chasing. Changing locations.

She listened to the second message:

> Clarke again. No reply? In DEEP SHIT! Karl was SHOT. He's in a hospital under military guard. P & J captured last night. Jude MISSING! A & I are at Church of HS. Need help to figure things out.

Abruptly, Wren ran to the service panel and put her shaking hand on the primary power source for the building. At the point she heard of Karl's fate, her eyes filled. The panic that struck her was the raw exposure she faced if anyone was coerced to name accomplices. *Did I waste time with the bot intruder? Are there more I didn't see?*

The fate of detection and consequence. She contemplated throwing the switch to go dark. That would leave a dead end for anybody attacking her fort. Or she could hunker down and put up a better offense to defend herself. She knew she could walk away, but if the government was serious about it, they could find her. Lacking nutrition, it took minutes for her to clear her head. Regardless of her choice, there was a lot to do.

After haranguing the Acoma leadership into submission, Colton had the look and feel of satisfaction. Pending outstanding investigations of a handful of civilians and the recovery of another, his operation was successful by his account.

"It's in the report, right?"

"Yes, sir. We detailed eyewitness accounts. The victim—"

Colton interrupted, "Tell me you didn't use the word victim."

"No, sir. The civilian was observed falling of the ledge. We have digital pics of the scene including close-ups of boot tracks. As soon as we recover the body, we'll match impression evidence and DNA. The body is down there somewhere because one of our GPS devices is somehow down there too. I'm waiting for the team to tell me when it's been retrieved."

"What's the contingency?"

"For no body?"

Colton stared nonplused, anticipating the obvious. The event had to move into a recovery operation as soon as possible to allow the government to make official statements.

"We calculate five days with injuries, the elements start consuming the body. We officially call the search on day six lifting the restrictions. We expect the locals to gear up, but they'll have to hand over any evidence. Either way we're clean."

"The locals are quarantined from the area until then?"

"Yes sir."

"Talk to me on day six."

"Yes sir."

The metal cartons taken from the area were shipped to DARON for safekeeping. With the government assets under the auspices of his team he could evaluate their meaning at a controlled pace. No obvious or logical connection had been discovered that explained why Franklin was sharing confidential modeling and why Worthington had sent the artifact images to the scientist. Regardless, Colton believed his trace on the scientist would give them more evidence to convict the scientist with treason. To close out his latest mission at the mesa, the NEADE boss planned to force plea bargains from all the others. A final report to his leadership would end the internal leaks, especially with the news of progress from the shadow team. They claimed to have figured out the missing detail on the seismic model, surpassing Shepard's team. It didn't matter that Shepard reported his team was only two weeks out from completion. Either way, the results from both teams would strengthen Colton's position.

Spiteful, Colton toyed with Shepard before he left, "I'll have that deliverable or your resignation."

The science of geology might hand me the ultimate gift after all, he thought boarding a jet in Albuquerque. *There's nothing left here but scraps.*

After pouring the bourbon in the glass of ice, Willis Colton paused, remembering the note he was given during the interrogation with Peter Childs. After reading it, he belted down the liquid contents and waited for the burning flavor to reach his stomach. It had to be a mistake. He looked at the note again,

Not all details in. Agent Jason Smith mortally wounded.

It was obvious the local police weren't happy left standing idle. Told their jurisdiction was moot against federal crimes, they listened while the feds rattled off question after question interrogating Jen Rawlins. The sworn affidavit dredged up the imagery of Karl landing in the pool, the flashlight blinding their faces when they were cornered, and the tunnel maze. After a two hour interview with Colton's people and then with the local Pueblo sheriff, she was given the clearance to leave, two days after she and Peter were hauled out of the ruins. With eyes swollen, Jen made it back to her room taking another dose of Tylenol, and lay back on the hotel bed, promising herself to call Wren when the pain broke. One of two phone calls she managed to make, her mother was at first panicked and upset; her own strength and vitality was already taxed beyond her natural limits. After the first call, Jen massaged the base of her skull with fingers. Her whole experience was like a dream transformed into a nightmare.

The second call was just as taxing.

Doug was pissed learning of their fate, "Don't tell them anything."

"I gave them a sworn statement so I wouldn't go to jail."

"Jen, you need a lawyer!" Doug reprimanded.

"When they shoot people, you start to cave in. It's the only way I could see Karl. I was told he's not in critical condition, but I want to see for myself."

"It's probably the same bastards that covered up my injury and took the drill bits. When are you coming back?"

"Not sure. I'll be the only one here. Peter is not going to wait around for full recovery because of Jude."

"You said he's still missing? So wouldn't he be looking for him?"

"The military says he…", and Jen choked up, "… fell off the cliff evading them. They're doing a recovery operation. Peter is so devastated he's flying out tonight to see his sister."

"He was probably pushed. We need to get an investigator up there."

"They cordoned off the area."

"They're covering up the fact you were ever there."

Jen blurted her next words out quickly, "They may be listening."

She had to suppress the urge to say out loud the elder hadn't lied after all. She wanted to yell that Amado knows Pueblo relics are significant to the world. She wanted to scream the words that the government doesn't know what they have.

"Doug. I have really have to go. I'll call you later."

Anticipating her visit to Karl, Jen finished packing so she could leave from the hospital. The call to Wren could wait a little longer. There was nothing she could do for any of them at this point.

After receiving critical care from the military, the Sky City facility was sufficient for recovery. Only cognizant for minutes at a time, Karl flashed in and out. He got a fuzzy glimpse of the room, his feet, and the IV. He felt the tearing pain on his scapula, entire shoulder, and left lung through chest muscle. Dizzy, he returned to sleep, null of full colored dreams. Bits and pieces of the present pinched its way through to the virtual screen his brain conjured for survival. One recurring synapse continued to seize his near consciousness. Like an out of body experience, immobilized with fear he tried to defend with arms and kick with legs. The encapsulation of frantic energy was like a dome over him, keeping him separate from another unearthly inculcation. He could see it and hear the words. He wanted to warn Jude.

The non-human form came closer and whispered, "K'aika! Samuti." [75]

---

[75] Mails, *The Pueblo Children*, 267. Meaning "Hello!". White, "New Material from Acoma," 342. Meaning "My son."

Peter sat numb. His mouth was turned down, reflexively tensioned to follow the formation of tears welling in his eyes. Pensively he grabbed the edges of the bed, the only neutral manifestation in his room. He would tell his sister that Jude was missing.

No. I'll tell Anne the truth!

Jude had perished and any pending news would be no worse than that. If he waited around for the duration of the search it would delay the inevitable news of mortal disaster. He needed to tell everything: how the pretense of a summer excavation escaped common sense; questions about who was involved and why he tolerated his friends' reckless judgment; the depth of the whole experience with the black books; and Worthington's death.

Peter shivered thinking of the consequences of his confessions. His sister would easily see that the centerpiece of her brother's failure was when he failed to call her about Jude's discovery of Worthington's suspicious death. Then she would interrogate him about everything else. She had every right. The relationship Jude had with Looks and his extreme sports would be challenged. And then it would get nasty.

Peter sat there alone and miserable, imagining how the rush of crushing emotion would tidal wave into his sister's life. Best friends beyond mere siblings, he *had* to admit the truth. Her anguish would explode and the ineptness of his mentorship would be the aftershock. Failing to protect her son, a subjective assault of accusations would follow. Peter could imagine her grief flooding him, the undertow of shame severing their sibling bond. A moral thought of the financial obligation crept into Peter's conscience. His grip intensified.

The deep anger he felt towards Karl was perplexing. Pointing the finger would be no consolation to his sister. *But I tried to stop it!* Why didn't questioning motives, fighting their decisions, and resisting their conclusions work? Why did everyone ignore the risk? His feelings towards Karl turned to outright malice. He used to call Karl a friend. A friend wouldn't go to extremes and blindly cause a fatal accident taking another's life.

"I kept telling him..." Peter clenched his jaw muscle. "...and telling him."

His tears dropped one after another.

When she reached her office, Angela opened a secured briefing document and reviewed the hard copy intercom between the craft and ground crews in Arizona.

"Unbelievable!" she complained.

Reading the dialogue regarding the weapons discharged, she immediately contacted the field commander and was told all the details, "Are you certain?"

"Yes Ma'am. At approximately one hundred."

The misplay could easily ensnare the CIA and lead arbitrary discovery to a narrowing introspective focusing on NEADE and NETL, including retaliation from the handicapped female college student.

"Goddamnit. Goddamnit!

Angela calculated the likely scenarios that had the potential to point back to her. There were more reasons to take evasive action with or without her partner.

His body still exhausted, Karl lay still hating what Jen had said. With raw emotions he didn't have the strength to scream, to kick. His condition had been upgraded from critical, with a concussion and bacteria induced infection from his open wound.

"It can't be! He ran out of there and I knew he could do it! He was going to make it out of there!"

Sitting by his side, holding his hand and rubbing his arm, Jen had told him. That Jude had died. That the family would be told by government officials that no remains had been found and no one could have survived the 500 foot fall. Based on GPS waypoints, and the ruggedness of the canyons, it could be weeks before remains could be located.

"They don't have the body. Can't you see it's a cover-up! Peter was there! He knows! They can't give up!"

"Peter already left to be with his sister."

And she repeated words again because Karl resisted what seemed obvious to others, "Don't do this to yourself! Like I told you, Peter is not going to get over this. He will not listen to you. And I think," she paused with a lump in her throat, wiping her eyes, "I think he will never forgive you. You need to let him do what he wants to do. What *he* thinks is right. What he needs to do."

Karl couldn't let the obvious intrude. It wasn't true. He wouldn't allow himself to forget what Amado told him: *The one who leaves the path will suffer.*

"If the old man saw the future then Jude is *suffering right now*! He's not dead!" Karl insisted.

The Forcing

Day 37.
Congressional Oversight Hearing. Washington, D.C.

NOW, FOR THE record, is it true you oversee a Pentagon funded agency referred to as NETL. Is that correct?"

Colton ignored the courtesy of a verbal answer and merely shook his head.

"For the record," the chairman filled in the blank, "the witness answered in the affirmative. Counsel, please instruct your client to verbalize his answers. Is it true that your conduct of official NETL business includes provisioning CIA agents to ferret out problems NETL encounters?"

"There is a staff of employees, under the direction of NETL. They work for NETL and carry out the charter that is defined."

"That's interesting and I'll tell you why Mr. Colton. Documentation in front of the members of this committee point to dissimilar activities that conclude NETL employees are unaware of the charter that is, in your words, *defined*. Let me state a few. I'm reading from a recent accounting of an operation in Arizona."

The chairman cited the situation report leaked days ago, "I'm paraphrasing this – you had three civilians placed under control of your agency, one of them severely injured by friendly fire. And a fourth individual, a real tragedy, died. And from a separate report, confirmed days ago, a Jason Smith, a CIA experienced agent, was murdered in an apparent carjacking while on duty. His personnel files are sealed, but unofficial correspondence indicates the young man was working for NETL."

The chairman paused, letting the whispers die down. Colton and his lawyer asked for a short recess. Somebody had decided to hang a noose around Willis Colton's neck.

"I'll grant the recess Mr. Colton. Before I do, please come back with answers. In the broadest terms, it's unclear to me how an agency vetting scientific research can be engaged in operations that ultimately risk and take lives. It's also interesting and at this point circumstantial, that you are directly or indirectly connected to these events. Let's break for lunch and return at three."

Colton rejected legal counsel's request for a debriefing, "Those clowns wouldn't have the pieces they do unless some one has turned. Get an injunction filed to lock out our records, and subpoena the committee for the evidence they have. You can keep them busy with that this afternoon."

Colton had other matters to close.

CHRON 19h18m46.659s

360320N 1120823W

I N THE EARLY morning, permitted backpackers and overnight rafters were the only warm-blooded mammals at the bottom to feel the quake. The Grand Canyon wilderness ecosystem of big and small mammals started migrating up canyon days earlier, as their generations had on like occasions, using their innate sensitivity to detect what humans and equipment gauges would latently record as a significant and geological anomaly. Undetected, the series of fracturing tectonic plates had moved into an acute alignment, taking over two thousand years to complete.

As recent as three hundred fifty years, the final geological specificity of failure was a crevasse, hidden underneath a shell of Zoroaster granite, over thousands of meters in length.[76] The one hundred ten meters of shell density formed cracks and began collecting random shard supplied by the abrasive fluid, which at peak times in the spring, reached nine thousand cubic feet per second. Seasonally, with continual peeling, the dome continued

---

[76] Ribokas, Bob, "Grand Canyon Explorer: Grand Canyon Rock Layers," http://www. bobspixels.com/kaibab.org/geology/gc_layer.htm#vs. © 1994-2000 by Bob Ribokas. Zoroaster granite was once the roots of an ancient mountain range that could have been as high as today's Rocky Mountains.

to thin. The passivity of cyclic freezing generated more fissures, weakening the structure over the span of one hundred years. A current day x-ray of the 423 meter segment would have implicated the divergence of younger plates that created a new rift. It went undetected, even with man's sophisticated tools. Earth's behavior presented yet another symptomatic catastrophic forcing, unknown to those living on the surface of the earth. The study of the science of the earth was too focused on the taking of resources. Humans were blind to what the earth was giving them: signals of consequence.

"Where the heck is he?" she whispered, trembling from the cold air while scanning the horizon. Tipping her head, she heard the down throttle of an engine as the fixed wing Cessna reached the necessary altitude above the south rim. The plane circled to land on the maintenance strip, taxied past the sole occupant on the runway, and parked. The pilot had motioned with his hand, pointing to the helipad, and immediately climbed out. Racing fifty yards to his Bell 206 helicopter he met his passenger at the front glass.

"Get a move on!" Harry yelled, fumbling with the straps on the tail prop, talking to himself and at Sarah intermittently. She could only hear portions of it.

"I can't believe my timing. I mean, it wasn't supposed to be done until tomorrow. You won't believe it!" the pilot reminded his passenger as he stowed away her gear, rushing from one side of the helicopter to the other. "Those guys never get done with the mechanics when they say they will! Who knows why I even bothered to check this morning and test it out. This was meant for us! I'm usually asleep! Hurry up! It's changing every second!"

Both climbed aboard as he helped with restraints, activating the aircraft at the same time. He paused to yell above the turning rotors, "You're ready with your camera, right?"

She lifted it up as proof.

Both climbed aboard as he helped with restraints, activating the aircraft at the same time. Sarah shivered, her body still cold inside her clothes as Harry talked into his mike while visually finishing his engine pre-start check, "Main rotor—clear!"

With main throttle open and flight idle closed, he checked the oil pressure. When it reached ten percent, he quickly engaged the main rotor and starter. Seconds later the pilot stabilized engine idle at sixty percent and incremented slightly. He nodded affirmative when the fuel boost pumps and hydraulics were activated. Instruments were the last visual he had to validate before take-off.

"Hang on! This is going to hurt!"

Utilizing his combat training, the craft shot up and forward. Sarah felt her chest compress and stomach tighten invoking nausea. As the nose of the aircraft led them over the structures below, the landscape jetted past in blurs as they raced into the shadowed mega basin of the grandest canyon.

Struggling with a bout of mental distortion, Sarah's leg and thigh muscles tightened. She began to crouch fetal-like, sensing they were free falling. It was the topography that sank below them. Harry signaled for his passenger to put the earphones on; she already missed part of the instructions, "....make a pass back to the east to get the sun at our backs. Then I'll come back against the current near the Clear Creek outlet, up towards what *used* to be Eighty-Three Mile rapids. You'll get a bird's eye view."

She managed to blurt out her altruism, "We should get down there as quickly as possible. There may be injured people."

Before landing and switching aircrafts he had radioed them with ten code, "I'm already ten minutes ahead of SAR. Their craft just came off maintenance. They have a long count to get through. It's coming up! Hold on!"

It felt like they were suspended in air trying to hit an imaginary corner. Adjusting, Harry banked to the left and pitched the blades to descend sharply.

"Eeeeh. That hurts!" Sarah winced. She had flown with the rescue team, but they were more delicate with maneuvers. Harry flew with combat skills. She pressed down on the pedals that supported her feet.

"Sorry. No tourists today. Barf in the bag, not on my glass!"

"Oh my God!" Sarah saw the earth-born anomaly. Her weak physiology became moot.

"That's what I'm talkin' 'bout!" Harry said.

She started taking pictures, concentrating less on her stomach and more on negating camera movement. The sequences of pictures she captured were suddenly new-age artifacts.

And to follow within twenty-four hours was a myriad of global alarms—official and unofficial; confirmed and unconfirmed; predictive and reactive; primary, secondary, tertiary, and redundant; private and public; scientific and layman— all were triggered in repetitious waves of broadcast to the anxious world.

"Do you want me to swing around again?"

"I got good ones! Let's get to the bottom and land. I can get more images from the ground."

"It might not be safe!"

"We have to take that chance. Anyone could be in trouble down there."

"Flight 718. We have a visual on the Grand Canyon at twenty-one. The confluence of the Colorado River looks impaired. Any reports?"

"Ten four. Stand-by."

Twenty seconds passed.

"Affirmative. USGS has reported an earthquake 360320N 1120823W. Six plus magnitude. At 0200."

Numerous video devices began recording the event in real time. Blogs and volumes of tweets had thrust the first wave of information out resulting in a textual flood of digital compression. Five hours after the first picture was transmitted from hikers' satellite phones and pictures from Sarah Cannes, virtual content exploded from a mere six to over ninety-two percent of total world wide internet traffic. The Hollywood breakup reported that morning was old news.

On the fifth floor of a run-down New York office building, the man sitting in a wheel chair watched three screens, tuned to the broadcast about the Colorado River. For once in a long time he was having fun, thinking of how the oil companies were going to get what they deserved.

"Imagine an oil company part of the solution?" he mimicked the voice-over, watching a commercial.

"My ass."

Bibliography

American Experience. "Gallery: Earth From the Moon." (Oct 6, 2005), http://www.pbs.org/wgbh/amex/ moon/gallery/index.html.

Bebout, Don G., and Charles Kerans. *Guide to the Permian Reef Geology Trail, McKit trick Canyon, Guadalupe*
National Park, West Texas. Texas: Texas Bureau of Economic Geology, 1993.

Black Hat. http://www.blackhat.com/main.html.

BP. www.bp.com/home.do?categoryId=1. Use download links, by energy type

Brown, Larry. "Unexplained Mysteries: COCORP revisited." http://www.scec.org/news/01news/es_abstracts/brown.pdf.

California Protea Association, "What are Protea." http://www. californiaprotea.com/protea.html.

Chapman, Jay, "California's Lost its Moho." GeoTimes, Web Extra (September 2, 2994), http://www.geotimes.org/sept04/ WebExtra090204.html.

Combs, Susan. "Oil and Gas: Slippery Slopes." Window on State Government (February 2001), http://www.window.state.tx.us/ specialrpt/rural/5oilngas.html.

Delta Mining and Exploration Corporation. "Diamond Exploration." http://www.deltamine.com/diamond_properties_exploration.htm.

DesertUSA. "Mesa Verde Nation Park." Digital West Media. http://www.desertusa.com/ver/du_ver_desc.html.

Dictionary.com. http://dictionary.reference.com/.

Dictionary of Earth Sciences, 2nd ed., Allaby and Allaby. Oxford: Oxford University Press, 1999.

DOB Magazine, "Nickles Energy Toolkit: Well Data Legend." http://www.dobmagazine.nickles.com/common/well_legend.asp.

Energy Information Administration. "International Energy Annual 2004." http://www.eia.doe.gov/iea/.

Farlex. "Holocene extinction event." The Free Dictionary, http://encyclopedia.thefreedictionary.com/holocene+extinction+event.

Flickenger, Rod. "Antenna on the Cheap (er, Chip)." O'Reillynet.com (July 5, 2001), http:// www.oreillynet.com/cs/user/view/wlg/448.

Guadalupe Mountains National Park, National Park Service, U.S. Department of the Interior. *Roadside Geology Guide.*
___. *Geology of the Western Escarpment.*
___. *McKittrick Canyon Geology.*
___. *Geologic Time & Rock Formations.*

Howstuffworks. http://wwwhowstuffworks.com

Hyperdictionary. http://www.hyperdictionary.com/.

Institute of Global Education, "Project Nature Connect", http://www.ecopsych.com/.

James, H. L. ACOMA: *People Of The White Rock*. 2nd ed, Introduction by Frank Waters. Atgeln, PA: Schiffer Publishing, 1988.

Lawrence Berkeley National Laboratory, "Oil & Gas Exploration & Production." Earth Science Division. http://www-esd.lbl.gov/er/oilgas.html.

Leadbetter, Ron. "Gaia." Encyclopedia Mythica. .http:// www.pantheon.org/articles/g/gaia.html.

LiceoCubano. "La Colonia Cubana Revista Mensual." (Febrero 17, 2008), http://www.liceocubano.com/spn/ secciones/fauna.asp#lnsects.

Lone-Star, http://www.lone-star. net/mall/txtrails/kilgore.htm.

Mails, Thomas E. *Dancing In The Paths of the Ancestors: Book Two of the Pueblo Children of The Earth Mother.*
New York: Marlowe & Company, 1993.

Malahoff, Alexander. "Loihi Submarine Volcano: A unique, natural extremophile laboratory." National Oceanic and Atmospheric Administration, http://www.oar.noaa.gov/spotlite/archive/spot_loihi.html.

Mills, Elinor."Mapping a revolution with mashups," CNET (November 17, 2005),
http://news.com.com/mapping+a+revolution+with+mashups/2009-1025_3-5944608.html.

Mineral Zone. "Minerals." http://www.mineralszone.com/minerals/.

Minge, Ward Alan. ACOMA: *Pueblo In The Sky*. 2nd ed, Forward by Simon Ortiz. New Mexico: New Mexico University Press, 2002.

Morton, G. "Oil headlines." http://home.entouch.net/dmd/oil_headlines.htm. Also see WorldOil.com.

Nabokov, Peter. *Architecture Of Acoma Pueblo: The 1934 Historic American Buildings Survey Project*. Santa Fe, NM: Ancient City Press, 1986.

National Aeronautics and Space Administration., "Earth Fact Sheet." http://nssdc.gsfc.nasa.gov/planetary/factsheet/earthfact.html.

National Geophysical Data Center. "Teachers Guide to Stratovolcanoes of the World." http://www.ngdc.noaa.gov/hazard/stratoguide/glossary.html.

National Institute of Standards and Technology, Computer Security Division, Computer Security Resource Center, http://csrc.nist.gov/publications/fips/fips197/fips-197.pdf.

National Native Americans Grave and Repatriation Act. "News From The National NAGPRA Program." http://www.cr.nps.gov/nagpra/.

National Park Service."Mesa Verde Management." http://www.nps.gov/meve/parkmgmt/index.htm.

National Park Service. "The Antiquities Act." U.S. Department of the Interior, http://www.cr.nps.gov/archeology/pubs/lee/lee_fpm.htm.

Orrell, David. "Science of the Living Earth:Gaia Theory." GaiaNet, http://www.bibliotecapleyades.net/gaia/esp_gaia06.htm.

Petroleum Strategies, Inc. "The Nash Books." http://www.petroleumstrategies.com/nash.html.

Petroleum Technology Transfer Council, "Drilling Well Classification System," Tech Transfer Tech, 2nd Qtr 2003,   Vol. 9, no 1 (2003), http://www.pttc.org/newsletter/newsletter_past/1qtr2003/v9n1p4.htm#2.

Rader. "Earth Structure." Geography4kids, http://www.geography4kids.com/files/earth_composition.html.

Ribokas, Bob."Grand Canyon Explorer: Grand Canyon Rock Layers." http://www. bobspixels.com/kaibab.org/geology/gc_layer.htm#vs.

Skinner, Les. "Oilfield Jargon." World Oil, September 2005), http://findarticles.com/p/articles/mi_m3159/is_9_226/ai_n15649426.

Space Today Online. "Space Terminology Glossary." http://www.spacetoday.org/Area71/spyterminologyglossary.html

TechWeb Network. http://www.techweb.com/.

The Cultural Landscape Foundation. http://www.tclf.org/index.htm.

The Foundation for the Advancement of MesoAmerican Studies Inc. http://www.famsi.org/.

USAID. "Annual Reports Library." http://www.usaid.gov/our_work/humanitarian_assistance/disaster_assistance/ publications/ annual_reports/index.html.

U.S. Department of the Interior, "Mission Statement", http://www.doi.gov/secretary/mission.html.

U.S. Geological Survey, "Metal Industry Indicators." http://minerals.usgs.gov/minerals/pubs/mii/.

Volcano World, "Submarine Volcanoes – Introduction, For Educators." http://volcano.oregonstate.edu/education/submarine/index.html.

White, Leslie A. "New Material From Acoma, Anthropological Papers, No. 32," Smithsonian Institution Bureau of American Ethnology Bulletin 136 (1943): 29–32,301–359.

Webopedia, http://www.webopedia.com.

Wikipedia. http://en.wikipedia.org/wiki/main_page.

Williams, David R. "Earth Fact Sheet." http://nssdc.gsfc.nasa.gov/planetary/factsheet /earthfact.html.

Acknowledgements

MANY PEOPLE HAVE been inspirational to me. Terry Groth has my heartfelt appreciation for his thoughts, wisdom, and comfort. He touched many parts of the book in review and during many night sessions white boarding the future.

I was fortunate to have a small pool of readers who volunteered to provide feedback. Many thanks to Tim Mitchell, Steve Brooks, Alison Monestario, Kris Gulbranson, Sally Albright, and Matt McKinney. The value of their guidance and commitment was important for the development of this story.

My family also sacrificed time. Their forfeiture was great and I love them deeply for their support and understanding.

And to the woods near my home – that freely gave advice when I listened.

Cover Image

Courtesy of the Image Science & Analysis Laboratory, NASA Johnson Space Center. The image, "Moonrise: Moonrise over the planet Earth" (Mission Roll Frame: STS103-703-M) can be found at http://eol.jsc.nasa.gov.

**An excerpt of consequence with,
RARE EARTHS
The unpredictable sequel to
An Earth Scorned**

Day 46.
Exiting la cuidad sagrada.
360453N 1090812W

ETWEEN THE TWO highest plateaus of sandstone crags, the main water trough extended across two-thirds of the lower levy shared with the helicopter. The ledge was only twenty-five yards away. Using cloud cover, the student stomach crawled past the partially disintegrated trough, to the edge of the cliff. Back to a crouching position, Jude strained his eyes, looking down and across the depths. He could see dark forms of rock, but everything was opaque. With the uplift of the wind current stronger at the edge of the plateau, the sweat soaked jacket dried quickly. The metal case tired his arms but he couldn't fail now. The exchange with Karl was understood. Peering over the edge, a single gust nearly took him off his feet.

Euphoria. Jude closed off images of capture to stay focused. Suddenly shadow was permanent and the stars were muted again. As the wind chattered the external liner of his jacket he considered his safety. Limited by cord length, Jude quickly tethered from the latches to secure the container to his torso, resting it on the front of his hips. He stood up, leaned at the waist bending his knees to test for clearance. A flat sounding knock triggered an impulse to turn around, but it would be fatal to his planned descent if he changed position to look. Knocking him off balance, another gust of wind pushed him forward. Euphoric feelings vanished. Hesitation cost him as the wind surged exponentially. The fog hid the details of his error.

Unprepared for another sudden gust, Jude became unbalanced, his upper body radically tilted forward. As his heels lifted, a surge of adrenaline coursed through his veins. Incapable of reversing direction, counteracting the weight of the container, he knew fighting it would put him at an immediate disadvantage. Instead Jude responded with elegance. The dark, wind, and rain became instantaneous threats to survival as his feet left the edge of the mesa.

One thousand one. At first clutching his cargo as the center piece of his aerial stunt, Jude elongated his frame to counteract rotation. Determined not to be a victim. Praying not to allow his free fall become a final tragedy. One thousand three. Unwilling to give up, Jude willed his impulses to quiet themselves and transformed his energy to respond. He had seen the sheer drop off in day light. How many seconds? Will my chute fail because of the wind gusts? The increasing velocity turned the rain into piercing shards, tearing at exposed skin. One thousand four. Am I too close to the wall?

Only guessing that he had enough downward wind speed to keep the chute behind him. And that the lines from his riser wouldn't twist because of his precious cargo. One thousand five. Only guessing, he was tracking away from the mesa wall and not towards it. Only guessing, Jude let go of the drogue to release the ram-air canopy. If any of his guesses were wrong, he would have no time to recover. Death would be certain.

Euphoria. A sheer second of calm. The moment when extreme downward thrust is harnessed by the canopy and the riser and lines reach equilibrium. Literally, a moment where the body is held in place as opposing forces negate each other. The mind can reverse panic within a second. Muscles and reflexes can easily resonate calm in ten tenths of a second. Production of endorphins and hormones can subside in a split second. But time was up.

The breath Jude sucked in was forced by innate response. His fear would have been much greater had he realized how close he was to the ground when his descent was halted by his canopy trapping air. His tenacity to thwart capture may have shattered if he knew he was only a few feet from the sandstone wall. Even the lights he saw flickering through the fog didn't have significance. In the one second, if he hadn't deployed his chute, the roar of wind that was upon him would have flattened the nylon baffles and collapsed the parachute.

Instead, his aerial feat to defy those in pursuit was hijacked by random force. Jude felt the powerful surge, almost tearing the container from his torso as the wind commanded the parachute, guiding it effortlessly in the direction of the jet stream. No amount of resistance or tactical maneuvering with toggles persuaded the unbounded air current to relinquish its command of the flight. Flying blind, Jude attempted to widen the slits of his eyes realizing he was gaining altitude. For those remaining on the top of the mesa, ten seconds had passed since they lost sight of their target. After the soldiers agreed the jump was fatal, the student had fallen four hundred feet, arrested his momentum and shot upwards at a forty-five degree angle. By the time the helicopter lifted off to respond to the injury at base camp, Jude was heading north, recovering altitude near equal to his original position. In the black of night, he was at the mercy of Earth's struggle to achieve its own equilibrium.

While his physical strength was tested, the sensory deprivation seemed indelible. He could hear everything, but for the volume of the wind, nothing. He could feel the lines tremor, an indication he was moving at rapid speed. Although the perverse trajectory was impossible to calculate it was too risky to try to view his altimeter. Jude's mind raced trying to force logic. This couldn't go on forever. But dawn had to be only minutes away. Something had to give or take. And then it did.

The first signal of abrupt change came with a scraping sound. At first shocked at his capability to even hear it, Jude's immediate response was to coil, lowering his head, rolling to his right to prepare for a frontal collision. In daylight, he would have reacted entirely differently to negate injuries. Any witness to his final approach would have decided the miscalculation was fatal. They would have seen the fully expanded parachute dropping precipitously, dragging the harnessed victim at almost horizontal level with the only device that could save him. The left edge of the chute glanced off the sharp imperfections of the broader portions of sandstone cliff. That intermittent compression smothered two air channels and increased drag to cause a tipping effect. At first in a bundle, Jude was bewildered when his body slammed into solid rock from the left side. No longer in an effortless free fall, he began fighting for his life.

Syrian Desert

315902N 400601W

THE SWELLING POOL of oil was unruly. Near sea level, the sand storms between Saudi Arabia and Iraq in the south Syrian Desert had masked a passive surge of liquid hydrocarbon. Bubbling to the surface west of Arar, the Kingdom's oil was flowing into Iraq, exploiting the boundaries of man and government. Every week, measurements were taken and samples analyzed. The KACST[77] Petroleum and Petrochemicals Research Institute struggled to meet the demands of Saudi Aramaco. Normally partners in cooperative efforts to streamline the extraction of oil, the two organizations had become divisive attempting to overrule the other with the best solution to recapture the asset. No one had discovered why this was happening.

"Sir, we're ready for you," reported the first lieutenant. Military analysts of CWIC had constant surveillance on the small reservoir of surface oil after reports of increased ground activity. [78]

The unit commander along with science personnel surrounded the terminal display, "These are uploaded from SAT. You can see the hybrid

---

[77] King Abdulaziz City for Science and Technology (KACST) is an independent scientific organization administratively reporting to the Prime Minister.

[78] Combined Intelligence Watch Center, within the Cheyenne Mountain Complex, hosted by North American Defense, NORAD.

images show an expansion of the pool over the last month. Nearly six kilometers. It's heading into Iraq."

"Lucky bastards," quipped the commander. "Like they don't have enough, so now they don't have to dig for it. What's brewing between Saudi and Iraq?"

"So far, there's comm from the official sites. Both are posturing cooperation. Underneath, Saudis aren't going to give up one drop without a fight."

The science officer instructed the console operator to display other unique illustrations, "Sir, the terrain maps out generally flat," he said pointing to the topology. "So gravity is playing a part in the direction of flow. It's like the oil is being squeezed to the surface."

"It that a guess?"

"Yes, but it's not uncommon to have oil flows shift over time."

"No earthquakes or anything to cause this?"

"No. My team pulled the data. From a tectonic point of view, the Arabian plate has been fairly stable. No spikes that would have prompted this outcome. The Saudis are probably scrambling to figure it out. We need samples from the deposit."

The commander showed his frustration, "We are sitting neutral but I can assure you somebody will need to nail this down. Iraq is going to poach and we're not completely out of harms way.

"One more thing," the science officer was duty bound to report. "This is an anomaly to current science. We don't know root cause, so we're flying blind right now.

"Meaning?" quizzed the commander.

"Our science could be irrelevant. At the rate the oil is surfacing, it could mean a forcing that is off the charts."

"Get a brief developed and send to a Mr. Colton in care of a small operation called NEADE"

"Sir?" the unit commander paused. "This is way under the radar."

"Willis and I were shoulder to shoulder a couple times, back when our trigger fingers counted for something. He should get a sniff of this."

Near Pole Bridge, Montana.

4846N 11417W

THERE NEVER WAS a decent telling of the weather in Montana. Nor could the land be counted on. At least that's how Mrs. Williams felt.

At the sink, the breakfast dishes dripped off in the rack, as the forty-eight year old wife finished cleaning the kitchen. The view out the double hung window, changing constantly throughout the day, kept her engaged with the duties of middle income drudgery, saddled with unplanned debt. Unconsciously she wiped silverware, moving it from wash water to rinse, and then to the strainer. Her external gaze saw the grass fields traced deeply by Angus bulls and heifers. The Cleft Rock and Hornet Peaks stood silent beyond their property line in Flathead County. Sometimes Janet Williams saw herself perched at the top of the peaks, her brown bangs floating in the wind free of the lower ground that held her captive. Free of their medical debt. Free of their son's leukemia. Inhaling slowly she couldn't see their future. She couldn't gauge their ability to keep the ranch they inherited from her parents. The phone chime broke the trance.

Cradling the receiver in her neck she continued to wash, "Hi honey. What did the doctor say?"

"Tyler's still in there taking it easy after his injection. The doctor says to stay with the protocol even if we can't afford it."

"Does he know we're broke? There's nothing else we can sell off."

"It doesn't matter. Right?"

"Joe. I'm on your side," she assured. There was stress in her voice and body. "We'll figure something out. At least we have each other."

"Well. You know the drill. I'll be leaving in about an hour. See you near dinner time."

"I know," the wife replied. It was a promise, sagging in its own weight of despair. The knife she held had been scrubbed shiny during their conversation. Blinking she looked out at the framed portrait of the earth.

She realized the cows had disappeared from her window portrait and a gray film cast over the length of visual perspective, "Drive careful. It looks like another storm is on its way."

Without trepidation she set the phone down on the counter listening to the minuscule sand rake the window panes. Like before, she had no answers. They were in a waiting game with the health of their six year old. Her gaze returned to Hornet peak. Their path through the maze of medical tests, repudiation, and doubt had victimized their lives. She took another deep breath. Maybe the offer on their dry acreage would go through. Everybody said they might as well hang on to it. Who would have thought their parcel of land was too small to bother with.

Those thoughts vanished as she suddenly composed herself. From the double magnetic knife bar, and all the large knives had fallen, bouncing on the counter with random direction. Jerking her hands out of the water, she saw a gash on her knuckle, "Great. One more thing," she complained.

She remembered when Joe hung the magnetic bar years ago claiming the power of a magnet never wears out. Slowly extending her arm she tapped it with a single knife as if to turn it back on. A gush of wind hit the side of the framed house. And when Janet laid the blade flat against the steel holder it failed to embrace the knife. The smallest of pebbles pelted the window.

"That's weird," she mumbled setting the knife down certain of the failure. *One more thing that couldn't break.*

Turned away from the window to retrieve a band aid, the sound of coarse scraping and meshing of steel instantly claimed her attention. And at that moment facing the changing panorama of landscape, she jumped back suddenly staring at the knife holder. Silently, water and soap bubbles dripped from the maze of blades that had welded themselves to the steel bar. More bizarre was the silverware that had somehow been pulled from the other side of the sink. The pots and pans hanging above her head were leaning towards the steel knife holder, invisibly controlled by its intense properties. The cautious step backward might have saved her life if it had been multiplied many times over. Unaware of the raucous conditions beyond the frame of her kitchen window, the resident could not have seen the minute specs of blood that splattered the side of the house seconds before. And then the larger portion of the mutilated Angus carcass, released from centrifugal force, surged through the double hung window shattering objects in the way.

Averaging twelve per year and only one funnel cloud recorded in Flathead County, the Montana tornado that gained major force from a downburst of wind, began cutting into the surface of the earth compounding its destruction by hurling collected debris. In it's aftermath it would be compared with the single deadliest tornado in world history that struck in Bangladesh over twenty years earlier. Spawning a void in atmospheric pressure, other supercells left permanent scars.

If she had survived, Mrs. Williams might have been curious about the behavior of the knives, and the metal silverware. She couldn't have known Gaussmeters through out the world, set to constantly measure the strength of earth's magnetic shield, tripped instantaneously in both directions and then normalized. In the aftermath of the detected void of Earth's magnetic field, scientific theories doubting the weakening of the magnetic force were instantaneously rejected. Science could no longer rely on the past. The land could not be counted on.

CHRON 21h47m1.035s

375327N 993343W

ACHIEVING THEIR SALVATION, the Lutherans filed out of the Zion church returning home to prepare late afternoon meals. Kristin hurriedly stripped off her church clothes, and reached into the dresser, pulling out pink cotton panties along with jeans and a button down blouse. She already convinced her mom she would go pick up her grandmother.

"You're leaving awfully early Kris. What's the rush?"

"There's not. You know how Oma is. Never ready. So I'll keep her on track."

"Good idea. Take the back road and stay off the highway."

Nothing was sweeter to her ears. Nearly sixteen, she almost listened to every word her parents said and sometimes followed their instructions.

"I will," Kristin replied, leaving the two-story farm house towards the driveway. *Good thing she never checks my pockets. He better be there.*

Prying the small tube out of her jeans jammed in there with a condom, the daughter of middle income farmers applied gloss to her lips as she drove pass field boundaries of corn and soybean. Steering away from the shoulder of the road she primped her damp brunette hair with the warm air current.

Billy used to tease her about how she kissed but that stopped after she gave him head. With the corn fields over six feet, practice made perfect. The farmer wouldn't find their embedded hangout until threshers cut the stalks at harvest. The spare plywood from a construction site, a couple blankets and old pillows stashed in garbage sacks, and a beer cooler would be hauled out in a couple weeks.

The teenagers could easily justify everything they did to escape boredom in the small town. Not the first or the last ones to be hooked, the infatuation and lust was something they could own. There was nothing else to do in Offerle. Nothing worth their time in the vast state of Kansas.

After parking on a short spur, Kristin checked her time, calculating they should have forty or so minutes to themselves. She could blame Oma for not being able to get ready. The elder wouldn't remember exactly what time her granddaughter arrived to pick her up. Leaving the car, the girl welcomed the cloud cover checkerboarding the golden tassels. A sunburn would betray her talents. One hundred yards into the dense foliage brought her to their space. She listened silently for her mate. Chirps and crows from sparrows and pheasants near and far. No sounds that would tell her Billy was close. She tilted her head towards distance traffic noise. She heard a car did stop instead of going by. Patiently, she sat hoping she didn't have to hike back out without pleasure. Her mind drifted anticipating the encounter. Rubbing her breasts, she thought of the other times. When pressed for time, they half stripped and used each other. Today, the sun felt good on her partially bared chest. She imagined his reaction if he came upon her laying there naked. Standing, she decided the surprise was worth having to get completely dressed again. Stripped from the waist up, her hands worked to get the jeans below her hips.

"Yaaaaaaa," Billy screamed as he bolted from her blind side and tackled his young mate to the ground.

Shocked with the outburst, Kristin covered her self, struggling to pull up her jeans, and hide her breasts.

"Jesus Billy! You scared the shit outta me! You were there the whole time?" she complained, gyrating to get lose from his grip.

"Sure. It took me longer to sneak in. I was going to jump out sooner, but you were doing a strip tease."

"Didja think for a minute that *might* not be funny?"

"Ah. Not really. I was getting into it. Let's keep it going," he insisted.

Kristin adjusted her jeans and grabbed her blouse. She was pissed, "Maybe not. Besides I only have fifteen minutes now, since you wasted time. I didn't want to be rushed. You always get to cum."

His look was not of self sacrifice as he mulled over another tactic. Getting a beer from the cooler, he offered her first sips.

"I can't. You know my Oma will smell it. She's senile but she still tattles."

Looking up through their slot to the sky, Billy lay back on his elbow chugging the drink. When the clouds began to dampen the sun's heat, Kristin warmed herself next to Billy. Both listened to the rattle of corn leaves vibrating at the will of a stronger breeze. All other sounds were drowned out.

"Maybe we should put the stuff back in the bags. I didn't notice any storm when I got here," she said. "I've got to get going anyway."

"Ya. I guess we can wait...tomorrow I have to do the ditches, but after dinner?"

"Maybe."

Suddenly, a large flock of sparrows announced themselves, swooping over head. Nearly touching the grayed-out tops of the corn, a second collection of birds swarmed them. Before Billy could scramble to his feet, to raise his arms, more birds came from the same direction.

"What's going on!" he whispered, trying to understand the noise coming towards them.

Spinning around, unable to completely set his feet, a deer burst into their opening. Staring at Billy, the animal paused a split-second, leaping over Kristin to evacuate from the open space. With slower reflexes the boy fell to the ground, landing on Kristin. At first he thought his balance was off. It wasn't the deer that made him fall. The ground shook violently for seconds.

"Shit! Did you feel that! Let's get the fu..."

No more words were finished. The threat was bigger than the abrupt invasion of wildlife. Frozen, both felt a shrinking of their being, caused by inborn response. Arms tensed as if the teenagers prepared to defend themselves. Looking intensely at each other, realizing fear had embraced the moment; their eyes darted to survey the circular boundary that was void of protection.

Billy slowly shifted his feet regaining balance to stand over Kristin. His mouth dry, his breathing belied his courage. It was a forced whisper to check sanity, "That deer. His eyes were freakin' out! Did you hear that noise? He must have been running from it!"

"A huge blow sound. Or more like a freight train," Kristin replied struggling with what she heard. "I'm dizzy."

"That's from the ground moving," Billy spoke loudly. "I'm going to check it out. Stay here."

"No way! I'm coming too!"

"Kristin. No! I'm just heading to that high spot where the irrigation rig is. That's all. You're safe. Listen."

They did. No other noise competed with the wind that was beginning to bend the plants.

"I'll be right back," Billy committed and ran out of sight.

Kristin could hear the corn stalks invade his path and then nothing. She counted seconds ready to follow, "Thirty. Thirty-one. Thirty-two. Thirty-three. Thirty-fo…"

The first after shock was so stiff it made her inhale, thrusting her body upwards. She landed on her butt as if she never moved.

"…ur," she uttered.

But like a whipsaw, the second wave of earth-born energy was guttural, first elevating then dropping her sharply into the ground as the density of soil undulated. The immense energy of downward thrust forced her upper torso to compress until it cracked. Her head butted into the shards of stalk extruding from the ground. She lay sprawled for moments near unconsciousness. Her mind fought to sort out the consequences.

Billy!

Painfully she rolled over. Blood filled the gouges in her face, spilling over and marking her blouse. Nausea and headache increased with movement. Handicapped with broken ribs she forced leg muscles to work. Kneeling with shallow breathing, Kristin looked to the spot where Billy exited, eerily tainted with the dull light and crassness of nature's anarchy.

"Billy!" she breathed the name, coughing.

She knew where he went. Among the other times they stole maturity, the small knoll gave them a vantage to the setting sun and early stars. Swiping at the corn, Kristin stumbled forward in the furrow, almost straight. More steps. With arms switching to cradle her side, more anxiety pushed her to run. Sensing the path they knew well, she had to go left and then more distance. She glanced at her forearms, covered with grit and the blood stains from wiping her face.

I can yell. I'm not sneaking. "Billy! Billy!" she thrust her voice, but the emotional urge to scream was greater then the physical ability. Crying interfered with repeating his name.

More steps. One more row over and she would start to go up hill. He would be there.

"Billy. Where are you?" she forced out, even louder, feeling the pain on the back of her throat and the throbbing of her sides.

Her feet felt the pitch of the ground and she looked down. *It was never like this!*

There was no time to retrace her steps. If she got turned around, her direction would eventually cross the highway. Determined to reach the plateau she hunched over meeting the raised ground with her hands. The erect stalks of corn leaned perpendicular to the earth that barely held their roots. Peering through the lower half of the plant she could see the horizon, darker than before, layered in a fog.

She grabbed the corn to pull her weight forward shifting her feet to gain traction. *It was never this steep!*

With a final surge, Kristin cleared the last crop row regretting her feat when solid ground gave way.

Gripping for life and yelling through tears, her fingers tore at the hearty corn leaves shredding them. Her hands thrashed at the remaining stalks, barely within her reach while feet frantically paddled the loose earth, free falling below her. Inexplicitly, Kristin had pitched beyond the sheer edge of raised surface that reigned above the vast crevasse. Biceps burned pulling weight upward against gravity until her hips piked over the loose scree. Fatigued, the female slithered to safety defeating her mistake.

Numbing as it was, she couldn't give up on the teenage boy who took her virginity when she gave it. She had to find her best friend that had replaced others and kept her secrets that had become milestones of their adolescence. She couldn't give up on him. But as she turned around gasping for air, spitting out muddy loam and blood, her feet pushed away in disbelief striking the ground as if to ward off the vision of mass destruction. Beyond her and across to the other side, the massive swath bore into the earth's surface varied in width no less narrow than fifty yards and at it's maximum as wide as two football fields. No survivors jumped out to surprise her.

"Billy," she whispered between short gasps for air, wincing. What they owned was gone. There was nothing else. Nothing else of value in Offerle.

Dazed Kristin cautiously scooted back towards the edge. Straining to see the bottom, scanning beyond the shards of iron ore and exposed ancient riverbed, she was seeing exposed rock substrate once covered by ancient ice sheets extended by the Kansan glaciation.

Volumes of sulphur vapor spiked the air. Released by exploited fissures, clouds of carbon dioxide floated from the depths. Cupping her hands around mouth and nose did not dissuade the vomit and dry heaving. The slow poisoning could easily claim another victim. Struggling to her feet unbalanced, Kristin could not see beyond the gaseous mix. She could not see in either direction how far the deep fissure extended. She could not see the adjoining fields or beyond that, the destruction of Offerle.

Slid off the concrete foundation, with half of the second floor in splinters, she could not see her family trapped inside, digging themselves out. Kristin couldn't hear her mother's cries as the splintered wall board frame was lifted from her crushed pelvis. Nor could she hear the frantic calls made from other residents, who had reported power outages and small fires. She did not know workmen scrambled to answer priority alarms ninety-six miles northeast. There, the Ellsworth Correctional facility had become another example of random destruction brought forth by mankind's greed.

Kristin sank to her knees exhausted and weak. Her fight to survive had separated one of the cracked ribs, and sharp ends severed muscle tissue causing internal bleeding. Thoughts engaged her to flee. She didn't want her parents to discover where she was. Why she was there. Then it seemed foolish to her. They would only care that she was alive. It was something they all could own.

Bibliography

Wikipedia. http://en.wikipedia.org/wiki/main_page.

Made in the USA
Charleston, SC
10 May 2010